BLIND ORDER

ELIZABETH B. SPLAINE

ISBN: 1545422338
ISBN 13: 9781545422335
Library of Congress Control Number: 2017905968
CreateSpace Independent Publishing Platform
North Charleston, South Carolina

ACKNOWLEDGEMENTS

I dedicate this book to my entire family, who has helped shape me into the person I am today: specifically my parents, Katie and Bill McMillan, my brother Brad, my in-laws, Jackie and Ed Splaine, and my wonderful husband, Kevin, and our three sons, Jake, Jesse and Max.

And also to Lisa Roots, who has known me forever and is the sister I never had.

And to my friends, many of whom took the time to read Blind Order before it had any chance of being published. In homage to their time and effort, their names are sprinkled throughout the book. They know who they are.

You'll never know the psychopath sitting next to you
 You'll never know the murderer sitting next to you
You'll think, "How'd I get here, sitting next to you?"

—Twenty One Pilots, from the song "Heathens"

Contents

Prologue

September 17, 1976

The shadow creeps deliberately down the hall toward her bedroom. The girl lies as still as a stone, body rigid and breath held, expecting the worst but hoping for the best. Abruptly, he is there, his reading glasses perched atop his slightly balding pate, a sickening smile on his pallid face.

She feigns sleep as he skulks slowly toward her and removes his glasses.

The girl opens her eyes and stares dully at the book on the nightstand, *Where the Wild Things Are*, which will never be read to her. Next to the book, folded neatly—because order is so important—are his reading glasses. She memorizes every detail of the glasses—the precise way they are folded, the thickness of the lenses, the round tortoiseshell frames—as he commences his nightly ritual.

Another shadow in the hall now, slightly smaller than his, stops just short of her bedroom door and pauses to listen, stifles a sob, and then runs away.

Salvation denied again.

Resuming her examination of his reading glasses, the girl absentmindedly wonders if her little sister receives the same special attention.

June 13, 1982

The flames lick the edge of the bedding, working to find purchase. The girl tilts her head, emotionless emerald eyes glazing over as she stares. Dressed in an increasingly furious concoction of yellow, red, and orange, Satan's sprites dance around their sacrifice.

"Who's going to hell now?" the girl wonders aloud.

PART ONE

The Awakening

CHAPTER 1

Present Day

The sudden change in light caught Linda Sterling unawares as she entered the bar. Darkness enveloped and momentarily blinded her, and she stumbled down two stairs leading to the main floor. Appearing out of nowhere, a young man materialized and cradled her elbow in his two hands, allowing her a moment to regain her composure.

"Hey, you okay?"

"Yes, I'm fine. Thank you."

Never taking his eyes from her face, the man's left hand drifted slowly from her elbow and down her slender forearm, finding a resting place among her long fingers while his right arm simultaneously snaked around her waist. Her eyesight restored, Linda returned his steady gaze with a cool one. He was a looker, for sure. Green eyes framed by long, dark lashes, black hair slicked back, cheekbones Michelangelo might have sculpted. Definitely the kind of man she would have dated—if she were dating anymore. Mistaking her scrutiny for interest, he tilted his head slightly and gently caressed her left hand, pausing when he discovered the solid band on her third finger. His eyebrows rose in a questioning gesture, and receiving no direction from Linda, he smiled slyly and resumed the gentle massage. A real gentleman, she thought. So much for chivalry.

Although used to the attention, she'd never warmed to it. People had always been drawn to her looks, but her parents had warned her early on that beauty is fleeting; it's what's inside that counts. "Your brain, your heart, your soul," Daddy had said as he tapped his head and chest to emphasize the point. Remembering her father enlivened her, and a thousand-watt smile brightened her face as she delicately disengaged from the stranger.

"Really, I'm fine. Thank you." It came out a little more vehemently than was warranted, but tonight she didn't have time for games.

Making her way across the floor, Linda eased off her wedding band and found a seat at the crowded bar. After depositing the ring in her wallet, she unfastened a button and adjusted her blouse so that it revealed lace and cleavage as she leaned toward the male bartender hurrying toward her.

"What can I get you?" His eyes wandered down her front, and she let them, pausing just long enough for him to get a good look.

"Cosmo, please. Not too sweet. Grey Goose if you have it."

"Course we got Grey Goose. Are you kidding me? Coming right up!"

As the bartender turned to search for the high-end vodka, Linda took the opportunity to examine his high end. Nice, she thought, involuntarily licking her lips. Very nice.

A commotion kicked up behind her, and she smiled, anticipating what was coming next. Brenda Forsythe had never been known for her physical grace and dexterity, and tonight was no exception. She approached the seat next to Linda, slammed her overstuffed purse on the bar, and flopped onto the stool with a grunt.

"How's it hanging, sister?"

"This is the way you greet your friend of twenty-five years? Really?" Linda asked.

"Gimme a hug, dammit. How the hell have you been? It's been forever since I seen you."

They embraced briefly, Linda acutely aware of eyes crawling over them.

"Good, I'm good. Here in town for a seminar, then it's back to the grind."

"Yeah, some grind. Hey!" This was directed at the bartender, who had mysteriously vanished upon Brenda's arrival. "Can I get a drink or what? This is a bar, right?"

The bartender placed Linda's light-pink drink—not too sweet—on the cocktail napkin in front of her, but not before shaking some salt onto the napkin.

Linda raised her eyebrows. "Clever. So the glass won't stick to the napkin, right?"

The bartender narrowed his eyes and said, "Yeah, you're right. The salt soaks up the glass's perspiration. Most people don't get that. I usually have to explain it. You must be pretty smart...or go to bars a lot." Big, flirty grin. Linda cut her eyes while gracing him with a half smile, avoiding his question and creating allure in the process.

"Hel-lo? I need a drink...please!" Brenda's hand slapped the bar.

The bartender stole his eyes from Linda's top and addressed Brenda. "Yes?"

"Bourbon, neat. And don't mess around with any of that cheap crap. I want Knob Creek."

"Of course, madam," the bartender replied in a faux British accent. Linda chuckled. Had to give the guy credit. He had a sense of humor. Confident.

Brenda faced Linda. "So, you're in town for what? A seminar?"

"Yes. I'm doing a presentation on the psychiatric effects of failed remission in pediatric carcinoma patients."

"Uh-huh. Really. Now in English, please."

"I'm going to talk about what happens to a child's brain, both physically and psychologically, when his cancer returns after being away for a while."

"God, that's awful. I don't know how you do it. Or why you do it."

The bartender broke the silence by placing Brenda's drink in front of her.

"So, you're some sort of doctor, then?" The bartender's eyebrows knit as if he couldn't quite believe that a woman so breathtaking could also be smart.

Linda raised her eyebrows and tried a humble smile. "Yes."

Brenda intervened. "Some sort of doctor? You betcha, mister. She's a psychiatrist and a cancer doctor. Because one medical degree wasn't good enough!" Brenda cackled at her own humor. "Hey, where's mine?" Brenda had stopped laughing and was staring at her napkin.

"Where's your what?" Linda asked.

"My salt? Where's *my* salt? You gave Dr. Fancy Pants salt but not me? Well, do you wanna know what I do for a living? I work at a dry cleaners! Now, where's my salt?"

Chastised, the bartender bowed slightly and picked up Brenda's glass to put some salt beneath it. As he lifted the glass, the napkin stuck to it.

"Now look what you done."

Linda placed her hand over Brenda's to draw her back to the conversation. "How's Sarah?"

Brenda's face momentarily contorted with sadness or frustration—or both.

"Oh, Lin, you gotta go see her while you're here. You just gotta. I don't know how much time she has left. She's in that nursing home, if you can call it that. Her ring got stolen—you know, the one with the small stones she always said were rubies but we both knew they weren't but we never said nothing 'cause we didn't want to burst her bubble? She loved that ring, and I'm sure one of the aides stole it. I can't prove nothing, but I know it. Poor Sarah." She finished with a heavy sigh.

"I'll go see her, I promise." Linda was quiet for a moment as she reflected on her childhood spent in various foster homes, culminating in Sarah's. A lot of people had tried really hard to get through to Linda after her parents' deaths. No one had made a dent in her emotional armor until she was placed with Sarah. Linda owed Sarah her life—literally. Yes, she'd go see her soon. But now...back to business.

"And you? You're doing okay? You look tired." Linda held Brenda's hand as she spoke.

"Well, I'll be honest, it ain't easy. I've been at the dry cleaners for nineteen years now, and I ain't making much more than minimum wage. But I'm okay." She slapped her hand down hard on the bar, grabbing attention once more. "You gotta count your blessings, don't you? I got my health, and I got my mind, and I have friends like you." She smiled and gripped Linda's hand.

"You always have me," Linda replied warmly and meant it.

Raised under very different circumstances until cruel fate threw them together, Linda and Brenda had encountered each other several times over the years as they were shuttled from one foster home to another. When they ended up being placed together in Sarah's home, they bonded as two young girls who have only each other to rely on could. Brenda had warmed immediately to their foster mother, desperate to find love and acceptance in a world that had displaced and then ignored her. Linda wasn't so easily charmed, however. She tested Sarah again and again, responding to her attempts at affection and kindness with harshness and delinquency. Sarah never gave up, though. She would wait patiently as Linda climbed through the window past curfew. As the teen slipped over the sill, Sarah would say only, "Glad you're safe. Sleep tight." Over time, Linda had finally relented, accepting Sarah as the mother she'd so tragically lost.

"How's Jonathan? And Catherine?"

"Thanks for asking, Brenda. They're great. What can I say? He's a wonderful husband, and she's perfection. That's why we had only one child. How could we have had another kid when my first one was perfect?"

Brenda laughed. "Nobody's perfect, Lin...well, maybe except you." She threw back her drink in one gulp and stood up. "Hey, bartender, can you take our picture? We haven't seen each other in forever, and I have to commemorate the occasion. How's that for a big, fancy word, eh, Lin?"

The bartender made his way back to the women, who were primping for their close-up.

"Okay. One...two...three! Great one, ladies."

"Thanks, buddy. Gotta go pee. Be right back."

As Brenda beelined her way to the restroom, Linda furtively perused the room. She swung around in her seat and pretended she was enjoying the music as she evaluated her options. There was a guy on the left. No, too tall. Straight ahead—too handsome, too strong. And on the right—too fat.

"Looking for something? Or some*one* perhaps? May I be of assistance?" The bartender interrupted her thoughts.

Linda turned slowly back around, leaning forward in the process. Sporting a Cheshire grin, his eyes dropped to her ample bosom, aided in their effort by

Victoria Secret's latest masterpiece, the Ultimate Push-Up Bra. She relished watching his mouth open slightly and listening to his breath quicken. Maybe *he* was the right one.

Abruptly she leaned back on her stool, titled her head to the right, and regarded the bartender with a critical eye. "I'm not sure you have what I'm looking for."

Mistaking her statement for verbal foreplay, he raised his eyebrows and accepted the challenge. "Oh, you bet I do. I got the goods to get the job done. I finish here at two. Can I meet you after?"

"I'll be long gone by then. I have to present in the morning, remember? Besides, you don't fit the bill." She waved her hand at him. He was dismissed.

Following the line of the bar to its curved mahogany end, she saw him. Sitting alone, hunched over an empty glass, caressing it as if it were a lover. Eyes slightly glassy, about five foot eleven, prematurely balding, with a paunch. She licked her lips. Luscious. Oh, they could have fun. He looks like he'll be leaving soon too, she thought. Perfect.

The bartender followed her gaze. "You're kidding, right?"

Jolted back to reality, Linda laughed throatily. "Absolutely. Yeah, sure. Just kidding." Standing abruptly, she buttoned her blouse and threw a twenty-dollar bill onto the bar.

"Hey, where are you going? What about your friend?"

"When she comes back, tell her I had a medical emergency. Something I had to do." Well, it was true. She did have to do this.

"Okay, bye. Nice talking to you," the bartender said dejectedly.

But Linda was already walking quickly toward the exit. As the door closed behind her, she heard Brenda yelling her name. Hurrying to her rental car, Linda got in and sped off, leaving Brenda standing on the curb, wondering why her very good friend had left so quickly without so much as a goodbye.

CHAPTER 2

Julian couldn't breathe. He desperately clawed at the dirt of his makeshift grave, but each time he moved some dirt, more would slide down to replace it. He wasn't going to make it. They weren't going to find him before he ran out of air. His chest was being crushed by the weight of the soil. Suddenly his face was wet, as if someone had wiped it with a damp cloth. It made no sense. Panic gripped him.

Julian awoke with a start and found he still couldn't move. It could have been due to the nightmare he had just experienced…or perhaps to the 120-pound dog lying on his chest and licking his face. How long had the mutt been there?

"Get off, Oscar! Down!" Julian wheezed, regaining his breath and composure.

Oscar obeyed immediately, with a groan sliding off the bed and onto the floor with a thud. Julian turned onto his right side and relished a long, deep breath before Oscar resumed efforts to get his master out of bed with a lugubrious lick across Julian's entire face.

"God, you need a mint." Another lick. "All right, all right, I'm getting up."

Oscar's tail responded to Julian's movement by thumping against the wall, harder and louder as Julian actually draped his feet over the side of the bed and found his slippers. Or…slipper.

"Oscar, drop it!" Another thud, smaller this time. Julian reached down and found the stolen slipper, slimy with drool, and slid it onto his other foot.

"Perfect start. Suffocation and drool. Why do I keep you, again?"

The Lab/English mastiff mix responded by pushing his large head against Julian's knee, his version of a hug.

"Oh, yeah...that's why, goofball." Julian ruffled Oscar's ears, sending him into a new cacophony of movement and sound.

Grabbing the guide stick he kept to the left of the bedroom door, Julian tapped his way down the nineteen wooden stairs that separated the first two floors of the Back Bay brownstone his grandfather had left him ten years ago upon his death. He followed the sounds of Oscar's nails clicking on the floor, which paused every few seconds as the dog made sure Julian was following him. Upon arrival in the kitchen, Oscar completed the morning ritual by sitting in front of his kibble bowl and whining. Well trained, Julian obeyed by filling the bowl and refreshing the dog's water as well.

As Oscar inhaled his breakfast, Julian listened to the news while brewing coffee. Nothing positive. Just the usual horror presented in a perky intonation with perfect diction.

"And sadly, there were no survivors of the crash. Names are being withheld until next of kin can be notified. And now to the weather...Bob, how long can we expect this great beach sunshine to last?"

Julian switched off the news. Talking heads—that's all they are. Why would someone want to do that for a living? To be on TV? Julian had been on television several times since making a career change and had discovered that it really wasn't a big deal. Or maybe that's because he couldn't see himself, as television isn't so important if you can't see. That's one thing he'd learned since being blinded years earlier in a horrific attack.

Julian dressed by choosing a shirt and slacks from his closet, which was arranged by rainbow color and divided by plastic separators designed by the blind for the blind. As Julian passed his hand down the line of hangers, he could feel when he reached one of the separators, which indicated he'd entered a different color zone of shirts or pants. Julian's closet had two levels—the top held shirts while the bottom was reserved for pants. Today he chose an electric-blue shirt and paired it with lime-green pants. As he'd become more comfortable with his blindness, Julian found that he preferred to wear loud colors. He liked to imagine how bright they were and what he looked like wearing them. It was one way for him to keep his color memory alive.

After saying goodbye to Oscar, Julian tapped his way to the subway station three blocks from his home. Using his prepaid pass, he entered the gates and waited patiently for the train. The rest of the trip was uneventful, and he arrived at the office ready for a full day of seeing patients in his adolescent psychology practice.

As Julian crossed the threshold, his assistant, Jesse, was just finishing a phone call.

"Uh-huh, I understand...no, I don't think so, but I'll check...yes, I know. I know! This isn't my first rodeo, honey. Just trust me, okay? Gotta go."

And then, spying Julian, he said, "Well, look what the cat dragged in. You look fantabulous in that blue! Where'd you get that shirt? Oh, yes...I bought it for you. No wonder you look splendiferous."

Is that even a word? wondered Julian.

Jesse continued. "And before you ask me if *splendiferous* is a word, it is. It's on my word-a-day calendar that Alex got me for Christmas, so ha!"

Julian broke into a grin. "Jesse James, you know me so well. The yin to my yang, the peanut butter to my jelly, the—"

"Yeah, yeah, save it, Julian. You're running late, and there's a new patient waiting in your office. You know, the one that was referred by Judge Tate for theft? Cute kid. Sad, though. Get to it."

"How about—"

"Some coffee? Already on your desk at two o'clock. Lid's loose on the top, as you like it."

Julian smiled. "Thanks, Jess. Oh, who was on the phone, by the way?"

"Phone?" Jesse had already moved on to something else. "Oh, no one. Nothing. Hurry up, you're late!"

Julian entered his office, expecting to hear the patient either stand up or acknowledge him in some way, as people usually did. Nothing but silence greeted him. Taking a cue from the boy, Julian crossed quietly to the desk, placed his briefcase on the floor to the right of the desk chair, grabbed his coffee, and then strode almost silently to the easy chair he used when working with patients. Placing a hand on the arm of the chair, he guided himself down into it and waited, crossing and uncrossing his legs while sipping his morning joe.

Minutes ticked by, and Julian could clearly hear Jesse speaking on the phone once more, this time talking to an insurance company that hadn't paid a claim. He waited patiently. After all, if this client wanted to spend the hour in companionable silence, that was fine with Julian. After years of working with children, Julian had learned many things. First and foremost, though, was that many kids who came through the door felt they had no control in their lives. Why not let them have some command during the office visits? So, Julian leaned back, crossed his legs at the ankles, sipped his coffee…and waited.

After a quarter hour had passed, the patient shifted on the sofa, causing the leather to creak and squeak as its occupant found a more comfortable position. Julian cleared his throat.

"So…" began his male visitor. Julian placed his almost empty coffee cup on the table to his left.

"So…what?" responded Julian pleasantly, palms spread in an open gesture. "What would like you like to talk about?"

"I heard your assistant say that your coffee was at two o'clock. What does that mean?"

"The blind use a clock analogy to describe where things are. So, when Jesse said that my coffee was at two o'clock, it meant that if I were seated at my desk, my coffee would not be directly in front of me but rather slightly right of center, where two o'clock would be on a clock face. Make sense?"

The patient ignored Julian's question and instead offered, "It must really, really suck to be blind, huh?"

Julian slowly brought his hands back into his lap while he uncrossed his legs once more. He didn't want his body language to appear at all "closed" to this boy who was testing him right out of the gate, so he leaned forward, elbows on his knees, and chuckled.

"I'm not going to lie to you. It can really suck, but not all the time." Short and sweet answer. Keep the onus on the patient to continue the conversation.

"Huh. I heard that some kid blinded you by knifing you in the eyes here in this office."

Julian recalled the details of the attack and involuntarily winced at the memory. He leaned back in his chair and sighed. "Yes, that's true."

"And I heard that he got off. That he only went to juvie for a little while. That he's back on the streets."

"Well, I don't know who your source is, but that part is false. Jeremy Walker is in prison for at least another five years."

It was true. The boy who'd attacked Julian ended up being tried as an adult and was currently enjoying another five years in MCI Cedar Junction in Walpole, Massachusetts. Each time Jeremy came up for parole, Julian attended the hearing, both to remind the court of the heinous crime and to ensure that his story wasn't forgotten throughout due process. Jeremy had been up for parole twice since the attack and had been denied both times based primarily on Julian's statements.

"Five years, huh? Well, that's a long time. I could be dead in five years."

Old words from such a young man. "What makes you say that? You're what...fifteen years old?"

"Yeah, I'm fifteen. And I say that because it's true. I could be dead in five years—or in jail with that kid you sent away."

"Just to be clear, I didn't send him away. What he did to me led to his being sent away. His actions led to the court's *reactions*, just as your stealing a car out of the police impound lot led to your being here today. Understand the difference?"

"Not really. All I know is that I don't got many choices, ya know? What are they? What're my choices? My dad left a couple years ago, my mom's never home because she's working two jobs, and I don't do good in school. I can't get a job because I'm too young. Everybody tells me I should be in school, but I flunked out. You tell me, Dr. Stryker, what're my options? 'Cause as far as I can see, I got nothing!"

"And stealing a car helps you how? All it does is either land you here with me or in juvie, right? Let's talk about your family."

"Like I said, not much to tell. My mom—"

"Sharon, right?"

"Yeah, right…Sharon. She works as an aide at the community nursing home in Lynn during the day and waits tables at night. And my dad, well…" His voice trailed off.

"You said your dad left a couple of years ago?"

"Well, not exactly, but ever since the…since my brother…" The boy struggled to find the right words. "Ever since my brother died, my dad ain't been the same, ya know? The final straw that broke the back, or whatever that saying is, was when my dad was laid off from his last job. He may as well not even be there. He just checked out…mentally, I mean. Whenever he's home, he's holed up in the basement. Won't let my mom or me down there. He's just pissed off all the time, ya know?"

The file that had been sent to Julian's office from juvenile court in preparation for this visit hadn't included anything about a dead brother, so Julian decided to learn what he could from the youth himself and discuss the issue later if it arose.

"Yeah, I do. What's he doing in the basement?"

"I don't know, and I don't care. All I know is that he doesn't give a shit about me or my mom anymore, so I don't give a shit about him."

"Is that why you stole the car? To get your dad's attention?"

"Hell, no! I stole the car because Robby told me I had to. He said I couldn't ride with the boys until I did…some sort of ritual or something like that. But obviously it didn't work out." Sounding deflated, he exhaled, the couch cushions creaking as he leaned back.

"Ride with the boys" was slang, of course, for joining a gang. Julian hadn't known there was a gang involved, as that information, like the boy's deceased brother, was nowhere in the paperwork. Seriously, who was in charge over in juvenile court these days? Julian made a mental note to ask Jesse to investigate. Meanwhile, the urgency of helping this kid increased substantially, knowing that he was on the brink of joining a "brotherhood." The gangs in Lynn were known to be hard core and full of violent offenders who were constantly in and out of places like MCI Cedar Junction.

"What if I told you there was a work/study program available to you that would allow you to go to school with support and learn a trade at the same time? Would you be interested?"

A long pause ensued in which the boy considered Julian's offer. On the one hand, he had a life that was going nowhere fast and parents who didn't (in his father's case) or couldn't (in his mother's case) take care of him. A relatively logical kid by nature, he quickly reviewed his remaining choices and found them to be lacking.

"Yeah, I'd be interested...I mean, I guess." He didn't want to sound too eager with this blind doctor. He still had a reputation to think about. "Sure, yeah."

Julian smiled awkwardly, suddenly realizing he'd forgotten the name of this young man. He couldn't subtly glance at the boy's paperwork to obtain the name, so he was left with no other option. Swallowing his pride, he said, "Listen, we were never formally introduced. I'm Julian Stryker. And you are?"

The kid chuckled and shook his head. "I may not be book smart, man, but I know a bluff when I hear one. You don't know my name, do you?"

Julian was caught. And to the kid's surprise, he owned up to the mistake by raising his hands in an "I give up" gesture.

"You got me," he said, flashing a big grin.

Not many adults admit when they're wrong, the kid thought. This guy's all right. "The name's Danny Sheehan. Good to meet'cha, I guess."

CHAPTER 3

"**D**r. Sterling, how lovely to see you again!" gushed seminar coordinator Evelyn De Groot. Linda rolled her eyes and took a deep breath before turning around slowly to address the sycophant. Evelyn waddled over to greet her esteemed guest, a foul perfume wafting slightly ahead of her. A full foot shorter than the five-foot-nine Dr. Sterling, Evelyn enclosed Linda in a bear hug around her waist. Repulsed, Linda raised her hands above her assailant and then slowly lowered them in a gesture of a hug without actually acquiescing to a full embrace.

"Evelyn...as always, it's a pleasure," Linda managed.

"Oh no, the pleasure is mine, Dr. Sterling. We were thrilled when we heard you were presenting this year. As you know, the American Psychiatric Association is working hard to create a more cohesive connection between us and the American Cancer Society. Your work in both fields goes a long way in cementing that bond. In fact, I wanted to talk to you about a unique opportunity in that regard. We're looking for someone to be 'the face' of our partnership." Evelyn lifted her arms and used the first two fingers of each hand to draw imaginary quotation marks around "the face" when she spoke.

"Anyhoo, we were hoping—well, *I* was hoping—that you and I could get together sometime over the next couple of days and discuss it. How about dinner this evening?"

"Oooh, Evelyn...I'd love to, but I'm meeting a friend of mine for dinner. Long story short, we grew up together, and I'd like to see her while I'm in town. Sorry." Linda flashed the smile she normally reserved for attractive men. Evelyn, momentarily caught off guard, paused a half second too long, allowing Linda the chance to slip away while saying, "I'm sure we'll talk later though, Evelyn."

Linda made her way to the conference room, where she was to present on the latest breakthroughs in carcinoma research. She was in a foul mood. Her most recent attempt to cavort with a male friend had been thwarted by a car waiting outside the bar where she'd seen him. After leaving the bar quickly to avoid dealing with Brenda, Linda had jumped into her rental, driven around the block, and parked a slight distance away from the entrance. Soon after, the man had exited the bar, only to get into a car idling right in front of Linda's. Her night had been ruined, and she'd not yet recovered from the disappointment. The last thing she wanted to be doing today was talking to a large group…and the last place she wanted to be doing it was in this hotel.

Entering the empty, overly air-conditioned room, she took note of her biography board on a tripod stand next to the podium where she would speak. Her gaze drifted over the rest of the space. Cloth-covered tables were arranged in a square U fashion, the podium falling in the middle of the open part of the U so all seats had a good view of the speaker. Gold-painted chairs were pushed in until they touched the table in front of them. At each place was a name placard, a pen and pad of paper, a small carafe of water, and a glass, in case her audience needed refreshment during the talk. She approached the podium and saw that she, too, had been supplied with a small carafe and a glass, which sat on the podium's shelf.

All was in order. Good, she thought. Order is important.

"Order is imperative," Linda said aloud, echoing the words her father had spoken often before he died.

Wandering to stand in front of her portrait, she gazed at it, head in hand and tilted to one side. Her smile in the picture was furtive, as if she had a wonderful secret she wanted to keep hidden from the world. The picture had been taken six years ago when Linda had just discovered she was pregnant. She and Jonathan had been told by reproductive experts that they couldn't conceive, so after mourning the news for several months, they had moved on like so many couples do, making a life for themselves devoid of children. And then, miraculously, she'd become pregnant and delivered a beautiful baby girl, Catherine. Linda smiled at the memory and glanced once more at the portrait. *Yes, my life is in perfect order, Daddy,* she thought. *Just as you would have liked it.*

Her reverie was interrupted by the arrival of the physicians attending her talk. Quickly placing her belongings behind the podium, Linda powered up the iPad that held her presentation. The techie guy appeared and connected her iPad to the overhead so that she could scroll through her presentation while she was speaking.

The doctors, primarily men, found their seats and were gawking at Linda as she stood pin straight at the front of the room, commanding everyone's attention without uttering a single word. Hands clasped demurely in front of her, a Mona Lisa smile poised on her graceful countenance, she waited until the last chair had been pulled in, the last glass of water had been poured, and the last throat cleared before opening her arms wide and unleashing a stunner smile in which flirtation met confidence that bordered on cockiness. As she welcomed each physician by name, she mentally ticked off his professional accomplishments, somewhat surprised to discover that she held the most awards, grants, and publications to her name.

Yes, all was in perfect order. So, why did she have that tickling sensation that started at the base of her spine, snaked around her midsection like a serpent, and slowly wound its way up until she felt it approaching her chin? Writhing around her neck, closing as it circled, it threatened to strangle her.

"What can you control?" her father had often asked. "When you feel out of control, determine what you can control, and focus on that."

Snapped back to the present, Linda Sterling briefly closed her eyes and pictured the gentleman she'd been with in Baltimore. He *had* been a true gentleman, even at the end when things were at their worst for him. Slowly uncoiling from her throat, the beast slithered back to its nest. Warmth spread from her cheeks down her perfect, lean neck and settled comfortably where she believed her soul was housed. A plan was forming in her mind, and with it came precious relief.

Opening her eyes, she sauntered to the podium, everyone's attention riveted on her heart-shaped derriere as it swung in rhythm with her stride.

Turning around to face her colleagues, she smiled and said, "Shall we get started, gentlemen?"

Chapter 4

Sarah Turnbull, as tiny and fragile as a sparrow, lay in bed, tubes connecting her to what remained of her life. Her eyes were closed as she drifted in and out of sleep...or consciousness...or both. Unwashed white hair surrounded her delicate head like a greasy halo, leaving the impression that she'd already passed and was simply awaiting the burial ritual that existed only for the purpose of assuaging the living's sadness and guilt. Bony hands perched carefully atop the bedcovers as if they had recently put down a good book and were eager to pick it up again as soon as their owner awakened. The myriad medical machines emitted persistent, irritating beeps, reminding her visitor that Sarah's situation was similar to the likely fate of all of us. We have no choice about getting old, but we damn well can determine how we arrive at death's door. That's the part we can control...at least somewhat, Linda thought.

Before entering Sarah's room, Linda had taken some time to discuss Sarah's condition with the physicians treating her. She wanted to understand the seriousness of the situation and what Sarah's prognosis was. The answers were "very serious" and "not good," respectively. The looks on their faces had spoken volumes, and Linda had chosen to leave it at that. Linda knew that Sarah was on medication for her heart, as she suffered from an ailment called atrial fibrillation, or AFib, a condition in which the upper chambers of the heart quiver or twitch quickly and create an irregular rhythm. The diagnosis was certainly not a death sentence, but it was serious and had to be managed appropriately. In addition, Sarah had recently suffered a stroke.

Given her advanced age and condition, Linda knew Sarah most likely didn't have much time left. She wasn't returning home, that was certain. At best, she'd end up living in the facility's 24/7 care wing. At worst…well, she'd die.

Gingerly, Linda took Sarah's right hand into her own, the crepe-paper skin shriveling under her touch. This hand, once so strong and determined, had lost all its strength and hung limply in Linda's tender grasp.

"Hi, Sarah. It's Linda."

There was no movement or response.

"I know it's been a while, but I'm here to see you. I wanted you to know that I—" Linda broke off, not knowing what to say.

How do you thank someone for saving your life? For giving you back everything you had lost? For loving you when no one else would? For never giving up on you? Linda wondered.

"I guess I just wanted you to know that…that I'm here. Thank you for all you've done for me. I love you." A single tear rolled down Linda's perfect alabaster cheek and fell heavily on the translucent skin of Sarah's hand.

"Also, I've done some things, Sarah. Some things that could get me into serious trouble. I just wanted you to know that I'm trying—really hard—not to do those things, but it's difficult. It's really, really hard. Even you don't know the whole truth. But…I wanted you to know that I'm trying." The tears were coming faster now, and to her own surprise, Linda didn't try to stop them. She spoke no more but just let them fall, one after the other, until they were spent. Leaning down, Linda kissed the back of the hand that had treated her with nothing but kindness and whispered a promise to return once more prior to leaving town.

Before she left the room, Linda slipped a small gold ring with three rubies onto Sarah's right middle finger. She had meant it to be for Sarah's pinky finger, but she'd had no idea how shriveled Sarah had become. Linda had purchased it earlier in the day to replace the one Brenda had said had been stolen by the staff. She smiled at Sarah once more, smoothed down the snow-white hair, and whispered, "I don't believe there's a God up there watching us, Sarah, but I know you do, so I'll pray anyway, okay? It's the least I can do. Bye, Sarah."

As she exited the facility, Linda noticed three support staff gathered in the small gazebo designated as the smoking area. Evaluating them for a minute without their knowledge, Linda saw three relatively short, dumpy women, all thirty-something with badly home-dyed hair in dire need of touching up, dressed in mall-bought scrubs designed to make them look more official. They gave Linda the impression of grown-ups playing at being professional. One of them was clearly in midstory, gesticulating madly with her cigarette. As Linda casually sauntered over, a warm, hearty smile fixed on her perfect face, they all burst out laughing at the story's conclusion. Linda stood abreast of the group, careful to position herself upwind to avoid the noxious fumes they were exhaling.

"Hello, ladies. How are you today?"

The storyteller turned and warily regarded Linda, the beautiful, graceful woman carrying a Fendi purse and sporting Jimmy Choos. Not many people like her around here, thought Sharon Sheehan, blowing smoke directly in Linda's direction. Sharon took a step forward, obviously the leader of the group. A long pause ensued in which Linda felt the women's appraising eyes dissecting her appearance. She waited.

"Afternoon," they finally relented in unison.

"Say, do any of you watch after Ms. Sarah Turnbull in there?" Linda gestured toward the facility.

"Uh, yeah...all of us, actually," Sharon offered, turning toward the other two women. "In different shifts sometimes, but yeah, all of us. Why?"

"And are you three the only support staff assigned to Ms. Turnbull?" Linda continued pleasantly.

They looked at each other, unsure where Linda was going with her questioning and clearly suspicious.

Sharon dropped her cigarette on the wooden floor of the gazebo, crunched it with her right clog, and then stepped down out of the structure so that she was facing Linda directly. Linda noted that the crushed cigarette was still emitting smoke.

"Yeah, sure, just us three. Why?"

"Well, I just wanted to tell you that I appreciate all you're doing for my friend in there. She looks as well as can be expected given her condition. So… thanks."

Linda watched as the three of them visibly relaxed. They'd obviously thought they were in trouble. Perhaps they're used to it, Linda thought.

Sharon gave her a warm, genuine smile and said, "Hey, thanks. We work our asses off in there, and nobody really ever says thanks or nothin'. Not a lot of perks in there, if you know what I mean."

"Really?" asked Linda innocently. "I would've thought the money you make from fencing items such as a ruby ring might make up for your obvious lack of income." She regarded them as one would examine a flea on a dog—fascinating yet needs to be exterminated.

"You need to know that Ms. Turnbull has received a new ruby ring, a real one, by the way. Did you know that the stolen ring wasn't real gold and didn't have real rubies?" By the looks on their faces, it was clear they'd not known. "Oh, I guess you haven't tried to sell it yet. Well, now you know. Anyhow, Ms. Turnbull has received a new, authentic ring from me, and I expect to see it on her finger every time I come here…which will be often."

Sharon had heard enough. "Oh, yeah? Well, I'm not saying nothin' was stolen, but if it was, we didn't do it."

Linda felt an uncanny calm flow over her, as if she were standing underneath a waterfall of tranquility. She gazed at Sharon for a moment, amused at the woman's naïveté. Smiling, she shook her head and took two steps toward Sharon, who involuntarily stumbled backward under the scrutiny.

"Just make sure she keeps the ring. I'm putting you in charge…" She cast a quick glance at the woman's name tag. "Sharon. Have a lovely day, ladies. Oh, and you really shouldn't smoke. You never know what might kill you, but why increase the odds?"

Linda glanced pointedly at Sharon before turning on her blood-red heels and walking away, back erect and head held high.

Sharon's gaze trailed Linda as she walked away. When Linda was out of earshot, Sharon turned to her two colleagues and said, "Okay, who did it?

Who stole the ring?" As they remained stoically silent, she stared hard at each of them in turn. "Which one of you stole the ring?"

No reply.

"Okay. Here's the deal. I worked really hard to get this job, and I don't intend to lose it because one o' you two bitches thinks she can make a buck off some old lady. You need to know two things."

She held up her right index finger. "One—Sarah Turnbull is all right and deserves better than she's gettin' from the likes o' you two."

The middle finger then went up. "And two—that lady that just was here was my son's cancer doctor. I didn't recognize her at first, but it's her."

The two women exchanged nervous glances.

"Yeah, that's right. She was mean right now because she thought that someone she cares about was being taken advantage of, which she *is*..." Sharon was into it now, leaning into the women and shaking her finger. "But that lady's a good doctor. She couldn't save my boy, but she tried really hard. I don't think she recognized me, thank the Lord, thinking that I stole her friend's ring, for God's sake. And I certainly wasn't going to tell her who I am. I'm so friggin' embarrassed right now."

The other two simply stood there, staring openmouthed at Sharon, who seemed lost in thought. Snapping back to the present, Sharon quipped, "Get inside. Break's over. And...keep it together, okay? No more stealing. I need this job."

Chapter 5

Julian had met with six patients throughout the day and was now dictating notes using his Dragon voice-recognition software. The computer would then type his words and read them back so he could verify their accuracy. This was one of many changes implemented when his sight had been robbed from him. Time-consuming, sure—but necessary and worthwhile.

As a sighted clinician, Julian had simply written all his notes post session, mostly by hand. However, after the attack that had blinded him, his loyal assistant, Jesse, had quickly realized how much his friend's practice had to change in order to continue functioning. Therefore, while Julian convalesced from multiple surgeries and therapy sessions, Jesse had revamped the entire office.

Starting with patient records, Jesse had researched, interviewed, purchased, and been trained on a digital medical management system that included scanning all paper records into electronic files and an integrated patient reminder-call application as well as billing and all pertinent financial record keeping. In addition, Jesse had reorganized Julian's office so that it was less cluttered and more logically organized. Coat rack stood to the immediate right of Julian's office door upon entering, the leather couch next to that. In front of the couch sat a beautiful mahogany coffee table that held a box of tissues on the right and a sound machine for blocking out stray noise on the left. Across from the coffee table was a matching mahogany end table that sat between two overstuffed arm chairs, one of which boasted a permanent indentation from Julian's butt. Finishing the room was Julian's cherished old mahogany desk that was home to more nicks, dents, and scratches than Jesse had thought possible. Jesse knew, though, that he couldn't possibly replace the desk, which had belonged to Julian's father before he had walked out on the family when Julian was twelve.

It was at this desk that Julian now sat dictating his notes when he heard the door to his office creak open. Through the crack, Julian could hear Jesse speaking to a patient, who based on Jesse's tone and demeanor was demanding to speak to Julian "right now!" Julian smiled, knowing that Jesse had the ability to talk people down as needed in order to protect his boss and friend. And all the while, the person on the other end of the line was thinking it was his or her own idea to call back tomorrow.

Julian's attention shifted back to his office door, where someone was standing completely still. Her perfume latched onto air particles that made their way seductively up Julian's nostrils and did a number on the limbic area of his brain, causing his breath to quicken and his heart to pound.

"Hello, gorgeous," he said with a grin, leaning forward in his chair, his fingers interlaced on top of the desk.

"I always like to see how long it takes you to recognize me," Alex Hayes smiled back, slowly making her way over to where Julian was now leaning back in his chair, arms spread wide, clearly inviting her to take a seat on his lap.

"You do realize that you can never change your perfume, right?" he joked.

Alex snuggled into his lap and laid her head against his shoulder. A tall woman at five-foot-ten, she was still no match for Julian's six-foot-two frame as she curled into him like a beautiful, graceful feline.

Julian sighed and decided to simply enjoy the moment. After all, it wasn't that long ago that he and Alex had shared a horrific case that had almost ended very badly. In fact, if it hadn't been for an FBI agent named Vinny Marcozzi, they would most assuredly be dead. They'd been investigating the murder of a rare book authenticator in Belize, and the chase had led them to Mexico, where they found themselves entangled in a bizarre vendetta between rival drug factions. If Vinny hadn't arrived during what turned out to be the final shootout, they most certainly would have been murdered, their bodies dumped in some shallow Mexican-desert grave. Worst of all, however, was that upon returning to Boston, they'd discovered the person who had reported the crime—a close, family friend of Alex's named Elizabeth Vandenholz—had been manipulating them all along. The whole ordeal, including their near demise, could have been avoided, and the case against Mrs. Vandenholz was still pending in Boston circuit court.

"Hey, have you talked to Vinny recently?" Julian asked.

"Marcozzi? No, but it's funny you should mention him, because he called and left me a message today. Why do you ask?" Alex pulled away and looked at Julian.

"Oh, I was just thinking about that whole Vandenholz thing and was wondering how he's doing."

"Well, I heard through Boston PD/FBI channels that he got a promotion due to solving that case. He's now special agent in charge of the upper US Northeast. That's probably why he called—to rub our noses in it." She laughed.

"Wow, good for him. At least somebody got something out of that clusterf—"

"Hey, hey, mister—watch it! You got something out of it too…me!" Alex hopped out of Julian's lap and crossed to the leather couch, which Julian's mother had given him upon his graduation from Boston University with a PhD in child psychology. The worn, faded leather creaked as she stretched out and then wiggled into a comfortable position.

Julian couldn't help but smile at the memory of the events that had transpired to bring them together. It had been a long road. When Julian's sight had been stolen, he'd thought his life was over. He lost not only his eyesight but confidence in himself as a psychologist. After all, he'd been seeing Jeremy Walker as a patient for a while—originally sent to Julian by the court system after being convicted of animal cruelty. Julian had thought that Jeremy was making good progress. How had he missed the sociopathic warning signs his assailant must have been exhibiting? What kind of child psychologist doesn't see an attack like the one Jeremy committed coming? Julian was so riddled with doubt about his own expertise that once he had worked through the initial depression associated with sudden drastic loss, he had returned to school to study criminal profiling.

Detective Alexandra Hayes had been assigned to Julian's case from the beginning. The successful investigation and eventual prosecution was due primarily to her expert handling and witness presentation. Post trial, she'd made herself quietly available to him as a friend, a shoulder to lean on, an ear for listening. Then, after he had completed his degree, she'd approached him to work with her and the Boston Police Department as a profiler. They'd worked many cases together over the years, but it wasn't until recently that they'd taken their strictly friendly, professional relationship several steps forward. That had been about a year ago, and both of them hadn't looked back. The one negative was that because they were in a relationship, Boston PD protocol decreed they could no longer work cases together. Although they regretted that fact, they both agreed that the perks of dating far outweighed the fun they had working together.

"Hey, did you hear me, Julian? Or do you disagree that you got something wonderful out of it too?" she enquired flirtatiously.

Julian crossed to the couch and knelt down on the floor. Reaching out and touching her hair, he slowly brought his left hand down around the angles of her right cheek, his thumb brushing the bone that created her royal aquiline nose. His thumb came to rest on her lips, through which he felt her breath quicken.

"God, you really are beautiful. You know that, right?" He felt her sly smile mature into a full-fledged grin.

"Sweet talker, that's what you are. Think it's gonna get you somewhere, huh?" She leaned forward, and their lips met.

"Hey, hey…" A voice broke in. "Do I need to get the fire hose again? Seriously, get a room, you two. Oh, wait…you have a room. In fact, you have two rooms—one in each of your houses. How about going there and letting me close up shop for the night?"

As always, Jesse had said all of this in one breath. The guy had lungs of steel.

"You're just jealous, Jess," Julian mumbled into Alex's lips.

"Damn straight I am!" he answered. "Where's *my* happy ending? Where's *my* better half? Where's *my*—"

"Okay, okay," Julian acquiesced, slowly rising, already missing Alex's touch. "Hey, can I get a ride home, Alex?"

"Sure thing. Grab your stuff, and we can stop by the North End on the way home for some Italian. Sound good?"

"Sounds perfect. Oh, Jess…Danny Sheehan's file is missing some really pertinent information. Did you know he had a brother named Jimmy who died of cancer?"

"Seriously? Oh, wow…sorry. I'll touch base with Amanda, the court clerk who helps me out. She'll fill in the gaps."

"Thanks. I'll want the name of his dead brother's oncologist so I can follow up with him regarding Jimmy's illness. Apparently it ripped the family apart."

"Got it. Anything else?"

"Just one more thing, Jess. Have I told you how awesome you are? Bring it in for a hug." Julian spread his arms wide, a Cheshire cat grin plastered on his face.

"I am not hugging you, Julian." Jesse stood, arms crossed, eyes rolling toward the ceiling. Alex chuckled, shaking her head.

"Yes, you are. Come on, bring it in. Alex, you too. Get in here."

"We should just give in, Jesse. You know he won't let up until we do." Alex crossed to Julian and tucked herself under his right arm.

Jesse squinted as he took in the ridiculous scene. Having left a broken, abusive home at the age of sixteen, William Stein had legally changed his name to Jesse James and had crossed the country in search of fame and fortune as an actor. He worked odd jobs, took some acting classes, and eventually made it out to LA. Finding no success on the screen, he made his way to New York to try his luck on the stage. After more years of waiting tables and odd jobs to make ends meet, he finally gave up and found himself back where he had started: Boston.

When Julian met Jesse, he was a broken man in desperate need of steady employment. With no office skills to speak of, Julian hired him anyway, intuitively sensing that he was smart and a quick study. Julian had never regretted the decision. Although standoffish and wary at first, Jesse had slowly made himself invaluable to Julian. And since becoming blind, Julian truly wasn't sure he could function without Jesse, a fact Jesse was aware of but never, ever highlighted. Julian had found the support he needed, and Jesse had found the "family" he'd never had. And, like most family, Jesse sometimes wished they would simply go away. Like now, for instance.

"Get in here, buddy," Julian pressed.

Jesse grimaced as he reluctantly entered the circle. Julian's left arm gripped Jesse like a vise, and Alex completed his humiliation by embracing him on the other side. They stood like that for a moment until Jesse broke away, waving his arms and saying, "Enough! Go...get out of here, you two! See you tomorrow."

If only Julian could have seen the slight smile on Jesse's face. It didn't matter, though, because not only had Alex seen it, but Julian had heard it in his voice.

CHAPTER 6

Linda stood naked in front of the mirror, her head tilted slightly to the left, evaluating her reflection. Her shoulders were broad enough and her belly relatively flat. A slender waist gave way to hips that flared gracefully—slightly wider than they'd been when she was younger, before Catherine had altered her shape forever. She cupped her full breasts and lifted them up, a slight pout forming on her otherwise flawless face. Perhaps some augmentation might be in order, or at least a lift, to alleviate yet another consequence of gravity and breastfeeding. She let her hands fall to her sides and focused her attention on the full bush of mahogany curls that formed a perfect triangle where her torso met her legs. She parted her legs and ran her right hand through the hair. Too long. Needs a shave. Her thoughts then drifted to her husband, Jonathan. He liked her smooth. And in truth, she liked it better that way too. Not the Brazilian wax style, but completely devoid of hair. All the better to feel him...really feel him.

Her phone vibrated, and she smiled as she recognized the ringtone. It was the song "Celebrate," by Kool and the Gang, that she and Jonathan had danced to at their wedding. Dorky, but it had significance to them, so they overrode their parents' objections and had the deejay play it anyway. It also meant they could avoid having to perform a slow dance in front of everyone.

"Hello, my darling. I was just thinking about you. You and that wonderfully large—"

"Hi, Mommy!" bubbled a voice across the air waves. "What're you doing? We miss you a whole lot, but Daddy took me out for ice cream and said that I can stay up as late as I want."

Linda smiled. It was a running joke between the girl's parents. Whenever they told Catherine to go to bed at a particular time, she would revolt. Standing with her little arms folded over her tiny chest, she would puff out her cheeks and spread her legs wide, as if this act of defiance would bolt her feet to the ground. They'd tried reasoning with her, bribing her, and then finally forcing her. Although the result was ultimately achieved, it never felt good to them. So, they'd resorted to reverse psychology, telling her that she could stay up as late as she wanted, no holds barred. Each time they'd incorporated this technique into the bedtime ritual, she'd fallen asleep by eight o'clock. Win-win.

"Hello, my love. Ice cream, wow! That's awesome. You sure do have a wonderful daddy. Sleep tight, sugar. That is, whenever you end up falling asleep."

"Thanks, Mommy. You sleep tight too. We'll see you soon. Here's Daddy."

"Well, that was close," Jonathan breathed into the phone. "What was that you were saying about my large—"

"We'll have to save it for another time, Jonathan," Linda snapped. "The mood's been broken. So, things are good there?"

Jonathan had been married to this woman long enough to know a mood change when he heard one.

"Yeah, all is well. How'd your talk go today?"

"Oh, fine. Just the usual mind-numbingly boring seminar stuff. Anyhow, glad everything's good. I gotta go. I'm meeting Brenda tonight for dinner."

"Okay. Lin?"

"Yes?"

"I love you."

Dr. Linda Sterling paused, hating Jonathan at that very moment for what she considered his neediness. He always insisted they complete a phone call with an "I love you," as if being successfully married for as long as they had wasn't proof enough of their love. He'd instantaneously altered her mood. Like a widow's funereal veil, blackness descended upon Linda's head and began its progression through her body, everywhere, all at once. The night was ruined.

"I love you too, Jonathan. Night," she growled.

She rang off and threw her phone angrily onto the bed. Turning slowly to confront her altered reflection, she glared at her face and saw lines that had been nonexistent prior to the phone call. Dark circles appeared under her puffy eyes. The blackness continued to ooze its way down as she shifted her attention to the rest of her reflection. Her body, tantalizing only a few moments before, had morphed into ugliness. It wasn't thin enough or tanned enough. Her breasts were far too saggy, and her hips were huge. Nothing was as it should be, and she screwed up her face in frustration. Desperately attempting to fend off the serpent that seethed deep and low in her belly, she dropped to her knees and threw her head into her hands. Still, the reptile assaulted her relentlessly, surging up and then back down, desperate to get out and find validity.

"No, no, no," she whispered. "Not now. It's too soon."

Dr. Linda Sterling started to cry, quietly at first and then in outright sobs. Inconsolable sobs. Crumpling to the ground in the fetal position, she thought about what her father would say, picturing him standing over her, riding crop in hand.

"Get up, girl. You think you have it rough? There are a lot of other kids a lot worse off than you! Determine what can you control, quit your whining, and get up!" The crop whipped down right next to her head, thankfully finding its mark on the floor and not on her. Her father continued, *"Now, get yourself in order, and get the job done. Get it done!"*

"But Daddy, please…it's too soon. Please don't make me do this… please," she begged.

"Linda, we both know that I can't make you do something you don't already want to do. Everything that you do, that has been done to you, has been controlled by you. You have either actively completed the task or passively accepted completion of the task by letting it happen. Now, what can you control? Get it done!"

The riding crop rose high in the air, forcing Linda to cower for cover closer to the bed.

"I—" The crop whooshed past her right ear, so close that she could feel the air on her skin.

"Said—" The crop *thwumped* on the bed.

"Get it—" The crop landed next to her left ear.

She held her breath.

"Done!" The crop landed on her right hand.

Linda gasped and glanced at her hand, which had been smashed not by her father's riding crop but by the telephone next to the bed. How had that happened?

Suddenly her head snapped up, tears drying as she stood up ramrod straight and stared into the mirror at her form once more. Her eyes had turned hard, pupils dilated, as she pursed her lips seductively. One hip jutted out to the side as a perfectly manicured hand poised on it just so. The other hand found a nipple and squeezed hard, her gaze never wavering. She spoke to the beautiful girl in the mirror who was removing her wedding band.

"Come on, honey. Let's do a little shopping before dinner."

⅄

Linda entered the hotel bar and immediately regretted the decision to shop so close to where she was staying. Three physicians who had attended her talk today were seated at the bar and waved at her excitedly as she entered. They motioned her to come over, two of them patting the seat between them. Not seeing a way out, she reluctantly sauntered over and arranged herself on the stool.

One of the men snapped—he actually *snapped*—at the bartender, who appeared in front of them, looking bored. Linda couldn't blame him. What must it be like for this man, whose meager reward for listening to pompous blowhards with overinflated egos droning on about their meaningless lives was a stray twenty dollars they *might* remember to throw on the bar before staggering up to their empty hotel beds? Depressing is what it must be like, Linda imagined, finishing the thought before ordering her usual cosmo.

Feeling a sort of kinship with the bartender, she smiled at the older gentleman, who looked upon her not with lust but rather with kindness and perhaps a little pity given her current circumstances. He casually glanced at the three men leaning toward Linda and then returned his gaze to Linda's eyes, an unspoken understanding between them. She knew that he understood her predicament and would do what he could to expedite her departure.

"So, Dr. Sterling...Linda, is it? May I call you Linda?" one of the windbags started.

"Of course."

"We thoroughly enjoyed your presentation today." This was directed at her ample bosom and not in the direction of her eyes or, say, her brain.

"Oh, I'm so glad," Linda responded dryly, the irony lost on the man. "Which part did you like best?"

"Well, actually, I wanted to talk to you about the patient you discussed, the seven-year-old with leukemia who regressed to toddler-like tendencies when..."

But Linda heard no more as her pulse raced and pupils dilated. She couldn't believe he was there, sitting alone in a booth against the wall. He was perfect—thinning hair, glasses, suit slightly crumpled. He looked tired as he banged away at the laptop's keyboard, his attention completely focused on the screen. His mobile vibrated, and he stole his gaze away from the screen long enough to verify the caller. He picked up the phone, but Linda could barely make out his end of the conversation.

"Yeah, I know. I got it," he said. Philly accent, Linda surmised. Or maybe Jersey or Maryland. But not from here is the point. Her mind raced.

"Okay, I can get it, but I'll have to get back to you because I don't have that information with me at the moment." Pause. "No, it's up in my room." Pause. "What, now?" A deep breath followed by an exasperated blowout of air. And then a grudging "All right, fine," followed by his hanging up, and then...

Her perfect man was suddenly standing up and stretching.

Her full attention returned to the three idiots surrounding her.

"Gentlemen, it's been wonderful chatting with you, but suddenly I'm not feeling well. I hope you'll excuse me?"

"I hope it was nothing I said," offered the man who had been talking incessantly. "I didn't mean to infer that you were erroneous in the conclusions in your paper. I just meant to say that—"

Mr. Perfect was powering down his laptop and packing it into its case.

"Wait…what?" Linda redirected some of her focus to the physician who'd been speaking. "Are you referring to my most recent paper in the *Journal of Pediatric Medicine?*"

Mr. Perfect downed the rest of his drink and was placing a ten-dollar bill on the table.

"Well, yes," replied the doctor. "And I hope I didn't offend you. I was just saying that I think it would be great if you would take a look at my research and perhaps incorporate some of my findings in your next article. Or I can publish without your opinion on the subject."

His coat slid onto his wonderfully average body as he turned toward the door, briefcase in hand.

Linda had been so adamantly sure of her current companions' lascivious intentions that she'd stupidly dismissed the three of them completely. She tried to focus on the researcher in front of her.

"It's you to whom I owe an apology, doctor…"

"Stevens. Richard Stevens, out of Johns Hopkins."

He was getting away.

"Of course, Dr. Stevens, my most sincere apologies for not recognizing you and for not taking your research into account. I would absolutely love to hear more about the thesis of your study, but right now I really do need to leave."

She stole a glance at the door, only to find that Mr. Perfect had just disappeared through it.

Returning her gaze to Dr. Stevens, Linda really looked at him for the first time. He was a serious-looking man—no, not serious…sincere—whose gaze was indeed falling on her breasts. But, she realized with sudden clarity, not because his eyes were hungering for what they couldn't have but because he had trouble making eye contact. He was most likely one of those brilliant people who were so socially awkward that they retreat into their own worlds.

When they're kids, they create an imaginary friend or place. And when they're adults, because imaginary worlds are no longer acceptable, they retreat into their work, which in Dr. Stevens's case happened to be in the same field as Linda's. Dr. Stevens chanced a glance at Linda's eyes, which had softened and now held genuine kindness.

"I hope you and I can discuss our work at a later date?" she offered, holding out her right hand.

He smiled shyly and proffered his hand as well, his grip limp and somewhat damp. "I'd like that," he said.

"I'll have my assistant get in touch with yours," Linda said as they exchanged business cards. "Count on it."

Linda darted out the bar entrance and glanced right and left, figuring she'd missed Mr. Perfect by about two minutes due to the exchange with Dr. Stevens. As she was walking toward the hotel's main entrance, though, she spied him talking to the young man behind the front desk. She made a show of checking her phone, reading e-mails, and composing pretend texts until she saw him turn and walk briskly toward the elevators. Unbuttoning another button on her blouse, she abruptly turned and headed for the same elevator, arriving slightly ahead of him.

When he appeared next to her, she angled slightly toward him, allowing him a full frontal visual of her. He didn't disappoint. His eyes traveled over her entire body, and once she was sure she had his full attention, she leaned forward to press the elevator button once more, her blouse falling dangerously open in the process. Her finger lingered over the call button as she slowly turned to him and said, "It seems like these things take forever, doesn't it?"

The third finger of his left hand was bare and didn't sport a white line indicating that he'd recently removed a ring, like so many men did at these conventions. His gaze darted up to hers, an embarrassed grin gracing his weather-beaten face. His sea-green eyes seemed tired but kind, and she momentarily lost her nerve. But then those salacious eyes found her blouse again, hardening her resolve once more.

"Yeah, forever."

Linda stared hard at the man, waiting for him to meet her gaze. After several moments, he finally met her eyes and was rewarded with one of her best smiles.

"My name's Ashley," Linda breathed, "and I don't mean to be blunt, but I find you very attractive. You seem very...what's the right word? Powerful. Yeah, that's it," she gushed.

Mr. Perfect stood up a little straighter, clearly unused to receiving such praise.

Blushing, he said, "Well...hello, Ashley. I'm Evan Donaldson, and it's nice to meet you. Really nice." He held out his hand to shake Linda's. She let it hang there as she moved a bit closer to him, forcing him to lower it or risk brushing it against her body.

"What do you do for a living, Evan Donaldson?"

He was starting to sweat, not believing this was actually happening to him. "Um...I'm a pharmaceutical rep. That is, I sell medical equipment and drugs to doctors and hospitals." He smoothed down his thinning hair.

"And your family must be missing you, huh?" A little closer still so that he could get a whiff of her perfume.

"No, no family to speak of in PA. That's where I'm from. Lancaster, Pennsylvania."

Linda leaned in close to him and whispered. "No family, huh? Well, what a shame."

The elevator arrived, and Linda turned away from him.

After ensuring no one was exiting the elevator, Linda locked her eyes on his and purred, "After you," gesturing him toward the elevator door. "I insist."

Evan Donaldson hurriedly entered as Linda surreptitiously perused her surroundings and then followed him in. The lobby was empty except for a woman arguing with the lone hotel employee at the front desk. They were both far too engrossed in their conversation to have noticed the frumpy man getting on the elevator with a stunning brunette.

Chapter 7

Alex took the winding off-ramp at forty-five miles an hour, fifteen miles an hour faster than the posted recommended speed, forcing Julian to grip the armrest with his right hand while bracing the other against the dashboard. As if that would protect me, Julian thought helplessly.

As the wheels skidded on the cement, the sound of squealing tires clawed its way through Julian's ear canals and into his brain.

"Nervous, Stryker?" Alex almost yelled, high on adrenaline from the drive in her vintage 1968 Mustang G6.

"No, no. I'm good," Julian whispered through gritted teeth, drawing a guffaw from Alex.

Alex suddenly slammed on the brakes, thrusting Julian forward against his seat belt, which strained under the sudden pressure. Her passenger remained stoically silent.

"Sorry about that, Stryker," Alex mumbled. "I didn't see the red light until we were on top of it."

"Well, of course you didn't, Alex. How could you when you approach it like Evel Knievel?" Julian answered quietly. Julian had long ago given up trying to alter Alex's driving technique. Instead, he had begun a new offensive: trying to understand why she felt the need to speed and perpetually push boundaries. Although she hadn't yet caught on that his tactics had shifted, she did wonder why he no longer hounded her about her driving.

"So, how's your mom?" Julian asked innocently.

Alex chuckled. "Is this in response to my quick stop? Are you torturing me with questions about my mother in retribution?"

"Please, Alex. I'm a psychotherapist. I think that if I wanted to torture you, I'd find more interesting and creative ways to do it rather than asking about your mother, for goodness' sake."

Alex turned to face him, wondering whether he was playing her or being serious. She decided it was the latter.

"Sorry again, Stryker. She's, uh...fine, I guess. Same stories, same questions. 'When are you getting married?' 'Why are you a cop?' 'Can't you just settle down?' Although..." She trailed off thoughtfully.

"Although what?" Julian pressed.

"Well, she does ask about you a lot and wonders how we are...the two of us, I mean, as a couple."

"And what do you tell her?"

"That we're just hunky dory, humming along. Dandy, even."

"Dandy?" Julian replied, laughing. "Who *says* that? *Dandy*," Julian repeated, shaking his head.

"Well, we are, aren't we?" Alex became serious.

Julian thought for a second and said, "Yes, actually, we are...dandy. Light's green."

"Oh, thanks." Alex pulled away from the light at an appropriate speed, her mind grounded and her soul soothed.

"Stryker?"

"Yeah?"

"You did mention my mother to torture me, didn't you?

"Yes, I did."

"But it didn't work, did it?"

"Well, we can look at it two ways, Alex. On the one hand, you could say that I was being a small person, hitting you in your weak spot—your mother—in response to your driving dangerously. Or, on the other hand, you could say that by mentioning your mother, I knew I'd draw out of you your biggest concern so that we could discuss it, thereby alleviating your stress and improving your erratic driving. Either way, we both win. You feel better and are driving less capriciously, and I have a happier girlfriend who will allow me to arrive at my destination alive."

Alex was quiet for a moment and then grabbed Julian's hand, squeezing it. "I'm gonna go with option number two," she said.

"Good choice."

"Hey, how'd you know the light was green, by the way?"

"What do you mean?"

"You told me the traffic light was green. How did you know?"

"I counted. When I was sighted, that stoplight drove me crazy because it's about ten seconds longer than most. So, I always counted at that light. It lasts seventy-three seconds exactly."

"You were counting as we were talking?" she asked incredulously.

"Sure. I have to do many things simultaneously now that I can't see. It's just part of the deal."

"Huh. You have so many talents," she said, meaning it.

"Oh yeah? Wait till we get back to my place. I'll show you some of my many *other* talents, young lady."

"Who you calling young? Or a lady?" she asked with a smirk, taking off again at breakneck speed.

They arrived at their favorite North End Italian restaurant, Giacomo's, and chose to use the parking valet, as it was four forty-five and the line of people waiting to enter was already rounding the corner. Like many North End eateries, Giacomo's was small and held few tables. Many of the restaurants simply closed when they were full. Arriving at four forty-five gave them a shot at being seated. If they'd arrived any later, they might have been looking at an Olive Garden Italian night instead of an authentic North End Italian night.

"Quick, Stryker, get out of the car and go to the end of the line so that we can get in before they shut the doors. Or, better yet, do your blind thing and get us to the front of the line."

Julian turned, fixed Alex with his best withering, sightless stare, and reminded her that "good people" do not take advantage of their handicaps to improve their positions in life. He then promptly exited the car, waited until she had moved forward to where she could no longer see him, and then tapped his way to the front of the line, where Giuseppe, the owner, always greeted guests. He hadn't gotten very far when he heard Giuseppe calling his name.

"Signore Stryker. Ah, no, no," he corrected himself. "*Doctore* Stryker, *come stai?* How are you?" Giuseppe approached Julian swiftly, placing one hand on each shoulder and kissing each cheek in turn. "It's-a been-a forever," he said in his singsongy Italian-accented English. Giuseppe had been in Boston for over thirty years but had managed to maintain his heavy accent as if he'd just arrived.

"*Come stai, vecchio amico?*" Julian gushed, returning the embrace and salutation.

"*Bene, bene, grazie. E dove e quella bella fidanzata di tuo, Alex?*"

Giuseppe, like so many Italian men, had a weakness for beautiful women, and Alex was no exception. Having reached the limit of his college Italian, Julian responded in English.

"She's parking the car, Giuseppe, but she told me she's looking forward to seeing you and to eating your fantastic food."

"Ah, *Doctore*, you-a flatter me," he said self-deprecatingly. "Come-a, come-a, I find-a you a nice-a table. Romantic, eh?"

Despite what Julian had said to Alex, he had no trouble accepting this slight favor from his longtime friend. He chose to view his being seated before others as a testament to his loyalty to Giuseppe versus a result of his blindness. Either way, he'd gotten a great table, but not without some under-the-breath comments from those in line he'd displaced. Not that he could blame them. Giacomo's was *the* place to eat in the North End.

Alex arrived ten minutes later, accompanied with a flourish from Giuseppe. Although she didn't speak a word of Italian, Giuseppe spoke to her as if she were fluent. Her English responses didn't seem to matter to him, as most of what he said was simple flattery.

As she sat down, the waiter approached and asked if they wanted their "usual"—homemade linguini with shrimp for Alex and mussels in a to-die-for *fra diavolo* sauce for Julian.

"Without question, my good man," Julian responded lugubriously. "And two glasses of your finest house red, please."

As the waiter departed, Julian turned to Alex and remarked, "Parking took a while."

"Yeah. Sorry it took so long, but Vinny called just as I was stepping out of the car."

"Again? What's so important that he couldn't wait for you to call him back?"

"That's what I asked him as I picked up the call. Apparently there've been several deaths with similar circumstances that he wants to run by us. And by 'us,' he means you."

"How many bodies?

"Four."

"In Boston?" Julian blurted, finding it difficult to believe that four people had died under suspicious circumstances without the Boston PD knowing about it.

"No, no. Let's see," Alex began as she consulted the notes section of her iPhone. "New York, Philadelphia, Hartford, and Baltimore."

"Over a period of how long?"

"A year."

"You said several deaths with similar circumstances. Is he thinking this is murder? And if so, why consult us? He's got a lot more resources at the FBI than we have."

"I don't think he knows *what* to think. Apparently he ran it up the flag-pole at the FBI and has been told to leave it alone, to leave it to the local PDs. But he said he just has a feeling about it. That something's not right about the deaths. That's all he kept saying."

Julian sighed deeply. Both he and Alex had enough on their proverbial plates without inviting trouble in the form of a case even the FBI didn't want to touch. But Julian literally owed his life to Vinny Marcozzi, and clearly it was time to pay up.

Their food and drinks arrived at the same time. Incredible smells wafted up from the plates, but the meals had to wait.

"What do you think?" Julian finally asked Alex.

"I think we need to see Vinny."

"Yeah, okay. Why don't you tell him we'll come down this weekend? We'll make a getaway out of it. DC is nice this time of year."

"Good try, Stryker, but I already invited him up here for the weekend."

Julian leaned back in his chair and crossed his arms over his chest. "Why'd you even ask me if you already had everything planned?"

Alex picked up her fork and started spinning pasta around it. "Well, we can look at it two ways, Stryker. On the one hand, you could say that I was sneaky and already had a plan to move forward with this potential case. Or, on the other hand, you could say that by raising the issue, I knew I'd draw out of you your biggest concern so that we could discuss it, thereby alleviating your stress and improving your ability to make the right decision to help Vinny. Either way, we both win. You feel better and are on board with the decision, and I have a happier boyfriend who has bought in to the process."

God, I hate it when my own logic comes back to bite me in the ass, Julian thought as he smiled and leaned forward to raise his wine glass in a toast to his beautiful partner's mental prowess. "Touché, my dear. Touché."

Chapter 8

Brenda Forsythe sat at a corner table facing the door so that she could spot Linda as soon as she entered. She had every intention of questioning Linda as to why she'd bolted out of the bar the other day without so much as a goodbye. Brenda was sure Linda had seen her chasing after her rental car, and still she hadn't stopped. Why would she do that?

As if on cue, Linda entered the restaurant, looking confident but slightly disheveled—a rare event, Brenda noted. Linda stood at the entrance, allowing her eyes to acclimate to the lowered lighting. Brenda waved her friend over and watched as she sat down heavily in the opposite side of the booth.

"Are you okay?" Brenda asked as she squinted in Linda's direction. Sure, she hadn't seen Linda in a while, but the person who sat across from her was very different from the woman she'd seen the other night.

"Yeah, fine. Why?" Linda raised her hand to get the waiter's attention.

Brenda noticed that two of Linda's normally perfect nails were broken. "Lin, look at me," she said.

"What? Why?" Linda responded, avoiding her gaze.

"Lin, have you been cryin'? Your nails are broken, your mascara's smudged, and your hair's all tousled. What's going on? Is it Jonathan?"

Linda looked away, afraid Brenda would see right through her.

"It is, isn't it? You always say your life's friggin' perfect, but ain't nobody's life that good. I knew it! That low-life piece of scum. Who is it? His secretary?

It's always the secretary. Like, she's so much better than you! How long he's been boffing her?"

Linda looked at Brenda as if she had lost her mind. Jonathan cheating on *her*? It was positively laughable! Or…was it? Linda recognized the burgeoning opportunity and grasped it as a drowning person would grab a life preserver. A real tear blossomed in the corner of her eye as she celebrated the beauty of her good fortune.

"Yes…yes, Bren. I thought I could hide it from you, my best friend, but of course you figured it out." The tears came freely now as Linda found a release from the ugly tension that had been screwed up inside of her.

Brenda reached across the small table and took Linda's hands in her own.

"Is that why you left the other night so quickly? I came out of the bathroom, and you were leaving. I even chased after your car and then asked the bartender if you'd said anything to him. He told me you had something you had to do. Was it Jonathan?"

Linda dabbed at her eyes with her napkin, looked Brenda directly in the eye, and said, "Yes, it was. That's the night I found out. Jonathan had called me and told me he had something serious to discuss with me. He sounded so concerned that I left the bar immediately. It was back at the hotel that he told me he'd been cheating on me for six months. I'm so sorry I left without saying goodbye. I was just so…I couldn't even—" She broke off and collapsed into sobs.

"Tell Brenda all about it, sweetheart. I have all night."

⋏

Evan Donaldson swam to the top of consciousness slowly, as if he'd been at the bottom of the ocean and had to fight to get to the top. Although he could see the light above the water, he couldn't quite get there—yet cool, fresh air was entering his lungs. He slowly closed his eyes, hoping that when he opened them again, he'd awaken from this bizarre nightmare.

Upon reopening his eyes, he realized he was indeed awake, but his vision was incredibly blurry. He was in a bed, partially propped up with what felt like multiple pillows. As he tried to turn his head, it felt as heavy as lead. It was all he could do to turn his eyes toward the clock radio playing music next to him, much less swivel his head. Every part of his body felt tied down, yet he saw no tethers. A rhythmic, repetitive *whoosh* that rose and fell in perfect time drew his attention. Sheer will and multiple attempts enabled him to slightly turn his head to the right, enough to discern what he thought looked like a ventilator. The same kind I sell to hospitals, he thought confusedly. With enormous effort, he visually followed the tube from the ventilator's body to its end, which he was horrified to discover was in his mouth. No— down his throat!

Blind panic set in as he struggled to free any part of his body from the invisible prison. In desperation, he clawed at the ventilator tube, trying to rip it from his throat. But all he managed was to move his fingertips, which lamely scratched against the white sheet that lay so pristinely under his paralyzed body.

⚔

"So, that's the gist of it."

Linda finished her imaginary tale of adultery as Brenda downed her third whiskey on the rocks. Linda had gone through three cosmos as well. The first one had been inadvertently spilled after one sip.

"Oh my goodness! How could I be so clumsy?"

"It's because you're upset, Lin."

The second had been furtively emptied under the table.

"Oh my God, Lin, you're going through those like water. Let's get you another."

And the third was currently being nursed, and Brenda was too drunk to notice.

"Well, he's an asshole, Lin. That's all there is to it. You're going to pack up your stuff and come back home to Boston to live with me until you get on your feet. You and Catherine, of course. I only got the one bedroom, but you and Catherine can take that, and I'll sleep on the couch until you find a place."

Despite the situation and her need to return to Mr. Perfect, Linda was truly touched. She reached across the table and said, "You and Sarah, Brenda."

"Me and Sarah what?"

"You and Sarah are the only two people who have truly cared about me in my entire life. I love you both so much." Genuine tears breached her ducts and rolled hotly down her cheeks.

⋏

A half hour had passed, and Evan Donaldson's eyes were moving more easily now. Manipulating his fingers like the legs of a spider, he had managed to crawl his right hand so that it lay atop his right hip. He was working on wiggling his toes when he heard a rap on the door.

"Hello! Housekeeping! Do you want turndown service?"

Evan Donaldson strained against his intangible shackles. With tremendous effort, he attempted to lift his head and scream. A quasi groan escaped his obstructed mouth, only to be muffled by the music and the hiss of the ventilator. He struggled to spiderwalk his fingers once more toward the ventilator tube.

"Housekeeping! Do you want turndown?"

Please! Please! Hear me! Evan Donaldson screamed in his head. In a burst of effort, he managed to hook one finger of his right hand around the tube connecting him to the machine. He then allowed gravity to pull his hand down, and with it came the tube, ripping out of his throat and freeing his mouth.

His scream erupted as a hoarse cough as the housekeeper announced, "Okay, then. Good night."

The housekeeper continued down the hall knocking on doors, and as Evan Donaldson listened helplessly, one tear trickled slowly down his partially anesthetized face.

⋏

"That's not true, Lin. It's not just Sarah and me who love you. Your parents loved you a lot before they were...well, before they died in that fire."

Linda gazed beyond her friend as if seeing the past unfold before her eyes—flames engulfing the bed where her father lay peacefully.

"You think so?" she asked absentmindedly, lost in the memory. "I'm not sure."

"What are you talking about, Lin? Of course they loved you—more than anything in the world. And so do me and Sarah. You can count on that."

Linda snapped back to reality. "Oh, before I forget, I stopped by to see Sarah, and you're right, she doesn't look well. When you see her next, you'll notice she has a new ring."

Brenda smiled. "That was sweet. But aren't you afraid it'll get stolen again?"

Linda smiled ruefully. "Something tells me this one will remain in place. Just a hunch."

Linda looked at her watch and made a show of yawning and stretching. She had already been gone too long and didn't want to risk failure once again. The man for whom she had abruptly left the bar the other night had been a bust, and she'd come too far tonight with Mr. Perfect not to reach her goal.

"Sure you're okay to drive, Lin?"

"Oh yeah, I'm fine. Thanks, Brenda, for caring so much." She looked at her friend as if seeing her for the first time. Prematurely graying hair in great need of a tint. Overdone makeup that didn't do much to hide the bags under her eyes. Wrinkled clothes that were slightly too tight. Linda was simultaneously disgusted and saddened.

"And you, Brenda? You going to be okay?"

"Me? Oh yeah, you betcha! A cab is out there with my name on it. Don't you worry about me! God knows you have enough to worry about."

Well, she's right about that, Linda thought.

⋏

As the housekeeper moved from door to door, realization dawned on Evan Donaldson. In his haste to alert the maid to his predicament, he'd neglected to take into account that the ventilator tube had been placed down his throat and into his lungs for a reason. Whatever was paralyzing his body also controlled the muscles that enabled breathing, making it more and more difficult to obtain a full breath. Minutes ticked by as he pawed at the sheets in a futile attempt to find the tube and reinsert it into his throat. Twitching like a fish out of water for too long, his mouth involuntarily opened and closed, gasping for whatever air it could get.

His brain running out of oxygen, Evan Donaldson's vision darkened, and his mind wandered to the good things in his life—his mom and dad; his cat, Buddy; the upcoming vacation he had saved so long for. Time seemed to pause as sudden bursts of white light exploded at the extreme edges of his vision, and a welcome serenity settled over him like a warm blanket. After several minutes, he stopped struggling and felt himself drift upward into the darkness. Then something wonderful happened. The brightest, most amazing white light appeared directly in front of him. Feeling euphoric, he gazed on its glory as it silently urged him forward to be enveloped by its warmth and comfort.

Evan Donaldson's brain still had enough firing neurons to register the sound of the door opening, but that same logical part of his brain reasoned that it was too late for him to be saved. That was okay. He was comfortable now in the light. It was warm and safe here. In fact, he was certain he didn't want to go back, even though someone was beckoning quietly to him.

"Evan, it's not time yet. I need you here to help me," a voice whispered in his ear.

Abruptly, the white light was blocked by a looming force that pushed air into his mouth.

No, no, no! Evan silently pleaded. *I don't want to return! Let me go...please!*

The entity backed away, and the light shone bright again, inviting him into its contented glow. Evan felt at once elated and at complete peace. As he walked into the light, his arms outstretched, the earthly voice quietly imposed itself once more.

"No, no, Evan. You need to come back. I need you here. You have important work to do before you go." The entity blocked the light once more to blow air into his lungs.

With enormous sadness and regret, Evan Donaldson was suddenly thrust back into the earthly realm. He slowly opened his eyes, half expecting to see God.

"Do you remember me, Evan? I'm Ashley," Dr. Linda Sterling said sweetly as she softly caressed his cheek wet with tears.

Chapter 9

"**S**o, how was last night in the North End with HRH Alex?" Jesse asked in a lascivious tone.

Julian didn't take the bait. "HRH? What does that mean?"

"HRH? Her Royal Highness, of course. She *is* a queen, Julian. I do not know what she's doing with the likes of you. Slumming, I guess."

"Hey!"

"JK, Julian. Just kidding. Now…to business. Your day is chock full of crazies, starting with Emily Beauchamp at nine, Nikki Solter at ten, and Jack Rafter at eleven."

"Who's Jack Rafter?"

"He's new. Referred by Judge Tate."

Judge Tate had been the adjudicator in the trial against Jeremy Walker, the kid who had blinded Julian. Prior to the attack, Julian had known Judge Tate as a fair, honest man who pulled no punches. After Jeremy's trial, Judge Tate had repeatedly reached out to Julian to check on his progress, and over the years, the two had become professional friends. Over time, Julian had amended his opinion of the magistrate to include someone who sported an incredibly large heart, a child advocate who would rather educate than punish.

"Okay. Oh, hey…speaking of new, did you get a chance to talk to Amanda, that court clerk, about the missing information in Danny Sheehan's file?"

"Yeah. Let me get it. Be right back."

While Jesse was gone, Julian picked up his phone and commanded Siri to call Stacey Goldberg, a social worker he'd known while at BU getting his PhD. Stacey and Julian had become good friends in school and had managed to enhance that friendship by creating a professional bond once they graduated. Stacey had come to Julian's aid more than once, and Julian liked to think he'd returned the favor for her.

"Hey, Stace, it's Julian Stryker. Long time no talk. How are you?"

"Julian! Oh my God, it's been…what? A year since I last talked to you! I'm great, really great. And you?"

"I can't complain…and even if I did, no one would want to hear it, right?" An old joke they shared from school, when they used to have to sit in therapy sessions with each other.

She laughed. "Exactly! What's up? To what do I owe the honor of this telephone call from the great Dr. Julian Stryker?"

Clearly, Stacey had gotten hold of some press that had circulated after Julian's case involving the FBI culminated in a shootout with a major Mexican drug kingpin. The papers had molded Julian into some sort of blind superhero: child psychologist by day and crime-fighting profiler at night. After riding the wave for a while, Julian had tired of the ridiculous questions and assumptions. The entire incident did have one positive outcome, however. It allowed Julian to raise awareness of blind people's rights and abilities. He hoped, for example, that maybe people would stop speaking too loudly when they met him, thinking that because he couldn't see, he also couldn't hear.

"Yeah, yeah. That's all in the past. Listen, I need a favor."

"Of course you do. What is it?"

"There's this kid, one of my patients…seems like a good guy but has been having a hard time of it recently. His brother passed away from cancer, and his dad's checked out. Mom works two jobs. You know the drill. Anyhow, I was hoping you could get in touch with him to talk about Rosey Tech."

The brainchild of Judge Tate, Roosevelt Technical High School was an institution that specialized in high-risk kids who had nowhere else to go. The last stop before juvie, it had redirected a lot of kids who would otherwise be in jail. While Judge Tate was running interference with local politicians who "didn't want a school like that in their backyard," Stacey had been busy writing grants to obtain federal and state funding. If it weren't for the two of them, the idea would have been squashed before it had a chance to get off the ground.

"Oh, Julian, you know there's nothing I'd like more than to help you out, but there are no open slots left. In fact, there's a waiting list as long as my arm to get in. Sorry, no go."

"Dammit! That's what I was afraid of. Can you put this kid on the short list, though, as a favor to me? I kind of promised him, and he really needs it. I feel like if he doesn't get something like this in his life, he might go the wrong way, you know?"

"Yes, Julian, I know. Unfortunately I know all too well. Anyhow, I'll add him to my personal list, but I certainly can't promise anything. What's his name?"

"Daniel Sheehan. I'll send you my complete file on him for your records. Thanks so much, Stacey. I owe you."

"You bet you do, Julian. And someday you're gonna have to pay up."

After ringing off, Julian turned to Jesse, who had returned with Danny's file and was sitting patiently on the couch.

"Is there a spot for him at Rosey?" Jesse asked.

"Not yet, but Stacey has a way of pulling through in the clutch. My gut says she'll make it happen."

"Well, I'm looking at Danny's file that Amanda sent over, and it says that Danny was an average student until about four years ago when his brother died of cancer. His mom and dad took it badly, of course, and kind of went in different directions, leaving Danny to fend for himself at the ripe age of eleven. Wow, poor kid," Jesse sidelined.

"Keep reading, please."

"Well, the father checked out—mentally I mean—and the mother ended up going back to school and now works two jobs to make ends meet. Still not a lot of focus on Danny, it sounds like."

"Yeah. We have to get him into that program at Rosey Tech. What was the brother's name who died?"

"James Sheehan. Jimmy."

"And the doctor's name who treated him? I want to talk to him."

"Hmm, let me see. Oh, here it is. Actually, Mr. Sexist, it's a woman, and she works at the Sidney Kimmel Comprehensive Cancer Center at Johns Hopkins in Baltimore. What was a kid from Boston doing at Johns Hopkins?"

"Must have been a clinical trial. That means the family had run out of options, and the trial was Jimmy's last hope."

"How could the Sheehans afford that? They don't seem like the kind of family that could fly to Baltimore at a moment's notice."

Julian shook his head. "Who knows, Jess? Maybe they borrowed money, maybe the trial grant had money to get them down there, maybe they mortgaged their house again. Parents will do anything to save a child, that much I've learned. What was the doc's name?"

Jesse returned his attention to Danny's file. "Dr. Linda Sterling. Ooh, Sterrrrling," Jesse dragged out the R into a purr. "Sounds kinda sexy, doesn't it?"

⋏

Linda sat quietly in Evan's hotel room, stroking his limp, graying hair. He had died sometime in the night, she couldn't remember exactly when. Sometime between their chatting and lovemaking, he'd suffered a coronary, a massive one by the look of it. She had looked on curiously as the drug had worked its magic to her intended end. That part always fascinated her, the actual violent ritual of death. No one goes willingly...or silently, she thought. At least they wouldn't if they could speak, but the first drug had taken care of that.

She glanced around the room and noted the time: 7:32 a.m. Goodness, she'd have to get moving if she were going to make her flight. She took one last look at Mr. Perfect and smiled.

"Goodbye, Evan. It was fun while it lasted."

Linda felt free and weightless, with not a care in the world. The ugliness that had writhed inside her for some time had been appeased, at least for now. It certainly hadn't been easy, though.

When they'd first arrived in Evan's hotel room, he had been a bit reticent, not quite believing that a woman of Linda's refinement would be interested in him. Indeed, he had been downright suspicious, forcing her to work harder than usual to gain his trust.

After two drinks, he had relaxed somewhat, allowing her to give him a massage and tease him a little sexually—hence her tousled hair and smudged mascara when she met Brenda at the restaurant.

But as time passed, she realized she was going to miss her dinner with Brenda, a key item in her alibi, so she'd hurried the process along by slipping a quarter of a crushed Rohypnol into his third drink. Her dosages were exact, as she wanted to cause enough drowsiness to move on to her next step but not enough to draw attention during an autopsy.

Removing a syringe from her purse, she'd then injected succinylcholine into Evan's superficial temporal artery, causing complete muscle paralysis, including his lungs. As luck would have it, Evan sold ventilators, so there was one in his room. Without it, she would have needed to hurry the process along, thereby missing his glorious ending, for death by suffocation didn't bring the same satisfaction and release as death by myocardial infarction, or heart attack. Although the games with Evan were not completed in her usual fashion, they'd worked out fine in the end. Better than fine, actually. Her father would be pleased.

Donning latex rubber gloves, she straightened objects in the bathroom and arranged Evan's clothes in the closet and in the dresser drawers. Although she'd taken great care not to touch many things, Linda removed the Clorox wipes she kept in her purse and carefully wiped each area and object she had encountered, tucking the used wipes into her purse afterward. Gathering her few belongings, she pulled the covers up to Evan's chin, smoothed back his hair, and caressed his face once more. After lowering the thermostat to sixty-two degrees, she completed the ritual by precisely arranging a pair of tortoiseshell reading glasses on the nightstand. Glancing once more around the room, she tiptoed to the door and listened for a moment, straining to hear even the slightest sound. Satisfied, she slowly turned the knob and peeked out into the hallway, first left and then right, careful to keep her face turned away from the hallway's one security camera.

After hanging the Do Not Disturb placard on the door handle, Linda walked briskly back to her own room, encountering no one along the way. She packed her suitcase, careful not to wrinkle her finest suit, and showered quickly, applied minimal makeup, and then dried her hair. Looking in the mirror at her entire reflection, she noted with satisfaction that the transformation from Ashley back into Dr. Linda Sterling was complete.

Again, her father would be pleased.

All was in order.

CHAPTER 10

Julian sat at his desk, eating the Thai food Jesse had had delivered to the office. He'd seen three patients that morning, all very different from one another. The first, Emily Beauchamp, was a fourteen-year-old girl referred to him by a female colleague who felt the patient would do better working with a male psychologist. Her file stated that Emily's arms were covered in small scars, indicating she'd been cutting herself for some time. Jesse had visually verified that for Julian. Once they got past the usual scrutiny most kids reserved for Julian because of his blindness, Julian was certain his cohort had made the right call in sending her to him. By the end of the session, she was talking openly about her lack of confidence and the outright, blatant bullying she experienced on a daily basis, both in the real world and online. He would see her weekly.

The second patient, Nikki Solter, was a seventeen-year-old straight-A student whose parents had sent her to Julian because they were worried about her anxiety level. After an hour with her, Julian had concluded that if she were any more normal, she'd be abnormal. As a senior in high school, she was applying to five Ivy League schools and was feeling the pressure that accompanied formulating submissions to those prestigious institutions. She told Julian that she felt better talking to someone other than her parents about her concerns and asked him if she could keep him "on standby" in case she needed to return. Julian loved it when patients devised healthy, logical next steps in a treatment plan. If only they all could be that easy.

Finally, there was Jack Rafter, the new patient referred by Judge Tate for animal cruelty. Julian had been down this road before, most recently with Jeremy Walker, who had acted on his initial sociopathic tendencies by experimenting on animals, cats specifically. It was well documented that many sociopaths began their horrific careers by torturing small animals, gradually working their way up to humans, as Jeremy had. Julian had been Jeremy's first and only human victim, thank God.

Meeting with Jack had brought up disturbing memories and images for Julian. As Jack described the torture of flies, tearing off their wings one at a time, watching them as they panicked and tried to fly first with only one wing and then crawling slowly away to die once the second wing was removed, he felt physically sick. Images flashed across his wrecked vision—Jeremy coming at him, knife raised, slashing him across his face, blinding him and breaking his nose in the process. He remembered hearing someone scream, shriek, and then—realizing it was himself—collapsing on the floor, ineffectually trying to defend what was left of his face. If Jesse hadn't pulled Jeremy off him, Julian most certainly would have been murdered in his own office. Jeremy had feigned remorse at the sentencing hearing, but it was clear to everyone—Julian included—that it was all an act for the benefit of the judge, who believed none of it. Rumors were that Jeremy still retold the stabbing story in prison, delighting in his one and only human sociopathic achievement.

Julian's current patient, Jack, was young—twelve years old—and because of that, Julian felt some reconditioning could possibly occur. He tried to be objective as he listened to Jack drone on, but it was difficult. He was to see him again the following week.

Julian returned his attention to the plate of pad thai he had been consuming while lost in his ruminations. Wow, this is good, he thought.

"Hey, Jess, where'd you get this food? It's awesome!"

Jesse appeared in the doorway. "New restaurant down the street. I'm glad you like it, because the guy who waited on me in the takeout section is two words: *gor* and *geous*! We'll be eating a lot more Thai, I daresay. Oh, I almost forgot—I texted Dr. Sterling's contact information to your phone."

"Thanks, buddy. And take it easy on the Thai guy...what's his name? He's not going to know what hit him." Julian smiled warmly.

"Mmm-hmm. You got that right. I didn't get his name yet. I decided to create a little mystery and suspense in this upcoming drama."

Julian shook his head and laughed. "You are nothing if not dramatic, Jess. Thanks for the number. I'll call her right now. When's my next patient?"

"Not till three, so you're good."

Jesse left, humming a tune Julian didn't recognize. Not surprising, seeing as Julian's idea of a Broadway show was *Les Misérables* or *Cats*. Both fantastic shows, but a little old school—"ancient," as Jesse described them.

Speaking into his phone, Julian commanded, "Read text message from Jesse James."

In response, the iPhone's internal computer voice named Siri said, "Sent today at eleven forty-five a.m. Here is Dr. Linda Sterling's contact information..." and proceeded to state Dr. Sterling's office phone number and address in Baltimore, Maryland.

"Siri, call Dr. Linda Sterling's office number."

Much to Julian's surprise, Siri replied, "Of course, Your Grace. Calling Dr. Linda Sterling's office."

Your Grace? wondered Julian.

"Jesse! What did you do to my phone? It's calling me 'Your Grace.'"

Jesse appeared at Julian's door once more, laughing so hard he snorted.

"So sorry, Julian. I had to do it! It's easy to program. I'll fix it by this afternoon, I promise."

Life certainly wasn't boring with Jesse around. Julian smiled and said, "Get out of here!" just as Dr. Sterling's assistant answered the phone.

"Dr. Linda Sterling's office. Lizzie speaking. How may I help you?"

"Hi, Lizzie. My name is Dr. Julian Stryker. I'm an adolescent psychologist in Boston, and I was wondering if I could speak with Dr. Sterling about a former patient of hers whose brother I'm currently treating. Is she available for a phone consultation?"

"I'm so sorry, Dr. Stryker, but she's out of the office at the moment. Actually, she was in Boston giving a presentation over the last few days and is expected back at the office today. In fact, she should've been back by now, but apparently her plane's been delayed. Shall I tell her you called and ask that she return your call as soon as she can?"

"Sure, that'd be great."

"Or, if you'd like, I'd be happy to give you her cell number. I'm sure she'd rather speak with you than sit for one more second waiting for that stupid plane." Lizzie giggled.

"Great idea. Thanks so much."

"Okay. Grab a pen and paper, and tell me when you're ready."

"Actually, Lizzie, could I ask you to text it to my phone? My number is most likely on your screen, right?"

"Yes, it is. I'd be happy to do that. Is that because you have really messy handwriting? I hear that comes with being a doctor." The giggle again.

Julian smiled and said, "Well, I certainly do have messy handwriting. I'm blind, so as you can imagine, my handwriting is really, *really* messy. Some might even say unreadable."

Lizzie was silent for a second and then said, "Oh, Dr. Stryker, I'm so sorry. I didn't know."

Julian was used to this response and took it in stride.

"It's okay, Lizzie. You didn't make me blind, so there's no need to be sorry."

Lizzie tittered nervously and then recovered. "I'll text you Dr. Sterling's cell number right now, Dr. Stryker. It's been a pleasure chatting with you. Have a great day!"

"Thanks, Lizzie. You too."

As Julian placed his phone on the desk, it dinged, indicating a new text message.

"Siri, read text message."

"Sent today at twelve forty-one p.m." followed by Dr. Sterling's cell number.

"Siri, call Dr. Linda Sterling's cell."

"Of course, Your Grace. Calling Dr. Linda Sterling's cell."

CHAPTER 11

A perky voice boomed through the overhead speaker. "Ladies and gentlemen, I'm sorry to inform you that flight 4131 to Baltimore has been delayed once more due to mechanical difficulties. I'll keep you updated as I'm informed of progress. Right now, we're looking at a departure time of one thirty p.m. If anyone has a connecting flight in Baltimore for which you'd like me to..."

Linda stopped listening as the announcement no longer pertained to her. Baltimore was home, so she wasn't in need of any connecting flight information. She returned her attention to the laptop on which she had been scanning news feeds in an effort to see if Evan Donaldson's untimely demise had been discovered.

Her eyes flew across the pages as she scrolled down. Nothing yet. She closed the laptop. Hopefully she'd be home before the first story broke the airwaves. That was always the plan.

Leaning back against the Naugahyde chair, Linda closed her eyes and allowed herself a momentary mental reenactment of last night and this morning. Evan hadn't understood why he had been chosen. None of them did. Not Sam Worthington in New York, Walter Croswell in Philly, Justin Simkins in Hartford, or Maxwell Cooper in Baltimore.

She smiled warmly, glowing as she reminisced. They were all so special to her. She could relive in minute detail all of their evenings together. That was one of her favorite parts. Squeezing her eyes shut to block out the airport chaos around her, she could almost smell their cheap cologne and feel the weight of their sweating bodies as they pressed themselves on her—against the wall, on the bed, in the shower—whatever and wherever they wanted. Because she loved them all. She really did.

Until she didn't.

And then…well, she needed to end it.

And like many other relationships she'd experienced throughout her life, it needed to end quickly. "Rip the Band-Aid off," her father used to say. "No use perseverating in your own grief or stagnation. Act quickly and decisively. That's how you remain in control and maintain order, Pippin."

Linda's eyes flew open. "Pippin," she said aloud. "That's what he used to call me. Pippin."

Funny that she'd just remembered the nickname now. Although her father often loomed in her conscious and unconscious thoughts, she'd forgotten that Pippin had been his pet name for her.

"Tired, huh?" a bass voice asked, too close for comfort.

Linda physically withdrew from the voice as she turned haughtily in her seat to face the man who had presumed it was okay to invade her personal thoughts and space.

"Excuse me?" Her left eyebrow shot up as she raised her chin and sat up straighter so that she looked down at him.

"Sorry. Didn't mean to interrupt. It's just that your eyes were closed, and I was wondering if you're tired."

Linda locked eyes with the man and then slowly leaned forward to glance at the chair on the other side of him. In it sat a very overweight woman in her late sixties, knitting what looked to be a sweater. She was humming quietly to herself and seemed very content. Linda actually envied her.

"Excuse me, ma'am?" Linda offered her thousand-watt smile as the woman's eyes focused on Linda's face. "This gentleman is looking for someone to talk to, and he made the mistake of thinking I was interested. You know how it goes, right?" Linda gave the woman a look that said, "Please help me get away from this guy who's hitting on me"—a combination of raised eyebrows, hopeful smile, and eye roll.

The woman looked Linda up and down and understood immediately. She laughed and placed her hand on the man's knee. "I'd be happy to engage in conversation, young man, since it looks like we're going to be here awhile."

Linda leaned in close to the man, patted his knee, and whispered, "See? I've found you a playmate. Have fun."

The man glared hard at Linda, who appeared innocent in response as her cell phone buzzed. "Oh, sorry. I have to take this."

As she stood up and walked away, Linda could hear the knitting woman say to the man, "So, where're ya from?" She was laughing as she slid her finger across the icon that appeared at the bottom of her phone screen.

"Hello?"

"Is this Dr. Linda Sterling?"

"Yes. Who's this?"

"Hi, this is Dr. Julian Stryker. I'm a child psychologist practicing in Boston. Your secretary, Lizzie, very kindly gave me your cell number. I wanted to talk to you about an adolescent cancer patient you treated about four years ago. His name was James Sheehan. Is this a good time?"

Linda glanced around her and noted that the gate across from hers had very few people in it. She quickly walked back to her chair, gathered her belongings, and hurried over to the almost-empty gate as she answered, "Sure, yes. This is a fine time, as my plane doesn't seem to want to take off any time today."

At the other end of the phone line, Julian chuckled and said, "That's what Lizzie said—that your plane was delayed. I have to admit I thought it was fortuitous that you were still in Boston, given that I'd like to speak with you about Jimmy and his family."

"Sure, sure. What would you like to know?" Linda asked, happy to be focusing on this side of her life, which was clinical—literally and figuratively. It was orderly, logical, and organized. And she loved it. "How can I help?"

"Well, I understand from my patient—Jimmy's brother, Danny Sheehan—that Jimmy died of cancer. What type of cancer did he have?"

"Before we begin, Dr. Stryker, may I ask if Mr. and Mrs. Sheehan signed a waiver that allows me to speak with you without violating federal patient privacy laws?"

"A fair question, Dr. Sterling. Yes, part of my initial patient paperwork includes a release that allows me to obtain information from prior treating clinicians. His mother signed the release, so we're all set."

"Okay. Thanks. You know you can't be too careful. There are a lot of wackos out there, if you know what I mean."

"I understand completely," Julian laughed, starting to like this woman.

"I don't have to search my mental database to remember Jimmy, even though it was four years ago. He was a memorable character, for sure. He was a bright, likeable kid, always with a grin on his face. And those freckles—oh my Lord! Adorable. I was heartbroken when we lost him. He fought hard, but in the end, it was just too much." Linda sighed deeply, reliving the horrible memory of his death—and her failure. "But to answer your question specifically, he died of pancreatoblastoma. Cancer of the pancreas."

"I've never heard of that occurring in children. Is it rare?"

"Actually, it presents more in children than in adults, but yes, it is rare. And the initial symptoms could be mistaken for so many other illnesses that it's often not diagnosed until it's fairly far along or even metastatic. If caught early enough, the prognosis is usually good. Surgery, maybe some radiation or chemo. But in Jimmy's case, as in so many others, his pediatrician mistook his vomiting, abdominal pain, and slight jaundice for the flu or a liver issue. By the time he got to me, the cancer had advanced so much that the tumor I removed was thirteen centimeters in diameter."

Julian blew out air on his end of the line. Thirteen centimeters was over five inches. He couldn't imagine a relatively small kid having a tumor that large in his body.

She continued. "Yeah, it was tough. I knew the prognosis for Jimmy wasn't good, but we moved forward aggressively in the hope that his indomitable spirit would carry him through. But obviously it didn't."

Linda became quiet, silently reviewing the mental movie of Jimmy's courageous fight. A tear appeared in the corner of her right eye. She never got used to failing, to losing those precious children. Her drive to save each one of them is what woke her up each morning, what made her face her failure over and over again. Until every once in a while, she won. A child lived.

"I'm sorry, Dr. Sterling, it sounds like you were very close to Jimmy."

Linda stood proudly and wiped the lone tear from her eye. "I'm close to all my patients, Dr. Stryker, and I never get used to losing them."

Julian paused and then said, very quietly, "Perhaps that's what makes you so good at what you do."

Linda knit her brow, pulled the phone away from her ear, and looked at it as if she could see the man on the other end of the line. Who *was* this man who was complimenting her?

Chapter 12

FBI Special Agent in Charge, Northeast Division, Vinny Marcozzi sat at his desk in Washington, DC, anxiously tapping a pen against the blotter on his desk. The *rat-a-tat-tat* sound carried into the open area outside his office, causing his assistant to appear at his door and smile tactfully before grabbing the handle and closing it silently behind her, leaving him alone with his thoughts.

Having been recently promoted to SAC, he oversaw all the special agents under him—probationary agents, special agents, senior special agents, supervisory special agents and the assistant special agent in charge (ASAC). His mother had once commented wryly, "My God, if the general public had any idea how many 'special agents' there are, they'd storm the government and demand their tax money back."

Not that each agent didn't have a job to do, but Vinny's recent rise in government bureaucracy had left him questioning why he had desired rank advancement in the first place. As a field agent, he had been at the heart of the action, making life-and-death decisions. Hell, not that long ago, he'd been in Mexico fending off a prominent drug cartel with his buddies Alex and Julian. Now, here he sat, staring blankly at the Presidential Commendation that hung on the wall opposite his large teak desk.

Vinny's eyes wandered about the room, settling on a picture that sat on the top shelf of a bookcase that extended the length of the right wall. It was not a picture of his family or his children, as he had neither. Rather, it was of

Mark Felt, a special agent who had started at the FBI in 1942 under Hoover's direction and climbed the ladder until retiring as deputy director in 1973.

Not many people knew Felt by name, but throughout his esteemed career, he greatly impacted the nation's safety and security, working espionage during World War II, bringing down crime bosses in the 1950s, and finally helping to urge along Richard Nixon's resignation during the Watergate scandal. Vinny tried to imagine what it must have been like for this loyal patriot to be forced to decide between the president he served and the country he loved. Perhaps it wasn't a difficult choice, but in the end, he chose his country by providing Woodward and Bernstein critical information that had led to Nixon's resignation. Most people knew Mark Felt only as "deep throat," but Vinny had done a lot of research on the man and had decided that Mark Felt stood for what is good about the United States, of what could be accomplished if petty differences were put aside. That's the way Vinny wanted to run his field office—but his superior didn't see things the same way.

Intent on creating relationships that would benefit both local police and the FBI, upon promotion Vinny had reached out to chiefs of police throughout the Northeast. He considered it "laying groundwork to enhance interdepartmental efficiency and effectiveness," or that's what he had written in the proposal that his boss, Deputy Director Joanna Langston, had grudgingly approved.

With the goal of staying ahead of the criminal curve, Vinny and his agents had urged local police to keep them informed not only of any potential crime-related statistics but also of any "questionable events" that may or may not be deemed legally criminal. And it was working. Recent statistics showed that his agents were receiving more tips that led to successful prosecutions than his predecessor had. Vinny's experience and independent research had shown that many high-profile cases were solved by good, old-fashioned police work coupled with strong "gut instinct." He had learned to trust the feedback of local cops, as their ears were to the ground. That was the only way to ensure the FBI remained relevant in today's rocky political climate, where dollars were vanishing faster than the ozone layer.

His boss, on the other hand, felt his efforts were simply "looking for trouble where there was none." She had repeatedly asked him why he was seeking problems for the bureau instead of focusing on being a strong liaison between it and the alphabet soup of organizations the federal government employed: the DEA, the CIA, the ATF, and so on.

In Vinny's mind, Joanna Langston was an Ivy League bureaucrat who had risen to her position by kissing the right ass. In contrast, Vinny refused to play the political game. Born and raised in the Bronx, he wore his upbringing proudly. He wasn't rude, but he was blunt. He wasn't always nice, but he was kind. In his heart, he believed Joanna was angry he had received the promotion to SAC, as he had been up against a blue blood who had gone through the academy with her. However, after the Mexico triumph that resulted in a Presidential Commendation, Vinny was a shoo-in for the position. Joanna had to work with him, but she didn't have to like it—or make it easy for him. And she took that position very seriously.

Mark Felt's enigmatic smile mocked Vinny from its silver frame as he mentally replayed the most recent conversation with Joanna, which hadn't gone well. Months of trying to make her understand his goals of outreach and diplomacy had resulted in nothing but anger and frustration on both sides. Eventually he had abandoned his efforts, and each party had quietly withdrawn to its corner to regroup. After this most recent bout with her, though, Vinny knew he was running out of time. He had to prove to her that his strategic efforts were worthwhile. Otherwise, she'd pull the plug on his program—and potentially on him as well. The pen continued to tap, its owner agitated but focused.

The disagreement an hour ago related to a number of questionable deaths from apparent heart attacks. As usual, what Vinny determined was worth the FBI's involvement was proclaimed a "waste of time" by Joanna. It had started with a phone call to Vinny from a Baltimore detective who was questioning cause of death for a body found in a hotel room. Vinny leaned back in his chair, closed his eyes, and ran his hand over his face as if to wipe away the crappy day. He silently reviewed his conversation with the detective.

"Last night I was called to the Days Inn, where I found a white, forty-five-year-old man in the bed, hair combed back, covers pulled up to his chin, reading glasses on the nightstand, as if he'd simply fallen asleep and never woken up."

"Okay. And?"

"Well, at first it didn't seem odd, right? But as I got more into the investigation, I had some questions."

"Okay. Go on."

"The autopsy determined—and I'm reading directly from the coroner's report here—that 'the victim had (a) engaged in sexual intercourse prior to his death and (b) passed away from a massive myocardial infarction, or heart attack.' Also, no leads from any hotel-staff interviews."

"What was his name?"

"Maxwell Cooper, a tire salesman from Delaware in Baltimore for a trade show. He arrived at the hotel alone, and staff didn't see him engage with anyone but this other guy, who he chatted with at the bar before eating alone. I talked to that guy and got nothing."

"Anyone go to his room? Any security footage?"

"No one reported seeing anyone arrive or leave his room except him, and apparently the software in the security cameras was being updated during his stay, so footage was unavailable."

"Of course," Vinny mumbled.

"Yeah, I know. But the weird part is that the hotel room was completely neat. I mean, no towels or underwear on the floor, bathroom supplies arranged precisely. And you should've seen the drawer and closet where he kept his clothes. Hangers exactly four inches apart. I measured it because it struck me as so odd."

"Fingerprints?"

"Very few fingerprints on doorknobs, faucet handles, TV remote, and so on. All were verified to be staff or former guests staying in that room."

"And you're sure that housekeeping didn't get in there to clean before you arrived?"

"Yup. We got in there first."

"Do you know the health history on the vic?"

"That's where it starts to veer from normal, Vinny. No history of heart disease, a nonsmoker, not a big drinker. According to his colleagues, Mr. Cooper was single but not one to engage in risky sexual behavior."

"What did the coroner rule it?"

"A natural death."

"So, why call me? Nothing sounds too out of the ordinary," commented Vinny.

"I'm not done. Based on what I found at the crime scene, I got permission from my boss to do a little more digging. I went to Mr. Cooper's workplace and found that his workspace was really messy compared to the hotel room. Papers piled high, empty soup cans and torn candy wrappers on the desk, pens all over the place. Human nature dictates that people tend to be messier when they know someone else will be cleaning up, right? Like in a hotel, for example. So, why would his hotel room be so neat when his workplace wasn't?"

"What about his house?"

"That's what I mean, Vinny. I found the same level of chaos there. A completely messy bachelor pad. I know, 'cause I got one myself. Also, I checked with the vic's primary physician, who validated that Mr. Cooper had no sleep apnea, cardiac arrhythmias, heart disease, or lung disease—all conditions that might contribute to a heart attack. His death came out of nowhere."

"I'm still not convinced," Vinny said.

"I know. I get it. Sudden heart attacks kill people every day, so given no evidence to the contrary, I closed the case as a natural death. Until I spoke with a friend of mine at the PD in Hartford, Connecticut, who told me about a bizarre case he'd encountered. Get this, Vinny—a salesman was found dead of a massive heart attack in his immaculate hotel room. After he and I compared details of the two cases, we determined that the circumstances and victims were too similar to be dismissed as coincidence. So, I talked to my boss again, and he gave me the okay to contact you."

Vinny's eyes popped open as his assistant entered his office, interrupting his reviewing thoughts.

"Hey, Vin, you okay? You seem a little…I dunno, off," she said.

"Yeah, Marcie. I'm fine. Just a headache, that's all."

"Is your headache named Joanna?" she whispered, looking behind her as she spoke.

Vinny couldn't help but smile. Somehow Marcie could make that type of insubordinate comment and make it sound so innocent, you weren't sure if you'd heard correctly.

"I plead the fifth on that one, Marcie."

"Okay. Well, just so you know, Alex called, and everything's all set for you to go to Boston this weekend. Plane ticket's booked—window seat, as usual. It'll be nice to get the gang back together, won't it?"

"You bet it will. Thanks. Oh…and Marcie? I hope you booked that flight on my personal credit card. I think I'm on my own on this one until I can prove otherwise to the brass."

"It's on your card, don't worry. But be sure to let me know when we switch it to the company card."

"Sadly, I'm not sure we'll get that far." Vinny blew out air.

Marcie pulled a face. "Are ya kiddin' me? Friggin' Vincent Marcozzi, fearless Presidential Commendation recipient on the case? You'll get it on the company card in no time," she finished, using her best Bronx imitation.

Smiling, Vinny shook his head as she exited and silently closed the door behind her. From her lips to God's ears, he thought.

CHAPTER 13

"Dr. Sterling? Are you there?"

Linda was still staring at the phone in her hand, wondering about the tinny voice coming through the speaker on her phone. How dare this person condescend to me? she thought. How dare he presume to know how I feel or what makes me an effective physician?

As if reading her mind, the voice continued.

"Dr. Sterling, I hope you're still listening. I certainly didn't mean to presume that I know how you feel or what it's like to be a physician in your position. I can't imagine what it's like for you on a daily basis, losing patients, fighting what probably feels like a losing battle. All I was saying is that you must be pretty special to have taken on this line of work—smart, empathetic, and extremely kind. I meant no offense."

Linda's eyebrows relaxed as she considered his words. Sure, he could be kissing her ass to get the information he wanted, condescending to her as so many male doctors did. But she didn't think so. He was basing his opinion solely on her choice of occupation and how devoted she was to her patients. He had no real reason to lie to her. No guise. His words were simply appreciative, and Linda wasn't used to that. Her gut told her this man was different—sincere, warm. Like her father. She made a decision and returned the phone to her ear.

"I'm so sorry, Dr. Stryker. I inadvertently pressed the mute button with my cheek. Of course you meant no offense. Your words were very thoughtful. I thank you. What other questions can I answer for you about Jimmy?"

"Can you tell me a little about his family?"

Linda sat down in one of the empty chairs at the gate and glanced at the overweight knitting woman. She was satisfied to see that the older woman still held the close talker hostage in a one-sided conversation. He looked incredibly bored. Serves him right.

"Hmm...let's see. Jimmy's family. Oh yes. His father was very engaged at the beginning of Jimmy's treatment. Present for the initial surgery. Even slept in Jimmy's room in a spare bed. The mother came and went as her schedule allowed. I got the feeling she was the primary caretaker of the kids. The other boy, Danny, was relatively young at the time and needed to keep a regular schedule, so the mom was in and out. But still committed and as involved as she could be. Danny didn't really talk much when he was visiting. I got the feeling he was overwhelmed. Understandable, of course."

"It certainly is. For a kid that age, losing a sibling can be devastating, as you can imagine. How were the parents as the disease progressed?"

"The mother became more engaged as she came to accept that she was going to lose her boy. Took time off work and stayed by his side until the end. The father, on the other hand, withdrew from Jimmy—and the family, now that I think about it. I remember thinking how sad it was that the father wasn't spending time with Jimmy, seeing as there was so little time left. I guess it was a blessing that toward the end, Jimmy was put into a medically induced coma. At least he didn't know that his father had checked out."

"Ironic. That's the same term Danny used for his father. 'Checked out.'"

"Well, that's what it was. One day he was part of the family, and the next day, he wasn't. It went downhill from there. I'm not sure what happened to the family after that. But I'm guessing it wasn't good, since you're calling me about seeing Danny as a patient."

"No, you're right. It's not good. Long story short—after Jimmy died, the father completely withdrew from the family. The mother went back to school and is working two jobs trying to keep them afloat. Danny tried to get his father's attention—to no avail—and turned to a local gang for comfort. He was referred to me by a judge who's willing to give him one more chance before juvie."

"Wow. Your job sounds as much fun as mine," Linda remarked dryly.

Julian laughed. "It has its good days and its bad days, but mostly good. You've helped me a lot, though, Dr. Sterling, as you've verified what my patient told me. I wanted to make sure I was getting the entire and true story before potentially going out on a limb for this kid."

"What do you mean?"

"I'm trying to get him into a work/study program that's currently full. So, if I'm going to pull in some favors and potentially owe some people who get him into this program, I wanted to make sure I was doing it for a kid who deserved it."

Linda was truly touched. It wasn't often she met other clinicians who were as committed to their patients as she was. Plus, she liked the sound of this man's voice. It was…soothing. A deep baritone that often paused for emphasis. A verbal touch on the arm, as if to accentuate a point. His voice reminded her of somewhere safe and far away.

"Dr. Sterling, did I lose you again? Is it the mute button, perhaps?"

"Ah, so sorry, Dr. Stryker. Please call me Linda."

"Then please call me Julian."

Julian. Linda rolled the name around her tongue, finding that it sat like a fine wine on her very choosy palate.

"Beautiful name," she offered. "Is it from your family?"

"Thanks. Yes, it was my grandfather's name. You don't hear it a lot, do you? Kind of makes me stand out, I suppose."

"Yes, I suppose it does." Linda was shocked to find that she didn't want their phone call to end. She tried to find a way to keep him on the line.

"Dr. Stryk—I mean, Julian?" she corrected herself. "Listen, you seem like a really good therapist. I mean, you clearly work very hard for your patients and are thorough and clinically competent."

"Wow, high praise, Linda. 'Clinically competent.' I really appreciate that," Julian said, laughing.

Was he making fun of her? Darkness descended like a screeching crow draping a black veil over her head, threatening to dismantle her fragile ego. She suddenly wanted to throw her phone across the walkway. She pictured herself reaching through the phone and ripping his throat out. Humiliated, embarrassed, and livid all at once, she abruptly stood and started pacing furiously around the chairs in a figure eight, again and again.

Julian stopped laughing, sensing the conversation had shifted.

"Hey, I was just joking, Linda. I appreciate what you said. It was truly very kind. It's just that no one has ever called me 'clinically competent' before as a compliment."

Linda stopped walking and pressed the phone hard against her ear. "Is that because you are *not* clinically competent?"

"No, no. I'm definitely clini—I mean, no one's ever said—" Julian cut himself off, unsure how to proceed. "I appreciate what you said, that's all. I should have left it at that," he concluded, sighing.

Linda's shoulders relaxed, and her grip on the phone softened as the darkness retreated. Perhaps it was simply a misunderstanding. Jonathan often told her she misinterpreted what people said. She read nastiness where there was none. She heard sarcasm where people meant humor. That kind of thing. For some reason, she was willing to give this man the benefit of the doubt. For now.

"That's okay, Julian. Perhaps I should have chosen my words more carefully. I'm not always good at reading people and their intentions. Perhaps that's why I chose this line of work. It's usually very black and white, if you know what I mean. I know that I couldn't live in your world, where everything's gray."

Julian sensed great sadness in Linda's tone. Deep-rooted melancholy born of being surrounded by death and dying. Of working so incredibly hard against almost insurmountable odds. Although Julian couldn't understand why someone would choose this path, he could certainly empathize with the impacts the choice made on their psyches. She continued.

"Julian, I know you're an adolescent psychologist, but I'm wondering if we might get together to talk sometime. I don't like to speak with mental health clinicians where I work. It's too close for comfort, you know? The last thing I need is for anyone with whom I work to think I'm losing it." She laughed nervously as she navigated this new ground.

Although Julian was somewhat taken aback, he agreed. "Sure...sure, Linda. We can do that. It'll be off the record, of course."

That was more than she could have hoped for. Off the record meant no paper trail.

A booming voice came over the loudspeaker to announce boarding for her flight. She was surprised to realize how fast the time had passed while she'd been on the phone with Julian.

"Linda, you still there?"

Linda watched as the elderly knitting woman collected her bags and started toward the gate door. Other people were quickly lining up to get on the plane, anxious to obtain some overhead baggage space. She had to get off the phone if she were going to make this flight.

"Linda?" Julian called out loudly through her phone's speaker.

"Yes...sorry, Julian. Listen, my plane was just canceled, can you believe it? How about I meet you somewhere for a late lunch, and we can start our... discussions. Will that work for you?"

CHAPTER 14

Brenda Forsythe sat slumped in the army-green chair next to Sarah's bed, head tilted and supported by her right hand. She dozed fitfully, dreaming of when she and Linda had been kids in Sarah's foster home. Her eyelids jumped as her eyes flew back and forth inside their sockets, seeing her past in a vivid recreation during REM sleep. Her rapid eye movement was accompanied by muscle spasms in her left hand, which would twitch and pull on the fragile hand it was holding. Sarah never noticed, however, as her medical condition made it difficult for her to maintain awareness for very long. Brenda's dream continued.

Linda was wearing a too-tight purple Jordache T-shirt she had managed to save from the fire that had ravaged her parents and her home. Her jeans were just as fashionable— high-waisted Calvin Kleins. Linda sat on the twin bed directly across from Brenda's in the room they shared, picking at the red polish on her fingernails. Leaning against the carved oak headboard, she curled her long legs to one side like a foal enjoying some inviting spring sunshine. That was Linda, even back then. Seemingly happy-go-lucky on the outside but wound as tight as a coiled cobra ready to strike on the inside.

Teenaged Brenda watched her new friend's eyes glaze over as Linda told her (for at least the forty-fifth time) about her parents and how they had died. Each time she retold the story, Linda added new details, slowly piecing together missing parts as her traumatized brain was able to recollect them.

As Linda spoke, Brenda reflected on her own story. It was simple, really. Born to a single, unwed mother, Brenda had been left on the steps of St. Joseph's Church in Lynn, Massachusetts.

The nuns had placed her in the orphanage, which would be her home until she was adopted at the age of five by Janet and Stan Baker, a well-meaning couple unable to have their own biological children. Brenda spent one glorious year with them, until Stan decided he'd had enough and walked out on Brenda and Janet. Janet, the only mother Brenda had ever known, assured six-year-old Brenda that the two of them would remain together and "make a go of it." That was her last memory as she fell asleep that night in her bed at Janet's house—and woke up the next day back at the orphanage. After that, Brenda had been bounced around from home to home, finally landing in Sarah's house with a foster mother who truly cared for her and a new "sister" whom she adored. Instant family. As far as Brenda was concerned, Linda could repeat her story every day—as long as Brenda was able to keep her instafamily.

Brenda sat enraptured by her beautiful friend's tale, trying to imagine the life Linda described before all "the bad" had happened, as they had come to refer to the fire and its aftermath. The way Linda told it, her life had been magical, an only child to loving, generous parents. Showered with gifts at Christmastime and her birthday. Sunday mornings spent in church and then family afternoon dinner followed by card or board games. Everything Brenda had desperately wanted her entire life.

As usual, in this version of the retelling, Linda was focusing on the day of her parents' deaths. She recounted once again how it had been a normal day, filled with school for her and work for her parents. As was her custom, Linda frequented the library after school. She arrived home at about five thirty to find both her parents sitting at the kitchen table, the air thick with tension.

Often at this point, Linda would give Brenda an anguished look as she continued. Her eyes welling up with tears, Linda would describe how her parents had sat her down and informed her that they were getting divorced. They still loved her, and it certainly wasn't her fault, but they would be separating the next day. Her father was going to remain in the family home with Linda, and her mother was going to get an apartment.

"It will be better for everyone, don't you think, Pippin?" Linda would mimic her father's voice, glazed eyes staring into her haunted past.

And then Linda would end the story abruptly, saying, "And then they died that night."

But in this version of Brenda's dream, the night Brenda was reliving in vivid detail in her fitful sleep at Sarah's bedside, new information was illuminated. After ending her story the way she usually did, with "And then they died that night," Linda added, "The way it should have been. Both of them, together under one roof."

Brenda's eyes were zipping to and fro under her lids while her hand gripped Sarah's tightly.

"What do you mean, Lin, 'the way it should have been'? You don't mean you're glad they died together under the same roof? You can't mean that."

Linda's glazed eyes snapped to attention as she stammered, "No, no, no, of course not. I don't know what I was saying. Just ignore me."

Brenda squinted at her friend. "You sounded like you meant it, Lin. You sounded really pissed off when you said it."

Brenda started at the *thud* made by her purse as it fell from her lap to the floor. She sucked air in quickly as she straightened up in the chair, disentangling her hand from Sarah's and using it to wipe drool from the side of her mouth. She really needed to get more sleep but couldn't find enough hours in the day to make ends meet and sleep too. Blinking hard twice, she forced her eyes to remain open as she reviewed her dream.

Brenda stared at the floor, trying to work out something that was bothering her, something that didn't fit into the story Linda had repeated so often. They were children when Brenda had first heard the story, so she'd listened to it with a child's ears, a child's perspective. But now, as it had replayed in her subconscious, something was askew. She closed her eyes again and rubbed them with the heels of her hands. What is it? she demanded of herself. What doesn't fit? And then she had it.

Why were Linda's parents sleeping in the same bed if they were separating the next day and filing for divorce?

"Brenda?"

Brenda's heart skipped a beat as she turned her full attention to the reason she was sitting in the God-awful, uncomfortable chair.

"Sarah, darlin', how are you?"

Sarah turned her head slightly to the right to gain a better view of Brenda. The effort clearly took a lot out of the frail woman, and she breathed heavily for several moments before she spoke again.

"I'm good, I guess. Glad you're here." Her rheumy eyes traveled over Brenda's weary face and settled on her anxious eyes. She gave Brenda a wan smile. "You look tired, Bren."

"What? Are you kidding me? Fit as a fiddle, I am, don'tcha know."

Sarah closed her eyes and frowned. "Do not lie to me, young lady." Illness had done nothing to dispel this great woman's inner strength. Her voice may have been halting and soft, but her words were as strong as the day Brenda had met her.

Brenda took Sarah's hand and held it against her cheek.

"Never could get nothing by you, eh, Sarah? Yeah, I'm tired. Working hard and not doing too good. But overall, I'm a lot luckier than a lot of other people. That's what you taught us, Sarah. Always be grateful for what you got, 'cause it all could go away tomorrow."

Sarah opened her eyes slightly and gazed knowingly at Brenda. "Linda came to see me."

"She said she was gonna. She's in town for a conference, but she's gone home now to that prick, Jonathan."

Sarah's gaze turned hard, and she seemed to gather strength. "Language, Brenda, language. No need for vulgarity. And what do you mean that Jonathan is a...what you said?"

"Aw, I don't want to trouble you, Sarah, but Lin told me that Jonathan's been cheatin' on her for a long time. Can you believe it?"

Sarah cast her glance downward toward the blanket that covered her feeble frame, her brow wrinkled in thought. Finally, she spoke. "Huh."

"That's all you gotta say, Sarah. 'Huh'?"

"Well, honestly, Brenda, I always thought it would be Linda who did the cheating. She's not comfortable in her own skin. Can't seem to settle anywhere, ever since she came to me at fifteen after her parents' passing." Sarah turned her entire upper body toward Brenda, a sense of urgency in her labored movement. "You'll need to look after her when I'm gone, Bren. Okay?"

Tears rushed to Brenda's eyes as she stroked Sarah's hand. "Don't say that, Sarah. You're gonna live forever. You're superhuman. You had to have been to do what you did for all of us stupid kids."

Sarah simply smiled in response and closed her eyes as she leaned back against the pillow once more. "Just promise me you'll look after her, especially if Jonathan's not around. My Lord, the luck that girl has had in her life.

First her parents being murdered and then her husband cheating on her. I know she's successful in her career, but really, how much bad luck can follow someone?" Sarah sighed, her energy nearly spent.

Brenda was puzzled. "Sarah, I think you're confused. You said that Lin's parents were murdered? They weren't murdered. They died of smoke inhalation during an accidental house fire."

Sarah gently shook her head back and forth. "No, Bren. Her father died in his bed, covers up to his chin, very peaceful. Her mother was found in Linda's bed—dead."

In Linda's bed? Brenda was aghast. "How did her mother die, then?" Brenda whispered.

Sarah turned her sad, nearly lashless eyes toward Brenda, tears suddenly appearing. "Forty-two stab wounds."

CHAPTER 15

Alexandra Valentina Hayes, debutante daughter of eminent Boston defense attorney Warren B. Hayes and his Russian immigrant wife, Svetlana Dmitrovich, stared absentmindedly at the decapitated head as the crime-scene techs completed the initial photography. She was sure the way of life she'd chosen wasn't her parents' first choice for her. An unmarried detective who saw blood and gore as often as her mother saw the inside of Newbury Street spas and salons, Alex had chosen her path at an early age and had never wavered. Not that her parents hadn't tried to dissuade her from this career choice. And goodness knows that although the decision to pursue her dream had come easily, the actual attainment of her badge had not.

But, like many women on the force, she'd started out determined and strong and had come out of the academy single minded and rock hard, both physically and mentally. Although women in law enforcement were more common now than in the past, she was aware of being held to a different standard than the men. Not a higher standard, perhaps, but a different one. Eyes always trailed her as she approached a crime scene, badge outstretched, her long legs carrying her forward with an air of authority and confidence. She had worked hard and had risen through the Boston Police Department at a relatively quick pace. Every award and promotion she'd received had been well deserved—and she knew it. She was self-assured because she was self-reliant, but she was not cocky. How could she be when she was dating Julian?

Alex smiled at the memory of meeting Julian for the first time and then frowned as she relived the moment she'd walked into the hospital room and saw his ravaged face. His eyes were gone, of course, but his nose had also been broken, and one cheekbone had had to be reconstructed. Although doctors had spoken with her ahead of time in order to prepare her for interviewing the victim, she hadn't anticipated how the savagery of the attack would affect her. Bile had risen in her throat as she'd gaped at Julian lying in the bed. Unsure how to approach him, she'd paused and then turned around to leave when Julian had said, "What…are you scared? Do I really look that bad? This is nothing. You should see the other guy." And then, to her complete astonishment, he had turned his head toward her and smiled. Well, sort of—smiled as best he could given his bandages and swelling. Despite all the injuries and pain, he had smiled and cracked a joke. How could she not respect a guy like that?

Julian had stood at the threshold of hell during his attack and then had stepped over the boundary during his recovery. Not surprisingly, his natural humor dissipated as the daily grind of mental and physical rehabilitation tore at his defenses. And then there was the fact that he'd lost one of his five senses. Not just any sense, but the one most Americans, when surveyed, said they'd be most terrified to lose—their sight.

Post investigation and conviction, Alex had remained at a polite distance throughout the year and a half of rehab but was often in contact with Julian's mother, with whom she had created a warm and lasting bond. When Julian had graduated with a degree in profiling, it had been his mother's idea that he join the Boston PD. When Alex and Julian started working together, neither was looking for a relationship, and maybe that's why it had worked. Alex had been divorced, and Julian was still very fragile. Creeping forward slowly over a period of several years, Julian's honesty and candor had drawn Alex in like a wounded animal to a haven. And Alex's strong spirit and powerful drive spurred Julian to accept nothing but the best from himself. They had been dating for about a year now, and life was good, solid, and calm. Well…their private lives were calm compared to their professional ones, that is.

"Something on your mind, Detective?"

Alex forced herself out of her reverie. "I'm sorry…what?"

"You were staring at the head as if it had said something confusing to you. Brow all crinkly, arms crossed. You okay?"

Alex uncrossed her arms and smiled at the crime-scene tech. "I'm fine. You done here, then?"

"Yeah, we're done. Want me to leave him? Or...what's left of him?"

"Please. I want to walk the grid again, make sure I didn't miss anything. Any sign of the body that goes with this head?"

"I haven't heard anything."

"Okay. Thanks, Johnny. Good work. See you soon. Say hi to Chelsea."

"I will. Say hi to Julian. I miss seeing his ugly mug around here," Johnny said with a grin.

Alex waved goodbye to Johnny and approached the dead man's head. Crouching down and leaning to the right, she noted that the eyes were open and the skin sallow. Inclining forward, Alex could discern slight indentations in the upper neck, indicating that the victim had been hanged and then de-capitated post mortem. Alex had once worked a case in which the criminal had killed the victim and then removed the head as a trophy, but she highly doubted this perpetrator had taken the body as a trophy and left the head. Too difficult to transport and hide. Without a body, it was impossible to prove that the hanging had killed this man, but the bulging eyes and pro-truding tongue were pretty good evidence that even if the victim had been injured prior to the hanging, it was the suspension from a fixed object that most likely killed him.

Alex's knees cracked as she stood up slowly. Too many seasons of prep-school lacrosse. As she rubbed her right knee, the one on which she'd worn a massive knee brace all those years, she said to the head, "Poor bastard. Not a good way to go."

"I can't think of one way that is a 'good way to go,' except maybe dying in your sleep."

Alex wheeled around, surprised and embarrassed at not having heard the person approach from behind. Some detective I am, she thought. Kevin McMillan stood appraising her, a half smile on his face, his hands casually tucked into the pockets of his perfectly tailored pants.

"How long you been there, Chief? And what are you even doing here, anyway?" Alex raised her hands to her sides and looked at their immediate surroundings to emphasize her point. They both stood in the middle of what passed for a field in the middle of Boston.

The chief laughed and said, "I was in the area, coming back from a mayoral briefing, and heard the call over the radio. Hadn't seen you in a while, so I thought I'd stop and say hi."

Alex raised her eyebrows as her head tilted down. "Really? Is that what it's come to between us?"

Chief McMillan took a step forward, palms up and out. "Listen, Alex, I know you wanted the chief position. Hell, a lot of people think you should've gotten it. But you didn't. I did. Our prior romantic relationship shouldn't get in the way of us having a good working relationship now. I mean, it's been over a year. You're happy with Julian now. And me? Well, I've got the job. What do you say? Peace?"

Alex stared hard into the eyes of her former lover and current boss. "Where's the olive branch?"

"What? What do you mean?"

"You're extending the proverbial olive branch," Alex said, smiling suddenly. "But I'd like to see an *actual* olive branch. Say, at a Greek restaurant? I'm starving. Want to get some lunch?"

Kevin evaluated her for a moment, trying to figure her out. He never could pin her down. That was one of the many reasons their relationship hadn't progressed. But it was the competition for the chief's position that had been the final blow. It had clearly worked out for the best, though, as word on the street was that Alex was as happy as she'd ever been, and Kevin loved his job.

His hands back in their pockets, Kevin shook his head while looking at the ground. Then he looked at her sideways. "Sure. Nothing says hungry like a decapitation. That'll always get the tummy rolling, eh?"

"You said it. Let's go."

They took Alex's car to Piperi Mediterranean Grill on Beacon Street, seeing as Kevin had been dropped off at Alex's crime scene.

"Pretty ballsy, Chief, being dropped off at the crime scene. You must have felt pretty confident that I'd agree to bring you back," Alex commented as they waited to be seated.

Kevin nodded. "Well, I figured I could at least get a ride back to the office. I hadn't counted on lunch, but this beats a dog at the food truck by far."

Alex smiled as a lithe, perfectly coiffed, early twenty-something hostess approached them. The young woman's eyes drank in the tall, manicured police chief in one long, languid glance. "Follow me, please," she practically purred, trailing her hand down Kevin's arm.

"Talk about ballsy," Kevin whispered under his breath to Alex.

They were shown a table by the window, allowing them a good view of the lunch crowd on Beacon, always good for people watching. Turning away from the window, however, Alex closed her eyes for about ten seconds and took in all the sounds around her, a habit she'd acquired through dating Julian. Kevin noticed and commented.

"Yeah, it's interesting, actually, Kevin. Try it. Close your eyes for ten seconds, and listen to all the sounds you normally don't hear because you're not paying attention to them. It's amazing what you can hear if you can't see."

Kevin closed his eyes, his brow furrowed. It was clear to Alex that he was taking this very seriously, as he did most things. He swiveled his head, first to the right and then to the left, absorbing all the sounds around him. After about fifteen seconds, he opened his eyes and smiled. "Wow, you were right. I'm going to do that more often. Is that a Julian thing?"

"Uh-huh," she said contentedly.

"Things going well, then?"

"Yes." Her smile said so much more than the word.

Kevin cleared his throat. "I heard some interesting sounds when my eyes were closed, but I think the most compelling was from that woman sitting over there." Inclining his head, Kevin gestured directly behind him without turning around.

Alex leaned to the left to get a better view of the woman in question. She noted the long brunette hair swept up into a French twist that looked careless but took a lot of skill to create. The woman's nails were short but manicured, and her pantsuit looked to be made of crepe silk. But it was her demeanor that held Alex's attention more than anything—confidence and power wrapped in an alluring package.

"And you haven't even seen her, Kevin. That woman could be wearing a burlap sack and she'd draw attention. What did she say that caught your attention?"

"It was her laugh, Alex. Throaty and deep, almost as if she knows something we don't."

PART TWO

The Struggle

CHAPTER 16

Linda sat at a lovely table that was equidistant from the bathroom and the kitchen—facing the door, as her father had taught her. "You always need to watch your back, Pippin. You never know who wants to do you harm. Always face the door if you can," he had instructed. She waited patiently, back erect against the chair, and stared absentmindedly at the empty booth across from her that would soon be occupied by Dr. Julian Stryker. Prior to ringing off, they had agreed to meet at one of Julian's favorite restaurants, Piperi Mediterranean Grill. Although Linda hadn't recognized the name, Julian had given her the address, and she had hopped into a cab tout de suite.

Her cell phone lay on the ecru tablecloth to the right of her water glass. She'd rung her husband in the cab on the way to the restaurant and left a message indicating that she wouldn't be returning home today due to flight issues. Knowing Jonathan, he would require a chat regarding the unexpected change. He'd told her recently that her job took her away too much and that their relationship as well as Linda's relationship with her daughter were suffering. Her response to his complaint was to remind him who brought home the large paycheck that allowed him the luxuries to which he'd become accustomed. After a heated argument, he'd agreed to her travel, provided they remain in more frequent contact. Hence her phone call to him and his anticipated response. As if he had heard her thoughts, just then her phone vibrated.

"Hello, Jonathan."

"Hey there. Just checking in to see when you think you'll be home."

"Well, I don't know the flight schedules off the top of my head, but I'll chat with Lizzie, and she'll get me on the most convenient flight. As it turns out, there's a psychologist here who's working with the brother of one of my former patients, so my flight cancellation was serendipitous, really. I'm meeting him to help him gain a better understanding of his patient and the family."

There was a long pause on the line. Linda assumed Jonathan needed a moment to take all this in.

"Well, sounds interesting. Catherine and I really miss you. She drew you a picture, which I'm texting you right now."

Linda's phone vibrated, and she pulled it away from her ear to view the picture he'd just sent. It was of the three of them—Linda, Catherine, and Jonathan—in front of their house. Linda noted that she was the tallest in the picture, a clear indication in her mind that Catherine thought her the more important of the two parents.

As it should be, Linda mused.

Jonathan interrupted her thoughts. "Please let me know when you're coming home."

"Sure thing. I need to get off the phone. I think I see the man I'm meeting."

"Okay. Love you, Lin, and I hope—" Linda pressed the red circle on her phone to end the call as Jonathan was still talking.

Linda couldn't believe her luck as she watched a tall, well-dressed man enter the restaurant and fix his stare on hers. His smile was broad and warm, highlighting white, even teeth. She stood and smiled, raising her chin and sucking in her stomach at the same time. The man strode toward her with confidence and a kind of grace one doesn't often associate with men. Not feminine—not at all, but rather as if he'd enjoyed childhood dance training that lingered as he traveled through life. Julian Stryker was exactly what she'd pictured in her mind. No, he was even better looking.

As he approached, she presented her slender hand. The man stopped abruptly and glanced at her hand and then behind him. As he turned back to her, she realized with horror that he hadn't been looking at her at all. She quickly peered at the table next to her and saw the woman the man had been focused on. Sitting quickly and grabbing her phone, as if the mistake had never occurred, she heard the man chuckle as he passed her table and seat himself. Black rage seeped from her pores as a strong, red blush rose from her heart, up her throat, and into her face. Fury blinded her as she pressed the icon on her phone to dial her assistant, Lizzie, who answered on the first ring.

"Hi, Dr. Sterling. How can I help you?"

The sound of Lizzie's perky, kind voice should have soothed her, but at this particular moment, it only enraged her more.

"Lizzie, do you really think that's a professional way to answer the phone? I can only hope you're not that brazen with other callers. Honestly! I know we've worked together awhile, but you need to do better than that if you expect to keep your job much longer. Get it together!" Her last words were spit across the miles, making the handsome man at the next table glance at her in disgust. Linda was far too wrapped up in herself to notice.

Linda heard a sniffle on the other end of the line. "Sorry, Dr. Sterling. I'll do better."

"Make sure of it! Now, you need to book me on another flight that leaves tonight, because mine was canceled."

"No, it wasn't, Dr. Sterling. I'm on Delta.com right now, and it says your flight ended up leaving late but is in the air right now."

Linda could barely see as an obsidian shroud encompassed her. "Lizzie, listen to me," she hissed. "I don't give a fuck what the computer says. My flight was canceled, and you need to book me on another one leaving later tonight. Is—that—clear?"

Lizzie had never been on the receiving end of her boss's venom. She'd seen it happen to others and had heard stories but had not yet experienced it herself. Unsure how to proceed, she wiped the tear off her cheek and simply said, "Okay. Anything else?" But Linda had already hung up.

Linda dropped her head into her hands, closed her eyes, and breathed in deeply, desperate to regain control. The serpent writhed low in her belly, awaiting the opportunity to lunge. The logical part of her brain reasoned that she was already risking her safety by remaining in the city where her latest "date" had occurred. The last thing she needed was to lose control and allow the black viper release once more. Too dangerous.

"Wow! Are you stupid or what?" Linda bolted upright and stared at the empty seat across from her.

When had her father arrived?

"I mean, what kind of a moron makes a mistake like that? You actually thought that man might be interested in you? You? Look at yourself. You're a mess, Pippin. A complete mess."

Suddenly, she sensed him standing, looming over her, riding crop in hand. *"You want to be successful? Get it together, and stop making rookie mistakes!"* The riding crop came down solidly on the table, making the water glasses jump.

"I'm trying, Daddy. Please don't be angry. I don't like it when you're angry," Linda whispered.

"You need to take care of business, or things are really going to fall apart around here," he said as Linda's eyes took in the entire restaurant.

Linda's gaze settled on the handsome man next her, who was staring at her as if she were quite insane. Linda quickly averted her eyes.

"Hey! Look at me when I'm talking to you, Pippin!"

Linda had no choice but to return her eyes to the empty chair where her father's presence seemed to reside. His voice had softened into a warm invitation. *"Do you know how beautiful you are, Pippin? I know beauty is fleeting, but you are simply exquisite, you know that?"*

Linda felt his large, warm hand cup her face gently. She closed her eyes and leaned into his touch. She loved him so much. And she knew he loved her too, especially when she was good to him. She wanted to be good to him... for him. She felt his lips brush against hers, lightly, a promise of what was to come if she were good. Her reward for so much hard work.

"Daddy, I love you—" The riding crop smashed against her water glass, sending it careening in a flurry of glass, water, and ice.

"Then do better, dammit! Work harder. There is nothing if not perfection! No mistakes!" The crop came down one last time, leaving her alone and trembling, her lap covered in ice water.

She slowly opened her eyes to find the restaurant's patrons staring in disbelief. She had no recollection of what she'd said aloud and what had been only in her head. It was a small blessing that her father had taken the black serpent with him, leaving her only a hollow shell to be filled with hard work and success. What else was there? Hard work leads to success, which leads to acceptance and love. It was a simple equation.

Dr. Linda Sterling smoothed back her French twist and smiled sweetly at the waitress who was rushing over to clean up the broken glass and water.

"I'm so sorry," she admitted. "I seem to have made a mess."

"Oh, no problem, ma'am. We can have this cleaned up in no time. Don't even worry about it. It looks like you have a cut on your arm from the glass, though. Shall I get you a Band-Aid?"

Linda glanced at her arm where the riding crop had hit her, leaving a slightly bloody welt as a memento of her father's visit. "That would be lovely. Thank you so very much," Linda responded, completely in control once more. "Listen, I'm waiting for a gentleman by the name of Dr. Julian Stryker. When he arrives, would you be kind enough to show him to my table?"

"Of course, ma'am. I'll let the hostess know to be on the lookout for him."

"You are too kind, thank you."

The waitress finished cleaning up the glass and gathered the plate and flatware to be replaced. She couldn't help but notice that the patron's knife had blood on its blade. Wrinkling her nose, she glanced once more at the statuesque woman sitting pristinely in the chair and then turned her gaze to the bleeding gash on Linda's arm.

Linda hadn't noticed, however, as she was smiling flirtatiously at the handsome man at the table next to her. She took absolutely no notice of his revulsion as he and his lunch date threw a twenty-dollar bill on the table and left.

CHAPTER 17

Alex and Kevin were discussing the severed head case when she heard a glass shatter nearby. Glancing over, she saw that the elegant woman with the throaty laugh was speaking with the waitress and smiling profusely. Alex watched as the couple next to the woman got up and walked out, whispering and glaring at her as they exited. I wonder what happened? Alex thought. The woman acted as if nothing out of the ordinary had occurred, but Alex's gut said otherwise.

"Alex, you still with me?" Kevin asked, waving his hand in front of her face.

"Sorry, Kevin. Something weird just happened over there. Just curious. You were saying?"

"I was saying that we can have Shawn, our in-house sketch artist, do a drawing of the head so that we can release it to the public without alerting them to the fact that the head is no longer attached to its owner. Sound good?"

"Yeah, yeah. Sounds good. Thanks. Hey, there's Julian. What's he doing here?"

Julian was tapping his way into the restaurant as Tiffany, the leggy hostess, did her best to guide him—using her entire body. Alex rolled her eyes. Julian's handicap elicited many reactions from people, but this was her favorite to watch—a woman falling all over herself trying to "help" him. Given his striking height, wavy dark hair, and lithe build, Julian's blindness gave him an irresistible vulnerability that many women found incredibly attractive. Perhaps that's why Alex hadn't divulged her feelings for Julian earlier. She didn't want to be "most women," so she had come across as tough and unemotional early in their relationship. It was he who had slowly drawn her out, helping her understand that she could be vulnerable, logical, and strong all at the same time and could achieve more growth—both personally and professionally—in the process.

Julian was doing his best to appease Tiffany without offending her. Alex sat back and observed as he gently peeled the girl's grabby hands from his arm while simultaneously laughing at something she'd said. He's so good, Alex thought. The young woman had been rebuffed and did not even know it. In fact, Alex would put money on the fact that the hostess had been left feeling better about herself than before Julian had walked in. Julian said something to her and was led to the table with the throaty-laugh woman who had caused a ruckus. Alex's interest was truly piqued.

"You going over there?" Kevin asked, turning around in his seat to take in the scene. "Wow, she's a looker, isn't she?"

Alex threw Kevin a withering stare. "Are *you* gonna go over there?" she asked dryly.

"No, no, I'd much rather be here with you, as I'm sure Julian would. I'm sure he's here on business."

"Hmm," Alex replied as she watched the woman greet Julian.

λ

Dr. Linda Sterling regarded the debacle that was unfolding in front of her at the hostess stand. The twit of a girl was practically mauling a poor blind man, who to his credit was clearly adept at handling situations such as this one. She tilted her head and regarded with fascination as he managed to untangle himself from the hostess's attentions, laughing all the while. Now that's confidence, she thought. He was a tall man with beautiful dark, wavy hair, cut to enhance its natural curl. His teeth were straight and even, and when he smiled, it felt relaxed and real. His nose was slightly too large and a little off center, which only added to his charm, and his clothing was of good quality and almost flamboyant. A man comfortable with himself and his world, even with his blindness. Linda was immediately drawn to him and realized with a start that she was doing in her head what the hostess was doing in real life. Forcing her attention away from him, she refused to succumb to his charisma. She was better than that—stronger, more in control. She was, after all, Dr. Linda Sterling, renowned oncology physician.

She glanced at her watch, and when she looked up again, the blind man was standing in front of her table, his hand extended and a big grin on his face.

"Dr. Linda Sterling, I presume?"

Linda was momentarily dumbfounded. No, she thought. No way. He would have mentioned his blindness. This can't be—

"I'm Julian Stryker. It's a pleasure to meet you in person."

Linda paused and glanced at the patrons around her. For the second time in ten minutes, they were all looking her way. So much for keeping a low profile, she thought.

"Get it together," her father hissed in her ear.

Linda stood and grasped Julian's outstretched hand in both of hers. "The pleasure is all mine, Julian. Thanks for meeting me. Would you like to sit down?"

Julian made himself comfortable, folding up his walking stick and placing it on the left edge of the table. The waitress appeared with a new plate and eating utensils for Linda. As she placed them, she said, "Hey, Julian! It's Lisa. Great to see you."

"You too, Lisa. How's Ryan?"

"Great! We're engaged. Can you believe it? And after only five years together!" she said with a laugh.

"Well, better late than never, right? I guess he didn't want to rush into anything." Julian gave her a big smile.

"Yeah, whatever. Anyhow, what can I get you?"

"Just water with lemon, please, Lisa. Thanks. Linda? Anything for you?"

Linda smiled warmly at Lisa and said, "Lisa knows that I like water." She winked at the waitress.

Lisa smiled thinly in return as she surreptitiously glanced once more at the cut on Linda's arm. "Oh, here's your bandage, by the way, ma'am." Lisa produced a Band-Aid from the pouch on the front of her apron.

"Many thanks, Lisa. Now, how about those waters?" Linda winked again, as if she and Lisa shared a secret. Understanding that she was being dismissed, Lisa turned and walked away.

"Bandage?" Julian asked.

"Oh, it was a silly mishap, that's all. I broke my water glass and cut my arm in the process."

"Your arm?" Julian asked, genuinely perplexed. "How did that happen?

"It really doesn't matter, now, does it, Julian? That's not why you're here. Let's get down to business, shall we?"

Alex continued to observe Julian as he approached the woman's table. It seemed as if Julian were meeting her for the first time. A handshake but no kiss on the cheek. Alex noted that the woman took Julian's hand in both of her own, a warm gesture...or perhaps overly forward? The waitress, Lisa, approached the table and chatted with Julian, laughing. But then her smile dropped as she glanced furtively at the woman. Lisa pulled something out of her apron and stared at the woman before walking away. Something's not right, Alex found herself thinking.

"First, is there anything else I can tell you about the Sheehan boy?" Linda asked.

"No, I think you gave me enough information with which to move forward. I really just wanted to make sure my efforts weren't going to waste."

"Did you get him into that program you were talking about?"

"Not yet, but my friend Stacey continues to work on it. I'm going to check in with her later to see how it's going. Thanks again, by the way, for your help. Now…" Julian leaned forward and placed his hands palms down on the tabletop. "How can I return the favor and help you? You mentioned over the phone that you wanted to discuss your job with someone other than your mental health colleagues—which I completely understand, by the way," Julian finished.

Now that she was face to face with Julian, Linda was reticent to reveal her true feelings. Unaccustomed to being exposed, she detested the sensation of vulnerability that accompanies any type of therapy. Although she held a double MD in psychiatry and oncology, there was a reason she practiced only oncology. Sure, she performed research in the field of psychiatry, but she didn't actively practice. She had been truthful in telling Julian over the phone that she didn't want to live in a gray world. No, she definitely preferred a black-and-white world, where order reigned supreme.

Julian sensed her change of heart and brought his hands together in an almost prayer-like gesture, elbows on the table. "I know what you're thinking, Linda, but you can trust me. It was clear on the phone that you're in need of talking with someone. Why not let it be me? Let me help you like you've helped me today." He smiled then—a genuine, kind, warm smile.

Linda paused and regarded this enigmatic man. Her father whispered throatily in her ear. *"Do not trust this man, Pippin. He'll be the end of you. Come back to me, and let's discuss next steps for us. Order is paramount. This man will cause nothing but chaos in your life."*

Linda waved her hand in front of her face as if shooing away a fly. Julian's smile was an invitation to be included in a club that accepts everyone, regardless of ability or social status or education. He didn't seem to care about anything but her well-being. He wanted to help her, to be her friend, like Brenda. She found herself leaning toward him, physically drawn by some unseen force.

Without warning, her father's presence enveloped her, his fury palpable.

"Do not speak with this man, Linda! There will be consequences if you do!" her father spat at her. The riding crop came down before Linda could stop it, upsetting her tableware and sending Julian's walking stick into the air, landing in Linda's hand. Or had she picked it up? She couldn't remember. She was losing control but felt powerless to stop the deluge of disorder that was raining down.

Julian initially jumped at the *thwack!* and then readjusted in his seat.

"What was that?" Julian calmly asked Linda.

"Ma'am, are you okay?" Lisa interrupted as she rushed over to the table. "'Cause you kind of don't seem okay," she added, glancing at Linda's arm.

"We're fine, Lisa," Julian answered, holding up a hand. "You know what, though? My friend and I are going to have to take a rain check on lunch. Thanks so much…and please say hi to Ryan for me," Julian finished, smiling.

When Lisa had gone, Julian paused and then addressed Linda directly. "Linda, I'd like to help you, but if you're not ready, I understand. If you choose to move forward, perhaps we should talk further at my office."

"I-I…I think that's a good idea."

"Good. I'm busy till four, but I can see you after that. How about four thirty?"

"Thank you, Julian. I'll see you then," Linda answered in a small voice she didn't fully recognize as her own.

Alex watched as Julian and his lunch companion chatted a bit and then become more serious. Julian had a neutral expression on his face as he spoke quietly to the woman, whose face suddenly contorted. Alex watched in amazement as the woman waved her hand in front of her face and then lifted her arms as if she were going to strike Julian. The woman's right hand shot out abruptly and grabbed Julian's walking stick, and before she could stop herself, Alex was out of her chair, running to help Julian. The walking stick came down hard on the table, causing Julian to jump. Then—silence. Alex froze in midstride, not knowing what to do. Julian gathered himself and spoke quietly once more to the woman and then to Lisa. Alex watched as he gathered his walking stick and satchel and strode confidently to the door, the hostess mute and reserved as he passed.

Chapter 18

Brenda Forsythe stood in front of the Lynn Public Library, staring up at the façade decorated in the Renaissance Revival design so popular in the late nineteenth century. The building was huge, and Brenda found herself wondering how much it had cost to build. Who had designed it? Questions she had never considered when she was younger, sneaking out of Sarah's house to meet her friends outside the library to smoke weed. In fact, she laughed out loud, suddenly realizing she had never actually set foot inside the building. I guess people do change, she thought to herself as she started up the broad stone steps.

She entered the inner sanctum gingerly, unsure of library protocol and feeling very out of place. A large, round desk was situated to her right, and a dreadlocked young man sat behind it, staring at a computer screen. Brenda paused, uncertain how to proceed.

"Can I help you?" the young man asked.

"Um...yeah, I think. I'm looking for some information on a fire. I mean, a murder. Well, a fire and maybe a murder that happened a long time ago, and I was hoping you guys might have something here. An old newspaper, maybe? Do you keep those? I mean, I guess they'd be really yellow, but I could still read them, right?"

Dreadlocks stared hard at Brenda. "How long ago are we talking?"

"1982."

Dreadlocks threw his head back and laughed. Brenda looked down at the floor. Coming here was a bad idea, she thought.

The young man stopped laughing when he realized Brenda was serious about her newspaper request. "Oh, I'm sorry. I'm sorry," he said. "I thought you were joking."

"This was a bad idea. I'm gonna go." Brenda turned and started to walk away, flushed with embarrassment.

"No, no, no. Please don't go. I'm sorry. I shouldn't have laughed. It's just that since I've been working here, no one's come in looking to read an actual newspaper. They're dying the same death as the dinosaurs, but the dinosaurs went more quickly. What exactly are you researching?"

Brenda had listened to him without turning around. She was used to not being taken seriously, so she had learned to play the role of a fool quite well. But that didn't mean it still didn't hurt every once in a while. She remained silent and still.

"Please, let me help you. I'm really sorry I laughed. My name's Dominic."

Brenda considered her options. On the one hand, she desperately wanted to know more about Linda's parents' deaths. On the other hand, she already felt stupid, and she could only imagine it was going to get worse when this kid Dominic realized she knew nothing about anything. She decided to look him in the eye to see if he was being honest about wanting to help her. She had always felt that if you looked someone in the eye, you would get a solid read on his or her intentions.

Turning around, she approached dreadlocks and stared directly into his eyes. Instead of looking away, Dominic broke into a gap-toothed grin that couldn't be denied. After a moment, she found herself smiling back and saying, "Well, Dominic, we have a lot of work to do, so let's get started. The name's Brenda, by the way."

Dominic led Brenda to a small room off the main part of the library that held only four computers. He explained to her that this was a study room created specifically for people who wanted privacy for reading or researching. He further explained that all newspapers dating back to 1912 were archived in files that could be found on the computer. Finally, he showed her how to use the Internet (until that moment only a phrase she'd heard batted around) to find related articles and documents pertaining to her research.

When he was confident she had a solid grasp of how to navigate these new waters, he asked, "Hey, why are you researching all of this, anyway? Are you in school and working on a paper or something?"

Brenda looked at him with sad eyes and sighed. "I'm trying to better understand someone I thought I already knew inside and out," she said dejectedly.

Dominic's gaze dropped to the ground. "Sorry to hear that, Brenda. You seem like a fine lady. I hope you find what you're looking for."

"Me too, Dominic. Thanks."

"I'm right outside if you need me, okay? Anything you need, just call my name, and I'll come in."

Brenda smiled her crooked smile and winked at him. "You got it, buster. Thanks."

Brenda started her quest, employing a hunt-and-peck method to type phrases into the search box on the Google search engine. Over and over again, she found herself wishing she'd paid attention in typing class in high school. Or in any class in high school, come to think of it. When she reflected on her time in school, she realized it wasn't that she hadn't *wanted* to learn. Her mind just couldn't stay on one topic very long before wanting to move on to the next one. She'd had a difficult time sitting still, and the teachers taught in ways that just weren't clear to her. Also, sometimes the letters in words would jiggle around, making it very hard for her to read. She was told at one point that she had something called ADHD and dyslexia. She wasn't sure what that meant, and Sarah was in no position to go to bat for her against the Lynn public school system. So, Brenda did the best she could and managed to squeak by with a D average to graduate on time. And college? Not even a possibility.

Brenda's first clumsy attempts at entering keywords turned up very little in the way of pertinent information related to Linda's parents. After several tries, she decided to enter Linda's name—Linda Adeline Sterling. Up popped numerous articles on her pediatric carcinoma research, an article about her wedding to Jonathan (the cheating lout), and a particularly interesting piece in the *Baltimore Sun* about her faculty appointment at the Sidney Kimmel

Comprehensive Cancer Care Center in Maryland. In it, Brenda discovered a plethora of awards and recognitions Linda had received throughout her years as a cancer doctor. The article left her even more in awe of her friend than she'd been upon entering the library. Linda never bragged about any of her achievements; that was one of the things Brenda liked about her. But Brenda hadn't understood the depth and breadth of Linda's achievements until now. The last sentence in one of the articles stated the following:

Who would have predicted that a young girl of twelve, cruelly or-phaned by fate, would grow up to have such a dramatic and long-lasting impact on the world?

Of course! Brenda slapped her forehead. In order to get information on Linda's early years, she should have been entering Linda's maiden name, not her married name. She quickly pecked out L-I-N-D-A-A-D-E-L-I-N-E-M-C-N-A-B-O-L-A into the search box, and the screen quickly filled with articles related to the fire. Brenda clicked on the first one dated June 14, 1982.

Fire broke out in the early hours of June 13 at the home of Mr. and Mrs. Sheldon McNabola, 345 Atlantic Avenue, Swampscott. Although the cause of the fire is still under investigation, it's safe to say that the entire home was destroyed. Fire chief Bill McCoy is working to de-termine if an accelerant was used, seeing as the fire was so aggressive and swift. Sadly, Mr. and Mrs. McNabola perished in the fire, along with their younger child, Michele McNabola, seven years of age. At this time, it's believed they died of smoke inhalation. The older child, Linda McNabola, twelve years of age, was the lone survivor and is being cared for by the Massachusetts Department of Children and Families until next of kin can be notified and care for her.

Brenda read the brief article several times, her brow furrowed. Linda had had a sister? She had never mentioned a sibling, but maybe it was just too painful for her. Poor kid. On the other hand, Brenda was relieved to read that Linda's parents had died of smoke inhalation as opposed to fouler means. Sarah must have gotten it wrong. Brenda clicked on the next article, dated one week later from the same newspaper, the *Swampscott Ledger.*

> This is an update on the fire that destroyed Mr. and Mrs. Sheldon McNabola's home at 345 Atlantic Avenue last week and claimed the life of three family members. In conjunction with the Boston Firefighters Association arson investigators, fire chief Bill McCoy has determined that the fire was, indeed, intentionally set. An accelerant in the form of gasoline was found throughout the debris, culminating in the master bedroom, where the body of Mr. McNabola was found, charred but lying on his bed in a state of repose. Crime scene investigators have also determined that Mrs. McNabola's body was found in young Linda's room and had been stabbed repeatedly prior to being burned. Finally, investigators found a large contusion on the head of the younger child, Michele, leading them to believe that she, too, might have already been deceased prior to the fire. The remaining child, Linda, is still in the care of the Massachusetts Department of Children and Families, as no relatives have been located. If anyone has any information related to this horrific crime, please contact the Swampscott Police Department at 781-585-1111.

As if watching a train wreck in slow motion, Brenda felt she had no choice but to read the last article dated August 31, 1982.

> This is an update on the gruesome murders and fire that were wrought on the McNabola family earlier this summer. Although the parents and younger child were laid to rest shortly after the appalling crimes, little Linda McNabola presses on with her life. Having no relatives able to care for her, she has been put into the foster care system and is hoping to find a forever home soon. You'd expect someone this young who has lost so much to be angry and bitter, but

she's not. On the contrary, she strikes this jaded reporter as resilient and determined. When asked what she misses most about her family, Linda doesn't hesitate before responding, "My father's love. He was my guide. He kept everything in good working order. I guess I'll just have to do that on my own now." On a more positive note, as sole heir to her parents' estate, she need not worry about her financial future. In addition, a fund has been set up in her name by anonymous well-wishers who want to ensure this bright girl has every opportunity to achieve her dreams. She'll need all the help she can get, having to go through life as an orphan.

Brenda sat back heavily in her chair and ran her hands through her hair. Tears welled up and spilled onto the keyboard as she imagined what it must have been like for her poor friend to have experienced such an ordeal. Of course, she'd lied about her parents' deaths to Brenda. She probably didn't want to have to answer the inevitable questions that would follow the real story. It would have been too painful.

But why lie about having a sister? And didn't Linda say that her parents were in the master bed together when the house burned? The article stated otherwise. Maybe that's the way she wanted it to have been, Brenda thought. Maybe Linda wanted to imagine that her parents' marriage was strong and intact when they died.

Dominic poked his head in the door. "Hey, I just wanted to make sure you were—oh…are you okay? You're crying. Disappointing discoveries?"

Brenda tried to smile and wiped her eyes on her sleeve. "Yeah, sort of." Then a thought struck her. "Hey, Dominic, you like working here? I'm kinda looking for a new job, and this seems like a cool place to work. Is it?"

Dominic smiled and said, "It's great, actually. The hours are good, and the pay is decent. And it's quiet, so I can study."

"Oh? What're you studying for?"

"I have my master's degree in library science from Harvard. That's how I got this job. Now I'm working on my PhD so that I can teach. That's my real goal."

Brenda stared openmouthed. "You need a friggin' master's degree to be a librarian these days?"

"It's not what it used to be, Brenda, so…yeah, sometimes," he shrugged.

She was quiet for a moment. "So, Hah-vud, huh?" she said in her best imitation of a high-class Boston accent.

Dominic smirked. "Yeah, Harvard."

"Wouldn't have guessed it in a million years, dreadlocks, but good for you, buddy. Don't think I'll be applying for your job once you move on. Don't quite got the…what do you call 'em? Credentials."

Chapter 19

Dr. Linda Sterling walked briskly down the sterile, antiseptic-smelling hallway toward Sarah's room. After the near disaster at the restaurant, she felt the need to touch base with the only remaining cornerstone in her life—the pillar who, according to the physicians with whom Linda had just spoken, would not be alive much longer. "A month, tops," they had stated rather coldly.

Linda entered the dimly lit room and quietly approached Sarah's bedside. She regarded the shrunken woman and was reminded of Mother Mary, another saint who'd raised a child under somewhat bizarre circumstances. No doubt when Sarah's time came, she'd be rushed up to heaven, led perhaps by St. Peter himself. She noted Sarah's breathing, halting and slow, as if her body had to fight for each small intake of air. Linda pictured Sarah's heart fluttering like a butterfly around a scented flower, never really finding its mark yet continuing to hover. What choice was there for the butterfly? To stop flying? It goes against nature. But Sarah had a choice. Wouldn't it be easier if her life were ended for her so that her suffering could end? Would Sarah want that? Linda wondered.

A small sigh escaped Sarah's dry lips. Linda turned to the nightstand, picked up some Chap Stick and applied it for her very gently. Sarah's eyelids fluttered and then opened, her eyes slowly focusing on Linda's face.

"Linda, my dear. You're back. Why?" The last word was whispered.

"I just wanted to see you again, I guess. You knew that I came before? I thought you were asleep the entire time."

Sarah gained some strength and smiled. "Brenda told me that you'd come. Thanks for remembering me."

"Remembering you! My God, Sarah, you're everything to me. Of course I'll always remember you."

Sarah lifted her hand and wiggled the finger that held the ruby ring. "Thank you for this."

"It's the least I could do, Sarah. I'm sorry that your original one was… lost."

"Oh, that's okay. We both know those stones weren't real," she said with a wink. Linda smiled.

Sarah's tone turned serious, and she put her stern face on. "I understand that Jonathan has not been kind to you."

Linda was confused. "No, he's great, actually. He and Catherine say hi, by the way."

"Really? Because Brenda told me that he cheated on you."

Linda had forgotten her lie, so she feigned embarrassment. "Oh…you caught me. You're right. He did cheat. I just didn't want to tell you."

Sarah's shrewd eyes narrowed and became tenacious. "You're lying to me, Linda."

Linda looked down at the floor. Sarah was the only living person who was still capable of making her feel like shit.

Sarah lifted her chin and continued. "When you were here last, you told me that you had done some things that could get you into trouble."

Linda's head shot up. When she'd confessed to Sarah during her last visit, she hadn't believed Sarah had heard her. But clearly she had. What to do now?

"It's me," Linda blurted. "I'm the one who's cheating. That's the bad thing I've done that could get me into trouble." Linda looked Sarah directly in the eye and silently dared her to challenge what she'd just said.

Sarah held her gaze for some time before finally relenting. "That's what I thought, and that's what I told Brenda. It was much more likely for you to cheat than Jonathan. That man doesn't have it in him."

Linda was shocked at Sarah's bluntness. Her face must have registered her surprise, because Sarah continued. "Linda, you know I love you, but you need to settle down. You're not comfortable in your own skin. It's as if you're always trying to be someone else. Trying to prove yourself over and over again to someone. And I have to tell you, when you get where I am, there isn't much that matters anymore except looking back and making sure you were a good person and tried to do the right thing all the time. If you can say that, then you'll be fine."

Linda's lip trembled as she felt the serpent awaken in her belly. *No, no, no!* she screamed in her head.

Sarah turned her entire body toward Linda. "Is there anything else you want to tell me, Linda? Anything else bothering you? My goodness, you're white as a sheet. Are you feeling well?"

Linda leaned into Sarah as she had when she was a girl. She felt bony arms wrap around her and long nails gently scratch her trembling back. Fat, bold tears began rolling down Linda's cheeks.

"I'm not a good person, Sarah, and I've done some bad things. And I can't seem to stop. I keep trying, but my father won't let me."

The serpent coiled itself around her waist.

The scratching stopped abruptly on her back. "What did you say, Linda? Something about your father?"

"He won't go away! He lives inside my head and keeps whipping me when I don't listen. I have to work harder, be better, and then he leaves me alone. For a while."

The snake tightened its grip around her midsection, threatening to continue upward, forcing Linda to take short quick breaths.

Sarah resumed her soft back scratching and quietly asked, "Is that the way he was in real life, Linda?"

"What? No! He was kind and loving. He rewarded me when I succeeded, when my room was orderly. He liked order. Order is imperative," Linda said robotically.

Sarah stopped scratching and pulled Linda away from her so they were facing each other. Placing a skeletal hand on either side of Linda's face, she looked deeply into her eyes.

"How did he reward you, Linda?"

Up over her chest, the serpent hissed toward Linda's slender, vulnerable neck. The pulse in her neck throbbed as the reptile closed in.

"With love."

Tears filled Sarah's eyes. She closed them as she asked the next question, dreading its answer. "What kind of love?"

The serpent burst forth in a fiery rage that consumed the part of Linda's brain that enabled logic. Her pupils dilated as she stared fixedly at Sarah, desperately hoping for redemption.

"Any kind he wanted."

Sarah's hands fell to her lap as she drew a quick breath. The past came rushing back to her in waves. Linda arriving at her home, organized and clean, seemingly devoid of feeling, which Sarah had attributed to her recent devastating loss. Linda's aversion to dating boys her own age, instead always seeking older boys, sometimes even men when they were willing to risk statutory rape charges, finally settling on Jonathan, a man whom Linda could control completely and without consequence. How had she missed it all these years? All the signs had been there, right in front of her. Had she been too busy? Spread her love too thin among so many needy foster kids? Sarah felt powerless and weak. And sad, so sad. And so very, very tired.

"Linda, what have you done? What is it that you're trying to stop but your father won't let you?" It was Sarah's turn to blanch. "What have you done?" she repeated breathlessly.

The serpent had settled on her scalp, slowly winding and tightening until she felt her head would implode. So much pain. Nothing but pain.

Linda felt confused. She had come to Sarah for reassurance, for forgiveness, yet she was hearing judgment and accusation in Sarah's tone. Her brow furrowed, and her pleading look became desperate.

"Look what he did to me today with his riding crop!" Linda grabbed Sarah's face and forced her head toward her bandaged arm.

"Linda, stop, you're hurting me!" Sarah whispered urgently.

"You need to understand! I don't *want* to do any of this, but he has to be stopped!"

"*Who* has to be stopped, Linda? You're talking in riddles!"

"My father, dammit! My father! Look what he did to me today!" Linda collapsed into the chair next to the bed, exhausted and broken. The snake lay at her feet, spent by its efforts to control her. Linda closed her eyes and willed it away.

Sarah lay in her bed, regaining her composure and her breath. For the first time in her very long life, she was scared. Not for herself, but for this damaged woman she'd taken into her home as a child and sworn to protect. After a time, she said softly, "Show me your arm."

Linda's red-rimmed eyes met hers, and in them she saw the little girl who had fought so hard to be recognized and loved. "Show me," Sarah repeated.

Obediently, Linda presented her arm for review. "Well, it's not too bad, is it? It'll heal well. Stand up, Linda."

Linda stood and approached her sometimes mother, always mentor, head bent in supplication.

"Linda, please look at me."

It took a full minute for Dr. Linda Sterling to gather the courage to look Sarah in the eye. When she did, she recognized that the judgment she'd seen earlier had been replaced by kindness.

"I love you very much. And because I love you, I'm not going to insist that you tell me what you've done to cause yourself so much distress. But I am going to insist that you speak to a mental health professional as soon as possible, because I'm genuinely concerned for your safety. And perhaps, if it's necessary, I want you to speak to a law-enforcement official about your actions. But only if it's necessary. Do you understand?"

Linda nodded, not trusting her voice. She knew she'd said too much, but once she'd started, she couldn't stop. There would be hell to pay with her father later, but right then, with Sarah's incredible strength shoring her up, Linda felt she could bear the burden and even, with a little luck, make it through unscathed.

"Okay," Sarah said, reaching out and stroking Linda's hand. "Okay. I'm tired now, Linda. I think I need to sleep."

"Of course, Sarah. Let me help you." Linda gingerly placed her left hand behind Sarah's head and guided it back to her pillow. She rearranged Sarah's blanket so it was tucked neatly under her chin and then smoothed the blanket so it sat evenly over Sarah's withered frame. She turned to gather her purse and looked once more at Sarah, who'd already slipped into a deep sleep. Her earlier fluttery breathing had been replaced by deep, even breaths, making her chest rise and fall in rhythm.

Linda touched Sarah's cheek once more and whispered, "I love you." As she turned to leave, she noticed Sarah's reading glasses on the nightstand. She glanced once more at Sarah and then at the glasses and was struck by the similarity between the way she chose to leave her "dates" and the way Sarah was tucked in. The hairs on her neck stood at attention as her father's omnipresence suddenly threatened.

Panicking, she backed away from the bed as her father's voice echoed throughout the room. *"Yes, Linda, it's almost time."*

Sharon Sheehan watched Dr. Linda Sterling race down the linoleum-tiled hallway, echoes from her clicking heels ringing in the air. The sound reminded Sharon of a ticking clock racing toward some unseen end. She's in a hurry, thought Sharon. And having heard some of the exchange between Sarah and her guest, Sharon wondered if Dr. Sterling was racing toward something—or away from it.

CHAPTER 20

Detective Alexandra Hayes sat at her desk, completing paperwork related to the severed-head case. Shawn, the in-house sketch artist, had completed a rendition of the head, and it was Alex's solemn responsibility to release the picture to the press in an effort to find the victim's family and garner any leads. Right now, the only lead was the head itself—which, after lying for several days in the field where it was found, didn't seem to have much to offer in the way of evidence. The head was now in the custody of the crime lab, whose techs were trying to determine time of death (based on blood-vessel atrophy), place of death (based on bugs discovered in the head's orifices) and cause of death (which to Alex seemed obvious, but she was just a detective, not a scientist, as the techs liked to remind her from time to time).

Alex sighed and read through the press release that Emily Cochran, Boston PD's public relations representative, had written that morning. Emily was a good writer, adept at maintaining a balance between fact and public interest. As usual, she'd done a bang-up job, and Alex picked up the phone to tell her so.

"Thanks, Alex. I appreciate the kudos. I don't hear a lot of that these days."

"Yeah, tell me about it," Alex replied. "What time is the press conference today?"

"It's in twenty minutes, and I'm hoping you'll do me a favor and attend."

"What? Oh, Emily, don't ask me to do that. You know how I hate the press," Alex moaned.

It was true. Alex's father was a well-known Boston defense attorney, notable for representing people no one else would touch. He was good at it, too, winning more than he lost and collecting big paychecks in the process. Nothing wrong with that, per se. But Alex had grown up with the press often sleeping in their trucks outside the house while her father was in the middle of prominent trials. She was often accosted on her way to school, cameras flashing while the vultures hurled questions at her.

"Hey, Alexandra, what's it like to have your dad represent scumbags all the time?" or "Hey, girl, your daddy's going to hell—you know that, right?"

Alex had learned to despise all of them. They touted the right to freedom of the press, all the while hiding behind their badges and microphones. It was as if they forgot to tuck some humanity into their back pockets when they got dressed in the morning.

"I know you don't like the press, Alex, but I think it's important that you're there—for two reasons. One, it's important for the public to see a woman of substance who carries a detective badge, and two, you have a way of connecting with people, getting them to open up. I'm hoping that quality will come across with the public and someone will come forward. Let's face it—a severed head isn't simply dropped into an open area in the middle of Boston without *someone* having seen *something*, right? C'mon. I need your help on this one."

"You clearly have me confused with Julian regarding the whole 'getting people to open up' thing, but…I'll be there. See you in twenty." Alex slammed down the phone. *Dammit!* she thought.

She leaned back in her chair and removed the plastic clip holding her long blond hair up in a bun. She combed her hands through the silky strands and shook her head to clear it. She couldn't get the image of Julian and that woman at lunch out of her mind. She and Julian had made a pact early in their relationship that they wouldn't butt into each other's professional lives. Since they were no longer working cases together, it usually wasn't a problem. But this circumstance seemed unique.

Alex wasn't concerned that Julian was cheating on her. On the contrary, she felt confident in his commitment to her and their relationship. No, it was actually bigger than that. Her gut instinct, the indescribable force that warns us when our very lives are threatened—often before our logical brains have had time to process the danger—was screaming that something wasn't right about the woman. Alex sighed, wishing she could pinpoint her concern. She certainly wasn't going to rely on "womanly instinct" when she broached the subject with Julian. She'd worked too hard in her career to base any decision on that load of crap. She'd have to keep mulling on what it was, exactly, that had her so riled up about this woman. Only when she was confident in her argument would she approach Julian.

She glanced at her Rolex, a birthday present from her parents, and realized she'd be late to the stupid press conference if she didn't hurry. She growled, "Dammit!" one more time, out loud this time, grabbed her jacket from the back of the chair, and headed down to the first floor, where she knew the circus would be waiting.

As she stepped off the elevator, a flash went off in her face. Instinctively she threw up a hand to shield herself and tore into the poor young camera-man who'd made the blunder.

"Watch it, asshole, or you'll get no more pictures! How's that sound, huh?"

Emily appeared out of nowhere and grabbed Alex's elbow, dragging her toward the podium. She whispered harshly under her breath, smiling the en-tire time, "Listen, Alex. I want you to be here for the reasons I already stated, but it kind of defeats the purpose of seeing a strong female presence up here if you can't keep your temper in check. Can you?"

Alex glared at Emily and then at the cacophony of reporters, photogra-phers, and journalists.

Emily continued. "You're looking at this all wrong. What you see as chaos, I see as opportunity. We are the conductors, and they are the symphony. It's our job to ensure that each section is tuned. Look over there." Emily pointed to a group of local Boston television reporters. "The TV stations over there are the strings; they carry the melody. The reporters from the *Globe* and the

Herald are the brass, and the photographers and cameramen are the tympani. By themselves, they sound okay, but when we direct them to play together, we achieve a symphony worthy of Carnegie Hall. We're the conductor; they are individual players, who achieve greatness only when led by us. You see?"

Alex was staring at Emily as if she'd lost her mind while she pondered what she'd said. Emily's symphony analogy was one that Julian would have used, and Alex found herself wondering if Emily had spoken with Julian regarding how to deal with her. Alex squinted at Emily and finally broke out into a grin.

"What you say actually makes sense," she said, acquiescing. "I'll try…but no promises," she added hastily.

"I'll take it!" said Emily. "Let's go."

They proceeded to the podium, where Emily made a general statement about the Boston PD's involvement with the severed-head case. After speaking for several minutes, she turned toward Alex.

"And finally, let me introduce you to the lead detective in this case, Detective First Grade Alexandra Hayes. She'll take some questions."

Alex advanced to the microphone with trepidation. She tried to envision the symphony as Emily had described. "Play them, or they'll play you" was the phrase that flew through her mind. It's not exactly what Emily meant, perhaps, but it would have to do.

From the *Boston Globe*: "Miss Hayes, what can you tell us about the case at this point in the investigation?"

"Well, it's *Detective* Hayes, and I can tell you that our in-house artist has created an incredible likeness of the victim in an effort to locate next of kin."

From Channel 12: "In similar cases such as this one, police have released unique characteristics of the body that might help in identifying the victim. Is there anything you'd like to share in that regard?"

"Not at this time."

From Channel 4: "Can we assume that the victim's fingerprints were not in AFIS or you would have used them to identify him by now?

"You can assume that if you like." Alex stole a glance at Emily, whose poker face gave away nothing. Alex was feeling more in control now, at ease with the give and take of the process. She pointed at a reporter for the next question.

From the *Boston Herald*: "I understand the victim had been subjected to the elements for several days before being discovered. Can you tell us how old the victim is and in what condition you found the body?"

"I'm not a medical examiner. Nor am I a scientist, as the crime-scene folks like to remind me." She paused, acknowledging some chuckles from the crowd. "But he seems to be between thirty-five and forty-five years of age. And as far as the condition of the victim's body…well, let's just say it was almost nonexistent."

The last line drew some gasps from this hardened group of ghoulish press. Oh yeah, we're having some fun now, Alex thought.

Emily almost tripped as she rushed to the podium to relieve Alex, who was becoming, in Emily's opinion, a little too cocky and loose with her verbiage.

"Ladies and gentlemen, we want to thank you for coming out today. We will of course keep you apprised of any updates regarding the case. So, please—"

From the *National Informer*: "One more question, if you don't mind, for Detective Hayes. Tell me, Detective, when were you going to let the public know about the serial killer that's lurking in our midst?"

The room fell silent. Alex blew air out, trying not to laugh. Lurking in our midst? Did he really just *say* that? she thought.

"I'm not aware of any serial killer in the area," Alex replied seriously.

"Really? Are you sure? Because my sources tell me that a body was found in a local Radisson that seems to match the descriptions of several other bodies that have been found throughout the Northeast corridor—all dead of apparent heart attacks."

"I'm sorry, who are you?"

"Brian Bosch of the *National Informer*."

Alex recognized both names. The *National Informer* was a rag that thrived on stories relating to fame seekers like the Kardashians and any *Real Housewives* TV show. And Brian Bosch was a veteran, king of all rag reporters.

"Well, Mr. Bosch, I've heard nothing about a serial killer in our area and certainly not one who kills via heart attack."

Another guffaw issued from the crowd, whose individual members seemed to share Alex's distaste for this man and his magazine.

"That's all for now, thanks."

Chapter 21

After seeing his three o'clock patient, Julian informed Jesse that Dr. Linda Sterling would be arriving shortly. He then sat at his desk and commanded his phone to dial Stacey Goldberg, the social worker who was trying to get Danny Sheehan into the Rosey Tech program.

Siri responded, "Dialing Stacey Goldberg, Your Grace."

Julian pressed the end call button and yelled, "Jesse! Get in here!"

"My Lord, Julian, the next town can hear you when you yell like that. I know you're blind, but you *do* remember that I'm just in the next room, right?"

Julian simply held out his phone to Jesse and said, "Fix…it…now."

"Fix what? Oh! Oops, I completely forgot. So, so sorry. Fixing it right now."

Julian heard beeping and popping sounds as Jesse adjusted Julian's phone to remove "Your Grace" from Siri's address book.

"All done." Jesse placed the phone back in Julian's hand. "By the way, I just saw Alex on the news, and she did pretty well with the press."

"Alex did a press conference?" Julian was shocked. She hated the press.

"Yeah, about a local murder. But at the end of the conference, Brian Bosch—you know, the guy from the *Informer*? He asked her about a serial murderer here in Boston. Do you know anything about that?"

Julian smirked. "Brian Bosch? Hardly worth taking him seriously. He probably asked the question so he could write about it in that claptrap magazine. If he asks a question, then in his mind it's a verifiable story."

"I don't know, Julian. He seemed pretty serious. Just saying."

The door to the outside office creaked open, and Julian heard Jesse's sharp intake of breath.

He turned to Julian and whispered under his breath, "If that's Dr. Linda Sterrrrling, then I'm willing to be a switch hitter and play for the other side. Guy at the Thai-food place be damned. She is positively gorgeous! My Lord!"

Julian set his mouth and said, "You know I love you, Jesse, but please stop talking and pretend for one minute that you're an assistant to a mental health professional who's about to see a patient. Okay?"

"Got it." Jesse exited to greet Julian's next patient, his right hand outstretched.

Encasing her right hand in both of his, Jesse gushed, "Well, you must be Dr. Linda Sterling. And let me say what a pleasure it is to meet such an esteemed physician. Welcome to our humble abode. Can I get you anything? Coffee, tea, water?"

Linda raised her eyebrows and stared at her right hand until Jesse finally released it. "Water would be lovely, thank you."

"Dr. Stryker is almost ready to see you. Please make yourself comfortable while I let him know you've arrived." Jesse handed her a bottle of water, which she accepted without so much as a thank you.

Jesse excused himself and slipped into Julian's office.

"It's a good thing she's gorgeous," he said, harumphing. "'Cause she sure isn't nice."

"And smart," Julian added.

"What?" Jesse asked, still peeved over Linda's dismissal.

"She's incredibly smart. Don't forget that," Julian said with a smile. "And she's not here as a consultant. She's here as a patient. Don't start a file on her, though. This one's on me."

Jesse leaned in and whispered, "Bad idea, Julian. I don't get a good vibe from her. I'm thinking you're going to want a paper trail on her."

"Don't be ridiculous, Jesse. Now stop stalling, and please show her in."

"All right," Jesse singsonged. "It's your funeral."

"Stop being so dramatic, Jess. Go."

⋏

Linda pushed the door to Julian's outer office open and strode in confidently. After leaving Sarah, she'd driven around for a while, finally finding some shade and comfort under an oak tree along the Charles River. She had replayed her conversation with Sarah and determined with 99 percent assurance that she hadn't said anything that could be construed as an admission of guilt.

But then her father had started asking her questions. *What had you been thinking when you went to Sarah in the first place? What did you believe you were going to find there?* Of course, she'd had no adequate answers for him, and he'd expressed severe disappointment in her lack of organization and judgment and told her that she'd have to do better. He wasn't angry, he'd said, but very dissatisfied with her performance thus far. She detested letting him down and promised right there by the river, with a beautiful summer sun making the water sparkle like diamonds, that she would try harder, work smarter, and remain one step ahead all the time. She'd told him that seeing Julian would aid her efforts, and he'd finally acquiesced to allowing the visit.

Appeased, he had then caressed her hair and spoken lovingly to her before whispering in her ear what would happen if she didn't follow through on her promise.

⋏

Julian greeted Linda as Jesse showed her to the couch.

"Julian, so lovely to see you again. Thanks for agreeing to see me on such short notice."

Julian smiled in response and then said to Jesse, "Thanks, Jesse. We'll be about an hour, I would think."

"Oh, no, no. Not quite that long. I do have a plane to catch."

As Jesse exited, Julian was struck by how different Linda seemed from the restaurant. It wasn't that unusual for people to put up barriers when they first sought therapy. They know in their hearts they need to talk to someone, but when they're actually seated across from a therapist, they balk. Julian was prepared to wait her out.

"Well, whatever time you can spare will work," he said, bowing his head and smiling. "Shall we get started? On the phone, you talked about the fact that the world in which you work is very black and white, not gray like mine. I think those were your words. What does that mean?"

"It's simple. In my profession, people either live or they die. You don't get the opportunity to heal them partially and let them live in that gray zone forever, the way you do as a psychologist. They either live, or they die. That's it."

Julian chose to ignore the dig about his profession. "What about when cancer patients go into remission? Sure, the cancer's gone, but they live with the risk of its return. Isn't that a sort of gray zone?"

"No, it isn't."

"Why"

"Because when cancer is in remission, it's gone."

"Until it returns."

"Or not," Linda countered.

"But isn't that the point?" Julian pressed. "That it could always come back?"

"You could say the same thing about a retrovirus, Julian. If you have a virus, and it goes away and then returns, is it the same virus or a different one? Does it even matter to the person who's sick? Of course not. So, when cancer is in remission, it's gone. There...black and white."

Julian leaned back in his chair. Dr. Linda Sterling was clearly not used to being challenged, and it was very important to her to win an argument. Good to know, he thought.

"Why did you choose to become a pediatric oncologist, Linda?"

"That's easy. Because I wanted to heal sick kids."

"But why kids? Why not adults?"

"'Cause adults are a pain in the ass. They lie, cheat, and steal. They treat other people like shit but expect to be treated like kings. Kids are honest and forthright. If they're angry, you know it. They let you know what they really think. I find that refreshing. Black and white. Orderly."

"You like things to be in order, Linda?"

"Don't you?"

"We're not talking about me, but yes, I do. In fact, because I'm blind, having things in order is imperative."

Linda froze. "What did you just say?" she whispered.

"I said that when you're blind, it's important to keep things in order at home and at work. You know, each thing needs to be put back in its place. Otherwise, you can't find it when you need it, or God forbid, you trip over it if it's left on the floor." He laughed.

Silence. "Linda? You okay?"

The therapy session had been conversational—entertaining, even. Linda had found Julian engaging and intelligent, not to mention incredibly handsome and understanding. He seemed genuinely interested in her opinion, and he was basing his decision to speak to her solely on her intellect and personality. He had no idea what she looked like. Amazing.

Her father's presence hovered protectively near, evaluating her answers as she gave them, urging her to maintain control and distance, praising her clear responses. Until…

"My father always said that."

"He said what?"

"That order is imperative. Not everybody understands it, but it's true. I know you understand. Without order, your world falls apart."

"Well, I wouldn't say falls apart, but yes, it's important to keep things organized." Julian paused, determining how far to push this woman he'd just met. "Is that why you're here today, Linda? Because your world is falling apart? Has something happened to make you feel like your order is dismantling?"

She started laughing then. It started as a low rumble in her throat and quickly escalated into a full bout of hysterical laughter. She laughed for a long time, and Julian let her have this release. He sat back in his chair and smiled, head tilted, until her energy was spent and she could focus and speak once more.

CHAPTER 22

When at last Julian heard a deep, cleansing sigh, he continued. "I assume your father is deceased."

"What makes you say that?" Linda asked.

"Because you said, 'My father always *said* that.' You used the past tense."

"Ah. Good catch. Yes, he's dead. Died in a fire when I was twelve. So did my mom."

"That must have been devastating."

"Not really. I mean, sure, at the time, I was devastated, but I ended up at Sarah's, so everything worked out the way it was supposed to."

"Who's Sarah?"

"She was my wonderful foster mother who never gave up on me. She's in Brookhaven Nursing Home in Lynn and apparently doesn't have much time left. I was there earlier today, and seeing her lying in the bed, so frail...well, I just wondered if it might be kinder to help her along."

Julian raised his eyebrows. "Help her al—"

"Do you believe in God, Julian?"

He was unprepared for this sharp turn in topic.

"Uh...yes, I do. Why?"

"I don't know. I wasn't sure there was a God when I was a child, but after my parents' deaths, I realized there is."

"What about their deaths made you believe that God exists?"

Julian heard the leather squeak as Linda rearranged herself on the couch. "It's like this. When death or other major seemingly negative life events occur, most people think God couldn't exist because he would never let those things happen. That's what I thought when I was a child. You know, like earthquakes and floods and things like child abuse. I see it the other way. God must exist because we have to go through those bad things to appreciate the good in life. See?"

"That's a very positive attitude you have, Linda. Were you in an earthquake?"

"No."

"Have you ever experienced a flood?"

"No, why?"

"You used those examples, so I thought you might have experienced them. So, what were the bad things you went through to see the good in your life?"

Linda paused, understanding that he was hemming her in. Her father roared in her ear, *"Don't do it! Don't do it, Pippin!"*

"You remind me of him, you know."

"I remind you of whom, Linda?"

"My father. He's kind and warm and generous, and he loves me so much."

"Was."

"Excuse me?"

"Don't you mean your father *was* kind and warm and generous?"

"Oh…yes, of course. Past tense, because he's dead."

"Let's talk about what happened at the restaurant today."

"Yes, I'm sorry about that. I've been feeling a little overwhelmed at work, and it comes out in strange ways sometimes."

"Can you give me an example?"

"Careful, Pippin, careful!"

"Well, sometimes I feel as if a black veil is covering my head, and then all of a sudden it lifts."

"That sounds like you're feeling depressed, which can often accompany feelings of helplessness or lack of control. Do you feel like you're in control?"

"At work, absolutely. Everything there is clear to me. Relationships are defined, and hierarchy is understood."

"And you're at the top of that hierarchy?"

"Of course. But outside work, things aren't always so clear and seem muddy to me. It's there that I feel out of control sometimes."

"And how do you handle that?"

"I look to my father for help. He used to call me Pippin, you know."

Linda had a sudden, overwhelming urge to tell Julian everything, to bring him in on the wonderful secret that until now had been shared only between her father and herself. She trusted Julian and wanted her father to like him as she did. No one had ever known about her father's pet name for her when she was a child, and sharing this secret was the first step toward absolution.

"That's interesting."

Linda was slightly offended. She'd taken this big step in their relationship, and Julian didn't seem to recognize its importance.

"It's not *interesting*, Julian. It's *cute*. That's how much he loves me."

"Do you know the story of Pippin, Linda?"

"I know it's a Broadway show…but no, I don't."

"Pippin was a prince who went to war to get his father's attention and love. When that didn't work, Pippin killed his father and took the throne."

"Huh…that *is* interesting." Linda regarded Julian thoughtfully and decided the tilt of his head was somewhat condescending.

"Why are looking at me that way? My father loves me a lot. He gave me a lot of attention, believe me."

"I do believe that he gave you a lot of attention. How about your mother? Did she pay attention to you as well?"

Linda shrugged. "She was clueless. No power whatsoever. Did whatever my dad told her. He treated her well, but in my opinion, she sold out."

"And how about you?"

"What about me?"

"Do you do whatever your father tells you? Have you sold out?"

Linda pierced him with savage eyes. This was not going the way she had planned.

"Fix this!" her father hissed in her ear.

"No. I'm my own person."

"Linda, do you ever speak to your father?"

"He knows! He knows. Get out now, Linda, you bitch! Get out!"

Shut up! Shut up! Linda screamed in her head. Her right hand rose to the side of her head, grabbed some hair, and pulled.

"It's okay if you do, you know," Julian continued.

Linda's entire body drooped. *You see, Daddy? I knew he'd understand.*

"Many people have conversations with deceased relatives or friends. It's a way of keeping their memory alive. Some people even imagine they hear their relative's voice speak to them as well. Do you do that?"

"Sometimes," she answered in the small voice from the restaurant.

"I see. You must really miss your father. It's been quite some time since his passing, and his memory is still so alive to you."

"Shortly after he died, I missed the order he used to insist upon, but as I got older, I realized I could create my own."

"Because order is imperative."

Linda broke into a wide grin. *Daddy, he really, truly understands.*

"I knew you'd get it," she said. "I just knew you'd understand me. I told him you would."

CHAPTER 23

The plane touched down at Boston's Logan International Airport at 7:33p.m., eleven minutes later than scheduled. Vinny's knee pumped up and down as he glanced at his watch for the fourth time in three minutes.

"You must have some big meeting or something, huh, buddy?" asked the gargantuan man seated next to Vinny. For the last seventy-four minutes, Vinny had battled with his neighbor for personal space in the ridiculously tiny area that passed as an airline seat these days. First he had fought and lost a crusade for the armrest, and then he'd waged an unspoken campaign for leg territory. Gallant efforts, but all for naught. Vinny was dying to get off the plane.

"Uh, something like that," he responded, keenly aware that the man wanted to engage in real conversation, which Vinny desperately wanted to avoid.

"What do you do for a living that's so important?" The man sounded belligerent.

Vinny narrowed his eyes and tilted his head to look at the man.

"I'm an FBI agent."

The giant laughed. "Yeah, right, and I'm the king of England."

"Well, it's nice to meet you, Your Highness. Now, can you please move so that I can get out of here?"

The mammoth openly evaluated Vinny, looking him up and down, his eyes finally resting on Vinny's battered briefcase. "No way you're an FBI agent. You don't have the look."

Staring straight ahead, trying to avoid an open confrontation, Vinny gritted his teeth as his knee resurrected its bounce, the only giveaway of his impatience. He waited until the man became bored with bullying, at which point his neighbor pried himself out of the tiny seat and lumbered down the thin walkway toward the exit.

Vinny's eagerness to exit the plane waned as he considered, not for the first time, what he was up against. Joanna's direct orders had been to leave the heart attack cases alone. After issuing that directive, Vinny had abruptly told her that he was taking some personal time to visit friends in Boston. She had leaned back in her chair, hands behind her head, and smiled. "This… personal time…wouldn't be related to the heart attack cases, would it?"

He had calmly raised his eyebrows in response and said, "Even if it were, it's personal time, so does it really matter?"

She had swiftly leaned forward in her chair and addressed him fiercely, her index finger a dagger that struck again and again.

"Understand this, Marcozzi. You don't like me. I get it. You don't think I deserve this job. Well, guess what? I don't like you either. Please give me a reason to demote you…or better yet, let you go. When you're in Boston, you are not on official FBI business. Therefore, you will not have—I repeat, *not have*—access to or the support of any FBI-related resources. Kapeesh?"

"Capisco."

"What? Was that some smart remark?" she quipped.

"No, no, Joanna. It's the Italian response to 'do you understand?' Yes, I understand. Capisco."

She glared at him, suspecting he was trying to pull one over on her, but Vinny's stoic face gave away nothing.

"Get the hell out of my office."

Vinny smiled at the memory while the logical part of his brain processed that he was completely on his own here in Boston. He had only his badge, his gun, and Alex and Julian, who weren't allowed to work a case together because of their personal relationship. Vinny shook his head as he gathered his belong-ings and walked up the Jetway. He was sure about two things: this case prob-ably wasn't going to work out in his favor, and that fact was…he had to try.

He took an Uber car to the Radisson that Marcie had booked for him. As the car pulled into the roundabout to drop him off, Vinny noticed two unmarked police cars parked in valet spaces. Black, nondescript Fords, side by side, government plates.

Exiting the car, Vinny made his way to the reception desk. A perky at-tendant whose name tag read "Brittany" blessed him with a smile that didn't quite reach her eyes. Good try though, Britt, Vinny thought.

"May I help you?" Brittany offered.

"Vincent Marcozzi. Checking in, please."

Brittany typed quickly on a keyboard Vinny couldn't see. "Yes, Mr. Marcozzi. I see you'll be spending three nights with us. Just so you know, your original room was given away by mistake, so we took the liberty of up-grading you to a suite. I hope that's okay." The smile appeared again and was gone just as quickly.

"That's fine. Thanks."

"Great. That's room four forty-one. Here's your key and your breakfast vouchers. Elevators are to your right. Have a nice stay, and please don't hesi-tate to let us know how we can make your time with us more comfortable." Strained smile, tilt of the head, a subtle dismissal.

Vinny laughed. "Thanks. Oh…hey, Brittany, can you tell me what those two unmarked police cars are doing outside?"

Brittany's eyes widened and then abruptly darted around the lobby, clear-ly agitated and concerned. She glanced behind her before leaning forward to whisper to Vinny, "Between you and me, you may want to find somewhere else to stay. I would if I were you. Apparently a guy died here last night. They *say* it was a heart attack, but if it were, why would they send two detectives to investigate?" She finished her breathless statement without blinking, her eyes glued to Vinny's.

Vinny's pulse quickened. "A heart attack, you say. Do you know anything else about it?"

Brittany checked the lobby again to ensure they weren't being overheard. "Well, I'm kinda good friends with a local reporter here, and he told me that he'd heard from some people in other cities that this has been happening there, too."

"Real-ly," Vinny drew out the double *L*, leaning conspiratorially into the counter with his hands on the desk.

"Uh-huh. *And* that the police are trying to hush it up because they think it's a serial killer but they're scared everybody'll freak out if they knew." She gave Vinny a look that said, "You know how the police are" and then rolled her eyes.

Vinny took the hint and frowned his agreement while nodding his head. "Listen, Brittany, do you have the number of this reporter friend of yours? Do you think I could talk to him about this? You see, I have an interest in this kind of thing. You know, tracking police investigations and following the police scanner, stuff like that."

Brittany was nodding her head sagely, as if she too shared a fascination with the macabre. "Yeah, I think that'd be okay. Brian's a cool guy, but a lot of people don't trust him 'cause he works for the *National Informer.* But that doesn't make him a bad reporter or a bad person, don't you think?"

Vinny inwardly winced at the mention of the tabloid. He had on more than one occasion had the opportunity to help reporters like Brian under-stand that their "work" often bordered on impeding a criminal investigation. Physical altercations had not been unwarranted.

"Of course not, Brittany. Of course not. And I'll just talk to him over the phone. I won't ask to meet or anything."

"I guess that's okay," she responded, writing down Brian's number on the back of one of Vinny's breakfast vouchers.

As Vinny made his way to the elevators, he turned once more to look at Brittany. She waved, winked, and then grinned. Vinny noticed that the smile made it up to her eyes this time.

After settling into his suite, Vinny sat in the easy chair facing the win-dow, absentmindedly watching the jets taking off and landing at Logan. After a few minutes, he dialed the number Brittany had written on his breakfast voucher. Brian Bosch, veteran smut reporter, answered on the first ring. Vinny did his best to convince Bosch that he was just a thrill junkie seeking information on the latest murder-related gossip, but Brian was smarter than he'd anticipated. After listening to Vinny's tale, Brian told him he'd need to call him back. And when he did, about ten minutes later, he'd learned that Vinny was an FBI agent and that he was in Boston visiting friends.

"How'd you get all that info so quickly?" Vinny had asked.

"Hey, Special Agent, you got your sources, and I got mine."

"Is her name Brittany?"

Brian had laughed. "She's a good girl, but she does like her gossip. She's an easy score when it comes to getting information."

Vinny silently cursed himself for using his real name when checking in. Any quick Google search would enlighten a curious mind as to Vinny's job and fame from the Mexico case he'd worked with Julian and Alex. Put that information together with the fact that he was curious about the current hotel death and wasn't using his badge as a means of access, and one could arrive at the same conclusion Bosch had.

Vinny said, "You know Brittany could lose her job for giving out the name of a guest staying at the hotel."

Bosch laughed mirthlessly. "Cut the crap. We both know that you're not going to draw any more attention to yourself than you have to, *Special Agent in Charge Marcozzi*. You have a hunch, and you're in Boston to verify it...or not. But what I don't understand is how you knew about this heart attack murder in the first place."

Vinny didn't want to lose any more face to this man. If Bosch found out that Vinny had simply stumbled onto the murder while checking into the hotel, the story Bosch would write would get Vinny laughed out of the bureau.

"Like you said, Bosch. You have your sources, and I have mine."

"Uh-huh. And if you're in Boston on official FBI business, why didn't you go directly to the police yourself? Why ask Brittany about it behind the scenes?"

Before Vinny could find time to fabricate a suitable response, the reporter came to his own conclusion, proving once more how dangerous it was to underestimate him.

"Unlesssss," he said, dragging out the *S*, forming an idea as he spoke, "you're not here on *official* FBI business. You're here on your own. But why not call in the Feebies?"

Vinny remained silent, knowing it wouldn't take long for Bosch to arrive at the correct answer.

"Ah…it's because you know they won't come. You're truly, completely on your own here in Boston," Bosch reasoned aloud, clearly not requiring help from Vinny. "But why?"

"Enough. Okay, you're right. I'm on my own, *right now*, because I'm conducting a preliminary investigation whose outcome will determine future FBI involvement, so—"

"Blah, blah, blah," Brian interrupted. "We both know that's Feebspeak for 'you're flying solo most likely because you pissed off a higher-up.' Am I right? Tell me, Vinny…may I call you Vinny? Did they let you keep your badge and gun?"

Vinny's pulse raced as he endeavored to turn the conversation to his advantage. After quick consideration, he decided to play the game by the rules Bosch had defined. He might be selling his soul, but he'd already spent serious political capital chasing this case in the first place. He closed his eyes and decided to go for broke.

"It seems we're both in a position to help each other out," Vinny offered.

"Now you're talkin' my language, Mr. FBI man. I'm listening," Bosch drawled in an almost lascivious tone.

Chapter 24

Alex stood outside Boston police headquarters at One Schroeder Plaza, her phone pressed to her ear as she updated Julian on her earlier triumph with the press.

"You should've seen it, Julian! I was awesome!"

Julian laughed out loud. He loved hearing her so jubilant in her success. "I know how much the press has bothered you in the past, so good for you! I'm proud of you! We should celebrate."

"Sounds good. Where and when?"

"How about you pick me up at the office right now? I'm about done here anyway."

Alex's phone beeped. "Hold on, Julian. Someone's calling." Looking at the caller ID that read "Vinny," she pressed the button that simultaneously put Julian's call on hold and opened the line to Vinny. "Hey, Vin. We're looking forward to seeing you this weekend. What's up?"

"Change of plans, Alex. What are you and Julian doing right now?"

"We were going out for dinner, why?"

"Because I'm already in Boston and need to talk to you guys pronto. Meet me at the airport Radisson bar in twenty minutes."

"What? Vinny?" But he had already rung off.

Alex returned to Julian and said, "Apparently we're not going out to dinner."

"We're not?"

"Nope. We're meeting Vinny at the airport Radisson bar in twenty minutes."

"What? Vinny's not supposed to be here until—"

"This weekend, I know," Alex finished. "But he's here now, and he says we have to meet him in twenty. I got the sense it's important. Ugh, hold on, Julian. I'm getting a text."

Alex drew the phone away from her ear and read the message that accompanied the two *bings* announcing a text on her phone.

"Heart attack victim found at airport Radisson. Local PD questioning homicide. You're lead on this. Get over there now. Kevin."

Alex looked up at the sunset and sighed. She returned the phone to her ear and said, "I just got called to a scene."

"Okay. Can you drop me at the Radisson on your way?"

"No need, actually. The body's at the Radisson as well. It seems to be a heart attack victim, but the local PD is questioning if it was a homicide."

Julian was quiet a moment. Why did that sound familiar?

Then it hit him.

"Alex, didn't the reporter from the *Informer* raise a question at the press conference about a serial killer murdering via heart attack?"

Alex's eyebrows knit in concentration, and her vision tunneled as she replayed the end of the press conference in her head. "Oh my God! You're right. We gotta get over there before that reporter does. I'm on my way to get you. See, Julian, see?" Alex was seething.

"See what, Alex?"

"See why I hate the press?"

✈

Alex screeched to a halt in front of the valet stand at the Radisson while a pimply, seventeen-year-old valet looked on. She exited the car, threw him the keys, and said, "Be careful with her, buster" before coming around to collect Julian from the passenger side of the car.

The hotel was exactly as you would expect, appointed with corporate, trendy items that were meant to make visitors feel at home but managed to achieve just the opposite effect. The space felt sterile, generic. Lots of business people in the lobby, on their phones and laptops, rarely looking up as they passed. The business-office printers were humming, the front-desk staff was busy, and there were no security guards to be seen. It was, summarily, the perfect place *not* to be noticed. Julian commented on the smell, pumped in with the air through some unseen duct. A hint of lilac, as if one were outside enjoying the beautiful summer day instead of stuck inside an airport hotel conducting mind-numbing business.

"May I help you?" a bubbly voice asked.

Julian turned toward the voice and smiled. "Yes, thank you. We're meet—"

"Oh my God. You're blind!" Brittany blurted.

Julian drew back in mock horror, hand to his chest. "Oh my God! Are you *serious*? I *am*?"

Alex wasn't in the mood. "Yes, he's blind, and despite his reaction, he was already aware of it. Now, we're here to meet a gentleman by the name of Vincent Marcozzi."

Brittany glanced around before whispering, "You mean the FBI agent, right?"

Julian leaned forward and beckoned Brittany closer before whispering back, "Is there another Vincent Marcozzi staying here right now?"

"No."

"Then he'd be the one. If you can call him for us, that'd be great. Thanks."

A short time later, Alex, Julian, and Vinny sat at a corner table in the bar, three friends quietly reminiscing about old times. Except their memories didn't consist of high school crushes and who was dating whom but rather the huge case they had worked together some years past involving drug kingpins and a sociopathic socialite who liked to manipulate law enforcement for her own entertainment. It wasn't glamorous, but it was *their* past together, and it's what made them into the people who sat at the table—stronger, wiser, and less gullible than they'd been prior to the case that took them to Belize and Mexico, ending in a shootout so dramatic it could have been the stuff of a mystery thriller novel.

"So," Vinny said taking a huge gulp of Diet Coke, "let me enlighten you as to why I asked you here. "

"Hurry it up, Vin. I got a dead guy upstairs waiting for me."

"Relax, Alex. He's not going anywhere."

Alex rolled her eyes. "Just make it quick. The only reason I'm meeting with you prior to walking the grid on the scene is because I'm hoping you'll give me some insight into the potential murder upstairs."

"Okay, okay. Listen, we have the following deaths via heart attack, in order, over a period of a year and a half." Vinny took a table napkin and spoke as he wrote:

1. Maxwell Cooper. Died January 12, 2015, at a hotel in Baltimore. Age—43 years. Heart attack.
2. Samuel Worthington. Died June 14, 2015, at a hotel in New York City. Age—45 years. Heart attack.
3. Walter Croswell. Died October 29, 2015, at a hotel in Philadelphia. Age—46 years. Heart attack.
4. Justin Simkins. Died February 14, 2016, at a hotel in Hartford. Age—44 years. Heart attack.
5. Evan Donaldson. Died July 13, 2016, here at the Boston Radisson. Age—44 years. Heart attack.

When he was finished, Julian paused and said. "That's it? Seriously, Vin, please tell us there's more than this."

"You don't see a pattern here, Julian?"

"I see five relatively young men who clearly didn't take good care of themselves, leading to early deaths." Julian shrugged.

Alex interjected, "What did your boss say when you ran it by him?"

"It's a her, and she said the same thing Julian did. She told me to leave it alone." Vinny blew out a mouthful of air and ran his hands through his thinning hair before continuing.

"She's looking for a reason to get rid of me. She actually told me that, can you believe it? That's why I'm here on my own. I had some personal leave that I had to use or lose. So…here I am."

Julian took in a long breath and leaned toward where he knew Vinny was sitting. "There must be more, Vinny. I know you. You wouldn't put your career on the line for something unless you really believed in it. So, what are you *not* telling us? Convince us to believe you."

Alex and Julian listened patiently as Vinny told them the background of how he had laid groundwork to collect friends and favors when he'd been promoted and that one of those friends had piped up regarding the seemingly strange coincidences of heart attack deaths in hotels over the one-and-half-year period. He reviewed each case with them in detail, presenting only facts and findings, trying not to draw conclusions for his listeners. After about ten minutes, he wrapped it up.

"Think about it. They're all white, approximately the same age; all un-married traveling salesmen in the city for a convention of some kind, either Protestant or Catholic; and all wear reading glasses. They were all found na-ked in the hotel bed after having had sex the night before. In all five cases, the men's reading glasses were found on the nightstand, covers pulled up to their chins. The hair was neatly combed back, and their hands were folded precisely across their chests in the area where the heart is."

"As if the perp feels remorse and is laying them to rest, so to speak," finished Alex.

"Exactly! Right, Alex! Yes!" Vinny almost jumped out of his chair. "How many people when having a heart attack would lie completely still in a bed so that their hair didn't get mussed or their covers didn't get pulled down? What are the odds that five heart attack victims would die with their hands folded perfectly across their chests? In *exactly* the same manner, across five different states? How many people would have their reading glasses situated on the night stand in *exactly* the same manner, without a book in sight?"

Julian was slowly nodding. Vinny was right. The odds of all those items occurring across five states was miniscule. Not even worth discussing.

"Where do we start?" Julian asked.

Alex placed her hands on the table. "Well, I don't know about you two, but I'm gonna start in Mr. Donaldson's hotel room here in Boston. I'm officially on the case already through Boston PD, Vinny. I shouldn't have even taken the time to meet with you before going to the crime scene, but curiosity got the better of me."

"Awesome!" Vinny pumped his arm. "Keep me in the unofficial loop, okay, Alex?"

"You got it, Vin."

Vinny turned to Julian. "Can you work on a profile of this killer, Julian? Any insight you can give me would be helpful."

"Absolutely...although I'm not officially working on this either, since Alex and I can't work cases together."

"Of course. Understood." Vinny punched Julian's arm softly.

"What are you going to do, Vin?" asked Alex as she stood to go.

He winced. "Well, in order to get some of the info I just told you, I kind of made a deal with a reporter for an exclusive interview about the FBI. Anonymous, of course," he hastily added.

Alex grimaced. "That's awful. I wouldn't want to be you. At least tell me it's with a respectable source like the *Times* or the *Globe*."

Vinny smirked. "Kind of. It's with Brian Bosch from the *National Informer*."

Alex's response, "You've got to be fucking kidding me!" was drowned out by Julian's laughter. Reverberating all the way to the front desk, it drew a smile from Brittany's face. A smile that reached her eyes.

CHAPTER 25

Julian remained in the bar after Alex and Vinny left. Alex said she'd return for him after speaking with the local cops and completing a preliminary walk-through of the crime scene.

Julian pulled out his phone and commanded it to dial Stacey Goldberg.

"Hello?"

"Hey, Stacey, it's Julian Stryker. Sorry, I know it's getting late, but I wanted to follow up with you regarding whether or not you were able to get Danny Sheehan into the Rosey Tech program?"

"Geez, Julian. You're persistent, aren't you? It's only been a couple of days since you asked."

"I know, I know. So sorry, but I'm worried about this kid, and I know what kind of pull you have over there. I really appreciate your—"

"Yeah, yeah. Save the ass-kissing for another time, Julian. I couldn't get him in. There just aren't any spots right now. I told you that before."

Julian was crestfallen. He didn't have a backup plan regarding Danny, and he'd been sure Stacey would come through.

"It's okay—" he started.

"Wait, wait, you didn't let me finish. I said there aren't any openings *right now*. But I know for a fact that the family of a kid who's currently in the program is moving to Oregon, so a spot will be freed up by the end of next month. Hope that'll work for you and Danny," she finished, clearly pleased with herself.

Julian slapped the table. "Yes! Yes! I *knew* you'd come through, Stacey. You're the best! And you won't regret it. Danny's going to really shine with the help of the Rosey program."

Stacey laughed. "You sure are some kind of child advocate, Julian. Seriously, if I were a kid in the system, I'd want you on my side."

Julian was all smiles, not because of the compliment but because he saw a bright future for a child who had suffered so much. That's what woke him up in the morning.

"Thanks again, Stace. I owe you big."

"Oh, don't worry. Someday I'll knock on your door to collect. In the meantime, say hi to Alex, and enjoy what's left of your evening."

"You too, Stacey. Thanks!"

Julian ended the call as the waitress approached.

"Clearly you have something to celebrate, sir. Can I get you anything?"

Julian smiled in her direction and said, "No, I'm all set, but thanks for offering."

He then commanded his phone to dial the Sheehan's home number. As the call connected, Julian reminded himself to thank Jesse for pre-loading all his patients' numbers into his phone. Jesse made Julian's job easier in so many ways, and Julian forgot to thank him sometimes. Some people would say that loading phone numbers is simply the job of an assistant, but Julian had known Jesse since before he was blinded. And the fact is, after the attack, Jesse took personal responsibility for ensuring his friend's successful return to adolescent psychology. Not only had he organized the office furniture to optimize ease of movement, he had also computerized all patient records and completed other tasks, like adding Dragon to Julian's computer for dictating and downloading all patients' phone numbers and home addresses to Julian's phone. Jesse had become invaluable to Julian.

Sharon Sheehan picked up after six rings with a groggy, "Hello?"

Julian felt terrible for waking her up but knew she'd want to hear this news as soon as possible.

"Mrs. Sheehan? This is Julian Stryker, Danny's therapist. How are you?"

"Um…fine. Who's this again?"

"I'm Dr. Julian Stryker, the child psychologist Danny was asked to see because of his…so he wouldn't…" Julian was having a hard time finding the right words.

"Theft? Because of his theft of a car? And so he wouldn't end up in juvie? Yeah, now I remember you. Yeah. So, how can I help you? Did Danny do something else wrong?"

"No, no, nothing like that, Mrs. Sheehan. I'm so sorry for waking you up, but I thought you'd want to hear some good news."

Sharon Sheehan blew out air on the other end of the line. "Good news? Yeah, I could use some of that. Not much of it going around these days, that's for sure." She yawned.

"Well, I have some for you. Danny's been accepted into a program at Roosevelt Technical High School. Well, he hasn't yet, but he will be within a month."

"And that's good news because…" she trailed off, not comprehending.

"Because my understanding is that he has been struggling in school. This program will allow him to remain in school, being educated by instructors who know how to teach kids who learn differently. *And*…he'll have the opportunity to learn a trade at the same time if he wants to."

Sharon was silent for a moment while she processed what Julian had said.

"Why did you do this?" she finally asked.

"Well, it's my job. But, more importantly, Danny seems like a really good, smart boy who has potential, and I didn't want to see that potential go to waste. I think if he had some guidance, he could be very successful in life. I know you're trying, but I also know the hard time you've had since your other son, Jimmy, died."

Sharon was quiet and then started weeping. Julian gave her a moment to collect herself.

"You're right. It's been hard, and it doesn't help that my husband doesn't seem to care anymore. Ever since Jimmy died—" Her voice caught, and she paused. "Ever since Jimmy died, it just hasn't been the same. He fought hard and had great doctors, but God called him home."

"I'm so sorry for your loss," Julian said, pulled into the grieving mother's anguish. "I didn't know Jimmy, but I agree with you about his having had great doctors. I ended up speaking with one, a Dr. Linda Sterling. I wanted to better understand Danny's background, so I contacted her for a chat. She honestly cared about Jimmy very, very much. She shares in your loss."

"Oh, I know she does. She's a great lady. She did all she could, but the cancer was too advanced. She cried when he died. I saw it. It was like she took Jimmy's death personally, like she had failed."

Julian reflected on his initial conversation with Linda and remembered her overwhelming commitment to her patients. Now that he'd met with her in person, he was beginning to wonder if her commitment was all-consuming. If perhaps she was losing a piece of herself each time a patient didn't make it, which from the statistics seemed frequent.

"Well, I just wanted to let you know about Danny's upcoming admission into the Rosey program. I'll make sure I give him the required paperwork when I see him for his next session. Please let me know if I can help in any other way. I hope things continue to improve for you, Mrs. Sheehan."

"Please, call me Sharon. And thanks, Dr. Stryker. I really, really appreciate your taking a chance on my boy. He'll make you proud."

"I don't doubt that, Sharon. Thanks for your time."

"Oh, by the way, Dr. Stryker, I saw Dr. Sterling the other day where I work."

"Oh? Where's that?"

"Brookhaven Nursing Home in Lynn. You know it?"

"No, but I bet it's a fine place."

"It's okay. Dr. Sterling came twice to visit a lady, but the other day, she seemed really upset. I hope she's okay. If you talk to her again, will you please tell her I say hi? She didn't recognize me when she was there, and I felt awkward reintroducing myself to her. Plus, I just don't want to drag up

Jimmy's death one more time. And talking to her would do that big time, you know?"

"I completely understand. Tell me, Mrs. Sheehan—"

"Sharon."

"Right, Sharon. Tell me, was Dr. Sterling visiting someone named Sarah?"

"Yeah, that's her. Awesome old lady. I don't know what the relationship is between them, but they seem very close. Dr. Sterling and some other lady named Brenda."

"Brenda," Julian repeated.

"Yeah. Anyway, please tell Dr. Sterling I say hi. And thanks again, Dr. Stryker. We'll talk soon?"

"You bet, Sharon. Have a great evening."

Julian rang off and thought for a moment. Linda had been at the nursing home the other day and, according to Sharon Sheehan, had been upset. And she had been upset at the restaurant with him. And she had been upset in his office. In addition, she seemed overly connected to her deceased father. Although Julian had initially agreed to talk with Linda as a professional courtesy, he was becoming concerned that there was more to her behavior than she had let on. Because he had no file on her, he wasn't legally obligated to maintain her confidence. However, he knew he was on shaky moral ground if he decided to move forward with the plan that was forming in his head. If he felt Linda was in danger of "serious and foreseeable harm," he could break confidentiality. Did he believe that?

He quickly reviewed the facts:

- She'd slammed his walking stick on the table at the restaurant without apparent cause or provocation.
- She'd used both the present and the past tenses when speaking of her deceased father during the office visit.
- She seemed to have a history of emotional overcommitment to her patients' outcomes.
- She'd continually changed the subject when he'd alluded to bad things that had happened in her life.

- She had clearly dismissed and exhibited disdain for her mother.
- She had a life-guiding belief that order is imperative.

Did he truly believe that Linda was in danger of "serious and foreseeable harm"?

Yes, he did.

Chapter 26

The head of security at the Boston airport Radisson sat stonily in his chair in the video control room. Alex had approached him, badge outstretched, asking to review camera footage from the night of Mr. Donaldson's heart attack. Alex now stood behind the security supervisor, arms crossed over her chest, staring intently at the black-and-white images on the screen. Mr. Donaldson's room was directly next to the elevators. And the one security camera on the floor was placed directly above his door, the angle making it almost impossible to see anyone entering or exiting. Did the perp know that? Is the guy really that smart? Alex found herself wondering.

Alex glared hard at the screen, willing it to give her some information she could use.

"Wait! Stop...go back," she directed the guard.

She had seen someone walking away from the elevators (and Mr. Donaldson's room), enter a room down the hall, and then return shortly thereafter with a roller bag. But other than that, no one entered the hallway until many hours later. She jotted a note to herself to follow up with the officers who'd first responded to the scene so that she could review interviews that had been conducted with guests staying on the same floor as Mr. Donaldson.

"Is that a man or a woman?" Alex asked the security guy.

"You mean the person pulling the roller bag? Hard to tell because the footage is so grainy, but it looks like a woman to me. See the sway in the walk? That looks like long hair tied up in the back, don't it?"

Alex leaned in close to the screen and found herself squinting, trying to get a better read.

"Can't you blow up the image, at least?" she asked, frustrated with the low-quality pictures.

"I could, but the picture would get more grainy then," he responded, turning to look at her.

"Ah, forget it," she said. "I'll see what the interviews produced, and maybe we'll come back to this." She nodded toward the screen.

"I'd be happy to come back and meet with you anytime," he offered, looking her up and down.

She regarded him dryly. "Really? Is that the best you've got? You need to bring more than that if you think you're going to get with this." She swept her left hand up and down her body and then walked out, whispering, "Asshole," under her breath.

She made her way to Evan Donaldson's room, where the forensic pathologist was packing up her bag, ready to leave.

"Any information that might break this case wide open?" Alex asked hopefully, clapping her hands together to emphasize the point.

Dr. Dolores Caruso sighed and gave Alex a tired smile. "I wish I could say yes to your question, but I'd be lying."

Alex's shoulders slumped. "Tell me what you know." Alex pressed the voice memo button on her phone so she could tape Dolores's report to send to Julian for his review—unofficially, of course.

"Based on body temperature and rigor mortis, I'm going to say time of death was between seven and eleven last night. Mr. Donaldson had engaged in sexual intercourse prior to his death but wore a condom, based on residual powder we found on his penis. Lividity shows us that he died in the position in which he was found—on his back in bed. There were no indications of foul play. Everything points to a natural death."

"Heart attack?"

Dolores shook her head. "You know I can't answer that until I get him on the table and run some blood work. I'll also talk to his primary-care physician to rule out preexisting conditions. But I can tell you that at first glance, it doesn't seem to be homicide."

Alex pursed her lips, and Dolores regarded her quizzically.

"Listen, Alex. It almost seems like you want this to be a homicide. Do you not have enough work? Because I heard that you caught the severed-head case. I'd think that would be enough to keep you busy for some time."

Alex sighed. "It's not that, Dolores. It's just that—"

"Alex, if you're looking for something that indicates this was anything but natural, there's simply no evidence to the contrary right now. And you know I've been doing this a long time." She smiled, raising her eyebrows.

Alex waved her hand in the air. "I know, I know, Dolores. I didn't mean to imply you don't know your job. Of course you do. It's just that this death might be the fifth in a series, if you know what I mean."

"No. I don't know what you mean."

Alex leaned in close and whispered. "There may be a serial killer out there who murders via heart attack, and Mr. Donaldson might be the fifth victim."

"In Boston?" Dolores drew back from Alex, raising her voice.

"Shh. And no—in four other cities…and now Mr. Donaldson." She pointed to the body bag, zipped up and ready for transport to the coroner's office.

Dolores stared at Alex and then at the body bag. "Well, causing a heart attack big enough to kill someone would require significant amounts of drugs. And those drugs stay in the bloodstream for quite some time. So we'd definitely see them on the standard toxicology screen we do back at the lab."

In her notebook, Alex wrote, "Tox screens in other deaths" and then returned her attention to Dr. Caruso.

"Okay. Please let me know when you have the tox screen done on Mr. Donaldson. If this *is* a serial killer, I want Mr. Donaldson to be his last victim." Alex pressed stop on her phone to cease recording and immediately sent the voice memo to Julian.

Dolores smiled. "I'll call you." And then to her assistants, she called, "Okay. Let's get out of here, people. We have work to do!"

They lifted the body onto a gurney and wheeled it out of the room. As was unspoken protocol in these situations, each police officer stood aside and silent as the body was removed. Alex always wondered at this phenomenon. No one ever said that she should be quiet and still as a dead body went by; it just sort of happened. And she'd learned over time that other people had the same reaction. When she had asked Julian about it, he'd told her that there were probably several reasons people did this. Perhaps seeing a dead body reminded folks of their own mortality and gave them pause. Perhaps the behavior was out of reverence for someone who will no longer grace the earth. Perhaps they were even thinking, "At least it wasn't me." Or worse: "What would happen if it *were* me?"

Alex was pulled from her reverie by a young officer stepping on her foot as he walked by.

"Hey, watch it!"

"Oh, sorry, Detective."

"Who's in charge here?" Alex asked him as she donned some plastic gloves.

The young man pointed down the hallway to a plainclothes cop named Raj Vettukattil, whom Alex had known since the academy. She was glad to see he was heading the initial investigation, as Raj was smart, fair, and honest. He wouldn't mind that she'd been assigned to take over his case, and she was sure she'd get his full cooperation moving forward.

Before approaching Raj, she took the opportunity to walk the hotel room herself. Dictating notes she would send to Julian, she started in the bathroom and was struck by how organized everything was. Toothpaste, toothbrush, shaving gear, comb, and deodorant were lined up perfectly on the counter. Mr. Donaldson's toiletry bag was in the drawer under the sink, as if he were going to be staying for a while. Towels were folded and hung on the towel rack, not the hooks. She opened the glass shower door and found the shampoo, soap, and conditioner lined up neatly in the caddy hanging from the showerhead, slightly used but caps on tightly.

Alex crossed to the closet directly across from the bathroom and found three suits with ties tucked into the jacket pockets. Next to the three suits were three shirts, each a different color. Alex stepped back from the closet and crossed her arms. Something wasn't right. She looked away quickly and then returned her gaze, a trick she had learned at the academy. By looking away and returning your eyes to the object in question, minute details often stand out. When she looked again at the clothing, the anomaly became clear. All hangers seemed to be exactly the same distance apart. Exactly.

"Hey, anybody got a measuring tape or ruler?" Alex called out to the remaining cops in the room as she snapped her fingers.

"I do," replied the young officer who had stepped on her foot.

He handed her a measuring tape, and she gauged the distance between each hanger. Exactly four inches apart, every single one. "That can't be coincidence," she said into her phone, more to herself than to Julian. After checking the pockets of each suit and finding nothing, she turned her attention to the rest of the hotel room.

Mr. Donaldson's closed suitcase lay on the luggage rack. She unlatched it and found nothing inside. Crossing to the dresser, she opened the top drawer and found three pairs of socks and three pairs of underwear neatly folded, as if nothing had been worn. Alex wrinkled her brow in thought. Mr. Donaldson was supposed to be checking out the day he died. He had already been at the conference for three days and had three days' worth of clothing with him. Yet everything was folded as if it hadn't been worn. She returned to the closet and leaned into the shirt section, careful not to actually touch the clothing. She drew a deep breath through her nose and detected the musky scent that's produced when laundry is dirty—leftover deodorant and cologne.

Someone—maybe Mr. Donaldson or maybe his killer, if there was one—went to great lengths to ensure that the room and its contents were in perfect order. *But why?*

Alex walked the rest of the room, noticing nothing of consequence except that Mr. Donaldson's reading glasses were folded neatly on the nightstand and no book was nearby, just as Vinny had mentioned.

Having exhausted her solo search, Alex walked down the hall to where Raj Vettukattil stood, talking on the phone. He ended the call as she approached.

"Hey, Raj, long time no see. What's shakin'?" Alex held up her right hand in a closed fist and bumped his right fist.

"Nothing, nothing, Alex. Good to see you. Don't tell me you caught this monster of a case?"

"Afraid so," she said. "What'cha got for me?"

Raj smirked and slowly shook his head. "Not much, my friend. Did you already see the security footage, if you can call it that?"

"Yeah. It was pretty much a bust. Did the tech get photos of the entire room and bathroom?"

"Tons of them."

"Prints?"

Raj raised his eyebrows and spread his palms wide. "Seriously, Alex? You're going to grill me on the basics? Of course we took prints."

"Yeah, sorry. I just don't want to screw anything up, you know? What else?"

Raj shrugged as he flipped open his iPad. He was one of the few officers who had made the transition into the digital age without kicking and screaming. Scanning his notes, Raj reported, "Forty-four-year-old white male, pharmaceutical rep from Lancaster, Pennsylvania, here for a work conference. Prior to retiring for the night, he was seen in the bar, sitting by himself and working on his laptop. The bartender said he took a call right before he left the bar, and that's the last time the bartender remembers seeing him."

"Was he a big drinker according to the bartender?"

"Nope. One drink each night he was here. Decent tipper, nice guy, the bartender said."

Alex thought for a moment. "What about housekeeping? How come it took so long for the body to be discovered?"

Raj consulted his notes, swiping through various screens until he reached the one he wanted. "The maid knocked twice, offering turndown service the night he was killed, but she heard no response, so she moved on. And this morning, housekeeping skipped the room until after checkout time because there was a Do Not Disturb sign on the door.

"Huh. Makes sense, I guess. Dolores said he had sex the night he was killed."

"Good way to go," Raj offered. Alex threw him a sharp glance.

"Sorry, Alex. But it would be, don'tcha think?"

Alex ignored the question. "Did anyone recall seeing a woman enter the room with Mr. Donaldson?"

"Maybe it was a man."

"What?"

"Maybe he had sex with a man," Raj offered.

"Okay. Did any of the people you interviewed recall seeing *anyone* enter this room with Mr. Donaldson?"

"Not so far, but we're still completing the interviews with the people who were staying on this floor."

"What about his phone? Did he call an escort service, by chance?"

"His phone calls, incoming and outgoing, are being analyzed at the tech lab right now. I'll let you know when I hear something." Alex ended the recording and forwarded it to Julian.

"Thanks. The bartender said he was on the phone prior to leaving the bar, right? Maybe we'll get lucky, and he was calling for a hooker."

"Yeah, right," Raj guffawed. "Nothing's ever *that* easy."

CHAPTER 27

Julian was traveling at an astonishingly low speed in the taxi, as traffic on Storrow Drive was crawling even at this time of night. It gave him time, however, to listen to the recordings Alex had sent and to compose a quick text to her, saying that although he had reviewed the voice memos, he had some other business to address and that he'd catch up with her tomorrow. It also offered him an opportunity to contemplate Vinny's request to create a profile on the killer, assuming Mr. Donaldson's death was a homicide and assuming it was related to the other four cases whose details seemed undeniably familiar.

According to Alex's findings, the evidence in Mr. Donaldson's room seemed to fit the details Vinny had recounted regarding the other four cases. In his mind's eye, Julian created a bullet-point list:

- In all instances, the men were visiting from out of town for a work-related conference.
- In each case, the hotel room was in pristine condition, as were the clothes, even though each victim had been staying in the hotel for several days prior to his death.
- And, it turned out, in the other four cases, the men's private work and home spaces were not nearly as tidy as the hotel rooms in which each was found.

If Mr. Donaldson's home and work cleanliness was found to be lacking as compared to the immaculate condition of the hotel room, then the bizarre circumstances surrounding all five deaths would be identical and therefore hard to ignore. Implications of foul play would have to be taken seriously.

Julian leaned back in the seat and closed his eyes, imagining himself inside the hotel room with the killer, assuming there was one. Statistically, most serial killers were men, so Julian started with that theory. Each victim had sexual intercourse prior to his death, but it wasn't necessarily with a woman, as condoms had been used in all five cases. Perhaps these men had consensual anal sex that had led to a heart attack. Julian dictated to the notes section on his phone to check with the other states' forensic pathologists to see if the other victims had any evidence of anal penetration. If the sex-leading-to-heart-attack theory held true, then it wasn't murder—unless the sexual partner knew of a potential underlying condition that would cause death via heart attack. And even if that were true, it would prove extremely difficult to substantiate in court. And, Julian further reasoned, the victim in Baltimore had been found to have no underlying heart disease or condition, so perhaps Julian could rule out this theory. Back to square one.

All five men had been found lying as if they had died peacefully, so if there were a killer, he somehow managed to convince them to lie down prior to killing them. Had they known they were going to die? If so, why was there no sign of a struggle? If the murderer had killed the victims elsewhere and then placed their bodies in the supine position on the bed, Alex would have most likely seen some evidence of that, and the body would have shown signs of having been moved. Furthermore, even if the killer had cleaned up after the murder, the victim's body would show signs of a struggle, such as fibers and skin under fingernails or bruising on the hands and arms from defensive wounds. No bruising or broken fingernails had been found, leading Julian to surmise that the men somehow acquiesced to their deaths. After all, he thought, in all the cases, gravity sent the victims' blood to pool at the bottom of the bodies, indicating (a) they had died in that position, and (b) the body hadn't been moved afterward.

He imagined himself lying on the hotel bed and allowed his mind to drift. It didn't take long before he pictured Alex with him in the bed. He smiled as she leaned over him, her long blond hair cascading on either side of his face. Sitting in the cab, he could almost smell her fragrance as she came in for a kiss...

His eyes flew open.

The killer must be a woman! She has sex with the men, positioning herself on top so that they're lying on their backs, and then somehow causes a heart attack post coitus. Julian mentally ran through the probability of his theory. Although history has given the world more male serial killers than females, the fact is that one out of six serial murderers in the United States are women, and some psychologists believe those numbers to be on the rise.

Of course! Julian reasoned. It has to be a woman.

"We're here, buddy," the cab driver stated matter-of-factly, interrupting Julian's thoughts. "That'll be thirty-seven fifty."

Julian reached into his wallet and pulled out a fifty-dollar bill from the section that held that denomination. "Keep the change. Hey, listen...can you please describe the entrance for me?"

"Can I what?" asked the irritated cabbie, turning around to look at Julian and realizing his gaffe. "Oh yeah...sure, buddy. Let's see. Uh, when you get out of the car, there'll be a curb to step up on. Uh, and then about, I dunno, fifteen feet until you reach another step up. And then it's a straight shot, about another ten feet or so, until you get to some glass doors that look like they open on their own. You know, the electric sliding doors? Anyway, then you'll be inside." He turned from the entrance to look at Julian. "Is that okay? Did I say it right? Are you going to be okay? Want me to walk you in?"

Julian smiled. "You did great, and I'm all set, but thanks for the offer."

Julian exited the cab and took note of the fact that the cabbie didn't leave until Julian had reached the glass doors, which did indeed open on their own. He smiled to himself. As much pain and anguish as his sudden blindness had brought into his life, it had delivered equally in kindness and generosity. He tried to remember that when he felt frustrated and cheated. Tapping his way forward, Julian noted the echo his stick caused each time it touched the tile floor. The space seemed large. As he moved, the echo altered slightly, as if he were approaching something solid in front of him. Stopping, he said, "Hello?"

No response. He moved forward carefully and heard heels clicking on the floor to his right. He stopped and faced the oncoming sound.

"Oh, I'm so sorry," a fiftyish-sounding voice boomed. "I just had to run to the bathroom. It always happens that way, doesn't it? You leave for one minute, and that's when someone comes in. Anyway…so sorry. Welcome to Brookhaven. My name's Mindy. How may I help you?"

Julian smiled and stepped forward, reaching a chest-high reception desk. "I'm here to see Sarah, please."

"Sarah. Does she have a last name? We have several Sarah's here."

Julian leaned forward and offered his most sheepish grin. "I have a confession to make. I don't know her last name. I'm here to see her for a friend of mine, but I never got her last name. Stupid, I know." Julian knocked on his head as if to accentuate his stupidity.

Mindy wasn't so easily fooled, however. She said, "Uh-huh. This *friend* of yours. She have a name?"

Julian weighed his options and decided in favor of the truth. "Her name is Linda Sterling, and my name is Dr. Julian Stryker."

Mindy cackled. "Oh, Linda! Why didn't you say so? She's classy. Been in here a couple of times. Did she ask you to come see Sarah? Fine old lady, that one. Smart as a whip. Never forgets a thing! I'll let the nurses know you're coming."

Mindy picked up the phone and alerted someone that Julian was on his way. She walked him down a long corridor that ended in a cul-de-sac from which rooms sprouted. Sarah's was the second on the right.

Julian thanked Mindy and waited until her footfalls had disappeared before knocking gently on Sarah's door. Receiving no response, he slowly opened the door a notch.

"Hello? Sarah?" He heard rustling of bedcovers and carefully approached. "Sarah?" he tried again.

Sarah sighed, yawned, and then groggily said, "Do I know you?"

Her breathing sounded labored, and Julian remembered Linda's statement that Sarah didn't have long to live.

He smiled, remaining where he was. It must be disconcerting to have a stranger in your room in the evening hours. He didn't want to scare her.

"You don't know me, and I don't know you, but I wanted to talk to you about someone you care for very much."

"Oh?"

"Yes. My name is Dr. Julian Stryker. I'm a psychologist, and I've been speaking with a woman named Linda Sterling."

Sarah clapped her hands together. "Oh, I'm so glad she reached out to you, Dr. Stryker! I wasn't sure she'd do as I asked, but clearly she did. I've been so worried, given the things she's been saying."

"You told her to speak with me?" Julian asked, confused.

"Yes. I told her she needed to speak with a mental health professional. She was saying some things that led me to believe she's in danger of hurting herself. In fact, I wonder if she already is."

"Is what?" Julian asked.

"Hurting herself! Did you see the mark on her arm? Oh, I'm so sorry," Sarah caught herself. "I got carried away. I'm so upset. I can't seem to think straight." She paused to catch her breath.

Julian empathized with this poor woman, who had clearly given so much in accepting children who had no other home. And to be repaid like this must be heartbreaking.

"May I please sit down?"

"Oh, yes, of course. Where are my manners? There's a chair to the right of my bed."

Julian felt his way around the foot of the bed and seated himself in the green Naugahyde chair. "Let's start at the beginning," said Julian, reaching out his hand.

Sarah took his hand as a tear ran down her cheek. For the next thirty minutes, she recounted the story of how Linda had come to live with her.

Although Sarah had fostered many children through the years, Linda had been different from the beginning. Sarah compared her to a feral cat unwilling to be tamed. Until one day, when her wild spirit broke, and she allowed herself admission into Sarah's loving fold.

"What caused the change?" asked Julian.

"I have no idea," replied Sarah. "I remember it like it was yesterday, though. It was a Tuesday afternoon in spring. She'd been living at my house for about four months, slipping out the window most nights to run around with whatever boy was her target at the time. She walked into the kitchen where I was preparing dinner and told me that she'd decided to stay and that she appreciated how hard I worked."

"And then what happened?"

"Nothing, really. It took her another full year before she could say she loved me, but when she did, oh, it was glorious!" Julian could hear joy in the old woman's voice as she relived the story.

"Her parents were killed in a fire?"

"Yes and no."

"What do you mean?"

"Well, her father died in the fire, most likely from smoke inhalation. But her mother was stabbed prior to the fire, and her sister died from a blow to the head and then was burned in the fire."

That was definitely *not* what Linda had led Julian to believe.

"Did the police ever find out who stabbed Linda's mother?"

Sarah hesitated before answering, "No. They never did."

"And her sister? Any conclusion on her death?"

Again, Sarah paused. "No."

"I see," said Julian. "Can you tell me about the mark on Linda's arm that you mentioned earlier?"

"It was a cut, relatively small but jagged, as if a sharp object had been drawn across her arm slowly."

"And you think Linda might have made the cut herself?"

"Well, it wasn't her father!" spurted Sarah.

Julian tilted his head and looked perplexed. "Can you elaborate on that, Sarah?"

"Linda said her father had done it to her, but I think she did it to herself. That's why I wanted her to see you. She said that her father lives inside her head and tells her to do things. She said she'd done some bad things and that she was trying to stop, but he wouldn't let her."

Warning bells were not just ringing in Julian's head. They were clanging like Big Ben on a Sunday morning in London.

"What kind of bad things, Sarah?"

"I don't know, really. She cheated on her husband, I know that. I think that's what she meant," she hastily added. "Hasn't she told you all this? You said she came to see you."

"She did see me, but she didn't tell me any of this. I know she likes things to be kept in order. That's very important to her."

Sarah looked directly at Julian and said, "Order is imperative."

Julian lifted his head. "That's exactly what she said to me. Order is imperative. And that her father used to maintain strict order but that she has to do it now that he's gone. What do you think that means?"

Sarah stared at her hands and wondered when they'd become so wrinkled and veinous. Holding them to the light, she gazed at them as if seeing them for the first time.

"Sarah, what do you think Linda means about keeping order now that her father is no longer here to do it for her?" Julian repeated.

Sarah glanced at Julian and wondered when he'd arrived. She then nodded her head, suddenly remembering who he was and why he was there. She was so tired, and her head hurt. Lifting a hand to her mouth, she was surprised to find that she wasn't breathing well. It felt as if something were lodged in her throat, blocking her airway.

"Sarah, did you hear what I said?" Julian prodded gently, lightly touching her hand. Sarah covered her face with her hands, and when she removed them, she saw Walter, her husband, at the foot of her bed, his right hand outstretched toward her. She smiled.

"What are you doing here?" she asked him.

Julian had felt Sarah's hand pull away from his and heard the change in her breathing. Thinking she was speaking to him, he said, "What am *I* doing here? Sarah, are you okay? Are you having trouble breathing?"

"It's time, Sarah," Walter communicated to her without speaking.

"Now? But, Walter, I have so much left to do," Sarah wheezed.

Julian was confused. "Who's Walter, Sarah?"

She didn't respond.

Julian called out toward the hallway. "Hello? Can someone come in here? I think Sarah's having trouble breathing."

"Come, Sarah. Look," Walter said, beckoning.

Sarah gazed past her husband to find her mother and father standing behind him. Mother was wearing her favorite apron, and father looked smart in his best suit. Their eyes were warm and welcoming, full of love. Knowing smiles graced their creaseless faces. At their feet stood Spots, her puppy who'd been hit by a car when she was seven years old. And...oh my goodness, there was Nana, her beloved grandmother, who had sat with her early mornings when they'd sipped tea like ladies and who had taught her how to knit and how to sneak cigarettes when she was a teenager.

Sarah was spellbound, one hand pressed to her heart while the other rested on her mouth, not quite believing the wondrous and powerful force that called her—and yet at the same time understanding that it was right and true. It was time. She heard a voice call softly and there, holding Nana's hand, was Martha, her very best friend who had passed way too soon in childbirth. And she was holding her baby, a boy. A boy! They were all there, standing next to the river she had enjoyed as a girl, its gentle waves lapping silently against their legs. Without saying a word, they were inviting her into their glorious world, where the sun shone brightly around them, warming the light breeze that blew across her face. She closed her eyes and allowed the soft glow to envelop her, enclose her in a shroud of euphoric warmth that seeped slowly inside her until she was one with it.

"Sarah, are you all right? Who's Walter? Sarah?" Julian was becoming concerned now, as her breathing was becoming more ragged. Julian was afraid that Sarah was suffering from dementia and perhaps experiencing some sort of seizure.

"Can someone get in here please!?" Julian yelled out toward the hallway. "Sarah, what do you think the phrase 'order is imperative' means to Linda?" pressed Julian.

"Sarah, you've done enough. It's time now," said her beloved Walter, leaning toward her. She inhaled his cherished scent and felt herself fading into his amazing, wonderful haze. As the impossibly magnificent bright white light approached, her body leaned back against the pillow as she was simultaneously lifted into the air. Nothing hurt anymore as she rose, free and light as a bird. She stopped breathing, for there was no longer a need for oxygen. Joining those she loved, she felt jubilation at being in their presence once more. Nothing mattered but that moment in the light, as part of the light.

"Oh my God," Julian whispered. "Someone get in here *now*! Sarah's stopped breathing!" Julian screamed.

As Sarah continued her ascent, she glanced down at Julian, who was leaning forward in his chair, gently shaking her body's arm. She was thoughtful for a moment, until she realized that it really was her time to go, just as it was Julian's time to move forward in his own life. She sent some white light toward Julian before gently ascending with her loved ones, her soul completely at peace.

Chapter 28

J esse sat in his desk chair, arms folded across his chest, staring at his boss through the open door that separated Julian's office from the waiting area. He glanced at the clock—11:50 a.m. Julian was seated in his own desk chair facing his window, head tilted back, either lost in thought or asleep. Since returning from the nursing home, Julian had been withdrawn and quiet, and Jesse was becoming worried. The morning patients had been canceled, and Julian simply sat in his chair, facing the window. He hadn't seen Julian this uncommunicative since the attack that had left him blind. Who do therapists talk to when they get down? Jesse wondered. Other therapists, he answered himself. Maybe he should call Hannah.

Hannah Hurwitz was a psychologist whom Julian had known since graduate school. She had been helpful to Julian on more than one occasion when he'd needed to consult on a patient or address a personal issue. He often asked her to cover for him when he went on vacation or away on a case. And…she had a huge, unreciprocated crush on Julian. Jesse smiled as a plan formed in his mind.

Approaching Julian's door, he knocked quietly.

"Hey, buddy. How ya doing? Anything you need?"

Julian turned toward Jesse's voice and said, "No. I'm good, Jess. Thanks, though," before returning his attention to the window.

"Uh-huh. Listen, Julian. I have two words for you. Hannah and Hurwitz."

Julian's head dropped. "That's three words, and do not threaten me with a session with her because you think I'm depressed. I'm simply working through what happened yesterday, that's all."

"Okay. Well, then, I was thinking that instead of speaking with Hannah, maybe you should keep your appointments today. I have several patients on the schedule for this afternoon, including Danny Sheehan. I know you wanted to tell him the good news about Rosey Tech."

At the mention of Danny's name, Julian turned fully toward Jesse.

"Do you think I killed her by asking her too many questions?"

Jesse smiled and sighed. "You and I both know that's not possible, Julian. Sarah was a very old lady who seemed to be under a lot of stress recently. None of that is your doing, though. She'd been extremely ill for some time, right? You can't kill someone by asking them questions, Julian. What's really going on?"

Instead of answering, Julian slowly shook his head. It took some time before he said, "I'm really not sure, Jess. Life's short, you know? You're here, and then you're not. Before she died, Sarah was having a conversation with someone named Walter. Turns out it was her husband who'd died almost twenty years ago. And yet, there he was, seemingly clear as day to her. It just makes you think…what are we doing here, and what happens after we die?"

Now Jesse felt truly concerned and vowed to call Hannah as soon as he returned to his desk. He sat down in the chair across from Julian's desk and leaned forward, placing his hand over Julian's.

"Julian, you and I have been friends for a long time now, so I'm going to tell you what you're doing here. You're an incredible psychologist who works mini miracles on some of the most damaged kids I've ever had the horror to come in contact with. You somehow manage to help them see that their present, horrendous circumstances are but a blip on the screen. You show them their self-worth so that they can see a future that previously felt nonexistent. That's what you do—every day, over and over, no matter the emotional toll it takes on you. In addition to that, as if it weren't enough, you help find bad guys who do bad stuff and put them away for a long time. That's what Dr. Julian Stryker does. That's who he is. That's why he's here. Now, as to the what-happens-when-we-die question, I have absolutely no idea and don't care at the moment, and here's why. I plan on being so tired from working my ass off here on earth that when my time comes, I'm going to say, 'Oh, thank God! I can finally get some rest.'"

Jesse withdrew his hand from Julian's and stood. "Now, Dr. Stryker, child psychologist extraordinaire, I believe you have a patient named Danny Sheehan coming in a little while, so get yourself together and focus. Your iPad with Danny's info on it is at twelve o'clock on your desk. Do you require anything else at this time?"

Julian had received the tongue lashing/pep talk silently, a small smile slowly forming on his chiseled face.

"You know, Jess, it occurs to me that perhaps you should return to school to become a therapist. Have you considered that?"

Jesse sighed theatrically. "Where would I ever find the time, Julian? Between your work drama and aiding your personal life, *you* tell *me*. Where would I ever find the time?"

"You're right, as usual," Julian said. Then, "Jesse James, once again you've proven yourself invaluable to me. Thank you for your friendship and your insight. And above all else, please do not call Hannah. This session you just had with me has put me back on the straight and narrow. Again, truly…thanks."

Julian heard him walk out heavily, mumbling as he went, most likely lamenting his choice of workplace, Julian mused.

Julian commanded his phone to call Alex, who picked up immediately.

"Hey, what's up?" she answered breathlessly.

"You sound out of breath."

"Yeah. I just came back from the ME's office, and I'm late for a meeting with Kevin about the severed-head case. What's up?" she repeated.

"Two things," Julian said. "I was calling to say I love you and also wondering about the ME's findings in Evan Donaldson's autopsy."

Alex laughed. "Wow. We are truly a romantic couple, aren't we? Okay, I love you too, and although the autopsy's not completed, Dolores has verified that Mr. Donaldson didn't engage in anal sex, had no obvious needle marks on his body, and had no history of any heart disease or condition."

"Did anyone check his home to see if he was as meticulous there as in the hotel room?"

"Funny you should ask, because the detective in Lancaster, Pennsylvania, left me a voicemail this morning, asking me to return his call. Apparently he's sending me photos of Mr. Donaldson's home and office."

"Okay. Any update on the tox screen and his phone calls prior to death?"

"Still waiting on both. Listen, Julian, I need to go. I'll talk to you later, okay?"

"Absolutely. Have fun with your severed head."

Alex paused before responding, "I always do."

As Julian ended the call, he heard Danny Sheehan enter the waiting room and greet Jesse. He waited until he heard the friendly banter decrease and then crossed to the doorway, smiled and said, "Come on in, Danny. Good to see you."

Danny laughed at that as he sauntered into Julian's office, repeating, "'Good to see you'...good one, doc."

That's what Julian loved about working with kids. Although there was often more drama associated with adolescent issues, they were far more honest than adults, not yet having learned the art of diplomacy and outright lying, even the ones who had gotten into trouble. Sure, they lied when they felt they had to. But once they felt safe with someone they could trust, the walls came down, and they were just...kids.

"How are you, Danny?"

"You know what, doc? I'm real good, actually."

Julian could hear the smile in Danny's voice, which drew a smile to his own face as well.

"Well that's great to hear, Danny. What's going on that's so good?"

"Lots of stuff, you know? I had a chance to hang out with the guys that got me in trouble in the first place. They asked me to do a ride-along. I'm not sure what they were gonna do, but I know they'd heard I was going to juvie, so they thought I was cool now. Anyways, they asked me to come along, and I just said no. I was terrified, but I said no!"

Julian was shocked. "You told gang members no? How did they react?"

"Oh, you know, they threatened me, my family. The usual. I was scared, but I held my ground and told them I had something better in my life now. I didn't tell them what it is. I like to keep it secret. Besides, they would've laughed."

Julian leaned forward, his interest piqued. "And what is that something you have in your life that's better?"

Julian could hear Danny exhale heavily while leaning back into the soft leather of the couch.

"I'm not completely sure, doc, but I think it's hope…with a capital *H*."

Now it was Julian's turn to lean back in his chair and smile. "And what, exactly, is hope with a capital *H*?"

"I don't know how to describe it. It's the kind of hope that someone gets who had none before that. It's not the hope that you feel when you want to do good on a test or be picked for a team. Naw…it's more than that. It's the hope of wanting to live again and be a part of something bigger than yourself. Does that make sense?"

Julian felt a rush of relief and warmth for this child who had endured so much. He still had a long road ahead of him, but hearing Danny's description of a future filled with hope, Julian was sure Danny was going to be one of the lucky ones who fought his way back into the functional world.

"It makes perfect sense to me, Danny. When my sight was stolen from me, I lost hope with a capital *H*. It wasn't until months later that I regained it. I understand what you're saying, because I've been there," he finished, smiling. "And more good news for you, Danny. You'll soon have a spot in the Rosey Tech program I told you about. Jesse has the paperwork for you to take home to your mom. I've already spoken with her, and she's excited."

"Wow! That's great, doc. Thanks. I'm glad to hear my mom was excited. That's the other good thing. My mom and I have been talking more lately… about Jimmy and life and my dad. I didn't realize how hard everything's been on her. And now with this situation at work…" His voice trailed off.

"What situation at work?" Julian asked.

"I'm not sure. She doesn't talk about it much, but I know she's really worried about some patient who died. Hey, she said you were there when it happened. That's weird, huh? Small world. Anyhow, she's worried about some doctor or something that knew this patient. I don't know exactly what's going on, but she's really stressed."

Julian's happiness at Danny's recent success vanished as he thought once more of Sarah and Linda Sterling's last conversation with her. Linda had lied to Julian about the ways in which her parents had died, and she had perhaps cut her own arm. In addition to those points, she felt she was communicating with her deceased father and insisted on…no, it was more than that—*demanded* order, whatever that meant. Each item by itself could be explained away, but together, they painted a picture of a precarious, obsessive personality bordering on schizophrenia. And yet her medical practice seemed unaffected. Or did it? he wondered. He resolved to contact Lizzie, Linda's assistant, as soon as he could.

Chapter 29

Brenda stared vacantly at the empty bed where Sarah had taken her last breath the day before. As Sarah had no family, funeral arrangements were left to Brenda, per Sarah's request. Not that there was much to do. Sarah, ever organized and thoughtful, had planned her funeral and accompanying services to the last detail, from flowers and readings to music to be played and sung. Brenda's job was to ensure everything was completed to Sarah's exacting standards.

Prior to coming to Brookhaven to arrange transport of the body, Brenda had taken time off work to contact and prepay all the people associated with Sarah's burial. Sarah had prewritten all the checks and signed them, leaving only the amount and the date blank. Finally devoid of activity to keep her mind busy, Brenda sat staring blankly at the empty bed, wondering how she was going to move forward at the age of forty-two...and once again an orphan. It troubled her that she couldn't cry. She'd thought that when she'd completed the arrangements and finally had some time to think about her loss, the tears would come, but they hadn't, and she didn't know why. Did she not love Sarah enough?

The closest person Brenda had to family was Linda, whom she'd counted as a sister until recent events had made her question Linda's honesty and... yeah, maybe even her integrity. However, Sarah had asked Brenda to watch out for Linda after she passed, so that's what Brenda would do.

"Excuse me. Are you Brenda?"

Tearing her eyes from the bed, Brenda focused on the woman in the doorway. She looked to be about Brenda's age, with big hair that rivaled the style Brenda had sported in the eighties. Her eyes were red, and her shoulders slumped, making her seem tiny.

"Yeah, that's me," Brenda responded sullenly, returning her gaze to the messy bed.

"I'm so sorry for your loss," the woman offered, slowly making her way into the room. "Sarah had been here for a while, and I had the opportunity to get to know her a little. She was a special lady."

Brenda considered the small, slumped woman standing on the other side of the bed. She looked her up and down.

"Are you person who stole Sarah's ring? The first one, I mean."

The woman's gaze dropped to the floor.

"No, it wasn't me, but I was in charge, so I'll take responsibility for it. I'll reimburse you if you like."

Brenda squinted at the visitor, trying to gauge her sincerity. She scrutinized the lady's uniform—frayed at the edges, with holes beginning to form at the knees—and determined that she had no more to offer financially than Brenda did.

"Nah, forget it," Brenda finally said, waving her hand in the woman's direction. "The ring was replaced, anyway."

"Yes…by Dr. Sterling, I know. Anyway, I didn't mean to bother you. I just wanted to stop by and say how sorry I am that Sarah's gone." She started to leave.

Something about the woman's demeanor, her kindness and honesty, made Brenda say, "Did you take care of Sarah a lot? I don't recall seeing you."

The woman offered a tired, weak smile.

"Oh, I've been here the whole time she was here, and yes, I took care of her a fair amount. But I have a lot of patients to take care of, so when you were here, I was most likely rushing among rooms."

"Oh. Must be tough, working here. All these people suffering all the time."

The woman smiled. "Actually, I like to think that my being here makes people feel better. That I'm helping, in some small way, to make their world better. It probably seems silly, but that's how I feel."

Brenda didn't think it was silly at all. She envied how confident this aide felt in her work.

"You know my name, but what's yours?"

"I'm Sharon Sheehan. It's good to meet you, Brenda."

"You too, Sharon. And thanks for taking care of Sarah. You're right. She was something else," Brenda finished as she looked at her feet. "And now she's gone."

"But she's in a better place."

Brenda looked up quickly. Sharon was smiling as she stared out the window at something far away. Brenda followed her gaze and saw children playing at the elementary school across the street. "Yeah, you know, people say that…but I'm not sure what it means."

Sharon looked at Brenda and said, "You know Brenda, I've seen many people pass here at Brookhaven, but I never truly understood what that phrase meant until my own son died of cancer."

Brenda drew a quick breath. "Oh, I'm so sorr—"

Sharon cut her off by holding up a hand in a "stop" gesture. "No, no. It's okay. I'm telling you this because when my son passed, I knew that his suffering had ended and that he was with God. It has to be better there than here, where he was in horrific pain. Do you understand?"

Brenda nodded slowly.

Sharon continued. "When you love someone, truly love them, you want to alleviate their suffering, right? Well, Sarah's suffering has ended. I know you loved her, and you'd want that for her. It doesn't mean you won't miss her and remember her as you knew her, but she's at peace. And what more could you hope for?" Sharon smiled warmly.

Brenda's face crinkled as tears formed and started rolling down her cheeks. They came quickly, and despite Brenda's earlier concern that she wasn't able to cry for Sarah, she was embarrassed that Sharon was seeing her fall apart. Because that's what it felt like. She was falling apart. She leaned forward on the bed and sobbed uncontrollably.

Sharon crossed to the bed, sat down, and placed a hand on Brenda's back, rubbing slowly in a circular motion, until Brenda's grief was spent. When Brenda looked up, Sharon was standing with a box of tissues and a knowing but kind smile on her face.

"It'll get better, Brenda. Trust me."

"Tell me about your son...unless you don't want to," Brenda added hastily.

Sharon's smile widened as she lifted her head and glanced at the ceiling. "Ah, where to begin. Let's see. His name was James Earl Sheehan, but we called him Jimmy. He was a character right from the beginning. He loved to cause trouble—not because he was a bad boy but because he was constantly trying to learn and figure things out. Once..." She laughed out loud as she remembered. "Once, he took apart our lawn mower because he wanted to figure out how it was built. He told me later that he was convinced he could build a better mower, so he took ours apart to analyze it."

"How'd that go?" Brenda asked, caught up in Sharon's obvious joy in retelling the story.

"Oh, not so good. My husband was furious because when he went to mow the lawn, the mower was in pieces." Sharon covered her face with her hands at the memory as she shook her head. "Joey—that's my husband—came into the kitchen and said, 'Do you know where the lawn mower is?' Well, you can imagine that my response was confusion. So I said, 'In the garage?' And he said—get this, Brenda—he said, 'Yeah, it's in the garage...and in the yard and in the bathroom and in Jimmy's room!'" Sharon broke into full gut laughter as she finished the story, doubling over in her amusement.

Brenda laughed too, picturing a lawn mower spread throughout the house.

"He sounds like he was pretty special, your Jimmy."

Sharon's laughter slowed until it petered out completely, and she looked thoughtful. "Yes, he was truly special. I guess that's why he left us so early. His candle burned so brightly when he was alive. Maybe he just used up too much fuel for him to keep going." Sharon turned to Brenda and took her hands. "Unlike your Sarah, who lived to a ripe old age and had the opportunity to make a difference in so many lives, yours included. How fortunate you were to have known and loved her!"

Brenda creased her eyebrows as she thought about what Sharon had said. "Yeah. You're right. I was lucky. And you know what? I still am, darn it. I got my health, I got a job, and I got a friend in Linda."

"Sterling?"

"Yeah, that's right. Dr. Linda Sterling, the sister I never had."

Sharon quietly said, "She was Jimmy's doctor, you know. She never made the connection between me and Jimmy, but it was good to see her again. No one worked harder to save my son."

"Yeah, she's a great doctor, but she seems to be going through something right now. Sarah was worried about her and told me to take care of her after she was gone. I just didn't think it would be so soon."

"Now that you mention it, I did see Dr. Sterling when she was last here visiting. She seemed real upset over the conversation she'd had with Sarah. Does she know about Sarah's passing?"

"No, not yet. I'll have to call her. I've been putting it off because I know how hard she's going to take it. But I need to call today."

Sharon patted the bed. "Okay. Well, I should probably get back to work. It was a pleasure, Brenda, and thanks for asking about Jimmy. When I talk about him, it's as if he's still alive to me."

"It was my pleasure, Sharon. You're pretty great at your job, you know that? Thanks for helping me out too. Maybe I'll see you around."

As Sharon left the room, Brenda pulled out her cell phone, scrolled through her contacts until she found Linda's cell number, and pressed it. It rang twice and then went straight to voicemail.

Chapter 30

The vibration of the cell phone roused her from the comfortable doze into which she'd fallen after having had sex. She glanced at the nightstand in time to see the phone's vibratic dance toward the reading glasses that lay there neatly folded, waiting to be used by their owner.

Rising, she perched herself on one elbow and peered down at the body next to her. She reached out and gently stroked the head's blond curls, slowly following their lazy waves until they ended at the owner's shoulders. Such beautiful hair, Linda mused. Such a waste on a man. Her hand continued its trek under the covers, down the chest of her partner, slowing as it reached the navel. The body's owner opened his sky-blue eyes and stared hard at her, willing her hand to do what he wanted. He was desperate. After all, it had been a long time—too long—since Linda had graced her husband with her body, and he was a hungry man. She'd been like a wild animal when they had made love earlier. He had the scratches on his back to prove it.

She smiled at him and kissed him roughly on the mouth. Slowly, her hand resumed its downward journey, pausing playfully near his groin, and then, without warning, she grabbed him—hard. Too hard. She leaned in close to his ear and whispered throatily.

"Who's in charge here, Jonathan?"

"Linda, you're hurting me. Let go."

"Say please."

"Please let go."

"I will, I will. But first, who's in charge here, Jonathan?"

"What are you doing? Let go!" He tried to get up, but her grasp held firm. Her tone turned hard. "Answer the question, Jonathan. Who's in charge?"

"What do you want to hear, Linda? That you're in charge? Fine! You're in charge! Now let the fuck go!"

She released her grip and rolled to her back, satisfied. Jonathan jumped from the bed and glared at her for a moment before entering their bathroom en suite. As usual, he said nothing about her behavior. She counted on that.

All of a sudden, the bedroom door blew open as a whirlwind of energy burst in.

"Mommy, Mommy, you're not gonna believe what Daddy said we could do today!"

Linda opened her arms wide, inviting her daughter in for a hug. "Well, I cannot imagine what Daddy said. You're going to have to tell me."

"He said that we could go to a pet store and pick out a puppy! Isn't that awesome! Can you believe it? I'm going to pick a boy puppy, and I'm going to name him PJ Flower. Do you know why I want to name him PJ Flower? Because PJ stands for Prince John, who was the villain in *Robin Hood*. Did you even know that? And Flower…well, just because I think flowers are the most wonderful things on the planet, don't you?"

Linda was horrified. How dare he make a decision like that without consulting me! she fumed. However, her face betrayed nothing. "You know what, beautiful girl? You run along and get dressed, brush your teeth, and wait for me downstairs. I need to talk to Daddy for a second, okay?"

"Okay, Mommy. But don't take too long because I looked it up on the computer, and the pet store opens in twenty minutes."

"Okay, smart girl. Run along." Linda patted Catherine's little behind as she scooted off the bed and ran out of the room, slamming the door behind her.

Jonathan reentered the room, a towel wrapped around his waist, his wet, golden curls glistening in the sunlight as he toweled them dry. "What do you want to do today?" he asked, oblivious to his daughter's recent visit and still miffed about Linda's prior power play.

"I'll tell you what I *don't* want to do today. Get a puppy." She looked at him shrewdly, arms crossed, as she evaluated his exquisite form. "Take off your towel," she commanded.

He stopped drying his hair and said, "Lin, I know you don't like animals, but—"

"That's completely not true, Jonathan. I love animals when they are behind bars and I can evaluate them from afar. I also love them when experiments are being conducted on them. It's something about the way they look at you in both circumstances. Like you're—"

"God?" he interjected, cutting her off. "Like you're God, Linda?"

"Don't be ridiculous, Jonathan. There is no God."

He closed his eyes and tilted his head back, clearly exasperated with her. He looks so cute when he does that, she thought. He opened his eyes and looked at her, worry creasing his forehead.

"Do you realize that you've described situations where you're in complete control?"

She looked at him as if he'd completely lost his mind. "Jonathan, they're animals. Stupid animals…and, yes, I am in control, because that's the way it's supposed to be. No, the way it *has* to be," she finished dismissively.

Jonathan sighed and sat down on the bed near her. "Listen, Lin, you're gone a lot, and it's just Catherine and me here. We could use some company, and with no siblings, it might be good for her to have a playmate. That's why I came up with the dog idea. Maybe I shouldn't have said she could get one without consulting you, but she was so excited about the idea that I just couldn't say no."

Linda gazed upon her husband's perfect form, leaned in, and whispered, "I don't think you heard me earlier. Take off your towel."

He whispered back, "Say please."

She pulled away from him, smiled alluringly, and then drew her arm back and slapped him hard across his left cheek. Stunned into silence, his head turned to the right from the force of the blow, he simply froze as she grabbed a fistful of his hair, leaned in once more, and calmly whispered to him.

"There is no way on this earth that I'm going to ever allow any animal to inhabit this house with me. They are dumb, filthy beasts who deserve the treatment they receive. They are messy, disgusting, and completely without order. Now, you're going to go downstairs and tell Catherine whatever lie you need to concoct to make her forget about this idiotic puppy idea. Is that clear?"

She released her hold on his hair and then used the same hand to stroke his cheek, which was quickly becoming flame red.

At the touch of her hand on his cheek, Jonathan jumped up and out of her reach. His eyes were wild, pupils dilated, and his chest was heaving. She couldn't help but notice that a vein in his forehead was throbbing, matching the same blood flow she could see in his carotid artery, also standing out in his neck. God, he's so beautiful, Linda thought, feeling herself becoming aroused. She dropped her head and cut her eyes at him seductively.

"Jonathan, let's stay in for a little longer. We can talk about this whole puppy thing later. Perhaps I overreacted. What do you say you drop that towel and give me a little sugar." She reached out her hand to him, wiggling her fingers, motioning him to come closer.

Jonathan subconsciously placed a hand on his stinging cheek as he said, "I'm worried about you, Linda. You've always been emotionally volatile, but recently I feel like you're really not yourself."

Linda pulled a face and sat up, pulling the sheet around her naked form. "I don't know what you mean," she said, meaning it.

Jonathan gawked at her. "Are you serious? You just hit me, for God's sake!"

"Jonathan, don't be so dramatic. That was a playful love slap, designed to get you going. I know it got me going. Come back to bed." She whisked off the sheet and splayed her legs wide.

"It's not going to work, Lin."

She flipped over and got on all fours, wiggling her derriere. "I know what my man likes." She started rocking back and forth and sighing. She glanced back at Jonathan, who despite his protests was becoming aroused. The towel fell to the floor.

"Better hurry up. Momma's getting impatient, and Catherine could come back any minute." She smiled at him lasciviously and licked her lips.

He continued to waver, not wanting to compromise his position in their argument but desperately wanting this woman, whose power over him was complete. He grabbed the towel and held in front of him in a final attempt at self-control. She laughed at him.

"Oh, honey, we both know you're going to give in. You can't resist me… never could."

She lay on her back and slipped two fingers inside herself. Arching her back and moaning deeply, she locked her eyes on Jonathan's.

He could stand it no longer. Throwing the towel aside, he lurched to the bed and devoured her. As he thrust himself into her again and again, she murmured in his ear.

"Do you love me?"

"You know I do."

"How much?"

"Enough to let you get your way all the time."

"Who's in charge?"

"You are, Linda."

"That's right, Jonathan." She stroked his back, urging him to climax. "Call me Pippin, Jonathan."

He pulled away from her and looked at her quizzically. "What? Why?"

"Just do it!" She raked her nails down his back, causing him to arch and cry out in pain.

"Okay! Okay! Pippin."

"No! No! Not like that! Talk to me, but call me Pippin. Tell me how much you love me."

Too far gone to understand this bizarre request, Jonathan immediately acquiesced.

"I love you to the far ends of the earth, Pippin."

Breathless grunts and thrusts.

"And are we getting a filthy beast of a dog?"

"No, Pippin."

Moaning, grunts, and thrusts.

"And who's in complete control, Jonathan?"

He climaxed and collapsed on top of her, exhausted and sweating.

"You are, Pippin."

She rolled Jonathan off her and grabbed his face between her two hands, squeezing hard.

"Damn right I am."

CHAPTER 31

Alex wasn't quite sure which hurt more—her eyes from reading and rereading interviews with guests staying at the same hotel as Mr. Donaldson or her head from the band of tension that was aggressively tightening like a noose around her crown. She leaned back in her chair, closed her eyes, and ran her fingers through her hair, massaging her scalp in the process.

Not one hotel guest remembered seeing Mr. Donaldson the day he died. In fact, save the bartender remembering that he was a good tipper, no one could even remember seeing Mr. Donaldson in the hotel at all, even when they were shown a picture of him. An average man leading an average life, Alex thought. Maybe he did die of a heart attack. Her desk phone rang. She sighed and picked it up.

"Alex Hayes."

"Detective Hayes, this is Detective Davey Rodriguez of the Lancaster County Police. I'm calling about the Evan Donaldson case. I left you a message but had a free minute so I thought I'd call again. Is this a good time?"

Alex laughed mirthlessly. "Detective, if your job's like mine, there's never a *good* time to talk. Please call me Alex. How can I help you?"

"It's actually how *I* can help *you*, Alex. I understand that you caught the Evan Donaldson case?"

"Yes, that's right."

"And your working theory right now is that Mr. Donaldson died of an apparent heart attack. Is that right?"

"Yes, that's right."

"I wanted to let you know that I was tasked with canvassing Mr. Donaldson's house and office space here in Lancaster."

"And what did you find there?" Alex asked anxiously, picking at a thumbnail.

"Nothing of note, actually. That's why I'm calling. Both places were kind of a mess. He was a bachelor and seemed to live his life as one. I can say that because I'm one too," he chuckled.

Alex found no humor in his words. "Go on," she urged.

Davey cleared his throat and got right to the point. "Half-eaten TV dinners in the trash, clothes and used towels in a pile on the bathroom floor. Bed unmade, mail strewn across the kitchen table. I could go on if you like."

"No, that's all right. I get the idea. What about his work?"

"Same situation there, except maybe not quite as messy. I spoke with some of his colleagues, and they said he was a really good guy, polite but shy. The women referred to him as 'sweet,' which is the kiss of death, if you ask me," he said with a laugh.

Alex ignored the comment as her mind fit these facts into the puzzle Evan Donaldson's death had become.

"Any heart medications found at his house?"

"What? Heart meds? No, just some vitamins and cold medicine."

"Any romantic interest people at his work might have mentioned?"

"I asked that, and the answer was always an unequivocal no. Apparently he was painfully shy and awkward around women. Same situation with his neighbors. Everyone remembers him as a kind, thoughtful man, an average guy."

"Okay, thanks, Detective. Can I call you if I have more questions?"

"Of course, anytime. Good luck."

"Thanks." Alex hung up the phone as her cell phone vibrated. She slid the icon on the screen to answer. "Alex Hayes."

"Hey, Alex, it's Dolores. I completed Mr. Donaldson's autopsy."

"Lay it on me."

"Well, as you know, there was no anal penetration, but Mr. Donaldson did indeed have sexual intercourse the night he died. We found traces of powder and lubricant indicative of his use of a condom that evening. In addition, we found traces of semen around the head of his penis. However, there's something you should know."

Alex's pulse quickened. "What?"

"He was sterile."

Alex grimaced in spite of herself. "Okay. But why is that important to the case?"

"It's not important in and of itself. What is important is *why* he was sterile."

Alex was becoming impatient. Sometimes Dolores liked to be dramatic, and now was certainly not the time. But she reminded herself that Dolores was a good person and an excellent medical examiner, so she waited her out.

"He had hypothyroidism, Alex. That explains a lot."

Although Alex was glad that Mr. Donaldson's medical condition cleared things up for Dolores, she on the other hand had absolutely no idea what hypothyroidism was.

"Care to elaborate for those of us who are, shall we say, medically challenged?"

Dolores chuckled. "Sure. Hypothyroidism occurs when the thyroid, which is a small gland in the front of your neck, doesn't produce enough hormones, causing the normal balance of chemical reactions in the body to become imbalanced. Now, early on, hypothyroidism can be tough to diagnose because its symptoms mirror those of so many other less serious conditions. However, if left untreated, over time hypothyroidism can cause health problems such as obesity, joint pain, infertility and...wait for it—heart disease."

Alex dropped her head into her hand. "Should he have been taking medication for this hypothy...thing? 'Cause no one found any meds anywhere."

"Yes, if he'd been diagnosed, he would most definitely be on medication to normalize his thyroid. But I think he'd not yet been diagnosed. He must have been dealing with the symptoms for some time, however, as I believe his sterility was due to the hypothyroidism, as was his heart disease."

Alex groaned. "You're telling me that Mr. Donaldson actually did have a heart condition?"

"Wait a minute, wait a minute," Dolores said. "Let me finish. Although Mr. Donaldson's heart did have some evidence of early-stage disease and technically could have caused a myocardial infarction, or heart attack, I don't believe that's what killed him."

"Wait, so he *didn't* die of a heart attack or he did? I don't understand," Alex huffed.

"Oh, he died of a heart attack, all right. A big one. But what I'm trying to say is that I don't believe his early-stage heart disease is what led to his myocardial infarction. Something else caused it."

"Like what?" Alex asked.

"I'm not sure," Dolores answered, sighing heavily. "His tox screen was clean except for some alcohol, which we've already accounted for. I found no needle marks indicating previous drug use."

"Yeah. That wouldn't have fit his character anyway, from everyone I've spoken to," Alex offered.

"So, I'm not sure what to tell you. There was one thing that was odd, though." Dolores trailed off as if lost in thought.

Alex waited, tapping her pen on her pad of paper, where she had been taking copious notes. She could stand it no more.

"What, Dolores? What was odd?"

"Well, the tissue in Mr. Donaldson's upper trachea was slightly lacerated."

Alex rolled her eyes. "English, please."

"It means, Alex, that his throat had some scratches in it."

Alex crinkled her nose as she pictured what Dolores was saying. "How could that happen?"

"I'm not sure exactly, except that something went down his throat that scratched it as it traveled."

"Could food do that?"

"Usually not, and I didn't find anything in his stomach that would indicate such trauma."

"So, whatever it was had been removed?" Alex asked.

"I would think so."

"Could he have been choked with something? Could that have caused a heart attack?"

"The stress of having something in your throat, knowing you can't breathe, combined with the actual slow asphyxiation and underlying minor heart disease might be enough to cause a heart attack," Dolores mused. "But you didn't find anything in his room that might have been stuffed down his throat and then removed, did you?"

"No, but we weren't really looking for that, either. I can't imagine he'd stuff something down his own throat and then remove it, can you?"

"Not really, unless it was a sex game gone wrong. You know, like one of those gags with a ball on it? Maybe the ball went down his throat? Or it was forced down?"

Alex shuddered involuntarily. If this were a natural death, it would be an awful way to die. If Mr. Donaldson had been murdered, it was horrific.

"Dolores, do me a favor. Can you please get in touch with the MEs in other cities where there were heart attack victims with similar circumstances? I want to know whether the other victims had thyroid issues…or any medical issues, for that matter. And I specifically want to know if they had…what did you call the things in the windpipe?"

"Tracheal lacerations."

"Yeah, that. I'll e-mail you the list of victims' names and cities. Please find out, and get back to me ASAP, okay?"

"Sure thing, Alex."

As Alex was replacing her phone in its hip holster, Kevin McMillan approached her desk.

"Afternoon, Detective. How goes things?"

Alex shook her head. "It's looking like Evan Donaldson's death might have been an actual, bona fide, natural heart attack, Chief. Turns out he had a heart condition. But it just doesn't feel right, you know? Especially with four other victims in other states matching the same profile and crime-scene description."

"Well, you're going to have time to dig some more, because I'm taking you off the severed-head case. Two decapitated bodies were found in Nashua, New Hampshire, this morning that match our guy's MO, so it's been kicked up to the FBI. They might contact you for information, but it's pretty much out of our hands."

Alex blew out air. "Can't say I'm too sad about that. I've got a strong gut feeling about this heart attack case. I think we're dealing with something much bigger than it seems right now."

Chapter 32

Dr. Linda Sterling exuded power, capability, and authority as her heels clicked toward her corner office with its mahogany desk. She waltzed by Lizzie, who begged her—to no avail—to slow down so she could deliver her messages. Holding up a hand to fend off the now-trailing Lizzie, Linda marched into her office, threw her cashmere wrap to her assistant, and proceeded to a large window that overlooked the oncology courtyard. She drew a deep breath as she watched patients lounging on benches, faces turned toward the sun. From her eleventh floor office, they looked tiny, insignificant.

"Unlike you, Pippin. You are truly rising to the challenge, aren't you?" her father whispered in her ear.

Linda smiled as heat crept up her cheeks. *What a pleasure to hear praise from you, Daddy*, she thought. She turned around to see Lizzie staring at her wide-eyed.

"What's gotten into you, Lizzie? Don't stand there gawking like an idiot. Hang up my wrap, get me some coffee, and give me my messages, in that order...please." Linda smiled her sweetest smile, causing Lizzie to falter in her response.

"Uh...okay, Dr. Sterling."

As Lizzie hustled away, Linda sank into her overstuffed leather desk chair, closed her eyes, and relived the moment she'd broken Jonathan's spirit the day before. The sex had been good. It was always good with him, but the psychological win had been magical. *God, he's so easy*, she thought. Like most men, I can lead him around by his dick. She laughed out loud, thinking how pathetic he was.

"What's so funny?" Lizzie had reentered Linda's office.

Linda jerked her head up and snapped, "Nothing, Lizzie. None of your business."

Contrite, Lizzie gingerly approached Linda's desk and placed her coffee on the blotter.

"Just the way you like it," she almost whispered. "A little cream, one sugar."

"Lizzie, Lizzie, why so glum? You look sad."

Lizzie flinched and looked at her boss quizzically. "I'm not sad, Dr. Sterling."

"Then whatever's the matter? You look terrified...or confused. Or both." Linda stared hard at her, a look of seemingly genuine concern on her perfectly made-up face.

Lizzie wasn't sure how to respond. Since she'd started working there three years ago, Lizzie had witnessed many sides of Linda—the brilliant, egotistical surgeon with her colleagues; the warm, caring physician with the patients; the loving, doting mother with Catherine; the tolerant, organized wife with Jonathan. But recently, these personae had begun to fray at the edges. Linda had become more egotistical and less caring, less doting, and less organized. She'd seen Linda's moods shift quickly in the past, like when a patient passed away, for example. But of late, Linda's moods seemed to shift as thoughts drifted through her brain. Like today, for instance. She'd arrived at the office angry and self-involved, and then, with a snap of her fingers, she was exhibiting true concern for Lizzie's well-being.

"Lizzie? Are you okay?"

Lizzie stared at her boss and stammered, "Yes...yes, Dr. Sterling. I'm fine. Thank you for asking. Um...here are your messages." She placed the pink sheets on Linda's desk next to her coffee and withdrew her hand, stepping quickly away. "Do you need anything else right now?"

Linda creased her brow and said, "No, that's all for now. Are you sure you're okay? You know you can talk to me if something is bothering you. Is there something at work that's making you uncomfortable? Or some*one*, perhaps?" Linda finished, raising her eyebrows.

Lizzie looked down at the ground. "No, Dr. Sterling. I would certainly tell you if there were. So, if that's all..." Her voice trailed off as she backed toward the door, shutting it quickly behind her.

Linda shook her head as she sipped her coffee and brought her computer to life. She reviewed some patient charts and was thrilled to note that most patients were either improving or remained unchanged—a small win with cancer. She stopped midsip, however, when she noticed that the lab results from one of her younger patients, Sabrina Cartwright, indicated that her white-blood-cell count was dangerously low. Sabrina had been undergoing chemotherapy and radiation, which could lower her count, but the recent drop was too dramatic for her current treatments to be the sole cause. Linda leaned back in her chair and returned her coffee cup to the desk. Restless, she stood up and walked around the office, arms crossed over her chest, thinking. Infection or the return of an aggressive cancer—those were the two choices, as she saw it. Both meant more treatment and inpatient hospital time for the beautiful little girl who reminded Linda so much of her own daughter.

Returning to her desk, she dialed the nurses' station on the ninth floor where she knew Sabrina's room was. It took four rings before someone picked up.

"Nurses' station, Pediatric Oncology, Katie speaking."

"Katie, this is Dr. Sterling. How's Sabrina Cartwright this morning?"

"Um, I haven't been in there today. Thelma's with her now, I think. Want me to have her call you?"

"No. Patch me through to her room."

"Are you sure? Because her moth—"

"I said patch me through!" Linda ordered.

"Okay. Hold on."

Linda waited while the call went through to Sabrina's room.

"Hello?"

"Thelma, this is Dr. Sterling. I was calling—"

"Oh, hello, Dr. Sterling, this is Jackie Cartwright, Sabrina's mom. How are you?"

Linda was caught off guard. "Oh…hello, Mrs. Cartwright. I'm well. And you?"

"We're fine. Why are you calling?"

"I was actually trying to reach Thelma. May I please speak with her?"

"Why? Is something wrong? Is my daughter okay? What's going on?"

Linda suddenly realized that the nurse who had initially answered the phone, Katie, had been trying to communicate to her that the child's mother was in the room. In her haste to receive an update on the patient's condition, Linda had ignored Katie's warning. Stupid! Linda thought. She couldn't lie to the mother, but she didn't want to panic her either, especially given the fact that she didn't yet know what they were dealing with.

"Sabrina's white cell count is low, Mrs. Cartwright. I just wanted to chat with Thelma and perhaps order an MRI and some more blood work, that's all."

"That's all? Are you kidding me? We've been around the block, Dr. Sterling. I know what ordering an MRI and more blood work means! That's doctor speak for you think my little girl's going to die!" She was crying.

Linda sat down heavily in her chair and closed her eyes. "Mrs. Cartwright, please calm down. That's not what I think. Let's gather more information before we jump to any conclusions. Also, isn't your daughter hearing you right now? Please calm down and give the phone to Thelma."

Linda heard rustling as the phone was passed to Thelma.

"Hi, Dr. Sterling. Thelma here."

"Well, that was awful," Linda said. No response from Thelma.

"Anyway, Sabrina's white blood-cell count is eight hundred and fifty. We need a CBC stat and an MRI to gauge any cancer growth."

Thelma had been a pediatric oncology nurse long enough to know how to react in these circumstances, especially in front of a patient and her mom.

"Of course, Dr. Sterling, I'll order them right now. Anything else?"

"No, that's it. I'll review the results from my office. Thanks, Thelma. And sorry for leaving the mess I know you're going to have to clean up." She was referring to the crying mother in the background.

"It's all good, Dr. Sterling. You have a great day!" She hung up, sounding upbeat and confident. Linda knew that Thelma's positive attitude was for Jackie Cartwright better than anything else. God bless nurses, Linda thought as she hung up the phone.

Turning her chair toward the window, Linda picked up her coffee and crossed her long legs. Her mind wandered from Sabrina to Catherine, and Linda wondered how she herself would react if anything were to happen to her little girl. Tears came to her eyes and her heart skipped a beat as she pondered the miracle that is a mother's love. Nothing could ever stand in its way. She would die to protect her and would kill for her daughter, if necessary.

"Sabrina Cartwright cannot die!" whispered her father.

"I know, Daddy. I know," Linda said aloud. "She won't."

"She'd better not. Your life depends on it, Pippin."

"I know! You don't need to remind me all the time. I'm doing my best!"

"Are you…really?" he said, mocking her.

Linda's cell phone buzzed, shocking her back to the present.

"Hello?"

"Lin, it's me, Brenda. Why haven't you called me back?"

"What do you mean?"

"I left you a message, Lin. Didn't you get it?"

Linda thought back to the vibrating cell phone waking her up while she was with Jonathan. An involuntary smile graced her beautiful lips.

"No, I didn't get the message. What's up?"

Brenda started crying. "I didn't know how to tell you in the message, and I still don't, so I'm just going to just say it. Sarah's dead, Lin. She's dead."

Linda's smile dropped as she blanched and stared into nothingness. The room narrowed as her vision tunneled into just a pinpoint of light. Her body started shaking, slowly at first and then picking up speed until she could no longer see straight. Somehow she managed to hold on to the phone, which had retreated from her ear and now sat limply in her hand on the desk. A tinny voice reached across the miles to revive her.

"Lin, are you there? Are you okay?"

Heavy as lead, the hand holding the phone, which seemed to belong to another person, returned to her ear. "I'm okay," Linda said numbly, her own voice sounding far away.

"I've made all the arrangements. The funeral's tomorrow. You're going to be here, right?"

"Yes, of course," Linda responded robotically. "I'll catch the next flight out. I need to go."

Linda clicked off the call and sat staring at the phone. "I killed her. It was me," she said to no one.

CHAPTER 33

Vinny, Julian, and Alex sat in an Indian restaurant not far from Julian's office. "You've got to try the curried chicken, Vin. It's awesome," Alex said, pointing to the picture on the menu.

"Spicy food doesn't sit too well with me, Alex," Vinny responded, waving his hands for emphasis.

"Then ask for it mild, you wimp," Alex chided him. "What about you, Julian? What're you getting?"

"My usual."

"Chicken Biryani it is," Alex laughed.

"What the hell is that?" asked Vinny, clearly not used to Indian cuisine.

"It's good is what it is," Julian said.

"The fact is that Mr. Doesn't-Cook-a-Lot doesn't know what it's in it because he's never made it. But he loves it when *I* make it for him," Alex finished, poking Julian in the ribs. "It's a chicken and rice dish with veggies and lots of yummy spices. A lot of work but worth it," finished Alex.

Vinny shook his head. "Yeah, you know what? Just order something for me that isn't too spicy, okay, Alex? I trust your judgment. You, on the other hand," Vinny said, pointing at Julian, "not so much."

Julian tried hard to look innocent as he recalled the last time he had ordered food for Vinny. They'd been in a Pakistani restaurant, and the first several bites had left Vinny gasping and searching for milk to assuage the burn caused by ghost peppers.

"Good times, good times," Julian mused, rubbing his chin.

"Yeah, whatever. All I know is, payback's a bitch, and her stripper name's Karma, blind man," Vinny challenged good-naturedly.

Julian laughed and suggested, "Shall we discuss the case?"

"Good idea, Julian. I only have so much vacation time left," said Vinny sarcastically.

"Hey, I almost forgot. How was your interview with Brian Bosch?" Alex asked.

Vinny rolled his eyes. "I gave him as little insight into being an FBI agent as possible but enough to whet his appetite for more inside scoop."

"Whatever that means," laughed Alex. "What did you get from him in return?"

"A lot, actually. He shared with me that he has snitches in almost every major city's police force and that as soon as he got wind of this Boston death, he started making calls. According to Bosch, the MO of the Boston death matches the other cities' victims."

"That's all well and good, but you're not going to take his word for it, are you?" Alex asked disgustedly.

"Of course not, Alex. I already made some calls to guys I know on the force in those same cities, and everything Bosch told me has been verified."

Alex looked skeptical. "Like what?"

Vinny pulled out a memo pad and flipped several pages. "All middle-aged men, slightly overweight and balding. No needle marks on any of the bodies. No history of heart problems or medications. All of them had sex the night they died. All of them wore a condom. All of them had folded reading glasses on the nightstand next to the bed where they were found. Covers pulled up to their chins. All rooms were immaculate, even though many of them didn't keep their personal spaces clean. All but one had clean tox screens."

"You spoke with detectives in Baltimore, Philadelphia, Hartford, and New York, and they all said the same thing?" Alex was shocked.

"Yup. Almost exactly the same story every time."

"Damn," breathed Alex.

The waiter approached and took their order, speaking a little more loudly than necessary to Julian, who sighed and smiled as he ordered his dish. When the waiter retreated, Julian turned to Vinny.

"What about security footage from the hotels?" asked Julian.

"Well, one hotel's camera was broken. The Boston footage is, as you know, not the best, and the other three hotels are e-mailing me the digital files."

"How'd you manage that without officially representing the FBI?" Alex asked, impressed.

"Let's just say they don't know I'm not on official FBI business," Vinny smirked.

"Wow, Vin. You're riding a thin line."

"You know what? I've worked hard and earned what I got. I'm not going to let some stupid bureaucrat decide the trajectory of my career."

Alex considered Vinny for a moment and asked, "Vinny, are you sure you're not pissed off because your boss is a woman?"

Julian drew a quick breath as Vinny physically drew back and narrowed his eyes at Alex. "Are you fucking kidding me, Alex? How can you even ask me that after everything we've been through? My boss is an ass-kissing, blood-sucking paper pusher who just happens to be a woman!"

Alex was already shaking her head and waving her hand in response. "Mea culpa. I'm sorry, you're right. That's not who you are. Forgive me?"

Vinny's eyebrows slowly retreated from their angry posture back to their normal position. He pursed his lips and said, "I'll give you that one, Alex, because I know you're under a lot of pressure with this case. But don't push it."

They were quiet for a moment. Julian broke the silence by saying, "So, you'll let us know about the security footage when you review it?"

"Yeah, you bet," Vinny answered, his voice back to normal again.

"What about witness interviews from the other cities?" Alex asked.

Vinny shrugged. "A fair number of people saw the victims in each case, but none of them recall seeing anyone enter or exit the men's rooms. All of the victims were salesmen in town for a conference of some kind, so clearly they were targeted specifically. Some had wives and children at home and some didn't, so that aspect doesn't seem to matter to the killer."

Alex reflected on her earlier conversation with Dolores. "I spoke with Dolores earlier, and she said that—"

"Who's Dolores?" asked Vinny.

"Oh, sorry. She's our medical examiner. Anyway, she said that Mr. Donaldson had something stuffed down his throat and then removed, leaving scratches in his throat."

"Sex game gone wrong?" asked Vinny.

"That's what Dolores suggested," said Alex. "Could be, but she wasn't sure. She's going to talk to the other cities' MEs to see if any of those victims had scratches too."

"What about the victims' phones? Any headway there?" asked Julian.

"Nothing interesting on Mr. Donaldson's phone. Just calls to his parents, his house sitter, and his local dry cleaner," answered Alex.

Vinny added, "Same situation for the other dead men. Some calls to home, work. One guy even had a voicemail from his kid on his phone, probably left while he was dying. It said something like, 'I love you, Daddy. Come home soon.' It was enough to break your heart, even for a guy like me."

Alex placed her hand on Vinny's arm. "You're a really good man, Vinny. You have a big heart. Julian and I know that more than most. You okay with this case? Is it getting to you?"

Vinny sat back and threw up his hands. "I know there's something really big here, and my idiot boss won't support me. The ironic thing is that if we nail this thing, her career could skyrocket. If she weren't so concerned about protecting her own ass, she'd see that the leads we have are real and that this heart attack killer isn't going to stop until we catch him. I just know it." He slumped in his chair.

Their food arrived, and they all took a break and ate. Halfway through his meal, Vinny spoke up. "Alex, you did a great job choosing my meal. What is it?"

Alex paused. "You like it?"

"I just said I did. What is it?" Vinny asked, stuffing another forkful into his mouth.

"It's called Doh Khileh. Just a pork-and-onion salad with a special garnish, that's all."

"Well, it's really good," Vinny mumbled, chewing.

Julian kicked Alex under the table because he knew what the "special garnish" was. Vinny thought Julian had been mean when he'd ordered him that spicy Pakistani meal? That was nothing compared to what he was eating right now.

"So, what kind of sick mind are we dealing with, Julian?" Vinny asked, wiping his mouth with his napkin.

"It's an interesting question, Vinny. Although most serial killers are men, I think we might actually be dealing with a woman."

Alex put her fork down. "Really?"

"Yes. I've been thinking about it and realized that the one thing that would make a man lie down for his own death would be sex. She lures him to his room, gets him to lie down on his back, has sex with him, and then somehow causes a heart attack."

"That's cold," Vinny shuddered.

"Yes it is. It takes a special kind of personality for this type of premeditated planning. Organized, smart, targeting the same type of man. Punishing him over and over yet manipulating him first by having sex. The intercourse itself is a conquest, proving that she's in control. Her victims aren't mousy, per se. But they're all middle-aged, paunchy, balding. Not the kind of guy you'd expect to act as an alpha. And I think she knows that when she targets them. Whomever we're dealing with most likely has some pretty severe father issues."

"Hey, I've had daddy issues, and you don't see me running around having sex with strangers and then killing them," Alex said.

"And I'm very grateful for that," Julian smiled, patting her hand. He continued. "In all seriousness, this person is very, very broken. I would imagine that she was most likely abused as a child. The fact that she has sex with her victims before killing them might lead one to believe that she herself was molested as a child."

"Assuming all of that is true, what's with the heart attack? Why kill that way?"

Julian shrugged. "Maybe her real dad died that way, and she's reliving the trauma."

Alex was confused. "Wait a minute. You said that you think she was sexually abused. Wouldn't her father's death be a relief because she would know she's no longer going to be abused?"

"Yes and no. Regardless of the fact that she was being abused, her father was still her father, and she loved him. Nothing's ever cut and dried when it comes to family and relationships."

"So, how's she causing the heart attack?" Vinny asked, wiping up the remaining juices on his plate with some bread and then popping it into his mouth.

"I wish I knew. It's got to be some kind of drug."

"The tox reports have been clean for drugs, Julian," said Alex.

"I know, but a drug-induced heart attack has to be how she's causing the deaths. Some drugs go in and out of the bloodstream relatively quickly, leaving little or no trace. I'm going to follow up with Dolores about that."

"God, that was so good!" Vinny gushed, patting his stomach. "I might even try making that at home," he said.

Alex laughed.

"Tell him," Julian said. "You have to tell him, Alex."

"Oh God…tell me what?" Vinny asked, looking from Julian to Alex and back again. "What did you guys do to me?"

Julian held up his hands in a defensive gesture. "Hey, I did nothing, Vin. It's all Alex this time."

Alex stifled a laugh. "You can try making Doh Khileh at your place, Vin, but I'm sure you're going to have a devil of a time finding the steamed pig's brain for the garnish."

Chapter 34

Lizzie worked nervously but quickly to find her boss a flight to Boston. She found it, somewhat disconcerted that Linda was standing directly behind her while she searched for flights online.

"I can find you a good flight and then have you approve it before it's booked, Dr. Sterling. You shouldn't feel like you've got to stand here while I search. It's kind of a waste of your time, isn't it?"

Linda leaned down so that her lips were brushing Lizzie's ear.

"Lizzie?"

Her typing ceased as every sinew in Lizzie's body stretched as tightly as a violin string.

"Yes, Dr. Sterling?"

"Do you not believe that I am capable of determining what is and what is not a waste of my time?"

"Yes, Dr. Sterling. I mean, no, Dr. Sterling. I mean—"

"Why are you not typing, Lizzie?"

"Sorry." Tears stung her eyes as she continued her search.

"You, my dear, are surrounded by complete morons." Linda's father said matter-of-factly.

Linda answered him in her head, keenly aware of Lizzie's presence.

Not now, Daddy. I can't deal with you and Sarah's death at the same time.

"Ah, but that's why I'm here, Pippin. You know that you killed her." He laughed. *"Not literally, of course, but rather with your reckless, disrespectful behavior. She simply*

couldn't take any more of your irresponsible actions, always thinking of yourself…so she called it quits."

That's not true! screamed Linda in her head.

"Oh, believe me, it's true," her father continued relentlessly. *"You're not capable of loving someone without hurting them. Consider me, your mother, your sister. How about Jonathan? Look at your little patient Sabrina, for goodness' sake."*

Linda left Lizzie and ran into her office, where she could continue the conversation in private, where she could speak out loud in order to make her father understand.

"What about Sabrina, Daddy? I'm helping her, not hurting her. That's why I became a doctor. To help people!"

Her father chuckled. *"Are you sure that's why you became a doctor—to help people, Pippin? Because it seems to me that a lot of your patients don't make it."*

Linda was becoming angry. It was one thing for her father to question her behavior with regard to the past or to guide her in dating exploits, but it was quite another to have him questioning her medical ethics.

"How dare you say that to me!" she whispered fiercely. "The field I chose comes with a lot of death. Those statistics have nothing to do with my abilities as a physician!"

"And why exactly did you choose oncology as your medical specialty, do you suppose?" he asked mockingly. *"Because you enjoy death! That's why!"* His laughter roared inside her head, exited her ears, and swirled around the room like a demented vulture.

"That's not true, not true," she groaned, grabbing her hair with both hands.

"It is true, Pippin. It is. But that's okay, because you've found what you're good at. Death. That's why you killed Sarah."

Linda was suddenly tired. She hadn't killed Sarah. Had she? She couldn't remember anymore. She sighed and shook her head.

She so badly wanted her father out of her head. The man who had been her anchor for so many years was now saying things that didn't make sense. She was a good doctor. She knew it. Why was he saying otherwise?

A sudden noise at the door startled Linda, and she looked up to find Lizzie gawking at her, a horrified look on her face.

"Dr. Sterling, are you all right?" Lizzie asked haltingly, one foot across the threshold in case she had to run away from the freak show she was witnessing.

"Careful," whispered her father.

Linda drew herself up to her full five-feet-ten inches and said haughtily, "Of course. Why?"

Linda's eyes followed Lizzie's as they perused her body, alighting on her right hand, which was holding a fistful of hair.

"Get out! Get out! Get OUT!" Linda screamed, lunging toward Lizzie and shoving her out the door.

"Now look what you've done!" she spat venomously at her father. "She thinks I'm crazy!"

Her brow wrinkling in confusion, Linda examined the hair in her hand and then slowly reached up to her own head. She carefully palpated her scalp until she found the spot where the hair had been ripped out. Wincing, she rested her hand on the ravaged area. The warmth felt good on the painful, exposed flesh.

"You're out of order, Pippin. Everything in your life is out of order. That's why this is happening."

"I know, Daddy," Linda said quietly, her eyes focused on the floor. "I'm trying to get my life in order, but I just don't know how anymore. Things feel like they're falling apart." Linda collapsed on the couch and hugged one of the designer pillows, sobbing.

Her father was silent as Linda exhausted her tears. When they were spent, he spoke soothingly, lovingly.

"You know what you must do, don't you?"

"No...please, Daddy. I told Sarah that I was trying to stop. Please don't make me do it again. It's wrong." She started crying again. "It's so wrong."

"It's not wrong, Pippin, if it makes you feel good. It will put you back in control of your life, your marriage, your career. It's what you do so well."

His voice echoed through her head, refusing to withdraw. As he continued to speak, his presence enveloped her entire body from the inside out. She closed her eyes and felt his breath on her face as he whispered.

"Do you remember that some people thought that our love was wrong?"

"Yes, Daddy."

"But it wasn't, was it?"

Linda didn't respond, the adult knowing instinctively that their relationship had been inappropriate but the child too afraid to answer. Her father answered for her.

"Of course it wasn't wrong. If it had been, you would have asked me to stop. And you never did, did you?"

Shame overcame her as Linda tried to remember if she'd ever asked him to stop. She didn't think so. She'd been so young. It had been so many years ago now.

"Now, Pippin, I need you to listen. Look at me."

Linda lifted her head, her eyebrows knit. She'd never actually seen her father during their conversations, so she wasn't sure what he meant when he told her to look at him.

"Daddy, I don't—" Linda's speech ceased as her father's countenance appeared before her. His head was large, too large, and it was hazy, as if she were viewing him through a screen. Breath trapped in her throat, she reached out to touch his face and found that her hand went through the haze. She withdrew her hand quickly and clutched it to her chest, eyes averted. She started whispering to herself, knowing that what she was seeing wasn't real but unable to alter the situation. She stole a glance every other breath to see if he had vanished. He remained, however, a patient smile affixed to his face as he waited her out.

After a time, she stammered, "Dad-dy, you can't be here. You n-need to leave."

"Pippin, you have made all of this happen. You have made me appear before you. Until now, the sound of my voice has been enough to guide you. But now..." He shook his head from side to side, his eyes never leaving hers. *"Well, now you need more guidance, so here I am. This is your doing, not mine."*

Linda closed her eyes. "If I do what you ask of me, will you leave me alone?" she asked in a tiny voice she no longer recognized as her own.

"Of course I will. I always do, for a time, until you need to restore order in your life once more."

Linda felt a massive weight settle on her as she acquiesced to her father's wishes. Without looking up she asked, "Where?"

"Providence, Rhode Island."

"When?"

"As soon as possible, Pippin. You need this. You'll feel so good afterward, and everything will be better, you'll see."

"Yes, Daddy."

Linda looked up as her father's hazy face evaporated. Feeling a mixture of relief and sadness, she rose and crossed to the desk, removed a small mirror from her purse, and commenced cleaning herself up, completing the transformation by brushing her hair so that the hairless spot could no longer be seen. After applying fresh makeup, she took a deep breath, smoothed her jacket and skirt, and crossed to the door. She planted a thousand-watt smile on her face and threw the door open.

"Lizzie, how's the Boston search going?" Linda asked a little too loudly as she breezed over to Lizzie's desk and sat down on its edge.

Lizzie's hands were shaking as she answered her boss without looking at her, "Um...fine. You have two choices for a nonstop to Boston."

"Change of plans, Lizzie. Turns out I need to be in Providence tonight for something. Book me a flight for this afternoon to Providence and then a flight out of Providence to Boston for tomorrow morning."

Lizzie looked at Linda and, despite Linda's efforts to conceal it, noticed that she'd been crying. She'd heard Linda talking in her office and wondered to whom she'd been speaking. But because Linda's emotions had been so volatile recently, Lizzie was afraid to ask, especially after what had happened earlier, so she erred on the side of caution and said nothing. Resuming the computer search, she offered, "There's a flight leaving in an hour and a half to Providence. If you leave now, you can make it." She clicked more flight options. "And tomorrow morning, there's a flight from Providence to Boston at ten forty. Shall I book these?"

"Perfect," said Linda with a smile, rubbing her palms together. "The timing will be perfect."

"Do you mind if I ask why you're going to Providence, Dr. Sterling? Is it for a talk? Do you need me to prepare any slides for a presentation?"

Linda had been walking back to her office when she turned around and stared hard at Lizzie, who shrank under her scrutiny.

"Yes, I mind if you ask, Lizzie, and no, I need nothing else from you."

As Lizzie watched Linda enter her office and shut the door, she resolved to find another job. She typed "monster.com" into her browser window and then "administrative assistant/medical field." She didn't know what was going on with her boss, but gut instinct told her that whatever it was, it wouldn't end well for Linda. And Lizzie was sure about one thing: she had absolutely no intention of going down with Linda's ship.

CHAPTER 35

A lex sat cross-legged in her desk chair, leaning forward and squinting at the computer screen. Her right forefinger rested lightly on the mousepad, ready at a moment's notice to click on the small square that represented "stop" on the video she was watching. Vinny had forwarded to her the security footage from three of the four other hotel murders with a note that said, "See what you think. Call me when you're done viewing these."

Although the security camera in the New York hotel hadn't been functioning, she had received footage from Maxwell Cooper's murder in Baltimore, Walter Croswell's in Philadelphia, and Justin Simkins's in Hartford. In all cases, the hotel had been relatively close to the airport, as the victims were all visiting for some type of trade show or convention in their respective fields. There seemed to be no connection between the men's professions and their deaths, as the jobs ranged from medical appliance representative to tire sales to cosmetics marketing director. However, being away from home on a work assignment was something they all had in common. That and their physical appearances and characteristics.

What just didn't make sense to Alex were the reading glasses that had been found at each scene. Although they were always found folded neatly on the nightstand, none of the men were reported by their colleagues and physicians as needing reading glasses. This specific detail troubled Alex more than any other, as she saw it as the killer's signature. Perhaps the killer felt compelled to leave the glasses, a final act that completed the death ritual. Or maybe it was simply a "screw you" gesture from the murderer to the police. Either way, the glasses bothered Alex because they were important but she didn't yet know why.

Alex tapped a pen against her thigh as she watched the camera footage related to Justin Simkins's murder in Hartford. As in the Boston case, the victim's room was located directly next to the elevator, the camera perched above it looking down the hallway. The sharp angle of the camera related to the victim's room made it almost impossible to see the door and consequently obscured direct sight of anyone entering or exiting.

Alex's eyes bored a hole in the computer screen, willing it to show her some useful scrap of information that might aid her in the case. She watched as people entered and exited the elevator, some clearly in a hurry, others standing and chatting after they exited. One couple was obviously intoxicated, groping each other as they made their way down the hallway toward a room. The man fumbled with the card key and then tumbled into the room with the woman literally falling on top of him, both of them laughing. Alex smiled in spite of herself and made a mental note to call Julian later. Maybe we could grope each other and fall into a hotel room, she thought.

Sudden movement on the tape caught her eye. Someone approached Mr. Simkins's room, paused at the door—sliding a card key, perhaps?—and then entered, the door closing behind the person. Several minutes later, the door reopened. Because of the camera angle, Alex could see only the right shoulder of the room's occupant. Based on the build and shirt type, it looked like a man, but she couldn't be absolutely sure. A swift flurry of activity occurred as someone else entered the room quickly and slammed the door. It was so fast that Alex couldn't determine the sex of the visitor, much less any other detail. She replayed the tape several times without gaining any insight.

Alex stared almost without blinking as the minutes clicked by on the tape's digital clock, waiting for Mr. Simkins's door to reopen. After about forty-five minutes, the door opened a crack, just enough for someone to peek through. It then closed again, only to reopen a minute later. Someone held the door ajar and then dashed out quickly, head and back bent, clearly aware he or she was on tape. Moreover, the person wore a fedora and a baggy coat, making it difficult to determine sex, weight, or height. Pausing and replaying the tape several times in slow motion, Alex was unable to discern any helpful information. Sighing, she moved on to the next tape: Walter Croswell in Philadelphia.

Again, the camera was placed above the elevator, but Mr. Croswell's room was halfway down the hall, leaving a full and unobstructed view of the hallway and his door. Additionally, the footage was relatively crisp. Maybe we're catching a break, Alex thought, pursing her lips in anticipation of seeing the killer. Twenty minutes into the recording, however, her hopes were dashed when the camera angle altered slightly upward, showing only the very end of the hallway, leaving Mr. Croswell's door no longer visible.

"What the hell?" Alex yelled at the screen, hands up in the air. "How'd that happen?"

As she continued watching the footage, twenty minutes later the camera angle changed once more to cover the area directly in front of the elevator. Sighing, Alex realized that the camera was most likely on a rotating schedule to allow full coverage of the floor, twenty minutes at a time. Just enough time for a killer to get the job done and move on without being seen, Alex thought glumly.

Alex completed the Philadelphia tape to ensure that the footage of Mr. Croswell's door, in twenty-minute increments, didn't shed any light on his killer. Satisfied she'd missed nothing, Alex focused on the final tape: Maxwell Cooper's room in Baltimore. She tapped her computer screen to play it and was immediately dismayed to see that although the camera was in a good position, Mr. Cooper's door was at the opposite end of the hallway, which stretched about thirty feet, leaving the picture somewhat indistinct.

Again, Alex watched people come and go silently as the tape played. Fourteen minutes in, she saw Mr. Cooper approach his door with someone. Alex paused the tape and stared hard at the screen. The visitor was wearing pants, flat shoes, and a nondescript light jacket with a hood. The guest was careful to avoid looking at the camera and seemed somewhat hunched over.

"Dammit!" Alex said, stymied once more. She tapped play again and watched as Mr. Cooper pushed the door open and then stepped aside to let his guest pass.

"Something someone might do for a woman," Alex said aloud.

While crossing the threshold, the visitor reached out a hand to touch Mr. Cooper on the shoulder.

Alex's pulse quickened as she leaned forward and reversed the tape, touched play, and watched the shoulder touch in slow motion. Pausing the footage, she zoomed in on the hand. Although the image was blurry, she could see long, elegant fingers and a small ring on the pinky. A woman's hand. She glanced at the time stamp on the screen: 7:35 p.m. Well within the time frame in which Mr. Cooper was murdered.

"Gotcha!" Alex whispered to the computer.

Holding her breath, Alex resumed normal playing speed and continued to watch the screen and the time stamp. The minutes crept by as she waited for the woman to exit the room. Almost exactly one hour later, Mr. Cooper's door opened just enough for someone to glance into the hallway, and then out came the woman, head down and back hunched. But instead of returning toward the elevator, she turned right, proceeding down the hallway and disappearing down the stairs.

Alex completed the footage in case the woman returned. For her efforts, she was rewarded with the sight of a housekeeper entering Mr. Cooper's room and then running down the hallway, silently screaming for help.

Alex stopped the recording and leaned back in her chair, shaking her head. A hand. That's all she had to go on. But it was a striking hand with a pinky ring. It might stand out once we have a suspect, but it certainly won't be enough to convict, she thought.

Her cell phone vibrated. Vinny's name appeared on the screen.

"Hey, Vin. Perfect timing. I just finished the tapes."

"What do you think?"

"I think that the hand stands out, but everything else is crap."

Vinny chuckled mirthlessly. "Yeah. I came to that very same conclusion."

"What about prints?" Alex asked, waving at Dolores who was approaching her desk at a brisk pace.

"I fast-tracked fingerprint ID with a friend of mine at the bureau, and she said there were at least seven sets of prints in the room, which is amazing, because I thought there would've been a lot more than that. Anyway, she said that out of the seven, only one was in IAFIS, and they were the prints of a former housekeeper who'd been fired for stealing a few weeks back. All other prints either weren't clean enough for an ID or weren't in the system."

Alex held up her index finger toward Dolores, indicating she'd be off the phone in a minute. Dolores smiled as she shifting her weight back and forth, clearly eager to tell Alex something.

"Well, at least we'll have some prints to compare our suspect's to if we ever get one," Alex said, rolling her eyes.

"Yeah, I guess so. Any feedback from the coroner about COD?"

"Yeah. Mr. Donaldson had a heart attack, all right. The question is, what caused it? And speaking of the coroner, she's standing in front of my desk, practically jumping out of her skin. Hold on, I'm putting you on speaker."

Alex touched the speaker button on her phone. "You're on speaker, Vin. Dolores is here, too."

"Hi, Dolores. I'm Vincent Marcozzi from the FBI, unofficially on the case."

"Good to meet you, Vincent. Dolores Caruso, chief medical examiner for Boston, officially on the case," she smiled.

"What's up, Dolores? You look excited," Alex said, moving things along.

"I was up last night at three in the morning, as I often am, because I can't sleep anymore. Aging is a wonderful thing. Anyhow, I was up at three and started thinking about what could cause tracheal lacerations like the ones I saw in Mr. Donaldson's throat. I knew I'd seen them before but couldn't put my finger on it."

"And?" prompted Vinny.

"Well, when I was a medical intern, there was a car-crash victim whose spleen was ruptured along with other internal injuries. His brain had smashed against his skull so hard during the collision that it had left him unresponsive.

Swelling ensued, and he was placed in a medically induced coma to allow the brain time to heal. Sadly, after three weeks on life support, his parents had to make the unthinkable decision to end his life and they graciously donated his organs for transplantation and his body to science."

Dolores paused for dramatic effect, her eyes darting back and forth between Alex and the cell phone resting on the desk. Alex held up her hands and raised her eyebrows at Dolores, urging her not so subtly to move on with the story.

"So, I happened to be the intern assisting in his autopsy, and I specifically remember the attending physician pointing out to me the state of the boy's larynx. There were consistent, oval lacerations in his throat caused by the tube that had been inserted in order to keep him breathing, albeit with the help of a ventilator. Now, although there are several items that when inserted down the throat could leave scratches, there's only one item that could leave the consistent, oval-shaped irritation I saw in Mr. Donaldson's trachea—a ventilator tube!" she finished triumphantly, slapping the desk for emphasis.

Alex's face betrayed her confusion and disappointment. She wasn't sure what she'd been expecting, but a ventilator tube was not it.

Vinny cut in. "Didn't Evan Donaldson sell things like ventilators?"

"Yeah, he did," said Alex. And then to Dolores, "Did any of the other victims have scratches in their throats?"

"I checked with the other cities' coroners, and all the other victims' throats were scratch-free," Dolores answered.

"So, for some reason, the perp changed his MO and used a ventilator," offered Vinny.

"*Her* MO," corrected Alex.

"Right, *her* MO," said Vinny.

"How do you know it's a woman?" asked Dolores.

"Security footage shows a female hand as the last one to touch Mr. Cooper in Baltimore. Also, Julian said that luring the victims into sex would dull their senses to the fact that death was right around the corner. Has to be woman," Alex finished. She thought for a moment.

"Dolores, can anyone put a ventilator tube down someone's throat?"

"Not really. I mean, technically, yes…probably. But if it had been done by someone who didn't know how to do it, then I would've seen a lot more damage to the laryngeal tissue. No, whoever placed the tube down Mr. Donaldson's throat knew what he was doing. Oh, sorry, what *she* was doing."

"So, we're looking for a woman who has medical knowledge who happened to be at a hotel where a medical conference was being held. Should be easy to narrow down," Vinny said sarcastically.

"Hey, at least it's a start," said Alex. "How many people attended that conference, Vin?"

Vinny laughed. "Only about four hundred and fifty."

"And how many of the attendees were women?" Dolores asked.

Vinny paused while he consulted his notes and sighed heavily. "Half. Long live equal rights and women's lib."

Chapter 36

Julian tapped his way into the office, to find Jesse wrapping up a phone call. "No, you hang up first." Pause. "No, you! Okay, we'll hang up at the same time. Ready? One, two, three…how come you didn't hang up?" He looked up to find Julian facing him with a smirk on his face.

"Yeah, okay, I really have to go. No, really. Talk to you later. Bye." Jesse placed the phone back in its cradle and cleared his throat. "So, Julian, you've got—"

Julian held up his hand to cut him off. "Important phone call?"

"Um…no, it was just the office supplies rep I told you—"

Julian shook his head and laughed. "Jesse, you've got to be kidding me! That's the best you can do? The office supplies rep? Really, give me some credit. I'm not a complete idiot."

Jesse sighed dramatically. "Okay, we agree on that point. You're not a *complete* idiot."

"Was it the Thai guy? What's his name?"

Jesse rolled his eyes. "Yes, Julian, it was 'the Thai guy,' as you so lamely put it. And his name is Oliver. He's brilliant, and did I mention that he's gor—"

"'Geous? Yes, you might have mentioned that," Julian said, finishing Jesse's sentence for him and shaking his head.

"Seriously, Julian, I think he might be 'the one,'" Jesse gushed.

Julian nodded and smiled. "One step at a time, Jess. We've talked about this. Don't get carried away."

"Mmm," Jesse said.

"What's 'mmm'?" Julian asked, head tilted to the side.

"I think you know what 'mmm' is, Julian. I may get too carried away, but methinks you don't get carried away enough. How long have you and Alex been dating now? Eight years or something like that?"

Julian shook his head, gently waving his hand for emphasis. "It's been a little while, and as usual, you're being dramatic and have changed the subject. I just don't want to see you get hurt…again."

"Don't you worry about me, Dr. Stryker. I'm just fine. Now, you on the other hand could use some assistance in the love department."

Once again, Julian had been drawn into an argument he knew he couldn't win. A half smile on his lips, he spread his arms wide and bowed theatrically to Jesse. "Game, set, match goes to you, my friend."

"Per usual," Jesse said flippantly as he straightened some papers on his desk. "Now, to business. Your three o'clock canceled, leaving you one free hour to catch up on notes and phone calls. After that, it's Jack Rafter. Remember him? The twelve-year-old potential sociopath who hurts animals?"

Julian winced. "Jesse, please don't refer to patients like that."

"Hey, I'm just playing the odds. I know the kid has a terrible home life."

"All right, thanks." Julian tapped his way into his office and sat down heavily in his desk chair. Although he wasn't looking forward to seeing Jack, who psychologically resembled his own assailant, Julian didn't like hearing the boy referred to as a sociopath either. Because of the changing nature of children as they developed and grew, ethically and legally Jack couldn't be labeled a sociopath until he was eighteen years of age. So, in his notes and on the billing paperwork, Julian had diagnosed Jack with a conduct disorder. Julian desperately hoped that a combination of clinical help and support at home would create a barrier between Jack and a diagnosis of antisocial personality disorder, or sociopathy, at the age of eighteen.

It wasn't just Jack who troubled Julian. The heart attack killer, as Julian had come refer to her, weighed heavily on his mind. Although women accounted for only a relatively small number of all serial killers in the United States, Julian was convinced that the murderer was a woman, and her method of death was disturbing. Heart attacks were not always quick and involved varying amounts of pain. In all cases, however, the victim would know he was going to die. That knowledge alone was a form of torture, and the perp knew that—in all likelihood relished it. Female serial killers usually target their victims and killed out of vengeance as opposed to the need to fulfill a sexual desire. Julian believed this murderer was getting revenge; the sex was simply a means to an end, a way to exert control and power over her victim.

His thoughts then drifted to Linda Sterling, whose recent behavior also caused Julian great anxiety. Having not followed up since Sarah's death, he felt somewhat irresponsible. Sure, he had no clinical obligation to Linda, but he'd started down a road and felt the need to walk the rest of the way with her, if for no other reason than she was a colleague.

He commanded Siri to call Linda Sterling's office number. Lizzie picked up on the second ring.

"Dr. Linda Sterling's office. This is Lizzie. How may I help you?"

"Hi Lizzie, it's Julian Stryker. How are you?"

"Hi, Dr. Stryker. I'm…good. How are you?"

"Well, that certainly wasn't convincing. Everything okay?"

"Um…yeah, it's fine. Everything's good. Can I help you with something?"

"Is Linda available? I wanted to follow up with her about a few things."

"Actually, she just left for the airport. She's flying through Providence on her way to Boston for a funeral. I'm sure you haven't heard, but her foster mother died recently."

"Sadly, I did know that, because I happened to be there when Sarah died."

"Oh!"

"Yeah. It was pretty awful."

"Why were you visiting Sar—" Lizzie cut herself off. "Oh, I'm sorry! It's none of my business! I do that all the time."

Julian smiled. "It's fine, Lizzie. I was visiting Sarah because Linda had mentioned her, and I guess I just wanted to meet her. She was a remarkable woman."

"Yes, she was. Dr. Sterling looked up to her quite a bit, and she's taking her death very, *very* hard."

Julian pulled a face. "What do you mean?"

Lizzie paused, unsure whether to trust this man she'd never met. But the knot in her stomach from the morning's interactions with Dr. Sterling made the decision for her, and she leaned into the phone, her voice barely a whisper. "Dr. Sterling has been acting very strangely recently. I shouldn't be talking about her like this, but you seem to care."

"I do care, Lizzie, and you're doing the right thing. What do you mean when you say she's been acting strangely?"

"Well, she was a little angry when she arrived at the office, and the morning only got weirder from there. She got the call telling her that Sarah had died, and she asked me to schedule a flight to Boston, but it was the way she did it that was so bizarre. She was...mean to me. Her behavior's been a little off recently, but today she was downright mean to me, screaming, hair pulling—"

"She pulled your hair!?" Julian asked, astonished.

"No, no, no. Not *my* hair. *Her* hair. She pulled some right out of her head. Oh, I really shouldn't be talking about this." Lizzie sounded nervous and started to cry.

Julian craved clarification. "You're telling me that Dr. Sterling pulled some hair out of her own head...on purpose?"

"Yes! And then she screamed at me to get out of her office. And then..." Lizzie faltered.

"Please go on, Lizzie."

"And then I could hear her talking to someone through the door. I know I shouldn't have been listening, but I was just so confused and concerned. I heard her say 'Daddy' and when she came out of her office, I could tell that she'd been crying, although she acted as if everything were fine. I thought her father was dead."

The hairs rose on the back of Julian's neck. Between his own patients and the heart attack killer on the loose, the last thing he needed was a client—or rather, a nonclient—who clearly needed real psychiatric attention. He resolved to address this with Linda during her visit to Boston.

"Dr. Stryker, are you still there?"

"Yes, sorry. Thanks so much, Lizzie. I appreciate your candor. I'll touch base with Linda when she's here in Boston and try to get to the bottom of what's going on with her."

Lizzie was sniffling. "Thanks, Dr. Stryker. Please don't tell her that I spoke to you. I need this job…until I can find another one, that is."

"I completely understand, Lizzie. Your secret's safe with me. Have a good day."

Julian rang off and sat back in his chair. He lowered his chin to his chest as he reviewed what he knew about Linda. She's a control freak with daddy issues, but was she beginning to lose touch with reality? Was her recent behavior affecting her medical practice? That's the million-dollar question, Julian thought.

He took a deep breath and commanded his phone to dial Linda's cell. It went straight to voicemail, and Julian found himself somewhat relieved. After listening to Linda's outgoing message, he left his own.

"Hey, Linda. It's Julian. I just wanted to touch base and see how you're feeling about…everything. Give me a call when you can. Talk soon. Thanks. Bye."

Julian told himself that he was being ridiculous, that Linda was going to be okay. That she wasn't losing touch with reality and wasn't putting any of her patients in harm's way. So…why wouldn't the hairs on the back of his neck relax?

PART THREE

The Reckoning

CHAPTER 37

Edward Townsend—Steady Eddie to his friends—had been a cab driver for exactly forty-six days. Prior to that, he'd worked construction, but two bad knees had forced early retirement from that profession. Having entered the workforce at sixteen years of age, he was not a well-educated man and, upon leaving construction, found his options lacking until a friend of his suggested he try driving a cab. He'd mulled over the idea with his wife of twenty-nine years, Jackie, and they had decided he should try it, not only for the extra money driving would bring in but also for the singular purpose of getting him out of the house.

Eddie rarely worked the night shift but had agreed to take a buddy's hours so that his friend could attend his daughter's dance recital. He hadn't even come to a full stop at the airport's taxi stand when a person quickly entered his cab and slammed the door. Pulling away from the curb, Eddie glanced at the taxi queue and was rewarded with people giving him the finger. Clearly his passenger had jumped to the front of the line, leaving those waiting in the queue frustrated and angry. Eddie peered at her in the rearview mirror and noted that she was smiling and waving at the perturbed crowd.

"To the airport Radisson please."

Eddie wrinkled his brow, wondering why some people thought they were better than others. His passenger lay her head against the seat and closed her eyes.

As you wished, Daddy, I'm here. I need your guidance now more than ever.

She waited, a small, anticipatory smile on her lips.

No response came. She tried again.

You told me to come, Daddy, and I'm here in Providence. Where are you?

Linda opened her eyes, thinking that perhaps she would see his face once more. Nothing.

She looked around the cab frantically. *Where are you?* she demanded in her mind, glancing at the driver, who regarded her in the rearview mirror with steely blue eyes.

She leaned against the seat and felt a hollowness in her chest. She knew what was coming and dreaded it.

As the cab slowed to a stop at a red light, Linda glanced out the window and saw a father pushing a little girl on a swing in a local park. The girl looked to be about seven years old and was throwing her head back, laughing. Linda's lips flirted with a small smile, which then vanished as quickly as it had come. Instantaneously, she was transported back to the age of five, and her father was pushing her on a swing.

"I can go higher, Daddy. Watch!"

Linda pumped her little legs in an effort to attain more height. As she flew higher and faster, her father laughed and asked, "Why so high, Pippin? What's up there?"

Linda looked down at him and said matter-of-factly, "I want to see God's face, Daddy!"

Her father's face quickly contorted into an ugly mask as he grabbed the metal chains of the swing, forcing her to a jerky, uneven stop.

Dragging her off the swing, he held her chin tightly in one hand while he spat out, "There is no God, Linda. No God! Do you hear me? I am your God. You'd do well to remember that!"

He'd then released her and sweetly asked if she wanted ice cream. Confused and terrified, she'd said yes to please him, but the truth was that she felt the same hollowness in her core as she did right now. It was at about that same age that her father had started giving her special attention.

She glanced again at the little girl, her braids flapping as she flew on the swing. I hope she's really happy, Linda thought. But then, is anyone truly happy?

As the cab pulled away from the light, Linda tore her gaze from the laughing girl. Staring straight ahead, her eyes deadened, and a sheer veil of black descended upon her. The crown of her head tingled as the darkness poured over her—slowly, like a thick, wet syrup. It caressed her skull, tightening its grip until she felt as if her head were in a vise. Continuing its sickening journey, it settled on her shoulders like a shawl of lead, finally coming to rest in her gut, which began to writhe like the serpent she knew would inevitably accompany her murderous odyssey. Transformation complete, she unbuttoned her blouse so that her bra was clearly visible.

The driver, who'd been surreptitiously ogling his stunning passenger throughout the trip, almost rear-ended the car in front of him as his eyes bulged at her state of near undress.

Linda braced her hand on the back of the front seat as the cab screeched to a halt.

"My goodness, Mr.—" Linda said, pausing to lean forward to see his name on the required placard, "Townsend, you should really keep your eyes on the road." She smiled lasciviously.

Eddie waggled his eyebrows in apology and started forward once more, glancing back every now and again. Each time he looked, he was rewarded with a smiling visage staring back at him. In fact, he found it odd that never once during for the entire rest of the trip did she look away from his eyes in the rearview mirror.

They arrived at the Radisson, and she paid Eddie in cash. As she exited the car, she asked him, "Are you happy, Mr. Townsend?"

"I beg your pardon, ma'am?"

"I said, are you happy? I mean, in your life, are you happy?"

He thought for a moment and said, "Yes, I am. Why?"

"Do you have a family?"

"Yes. A wife, two boys, and a girl."

"Do you love them?"

"Yes. Very much."

"Do they love you? Would they say that you're a good father?"

He thought again and answered. "Yes, I believe they would."

She leaned forward toward his open window, bending at the waist, her shirt falling open. Eddie fought to keep his eyes level with hers. She waited him out, head tilted, one eyebrow raised. She shifted her weight so that her heavy breasts jiggled.

"Are you sure that your family would say you're a good husband and father?" she leaned closer, whispering in his ear.

Steady Eddie Townsend nodded dumbly, eyes locked straight ahead, desperately avoiding her chest. This kind of crap never happened in construction, he thought to himself.

Linda drew away from him and saw that despite his best efforts to not engage with her, his crotch had a different plan. She smiled and leaned in once more, noticing for the first time a pair of reading glasses on the dashboard. She stopped short and stood abruptly, her smile evaporating.

"You're a lucky man, Mr. Townsend, because I believe you. You would have died to know the things I would have done to you if you'd answered differently...just *died*," she finished dryly.

Relieved, Eddie kept nodding his head, not quite believing what had happened. She handed him an extra twenty dollars and patted the roof of the cab.

"Take care of yourself, Mr. Townsend, and keep being the great man your family thinks you are, okay?"

"Yes, ma'am." He sped off before either of them could change their minds.

Linda turned and walked with purpose toward the front doors of the hotel, which opened electronically with a *whoosh*. Stale, overconditioned air bombarded her as she strode confidently to the front desk.

"Good afternoon, madam, how may I help you?" a young blond woman asked.

"Dr. Linda Sterling, checking in for one night."

"Of course, Dr. Sterling. Welcome to Providence."

"Thank you. Tell me, are there any conferences or trade shows being held here right now?"

"Um...no ma'am, but the Hilton down the street is hosting a huge conference today and tomorrow for techies—computer software, you know, things like that," the clerk offered helpfully.

Linda's eyes flashed, momentarily widening before settling on the girl's name tag.

"Well now, Ashley, thank you so much for that information. You know, I've always loved the name *Ashley*. If I ever had a daughter, I always said that would have been her name."

Ashley blushed and said, "Thanks, Dr. Sterling, that's very kind."

After checking in, Linda explored her room. Queen bed with an over-starched spread; sterile mauve walls with store-bought artwork housed in inexpensive faux-gold frames; desk against the wall near the window with all the usual business accoutrements: charging station, blotter, pad of paper with pen, magazine with local attractions/eateries, phone, and so on. She sauntered to the window and whisked aside the heavy drapes and underlying sheer curtain to reveal a stunning view of the parking lot. She smiled to herself. Having been in so many of these rooms over the years, none of this mattered. She was here for a purpose and would not be sidetracked or deterred from her goal.

Turning to the mirror over the desk, she caught a glimpse of herself and stopped short. Her visage looked tired. No, more than that. She looked... worn. Beaten down. The bald spot on the right side of her head shone clearly in the waning sunlight coming through the window, and she subconsciously rearranged her hair to cover it. Her gaze shifted down as her eyebrows came together in thought.

How had it come to this? She had everything the world had to offer: a successful career, a beautiful daughter, a loving husband. And although Sarah had passed...beloved Sarah...she still had Brenda, who was as loyal and trustworthy as they came. Thinking of Brenda made her smile, and she regarded her countenance once more. Looking deep into her own emerald eyes, she noted that a sparkle still resided there. A glimmer of hope, perhaps, for a more normal future? Searching further into her soul, she realized a strength and determination she didn't know she possessed. She had confided in Sarah that she was trying to stop, that she knew her behavior was wrong. So, right there in the hotel room, on the spot, she made a decision that she was going to stop dating. She resolved to return to her husband and settle into the incredible life she'd built. Smiling into the mirror, she decided she didn't look so tired anymore.

Her phone buzzed, indicating that a voicemail awaited her. Feeling secure and confident, she dug the phone out of her purse and noted that Julian had called. Smiling, she was about to play Julian's message when her phone rang. She abandoned the voicemail and slid the icon to answer.

"Dr. Sterling, this is Carla at the hospital. I have Sabrina's numbers for you."

"What do you mean, 'Sabrina's numbers'?"

"You had asked me to perform stat blood work on Sabrina Cartwright to determine why her white cell count is so low, remember?"

"Did I?" Linda asked, placing her hand to her forehead. God, that seemed like so long ago. When was it, exactly? Linda wondered.

"Dr. Sterling? Are you there? I have the results. Is this a good time?"

"Uh…sure, yes. Go ahead." Linda drew courage from her recent decision to return to a traditional life.

"Well, since you asked me to test her blood, her white count has dropped even further. The MRI and CT showed that the cancer has spread to her lungs and twelve of twenty lymph nodes. It looks metastatic to me, but I'll forward you the info so you can review it per usual, okay?"

Although the logical, medical side of Linda had known this might be the result, the maternal part of Linda took the information badly. The room started spinning, and she couldn't seem to get enough air. She dropped herself into the desk chair to avoid passing out.

"Dr. Sterling, I need to go, but I wanted to let you know immediately because I know how much you care for Sabrina. What should I tell her mother? She's waiting for the results."

Linda was having trouble focusing. "Uh…um, tell her nothing, Carla. I'll take care of it."

"Okay. I'll send you the test results so that you can review them yourself. Bye."

Linda was left staring at the screen as it faded to black. Another one's going to die, she thought helplessly. Another innocent child is going to leave this earth because of my lack of control and ability.

Her phone buzzed again, reminding her that she had a voicemail waiting. Numbly, she pressed the play button. Like the beam of a lighthouse reaches a lonely ship on the sea during a harsh winter storm, Julian's voice reached out to her. "Hey, Linda. It's Julian. I just wanted to touch base and see how you're feeling about…everything. Give me a call when you can. Talk soon. Thanks. Bye."

She'd forgotten about Julian. He would help her, she was sure. She would tell him everything, and he would help her sort it all out. Of course he would understand why she'd taken action, starting with her parents and her sister. He would explain to the authorities, and she could go back to the incredible life she'd created. It could happen.

The laughter started low in her belly, almost a chuckle, really, and built until she could no longer control it and tears were streaming down her face. Dr. Linda Sterling looked hard at her reflection and realized she'd never felt so lonely in her entire life. Not when she was six years old and the special attention had become a regular occurrence, not when she was a teenager and her parents and sister had gone away, and not even when Sarah had died.

"Maybe it's time for me to go away," she stated to her reflection, once more haggard and disheveled.

"Don't be ridiculous, Pippin. You're always so incredibly dramatic. What you need is…well, you know what you need to restore order in your life. Frankly, I'm getting a little fatigued of having this same conversation again and again."

"Me too, Daddy. That's why I think I need to leave."

"If you mean that you intend to kill yourself, then I have to tell you that I simply will not allow it."

She laughed out loud. "You can't control that, Daddy. You may have controlled a lot of things in my life, but you cannot control my death."

"Oh, but I can, Pippin." His voice softened. *"Do this one last thing for your father. Go to the Hilton. Relieve your stress. Get your life in order. You'll feel so much better. You know you will."*

While he spoke, he was stroking her long, languid neck. Linda could feel his breath on her throat and closed her eyes. His touch was soft, luring her to that dark place where she found so much power and release.

"You are so incredibly beautiful," he whispered. *"Do this one last thing for your father, for yourself. I love you."* His voice trailed off.

The serpent awakened within her and started its tantalizing descent at her throat, working its way slowly across her chest and torso before settling into her loins. An eternity passed before she reopened her eyes, pleased to see that her appearance was now completely in order and ready to hunt.

Chapter 38

Jason Quinn certainly wasn't stupid, although he worked hard to come across as thickheaded and single-minded. Having graduated from Stanford at the age of nineteen, he'd gone on to receive a master's degree in journalism from Georgetown and then settled himself into the DC area with a prime job at the *Washington Post* as its junior crime reporter. He'd made himself available for any crime-related story, at any time, and ended up working nights and weekends, rewarded for his efforts by being promoted to the top crime post upon his predecessor's retirement.

Jason enjoyed a reign as the golden-boy reporter who could write no wrong. His private life rivaled his professional one in its zeal, landing him not once but twice in jail for DUIs. Was it laziness, ego, alcohol, or all of the above that led him to compose a story in which he plagiarized an entire paragraph from an article printed fifteen years before in the same newspaper? Not surprisingly, Jason's heralded rise vaporized, and he found himself at first jobless and then homeless.

Never one to wallow or stand still, Jason worked diligently, seeking employment at rival newspapers. Encountering nothing but rejection, he turned toward news magazines in search of redemption, to no avail. Apparently word had spread of his fall from grace, and he became desperate to find employment in his field. As he was being ushered out of *Newsweek*'s offices, one of the security guards had offered him some flippant advice: "Why don't you go to the *National Informer*? I'm sure they'd be glad to take you in."

And they *were* glad. Actually, they'd been thrilled when he had approached them for a job, taking him on immediately and paying him not only a generous salary but adding substantial bonuses for meaty stories. What did it matter that he often had to chase ridiculous celebrities and take some "creative license" with his stories? His only stipulation upon accepting the post was that he would alter his name to protect all the kudos he'd earned as Jason Quinn. Thus, Brian Bosch was born.

Using the same natural instincts and work ethic he'd applied to stories about Kim Jong Il and Whitey Bulger, Brian rose quickly to the top of the smut-rag food chain and was currently heralded as its top reporter in the United States. Having become immune to the sniggers and disdain that were palpable when in a room with "real" reporters, he'd turned their derision into fuel for continued success. Brian Bosch was first to the story every time.

However, after leaving the *Post*, many of his contacts refused to return his calls, so he'd developed new ones, paying them when necessary. Recently his hard work had once again come to fruition, as several of his police contacts around the country had verified the potential existence of a person killing middle-aged men attending trade shows, all of them via heart attack.

Thanks to his enterprising young friend Brittany at the front desk of the Boston airport Radisson, he'd been able to gain informational access to the most recent Boston murder. Her lead, coupled with the fact that Vincent Marcozzi was in Boston investigating a local death, had verified for Brian that the Boston death was undeniably similar to the other cities' deaths. And although it was clear from Alex Hayes's response at the press conference that she knew nothing about the other heart attack victims, it didn't matter. Brian had been hoping to publish the story with a quote from Detective Hayes, but instead he decided to attend a trade show in the killer's death zone and get the public's reaction to a potential serial killer in their midst. Now *that* would make a good first installment of this developing story.

And so it was that he found himself in Providence, Rhode Island, at a Hilton hotel, his nose to the ground amid a sea of middle-aged men (and women) showcasing their products at a medical technology trade show. He worked his way around the large, open space until he understood the layout and then approached a booth that had a large, multicolored placard across it that read "MediWrite."

"Excuse me, sir. My name is Brian, and I'm covering the trade show for a national paper. I was wondering if—"

"The *New York Times*?"

"Excuse me?"

"Are you with the *Times*?'

"No, but I was wondering—"

"The *Washington Post*?"

"No, sir, it doesn't matter. Anyway, I was just wondering if I could get your reaction to the possibility of there being a serial killer stalking trade-show participants."

"A what? A serial killer? Here?" The man whipped his head back and forth as if a knife-wielding maniac might emerge any second.

Brian smiled encouragingly. "Not necessarily here, sir. But there is a significant possibility that someone is targeting middle-aged men who either work at or are attending trade shows on the east coast of the United States. What is your reaction to that?"

"How do you know that a killer—"

"Please just answer the question, sir."

"What's my reaction to that?" The man scratched his head. "Well, I guess I'd have to say that's bullshit! I come from the great state of Alabama, and as you can see…" The man drew back his jacket to reveal a very large pistol tucked into a hip holster. "If someone approached me with intent on doing me bodily harm, well, I think he'd find himself on the business end of this here baby girl." The man patted his gun. "That's her name, by the way, Baby Girl, with a capital *B* and a capital *G*. You got that?"

While the man leaned into Brian to squint at the notepad on which he'd been taking copious notes, Brian took the opportunity to glance around the room quickly, ascertaining that no one had seen the man reveal his large and very illegal gun.

Brian couldn't have planned the man's response any better. Not only had he obtained a great quote, but he'd stumbled onto a gun-toting redneck. Leave it to the Amendment Two crowd to get the blood boiling, not only about a serial killer but about guns in general.

Brian held out his hand. "Thanks you so much, Mr.—?"

"Gunther. Artimer T. Gunther from the great state of—"

"Alabama. Yes, I got that. Thank you, Mr. Gunther. Have a great day, and keep your eyes open." Brian winked and smiled before moving on.

Brian spent the rest of the afternoon interviewing trade-show participants and learning about leading-edge technology that was already having a positive impact in the medical community. His personal interest was piqued at one booth, where scientists from Singapore had actually created a mini midbrain, which was being used to help researchers conduct studies on and develop treatments for Parkinson's disease. His own mother suffered from the malady, so he was heartened to discover that leaps in research were being made.

After several hours of roaming, Brian reviewed his notes and determined that he had enough information to move forward with the story. Smiling, he made his way to the elevator, ready to enjoy some room service and writing. While waiting for the elevator, he glanced to his left and noted that the hotel bar, Flanagan's, was abuzz with activity. Music spilled out into the main lobby, and Brian couldn't help but laugh when he heard a group of people, clearly inebriated, singing along with DNCE's "Cake by the Ocean." The elevator arrived, and he stepped in, smiling at a boy holding his mother's hand. As the doors began to close, he thought better of it and hopped off at the last minute, saying "Forgot something!" to the surprised woman, who was looking at him as if he'd lost his mind.

Making his way into Flanagan's, Brian found a seat at the bar, wedging himself into a single seat between two drunk men arguing about baseball and a couple who based on their intoxication and rising hormone levels clearly needed to find a hotel room...and fast. He ordered a gin and tonic and tapped his hand on the bar in time with Pink, who was ordering her loyal subjects to "Raise Your Glass" in her crooning alto.

"You are so wrong, my friend!" announced the man next to Brian as he poked his cohort's chest. "Manny Ramirez left the Red Sox because he was lazy and he knew they were going to trade him! Didn't you see him always jogging to first base? The man couldn't have run away from the bulls at Pamplona if he'd had to! Am I right?"

Brian shook his head and marveled at the wonder that was sports. It could bring people together and divide them just as quickly. "Am I right or not?" the man next to Brian repeated.

Brian suddenly realized the man had been speaking to him. "Oh, you're talking to me? Uh...yeah, actually, I agree with you. Manny wasn't a real loss to the Sox."

Clearly Brian had given him the desired answer, because the drunkard slung his arm around Brian's shoulders and leaned in, veering the conversation away from Manny toward another Red Sox player who was equally as contentious among fans—David Ortiz. As Brian strained to pull away from the inebriate, whose breath reeked of alcohol, he caught a glimpse of a woman arguing with a fellow in a booth about twenty feet away. Although the music and conversation were too loud in the bar for Brian to hear the exchange, the man was clearly very angry with the woman.

He was leaning across the small table with his teeth bared as he alternatively glared and then said something to her. In response, the woman placed her hands on the table and leaned forward to ensure that the person across from her heard what she said. Brian watched as the woman's lips formed the phrase, "Fuck you." The man paused, face contorted into an ugly mask, and then quick as a snake strike grabbed the woman's left wrist and twisted hard. Her response was just as swift as she snatched up her glass with her right hand and whipped what was left in it into the man's face.

Before he could analyze what he was doing, Brian had disengaged himself from his drunken friend and appeared at the booth where the altercation was occurring. His sudden appearance caught both occupants off guard and caused a momentary hiatus in the argument.

"Everything okay here?" Brian asked nonchalantly.

The man looked Brian up and down as he swayed in his seat, still gripping the woman's wrist.

"Who the hell are you?' he demanded.

Brian squinted at the man and said, "Who am I? Your worst nightmare, buddy. Let go of her wrist, and get the hell outta here before you really piss off the lady and she throws more at you than just her drink."

The man stood quickly and had to grip the edge of the booth to steady himself. He mumbled something unintelligible in Brian's direction and then turned to the woman and whispered, "Biiiitch!" before stumbling toward the seat at the bar Brian had vacated.

They both watched the man leave and then turned to each other, Brian smiling and the woman scowling.

"So, now it's your turn?"

"I beg your pardon?" Brian asked.

"It's your turn with me?"

Brian hadn't noticed until this moment how incredibly beautiful the woman was. Her rich brunette hair was swept up into a twist that accentuated her elegant, graceful neck. Her eyes, emerald green and accusatory, were boring into his, and he found himself unable to respond.

"You think that you can rush in and save the day and that I'll...what? Have a drink with you? Chat with you? Sleep with you, for God's sake?"

The spell was broken, and Brian dumbly shook his head. "Uh...no, I was just trying—I just thought you needed help."

She laughed without humor. "Listen, buddy, when I need help, I'll ask for it. And certainly not from the likes of you." She waved her hand dismissively.

Looking back on that moment later, Brian would wonder why he hadn't just walked away, why he'd seen her response as a challenge instead of a rebuff. He slipped into the booth and leaned across the table good-naturedly.

"Well, it looks as though my seat at the bar has been taken, so how about you and I have that drink right here. My name is Bri—" Brian stopped short, sensing this woman's power and intelligence and not wanting her to know what he did for a living. "My name is Jason Quinn," he finished.

She glared at him for another moment and then offered him a half smile that hinted at the rare beauty to be found in a full grin. "Are you sure that's your name?" she asked, turning her head and tilting an eyebrow.

He'd been caught and knew it, but he couldn't go back now. "Yeah, I'm sure."

"Well, Mr. *Quinn*, my name is Ashley, and it's truly a pleasure to meet you."

Chapter 39

Brenda sat at Sarah's kitchen table, sipping some sherry she'd found behind a can of sardines in a corner cabinet. Taking a big gulp, she smacked her lips together as the liqueur slipped down her throat.

"Don't quite get what all the fuss is about," she said aloud, holding the crystal glass up to the sunlight peeking through the dirty kitchen window. The cut of the crystal bent the dim light into a prism that exploded in a rainbow of colors against the dingy ivory wall.

"Ah, Sarah, there you are," Brenda smiled, holding the glass up to the rainbow in a toast. "You always were full of sunshine and rainbows. I miss you already—" She broke off, allowing some tears to fall while she gulped down the rest of the drink.

"Now to business, Sarah. You told me to sell your stuff and your house, and that's what I'm going to do. But if you don't mind, I'd like to go through and see if there's anything I might like to keep in remembrance of you. And maybe I'll grab something for Lin, too—that is, if you don't mind."

Brenda waited, honestly believing that Sarah would give notification, a sign perhaps, of any discontent with Brenda's plan. When none came, Brenda pushed herself out of the 1970s-style mustard-yellow vinyl chair and rubbed her hands together.

"Let's start in the family room, shall we?" Brenda wandered into the space where they'd spent so much time as a makeshift family. Grabbing a box, she started gently placing items, one by one, on top of one another, until she had filled it to the top. She glanced at the box and realized with dismay how quickly an entire life that had been devoted to helping others could be shut away and forgotten.

"But not up here, Sarah," Brenda said aloud, tapping her head for emphasis. "Don't you worry, Sarah. I got you right up here...forever."

Meandering to the mantle, its chipped paint lending it a marbled look, Brenda touched each frame that held pictures of her foster siblings throughout the years. She paused at a rusted metal frame that held a close-up of an unsmiling little girl, eyes slightly to the left of the camera lens because she couldn't bear to look anyone in the eye when she'd first come to Sarah's. Brenda was seventeen when Ruthie came into their lives, a scrawny, undernourished five-year-old who used to steal food and hoard it in the one dresser drawer allotted to her. Brenda found the food one day while putting away laundry and reported it to Sarah, who simply nodded.

"I know," Sarah had said. "It's okay, Brenda. One day, not long from now, Ruthie will realize that she'll always have a meal here and that no one's going to take her food away. When she's ready, she'll put the food back."

Brenda smiled at the memory of the day she'd been in the kitchen cutting vegetables for dinner when Ruthie had entered, her arms full of small cans and crinkly packages, to announce that she'd "found" all the food in her drawer and that she wanted to put it back where it belonged.

Continuing her trek down memory lane along the mantle, each picture brought memories flooding back to her. Most children who entered Sarah's world came in abandoned, abused, or forgotten, but exited however many years later stronger, smarter, and kinder.

Kindness and patience, Brenda thought. That's what Sarah lived, every day, in every gesture, action, and word. She gingerly removed each picture from its frame, placing the photographs in a small pile on the scratched, faded coffee table nearby. As she did so, she vowed to use her newfound computer skills to search for each of her former siblings to see how they were doing. Or at the very least to tell them of Sarah's passing.

Brenda arrived at the last picture in the row, a four-by-six black-and-white photo of a tall, gangly beauty with her arm draped haphazardly over the shoulders of a shorter, stocky girl. In the photo, Brenda wore a large grin that left nothing to the imagination whereas Linda graced the photographer with a prim look that promised she was holding something back. Lifting the picture from the mantle and peering at it, Brenda decided that the girls' poses really captured who they are. While I put everything out into the world and hope for the best, Brenda thought, Linda holds back and waits for the world to come to her, on her terms.

"Some things never change, I guess," Brenda said with a sigh, removing the keepsake and placing the frame in another packing box. She turned her attention to the cherry-stained bookcase to the right of the mantle. All the great authors were standing side by side, once upon a time daring Sarah's misfits and orphans to conquer them. Brenda ran her hand along their mostly leather spines and smiled at the memory of Sarah's gathering her heathens around her to read Dickens. Most of the kids, Brenda included, couldn't be bothered to slow down long enough for a good story, but Sarah would insist they flock around her on winter evenings as she used various voices to weave a tale of intrigue or woe that inevitably left the children with their mouths agape and asking for more. Brenda shook her head. Sarah really was a peach.

Her hand rested on a dark-burgundy leather-bound volume she didn't re-call seeing before. Feeling nostalgic, Brenda removed the book to peruse the pages and found that the author was none other than Sarah herself and that all the writing was in Sarah's own hand. Flipping quickly through the book, she noted that each page had a different date and that the last page was dated three months prior, right before Sarah had gone into the nursing home. She quickly flipped back to the first page and realized it was dated several years ago.

Brenda stepped back from the bookcase and examined the entire struc-ture, which held at least two hundred books. Squinting, she looked only for volumes that didn't have titles on their spines and, counting quickly, esti-mated there were about twenty-five. Brenda worked diligently to pack all the regular books into the moving boxes and sealed them shut before gathering the journals, all of which were bound in the same dark-burgundy leather. With the volumes scattered around her on the couch and on the coffee table, she sat down heavily, picked up the most worn, faded journal, and started to read.

November 7, 1941

Walter gave me this journal for my birthday. He told me that I'd know what to do with it, but I don't. I guess I'm supposed to write in it each day, expressing my innermost thoughts and secrets. Ha! With all that's going on in the world, I can't imagine that my concerns would rank highly enough to warrant putting pen to paper. But with that in mind, let me just say that the megalomaniac that's currently residing in Germany, the person whom President Roosevelt dismisses as a crackpot, seems to be making significant headway with regard to taking over Europe, especially with Mussolini in Italy. My friend Gerthe in Germany, with whom I have shared a pen-pal relationship for ten years, is no longer responding to my letters, leaving me to wonder if her Jewish faith has placed her in harm's way. I continue to pray for her daily.

December 12, 1941

History will dictate why I have not recently been able to capture my thoughts in this journal. My tears stain the page as I recall the horrific events of only five days ago. My beloved Walter has been called to action and will be leaving for Europe as a US soldier of the army. He won't say it, but I believe he is scared. He feels it's his patriotic duty to go, and of course he must go, but…I have a strong feeling that if he goes, he may not return. I write these words in the hope that if I expel them from my thoughts, the fear inside me will dissipate.

January 29, 1942

I cannot contain my excitement any longer and must tell someone, anyone, my wonderful news, even if it is just this silly little book! Walter and I are expecting a child! We weren't sure I could become pregnant, but clearly the Lord had different plans! Following my writing the news here, I will be writing Walter a letter forthwith. He will be absolutely dumbfounded. I miss him terribly as he's been gone for six weeks, but I hope this incredible news will see him home safely to meet his son (or daughter!).

May 5, 1942

No, no, no, no, no! I refuse to believe it! Never! My neighbor told me the rumor about heavy fighting and significant casualties, but I cannot believe it! I will not believe that the Lord would take my Walter away from me. Forgive me for saying this, but…anyone but Walter!

May 7, 1942

The telegram came today, along with two uniformed army soldiers to deliver it. I still cannot form words to express how I'm feeling.

May 13, 1942

I received a letter from Walter today dated April 22. Ironically, he asked me if I was still writing in the journal he'd given me. Walter is dead, of course, leaving me alone with this bundle in my ever-growing belly. I'm told he died a hero in Great Britain. As Germans were shelling London in late April, Walter ran to retrieve a fallen soldier and was hit with shrapnel, dying instantly, they told me. I'm numb, literally. I can't feel my legs and cannot cry.

May 17, 1942

I can't seem to stop crying. What am I going to do without Walter? How am I to support myself? Many of my friends have taken work at local factories, but I cannot given my circumstances. The stress is overwhelming. I have exactly $59.46 left in my bank account.

May 31, 1942

I lost the baby. The doctor said it was rare to have a miscarriage at five months but that it does happen from time to time when the mother is under extreme duress. He then left me alone in the room for what felt like years until a nurse came to sit with me. I wonder if more women will ever be doctors? Maybe then, since they know what it's like to be pregnant, perhaps they might be a little more empathetic when a baby is lost. I don't know what to do now. My little family is gone. I am an orphan of sorts.

Brenda lifted her head and stared blankly. She'd known that Sarah had been married to a man named Walter but had known nothing about how he'd died. Nor had she known that Sarah had lost a baby. When Brenda was about sixteen, she'd asked Sarah why she had no children of her own. Sarah had hugged Brenda hard and then looked deeply into her eyes before responding, "Brenda, my love, you and the others are my children. You're all I need."

Brenda closed the journal and ran her hand along the soft cover, remembering that Sarah had been a teacher prior to becoming a full-time foster mother. She must have decided to devote her life to children after losing Walter and the baby, Brenda thought. First as a teacher and then as a full-time foster parent.

Suddenly, Brenda realized that Sarah must have journal entries about her. She rifled through the rest of the books until she found 1982 and then paused before opening it. After all, she was invading Sarah's personal memories going through her belongings like this. On the other hand, Sarah had asked Brenda to take care of everything upon her death, so perhaps she knew that Brenda was going to see the journals. Either way, Brenda's need to know overcame the slight guilt she felt at rummaging through Sarah's past. She threw open the journal and searched the dates. Ah, there it was!

September 13, 1982
A little girl named Brenda Forsythe joined our motley crew today. She's a warm-hearted soul who's never met a stranger. I've no doubt she'll fit right in and will enjoy taking care of some of the littler ones. Poor, poor Brenda was abandoned not once but twice. Something tells me she'll pull through, though, and be the stronger for it! I will ask God this evening to take her under his wing so that one day she can fly on her own.

Brenda reread the entry several times, not quite grasping how she felt about it. *Poor, poor child was abandoned not once but twice.* Unwanted and unloved was how she'd come into Sarah's home.

Something tells me she'll pull through and be the stronger for it! That was Sarah. Brenda smiled as she realized that Sarah had willed Brenda to be strong. She wouldn't have had it any other way. Brenda returned to the entries and skipped through them until she found her name once more.

January 20, 1983

Brenda was warm and welcoming to our newest addition, Linda, whose family was killed in a house fire. Brenda seems to have found a best friend in Linda, whereas Linda is hesitant and untrusting to anyone, including Brenda. It'll take some work, but I'm sure she'll come around.

March 8, 1983

Linda sneaked out of the house again last night, trying my patience for the eighth time in a month. I'm having her see Dr. Amelia Clarke to determine the underlying issues so that I can better aid her in becoming the young woman I know she can be. She's smart as a whip and incredibly beautiful, and she knows it on both counts. A little humility might do her well.

April 24, 1983

I am becoming genuinely concerned about Linda's mental health, as she talks about her father as if he were still alive and spends time staring into nothingness, as if her mind has left her body. Dr. Clarke tells me that she believes Linda was sexually abused by her father. Linda has not said this, but Dr. Clarke believes it to be true.

May 1, 1983

I am distraught! I'm simply coming undone, and this journal is the only means of release! Dr. Clarke told me today in confidence that she believes Linda might have done harm to her family prior to the fire. It turns out that her mother had been stabbed and her sister had been bludgeoned before the fire was even started. What does this mean for Linda? Does it mean that her family's killer is somewhere out in the world and might be coming for Linda? Or does it mean that perhaps…no, I can't bring myself to write it, but you know what I'm thinking. Please, God, give me the strength and patience to help this wounded soul find your path once more, no matter what she's done.

Brenda gaped at the words as they swam across the page. Sarah's scrawled longhand became blurry as thoughts swirled and smashed into one another in Brenda's mind. She resisted the urge to call Linda. Brenda wanted to have this conversation in person, to see Linda's face as they spoke. She didn't want to believe. No, she *couldn't* believe that the friend she knew was capable of such extreme violence.

Chapter 40

"How do you like your gin, Mr. Quinn?"

"Straight up is fine. Thanks."

Brian was admiring Linda's derriere as she prepared his cocktail at the mini-bar. It hadn't taken long before he'd asked her to accompany him to his room. A little light conversation aided by gentle rubbing of her foot on his lower leg had sealed the deal, and they had vacated Flanagan's quickly and with intent.

Linda reveled in this part of the process: the foreplay. The anticipation, knowing what was coming—the control, complete domination, and finally the release—brought blood rushing to her cheeks. After completing his drink, she turned and fixed her gaze on him through her impossibly long lashes.

Placing one foot in front of the other, maximizing hip movement, she advanced toward him agonizingly slowly. Offering him the drink with her right hand, her left hand cupped his chin, lifting slightly so that he was staring directly into her eyes as she slowly unbuttoned her blouse. Brian was mesmerized as she drew the edges of her shirt back and placed her hands on her hips, fully exposing her curvaceous belly and breasts.

"How do you like it?" she asked, lips pursed.

"Beautiful," Brian breathed, not quite trusting himself with any other response.

Linda threw her head back and laughed. "Not me, Mr. Quinn, the drink. You haven't even tried your drink."

She proceeded forward and placed her mouth near his ear, whispering, "You need to relax. You're way too tense. How are you and I going to have any fun if you don't relax?" Her tongue darted into his ear and then traced the outside of it, culminating in a playful nibble on the lobe.

She drew back and gazed at him, her emerald eyes taunting and mocking at once. He threw back the drink in one large gulp and finished by wiping his mouth on his sleeve.

"How undeniably charming," she forced a smile. "Would you like another?"

"Yes, please."

She returned to the minibar, sensing her father's pride in how quickly and efficiently she had gotten her guest under control. Glancing at her watch, she felt confident she could complete her date, get a good night's sleep, and be on the plane to Boston in the morning.

"So, what do you do for a living, Ashley?" Brian's voice interrupted Linda's thoughts.

She returned to him, handed him the drink, and sat on his lap, her right hand around his shoulders and her left one slowly unbuttoning his shirt. She leaned into his neck and started kissing it, commencing at the base and working her way over until she was kissing him full on the mouth. After a time, he drew away and looked at her.

"You are remarkable," he said, slightly out of breath.

She smiled and said simply, "I know," before resuming her exploration of his body.

"But you didn't answer my question."

She pulled away and examined him straight on, determining that he was serious.

"What does it matter what I do for a living, Mr. Quinn?"

Brian shrugged. "It doesn't, I guess. Just making conversation."

Linda looked at him as if he were quite insane. *"Making conversation?"* she said, mocking him. "Is that why you're here? Because if it is, then perhaps you should leave."

She stood abruptly, gathered her open blouse around her, and glowered at him. Brian was immediately transported to the circumstances under which they had met at the bar and suddenly regarded her in a new light. Or perhaps he became able to see past the delicately composed façade. He wasn't sure why. Perhaps it was all his years interviewing people for stories, working to get at the truth amid a cacophony of lies. Or maybe it was the fact that she wouldn't divulge her line of work or that she was used to getting her way, and when she didn't, the spoiled brat emerged, down to the pout that currently sat on her luscious, full lips. For whatever reason, Brian's inner brain bristled at the idea of continuing the evening together.

"You're married, aren't you? Ashley probably isn't even your real name, is it?"

He could tell she hadn't been expecting this turn of events by the flash of anger that suddenly invaded her entire person and exited just as quickly, as if a powerful force had swept through her, leaving a bizarre mantle of calm in its wake.

Her eyes narrowed as she responded quietly. "What gave me away, Mr. Quinn?"

He smiled in response, shaking his head. "You've clearly not done this before. Cheated on your husband, I mean. You should get your backstory ready for your one-time lovers, something believable but forgettable. You know, like maybe you're a housewife, and your husband doesn't appreciate all the work you do around the house. Something like that."

Linda nodded her head sagely, as if his input were valuable to her. "Okay, okay. Let me try…how's this backstory? I'm a double MD whose husband doesn't appreciate all the work I do to support the family. I kill people because it makes me feel good and relieves my extreme stress." She tilted her head, small smile on her lips. "How's that?"

Brian shook his head. "No, no, no. Too complicated and completely not believable. Ooh…" Brian trailed off, suddenly light-headed. The room started spinning, and he saw two women standing in front of him. "I don't feel good, Ashley."

"What's wrong?"

"I dunno." Brian was slurring his words, beginning to sway back and forth. His glass, devoid of gin, fell to the carpeted floor with a dull thud while his head slowly drooped toward where the glass lay. "Did you put sumthin' in my drink?" he mumbled.

Suddenly Linda was by his side, stroking back a stray lock of hair that had fallen across his forehead. "Let go, Mr. Quinn. Let the drug do its work so that I can complete mine. Just let go."

Brian struggled to maintain focus as he lamely pawed at her to get away. His attempt to rise resulted in his crumpling to the floor, where he managed to roll over onto his back as a terrifying realization overtook him.

"Oh my guh…oh, ma guh…it's you. You're the har attack killer!" Brian's voice was a mere whisper now, but his eyes were bulging.

"Don't be ridiculous, Mr. Quinn. You yourself told me that my backstory was—what did you say, again? Oh, yes…my backstory was 'too complicated and completely unbelievable.'"

The last thing Brian saw before passing out was Linda's beautiful smile hovering over his face, close enough to kiss him good night.

CHAPTER 41

"**W**ell, well, well. The gang's all here. How fun for me," Jesse said, rolling his eyes. "What does everyone want to drink? Coffee, tea, or water?"

"Coffee."

"Coffee, please."

"Water, my good man."

"Julian, what do you want?"

"What types of teas do we have, Jess?"

Jesse sighed theatrically. "Seriously, why do you always have to be a pain in my a—"

"Jesse, we have company!" reminded Julian.

"These people aren't company, Julian, for goodness' sake. It's Alex, Vinny…who looks fabulous by the way—"

"Thank you, Jesse," Vinny smiled.

"You're so welcome. And Dr. Caruso, who's been here so many times I feel like she should get a paycheck from you."

Julian sighed. "Fine, I'll take a coffee, then."

"Perfect. Back in a flash." Jesse left Julian's office, leaving the door open.

"Does he always get his way?" Dolores asked.

"You know what? I used to fight him, but I found it's just easier to agree with him. We get more done. I still fight on the important things, though."

"And lose!" Jesse singsonged from the waiting area.

Julian laughed. "And often lose. Okay, let's get down to work. I wanted to get together to catch up on what each of you individually has been doing regarding the Evan Donaldson case. Vinny and Alex, before you arrived, Dolores and I were discussing drugs that can create a heart attack but leave no trace. Dolores, can you update these two on what you told me?"

"Sure. There are several ways to cause a myocardial infarction, or heart attack, powerful enough to kill a person, but our gal has found a way to complete her task while leaving no trace, either *on* the body or *in* the body."

"What does that mean—on the body or in the body?"

"Good question, Alex. There are no obvious markings on the skin of Mr. Donaldson's body that would indicate either trauma or an external force being applied to cause his heart to stop working."

"What kind of external force?" Vinny asked.

Dolores raised her eyebrows and slowly shook her head. "It could be something as dramatic as a defibrillator…you know, the paddles you see people use on TV to get someone's heart working again? Well, those could impose an electric current strong enough to stop a heart as well, but I would've seen markings on his skin if that were the case. But I was actually thinking about an external force such as an injection of some kind."

"I don't suppose you found any needle marks?" Alex asked dully.

"Like I said, I didn't find any obvious marks on his skin."

"You mentioned something about *in* the body too?" Vinny stated.

"Yes. His blood chemistry was slightly high for alcohol and potassium chloride, but otherwise was completely normal."

"I understand why his tox results were elevated for alcohol, considering his time spent at the bar prior to being murdered, but what would cause high potassium chloride in his blood?" asked Julian.

Dolores shrugged. "Could be a host of things, Julian. Usually a high level of potassium found in the blood is a sign that a person's kidneys are no longer functioning efficiently. High levels could also be created by extreme use of alcohol and/or drugs. But in Mr. Donaldson's case, his kidneys were healthy, and we know from interviews that he wasn't a heavy drinker and never used drugs. And let me reiterate that his potassium chloride levels were only *slightly* elevated. I'm just not sure it's relevant."

"Drinks are here!" announced Jesse a little too cheerfully given the current discussion. He passed each person a drink and placed Julian's on the coffee table in front of him—"Twelve o'clock, Julian"—and was gone as quickly as he had come, quietly closing the door behind him.

"I don't know, Dolores. Considering we have little else to go on, I'm thinking the higher potassium chloride level in his blood might be relevant. It's a place to start, anyway," Vinny finished, looking at each person in turn for support.

"Okay," started Julian, warming up to Vinny's idea, "can a really high level of potassium chloride kill someone, Dolores?"

"Absolutely. Hyperkalemia, or high potassium in your blood, usually builds slowly over time, eventually causing heart palpitations, abnormalities, and finally death. But it takes a while for the levels to build up, Julian."

"Well, that's no good for our case, is it?" Alex said dejectedly.

Dolores pursed her lips in thought. "Wait a minute, Alex. If someone were to inject a large amount of potassium chloride directly into a person's vein, a myocardial infarction is very likely to occur, and pretty fast."

Alex shook her head. "But if the perp had done that, we'd see even higher levels of potassium chloride on the toxicology results, wouldn't we?"

Dolores took a sip of her coffee. "All of us have potassium in our blood. We need it to survive. If we take in more than we need, our bodies metabolize what we can use and then the rest exits as waste. Depending on how long our killer spent with Mr. Donaldson before he died and how much potassium she injected into him—"

"Wait a minute, Dolores. You told us that you found no needle marks on his body, so how could she have injected him?" Vinny said.

"I'm sorry," she started, waving her hand in the air. "Let me be clear. The only way to kill someone using potassium chloride is to inject it. Pills wouldn't be strong enough. And you're right, Vinny. I found no needle marks on the body. Not between the toes, behind the ears—all the places people might use in order to hide needle marks. I don't know what to tell you, but

I think we're back at square one. Perhaps the potassium chloride thing isn't relevant."

"What about the scalp?" interjected a voice from the doorway. Jesse had opened the door and had been listening, unnoticed.

Julian turned toward his voice and smiled. "Jesse James, sometimes you say things, and I think, Wow! What an idiot! And other times, like this one, I think, Wow! You're amazing!"

Vinny, confused, ignored Julian's comment and asked, "What about the scalp?"

Dolores was already nodding her head. "Jesse, if you ever get tired of working with Julian, give my office a call. You're right. It's extremely rare, but a scalp injection could have occurred."

"Did you check Mr. Donaldson's scalp?" Alex asked, leaning forward in her seat.

"Sort of. You see—"

"What the hell does 'sort of' mean?" demanded Vinny a little too loudly.

Dolores appeared wounded as everyone stopped and stared at Vinny, who immediately apologized and sank back into the leather couch. Running a hand over his stubbled face, he grimaced and said "Listen, it's been a rough couple of days. I'm sorry, Dolores. I didn't mean to jump down your throat like that. I know you're doing the best you can."

Before continuing, Dolores paused and glanced at Alex, who nodded as if to say, "It's okay. I'll explain later."

"I did check Mr. Donaldson's scalp as much as I was able, leaving his hair intact. Normally I would have shaved his head to complete a thorough skin investigation, but his parents specifically requested that his hair be left alone. They plan on having a viewing and didn't want him wearing a wig of any kind."

"What about the other victims? Did you happen to ask those cities' medical examiners if they found any needle marks on those folks?" Julian asked.

"I did, actually," Dolores sighed. "Their answers were all no. All the other victims had their heads shaved and examined, and none of them found any needle markings at all on the bodies or the scalps of the vics."

"God, this is so frustrating!" Alex said, slamming her fist on the coffee table and causing Julian to jump in his chair. "Sorry, Julian," Alex mumbled, "but I feel like we've gotten nothing for so much work. Nothing on the security tapes except a fucking pinky ring, nothing from any of the autopsies. Hey, Vinny, were you able to run down the names of the female trade-show participants in Boston? Did anything pop from that?"

Vinny shook his head, his face as long as a hound dog's. "I ran all the names, and the worst offender had four unpaid parking tickets, that's it. Interviews have turned up zilch. Believe me, Alex, I'm as frustrated as you are. I'm running out of time, my ass is really on the line here, and we got nothing. Absolutely nothing."

CHAPTER 42

Brian Bosch, a.k.a. Jason Quinn, lay prone on the bed in his hotel room. His head felt like it had been slammed with a sledgehammer, and as hard as he tried, he couldn't recall why. His last memory was jumping out of the elevator and smiling at the mother and her child. Then where had he gone? Ah, the bar. Did I drink too much? he wondered. Brian closed his eyes and desperately tried to remember as visions swam through his head. The bar, a woman, a disagreement, flirting, gin in a glass here in this room and—

His eyes popped open as he heard the bathroom door open.

"Oh, you're finally awake. I thought you were going to miss all the fun. Well," she chuckled, "the rest of the fun."

The woman—Ashley, he suddenly remembered—approached the bed and leaned in to kiss him. A towel graced her lovely body, and even under the circumstances, he could still appreciate her beauty.

"Still a bit groggy? It's understandable. I put a fair amount of Rohypnol in your gin, Jason...or should I call you Brian?" Her head tilted as her smile disappeared.

Brian was confused. She'd given him Rohypnol, the date-rape drug? *Why?*

"You're probably wondering why I gave you a Roofie," she said, as if she had read his mind. "I needed you groggy so that I could do this."

As she opened her purse and pulled out a syringe, terror seized Brian. His mind flew back to the words he'd mumbled prior to passing out: "You're the heart attack killer!" He blanched, realizing with horror that he was in the presence of pure evil.

As he attempted to rise, nausea and vertigo impeded his feeble efforts. Linda mocked him and imitated his trying to get up.

"It's no use, honey. I've done this before, and I know my dosages. Speaking of which…"

Linda held the syringe up to the lamplight, flicked it twice with her finger, and pushed the plunger slightly, allowing one drop of succinylcholine to ejaculate. "We wouldn't want any air to get into your artery when I give you this injection. That would cause a premature death and, honestly, would be so disappointing to me." She pulled a pouty face.

Brian was trying to shake his head, his brain racing to figure a way out of this nightmare. His eyes darted back and forth in their sockets, searching for something that might help him.

"Shh…it's okay, really," Linda breathed, coming closer and sitting next to him on the bed. "It's going to be better for both of us if you just relax." She stroked his thinning hair and smiled as she gazed lovingly into his eyes. "You think you don't want this, but you actually do. Otherwise you would have asked me to stop. And you haven't asked me to stop, have you?" she asked him, her eyebrows raised.

Brian moaned. It was the best he could manage.

Linda smiled and kissed his flaccid lips. "That's what I thought. Now, here's what's going to happen. The drug in this syringe is succinylcholine, or sux, for short. It will paralyze you by working at the junction of the nerves and muscles in your body."

Brian tried to rise again and was rewarded for his efforts by accidentally moving closer to Linda, who waited patiently, watching him struggle.

"May I continue, please? Anyway, although you'll be awake the entire time, this drug will paralyze your entire body, including your lungs, so you could asphyxiate very quickly. But I don't want you to worry, because that won't happen to you, I promise."

Linda smiled again, feeling Brian's relief flow over her, energizing her.

Brian's eyes relaxed somewhat as he realized that although Ashley was a crazy, sick son of a bitch, she wasn't going to kill him. As his mental clarity increased, he vowed that when this nightmare was over, he would write a kick-ass story about this experience that would land him back on top in the reporting world and make all those assholes who turned their backs on him suffer. After that, he was going to track this insane bitch down and exact a vengeance that would ruin her career and her life. He almost smiled.

Linda noted Brian's attempt at a smile and placed her hand on his heart. "That's the spirit," she said. "We should both enjoy this, because before we know it, it's all going to be over."

Before he could react, she leaned forward, grabbed his hair with her left hand, and yanked his head to the right. The syringe appeared before his eyes and disappeared to his left, and he felt a sharp sting and then warmth as the drug entered his temporal artery, above his left ear under his hair.

Releasing her grip on his hair, she eased his head back to the pillow. "This should take effect relatively quickly, although I used a small dose to give us some time."

Feeling a chill as the drug worked its way through the veins and arteries in his body, Brian focused on the sensations the drug created, because he needed to explain it clearly to his readers when he wrote his story. His mind clearer now, he started thinking about other information he'd need for the article.

"W-w-w...," he stammered.

"Wow?" Linda asked. "Yes, I know. Sux works fast."

"W-w-wh..." Brian tried again.

"Why?" Linda finished for him. "That's not so easy to answer, Mr. Quinn...or should I call you Mr. Bosch? I had some time to check you out while you were napping, and I discovered that you have quite a history in the newspaper biz, and now you're with the *National Informer*. Tsk, tsk, tsk. Cheating and plagiarizing...not impressive, Mr. Bosch, not at all. But to answer your question, it's not that I *want* to do this, Brian, it's that I *must*. I have no choice, really."

"Y-y-yeh..." Brian stammered.

Anger flashed in Linda's eyes, bright green and laser-like as they bored into Brian. "No! You're wrong, Brian! I have no choice! None at all! Sarah may have thought I did, and even I might have thought I did at one time, but it's become clear to me now that I *don't* have a choice. This MUST be done to regain and maintain order in my life! Once this is done, he'll leave me alone, and I can...I can...I can be normal!"

She thrust herself from the bed and paced furiously back and forth, from one side of the bed to the other. Her fingers ran incessantly through her hair, and Brian saw strands coming out as she raked her nails through. Throwing the towel to the floor, she halted in front of the full-length mirror.

From where Brian lay on the bed, he could see the side of her face as she examined her body, commencing at her feet. By the time her inspection finished, her visage had contorted into an ugly mask that he no longer recognized, and for the first time in this horrific process, he felt truly afraid for his life. As she turned and approached him once more, he recognized that she wasn't the same person he'd seen several minutes earlier. She was mumbling to herself, and Brian was able to discern the same phrases over and over again. "I know, Daddy! Order is imperative! I know!"

Suddenly, she sank to the ground as if struck by something. When she rose once more, Brian saw that she had dug her fingernails into her abdomen and was scraping them across slowly, leaving a trail of jagged skin and blood in their wake. Even more terrifying, she was completely silent, and her face had morphed once more into a mask of serenity. Mascara streaked her cheeks, but a thousand-watt smile graced her countenance, and her eyes exuded peace.

Brian's body started involuntarily shaking. As his bladder and bowels released, he managed to turn his near-paralyzed eyes away from the horror he knew was coming. There would be no story rocketing him once again to the top of the reporting food chain, no vengeance on this clearly sociopathic freak show hovering over him.

"Brian, Brian, sweetheart, you've created quite a mess, my love. But I don't mind. I'll ask you once more, though, just to be sure. Do you want me to stop?"

Brian stared without blinking because his eye muscles were completely paralyzed. He was finding it difficult to breathe, as she'd said would happen.

"Any sign at all, and I'll stop."

She waited.

"No? Then let's proceed. I see that you can't breathe very well. You're probably concerned about that, but I'm a woman of my word, and I told you that you wouldn't die of asphyxiation."

She produced another syringe. Brian's eyes were stinging due to lack of moisture, and he desperately wanted to fill his lungs with air.

"This last drug will take care of everything, Brian. I'm going to inject it into the same artery I did before, okay? You're going to feel better soon."

For some delirious reason, he believed her and eagerly anticipated the injection. As the drug entered his bloodstream, it traveled quickly to his heart, which started spasming. Despite his paralysis, he could feel his heart beating fast, too fast, and then pain spreading across his chest, down his left arm, and up into his jaw. His vision fractured into a thousand small points of light, and before his consciousness imploded into nothingness, Linda appeared before him, a look of euphoric tranquility on her perfect face.

Out of respect, she continued to stroke his hair until the light had completely faded from his eyes. A sense of loss overcame her as the magical moment dissipated, so Linda sat quietly, reliving the ecstasy of the moment he'd realized he was going to die. In her mind, she could recall the emotions that played across his eyes: first confusion, followed by understanding, then fear, pleading and, finally, resignation. She lived those emotions with him yet with the knowledge that she alone dictated his future. His powerlessness fueled her need to control and dominate, building and writhing until the moment of the final injection, when all her pent-up frustration and self-loathing fluttered away as he expelled his last breath. She was whole again, her world in order once more.

Linda closed her eyes as she reflected on the only other thing that gave her this kind of thrill. When she could save a life, when a child was going to live because of her skills as a physician, she felt whole and calm, in control.

Linda's eyes snapped open as reality smashed her composure. She hadn't contacted Mrs. Cartwright to alert her to Sabrina's declining health. Linda looked around the room and then at her watch.

It was 11:37 p.m. She'd have to clean up here, go back to her room, get some sleep, and then call Mrs. Cartwright first thing in the morning on the way to the airport. Her hands clad in latex rubber gloves, she went about the room, tidying up here and there, arranging the hangers in the closet so they were equidistantly apart, organizing his toiletries in the bathroom, position-ing his underwear and socks in the drawer, and finally wiping down the room for fingerprints, placing special emphasis on Brian's gin glass, which she had touched. Tucking the used Clorox wipes into her purse, she turned down the room's thermostat to sixty-two degrees and then returned to Brian's side to kneel next to his body. She reached into her purse and removed a pair of round, tortoiseshell-framed reading glasses. Placing them gently on the night-stand, she smoothed down Brian's hair and arranged his covers so that they came up to his chin.

"So sorry to have to leave you so soon, my love. You'll always be very special to me."

Kissing him lightly on the lips, she whispered, "See you in hell."

CHAPTER 43

L inda awoke at 6:43 a.m. without needing an alarm. She sat up and smiled as the morning sunshine peeked through the heavy hotel curtains. Starting with her toes, she spent several minutes stretching each muscle in her body until she felt completely relaxed.

"Maybe I should book myself a massage," she said aloud. "I've certainly earned it."

Throwing back the covers, she hopped out of bed and made her way to the bathroom, where she showered quickly and blew her hair dry. She then stood in front of the mirror, deciding how to wear her hair. After all, to-day was Sarah's funeral. Linda wanted to look dignified and smart, as Sarah would have insisted on that. Deciding on a French twist, she swept up her locks and had them pinned beautifully in less than a minute. She applied a light base with SPF 30, minimal blush, some light eye shadow, and waterproof mascara, in case waterworks started at the funeral. She crossed to the closet and removed the silk-and-cotton suit she had brought with her. The color was a deep, rich green, Sarah's favorite color on Linda because it matched her eyes, Sarah used to say. She dressed quickly and then evaluated herself in the mirror. Satisfied, she packed her suitcase and made her way downstairs to the front desk, where Ashley, the same clerk from the night before, greeted her with a grin.

"Good morning, Dr. Sterling. How lovely you look in that beautiful suit! Going somewhere special today?"

"I am. I'm going to the funeral of a very good friend of mine today. She raised me, actually," Linda finished, her voice faltering a little.

"Oh, I'm so very sorry to hear that. Hopefully she lived a good life?"

Linda looked at Ashley thoughtfully for a moment before answering. "She lived the best of all lives, Ashley. She was the most wonderful, loving, giving, selfless person I've ever met."

"Well, we could all take a lesson from her legacy, then, couldn't we? Sounds like a special lady."

"She was," Linda said, smiling.

"Checking out then?"

"Yes, thank you."

"Did you make it over to the Hilton last night?" Ashley asked as she processed Linda's credit card.

"I beg your pardon?" Linda asked, caught by surprise.

"The Hilton. You had asked me if there were any trade shows in town, and I had told you that there was one at the Hilton."

"Oh, that," Linda scoffed. "I was simply trying to avoid the trade shows. They're such a nightmare with all the people and traffic, you know? That's all. No, I certainly would never seek one out."

Ashley nodded. "Now, that makes more sense to me. I agree. It seems like many of the attendees use the show as an opportunity to act out and misbehave, if you know what I mean."

Linda gave Ashley her most precious smile. "I know exactly what you mean, and I couldn't agree more, my dear. Have a great day."

Linda caught a cab in front of the Radisson and ordered the driver to the airport. As she settled into the seat for the short ride, her phone buzzed, indicating a new voicemail. She pressed the play button, and Catherine's breathless voice spoke loudly and without pause.

"Hi Mommy I miss you so much when are you coming home because Daddy and I are going on a trip I told him that you should be coming too but he said it was just for him and me but I'll see you soon I'm sure and I'll bring you something back from Disney World okay bye I love you!"

As Linda was registering what Catherine had said, Jonathan's husky voice came on the recording.

"Listen, Lin, Catherine and I are going to Disney World for about a week. I just need to think things through. It's just that you…it's just that we…listen, I can't do this anymore. I can't be a single parent all the time. It might be okay if when you came home you were actually…home, but you're not. It's like your mind is somewhere else all the time, and you're not the same person, Lin. You've changed. Or maybe I've changed…I don't know. The last time we had sex, you were really mean…cruel even." Jonathan paused and took a deep breath. "Let's talk about this when Catherine and I get back from Disney World. I'd ask you to come, but I know you'd have something more important to do."

The line went dead, and Linda's arms went numb. He's taking my baby away from me, she thought. That sniveling coward waited until I left and is stealing my child. Who knows if he'll even return? Maybe they're not going to Disney World. Maybe he's kidnapping her and going to South America or Europe. How dare he! Who the hell does he think he's dealing with? The fucking moron!

She vowed to hunt him down, get Catherine back, and divorce his ass as soon as possible. God knows he could be replaced by next week.

Hell, he'll be lucky if I don't have him killed.

That brought a smile to her lips.

Perhaps I'll do it myself. Now *that* would bring some release.

"That'll be seven fifty, ma'am."

Linda paid the driver, exited the cab, and made her way through security to the gate for the flight to Boston. At the gate, she settled into a seat partially secluded from fellow passengers, opened her laptop, and scrolled through her e-mails until she found the one from Thelma that contained the test results for Sabrina Cartwright.

Opening the lab report, her eyebrows knit in concentration as she processed how dramatically Sabrina's blood had changed for the worse in less than a week. Linda then opened the MRI report and read the radiologist's notes, which indicated that Sabrina's cancer had spread to her lungs and several more of her lymph nodes. As if that weren't enough, Sabrina had contracted a serious infection, not uncommon when undergoing chemotherapy and radiation. Linda hung her head in despair and focused on her breathing.

Once she felt she had her emotions under control, she dialed Mrs. Cartwright's cell number. Part of her wanted the call to go to voicemail while the other part wanted to share the awful news, as if relaying it would unburden her of the responsibility of Sabrina's life.

"Hello?" Mrs. Cartwright answered cheerfully.

"Mrs. Cartwright, this is Dr. Linda Sterling. How are you today?"

"Well, I was doing well until I just heard the tone of your voice, Dr. Sterling. Why are you calling?"

Linda looked down at the floor and rubbed her forehead with her left hand. "It's Sabrina's white blood-cell count, Mrs. Cartwright. She has several things going on in her body right now."

"I know, Dr. Sterling. The girl has cancer. I'd say that's a lot going on in a little seven-year-old body, wouldn't you?"

Linda shook her head. She needed to think clearly and explain things properly. This mother deserved nothing less.

"Let me start again. Because Sabrina has been undergoing chemo and radiation, the number of white blood cells in her body—the ones responsible for fighting off infections—has decreased. If the white blood cells decrease too much, an infection can occur, making them rise once more. This is what's happened with Sabrina. We thought her body was winning the fight against the cancer by creating more white blood cells, but it turns out that the rise was due to an infection. In the meantime, the cancer was spreading and is now in various other parts of her body. Does this make any sense?"

Linda listened to Mrs. Cartwright's even, measured breathing on the other end of the line. She could only imagine what was going through this heartbroken mother's mind.

"Do you have children, Dr. Sterling?"

Linda had made similar calls many times and had dealt with various responses—anger, resentment, sadness, disbelief—but this was the worst of all: personal pragmatism. Mrs. Cartwright was about to give up, not on Sabrina, but on Linda. She was going to let go of the one buoy in the horrible storm that is cancer: hope. Linda represented hope, and Mrs. Cartwright was going to forgive Linda that mantle of responsibility. Linda wasn't sure she could take it.

Thinking of her perfect little Catherine, Linda's hand covered her mouth.

"Yes, I do, Mrs. Cartwright. A little girl."

"And what is your little girl's name?"

"Catherine."

"And how old is your little Catherine, Dr. Sterling?"

"She's five years old."

"I see. Well, I hope you cherish every second you have with her, Dr. Sterling, because before you know it, she'll be grown and gone. I know I've enjoyed each moment I've been privileged to have with my lovely Sabrina. Did you know that we named her after a character that Audrey Hepburn played in a movie of the same name?"

Linda smiled weakly. "No, I didn't know that."

"Yes. My husband and I are big Audrey Hepburn fans. The grace and dignity she showed throughout her life is rivaled only by the strength and courage my little girl has shown throughout this unimaginable ordeal. You know, in a way, it's almost comforting to know that it'll all be over soon. I hope you don't think that sounds morose or melodramatic, but it's true. Her pain will end soon, won't it?"

By answering yes, Linda was acknowledging that she, too, was giving up. But she couldn't lie to a woman who had already suffered so much.

"Yes. I'd say Sabrina has about two weeks left based on the cancer's aggressive growth. Mrs. Cartwright, I'm so—"

"Sorry? Is that what you were going to say, Dr. Sterling? Don't be sorry. I appreciate what you're saying, but you tried your best. If it weren't for you, Sabrina wouldn't have blessed our world for as long as she has. You extended her life, Dr. Sterling. I'm sure about that. Don't you ever be sorry for trying your best."

"There are some things we could try. There's a clinical trial underway in—"

"Dr. Sterling, please don't. I've thought long and hard about this potential outcome, and I'd prefer that the time Sabrina has left be as pain-free as possible. I want her to die with dignity, under circumstances she dictates, as much as that's possible. Do you understand?"

Linda squeezed the bridge of her nose, staving off the tears she knew were imminent.

"I do, and I respect what you're saying. I'll call Thelma at the hospital and update her on our conversation. When I return, we'll all sit down and determine how to make Sabrina's transition as pleasant as possible, okay?"

"You are truly a godsend, Dr. Sterling. Your compassion is what makes you stand out as a physician and a human being. Please don't forget that."

While Mrs. Cartwright pressed the end button on her phone and entered her daughter's room to tell her the news, Linda sat quietly in the terminal, staring at her computer screen, slow tears rolling down her face.

"Well you've done it again, Pippin. You've managed to kill another child with your incompetent medical practices."

Linda leaned forward and placed her head in her hands. *I can't deal with you right now, Daddy. I did what you asked in Providence, so please leave me alone.*

"Don't you understand, Pippin? I'm never going to leave you. Ever."

Linda lifted her head, and he was there, standing in front of her, an accusatory look on his face, arms folded across his chest.

"Catherine and Jonathan are gone, Sarah's dead, and Sabrina is dying. Your life is out of order, and you've lost the ability to control anything."

Linda scowled at her father and snarled, "Leave me alone, or else!" in a voice she didn't recognize as her own.

He laughed at her then, the strong, hearty laugh she remembered from her childhood before everything went so horribly, horribly wrong.

"Or else what?" he asked her, genuinely amused.

She glanced around and saw that people were staring at her. Wiping the tears from her face, she removed a tissue from her purse, blew her nose, closed her laptop, and gathered her belongings. Standing up and throwing her head back proudly, she responded, "Test me, and you'll find out."

CHAPTER 44

Vinny's cell phone buzzed at 11:03 a.m., indicating he had a text. It read, "Call me ASAP. Steffy."

Vinny dialed immediately, and Steffy answered on the first ring, as if she had been waiting for the call.

"Hey, Vin, it's been a while. How are you?"

"Good, I'm good, Steffy. How's the Providence PD going for you? The guys still giving you a hard time about those smokin' hot legs you got?"

"Not now, Vin. I'm calling because I got some news for you on the down low. You know how you said I should contact you if I ever ran across something the Feebs might like a piece of? Well, I heard through the grapevine that you're unofficially looking for some heart attack serial killer, and I think he struck here last night."

Vinny's heart began to race, and he felt flush. "Why do you say that?"

"Well, some dude bought it last night in a local hotel. Maid found him this morning laying in bed like nothing happened. Covers up to his chin. But I know about the reading glasses the perp leaves as his calling card, and there they were on the bedside table."

"What about the closet and drawers and bathroom?"

"What do you mean?"

"Were they ridiculously organized? Hangers exactly so far apart? That kind of thing."

"Uh…I'm not sure 'cause I wasn't called to the scene, but I can check and get back to you."

"Do that. And…Steff?"

"Yeah?"

"Let me know if there's any security video available."

"Got it."

"I owe you big time."

"Don't you worry, Vin. I'll collect. Count on it."

Vinny rang off and dialed Alex, who answered on the third ring, sounding epically pissed off.

"Alex Hayes!" she almost yelled into the phone.

"Bad day?" Vinny asked.

Alex breathed out heavily. "The day was fine until my friggin' mother called and got on me about my relationship with Julian—why am I not married? Do I know how old I am and that my biological clock is going to eventually stop ticking? That kind of bullshit. Of course I know how fucking old I am!"

Vinny rolled his eyes.

"Yeah, sounds awful. Listen, Alex, I just got a call from a friend of mine in the Providence PD—"

"Rhode Island?"

"Yeah, Rhode Island. And she told me that our gal killed a guy there last night in a local hotel."

"Huh. She's ramping up her timetable, killing more frequently. What are the details?"

"Same MO. Glasses on the nightstand, covers up to the chin. Steffy's checking into security footage and if the bathroom and closet were neurotically organized."

"Okay. You going down there?"

"I'll be on the next flight out of Logan. Want to come?"

"I'd like to, but I haven't spent much time with Julian recently, so he and I are having lunch at one. You good without me?"

"Yeah, yeah. It's fine. I'll keep you posted."

Alex hung up and called Julian's office.

"Dr. Julian Stryker's office. This is Jesse. How may I help you?"

"Well, good morning, Jesse. You sound chipper. Is it because of Mr. Right? Or should I say Mr. Right Now?"

"Clearly you've been hanging around with Julian too long, because you're starting to develop his horrendous sense of humor, Alex. Work on that, will you, please? Now, what can I do you for?"

"Is Julian around?"

"He's with a patient right now. Oh, wait…their session just ended. They're walking out. Hold a sec."

Alex heard the familiar chit chat that accompanied Julian's goodbyes with his patients. She then heard a click, brief music (Bee Gees, she thought), and then Julian came on the line.

"Hey, you. What's shakin'?"

"You really need to change your hold music, Julian. Really, the Bee Gees?"

Julian laughed. She loved the sound of his laugh. It was so genuine and deep. One of the many, many things she loved about him.

"Is that why you called? To harass me about my music?"

"Yes. That and to tell you two more things. My loving mother called this morning, obsessing about our relationship. Do you mind if she joins us at lunch today so that she can be reminded of how perfect we are together just the way we are?"

"I don't mind. The question is, do you?"

"Of course I mind, but if this'll get her off my back for a while, then I'm up for it."

Julian smiled. "Sure. Whatever makes her and you happy."

"Thank you. And secondly, Vinny called to say that psycho bitch struck again in Providence. He's on his way down there. He'll keep us informed."

"Wow. She's really stepping up her game, isn't she? Definitely increasing her kill rate. Something must have happened to trigger the change in her pattern. Vinny should be really meticulous on this one, because the fact that she's killing more frequently means that she's more likely to make a mistake. Let's just hope he can get to her before she kills again."

"She's unraveling?"

"Big time. We should expect another kill soon, and it may not follow her familiar pattern. If she's becoming this unstable, then she might kill by opportunity versus planning everything out as she's done so far. The next victim, if there is one, may be her most gruesome yet."

"God, this is awful. The fact that these men *know* they're going to die is horrific. She's really twisted and sick, isn't she?"

"Yes and no. Her acts are cruel and inhumane, but remember—she's most likely fueled by something that happened in her past, maybe over an extended period of time."

"So, we should forgive her?" Alex asked in disbelief.

"No, of course not. But I don't think we should so easily dismiss her as a monster, either. She's so broken that she needs to kill in order to feel better... for a short time, at least. The positive feelings she gets from murdering are most likely becoming less fulfilling—hence the need to kill more frequently to obtain that high. Eventually, no amount of death will be enough, and that's when she'll either explode or implode."

"What do you mean?"

"Well, history shows that one of three things happen with people like this. One, they go on a rampage murder spree that results in suicide by cop, or two, they kill themselves before the cops get the chance to kill them."

"Either way, she'll be dead, and the world will be a better place."

"That's a simplistic view, don't you think, Alex?"

"No, Julian, I don't. When you do what I do for a living and see the worst that human nature has to offer day in and day out, you become a little black and white on issues. Gray is a dangerous place to live."

Julian chuckled.

"What's so funny?"

"A patient whom I'm unofficially seeing right now said the same thing not so long ago—that she couldn't live in my gray world. You two are kind of similar, now that I think about it. Beautiful, driven, intelligent—"

"Hey, buster, don't get any ideas."

"Never in a million years would I think about trading you in. I'd inevitably be trading down, and why would I want to do that?"

"Good to hear. Well, I gotta go. I'll pick you up for lunch at one at your office, okay?"

"Sounds good. I love you."

"I love you more. See you. Oh, wait…Julian?"

"Yeah?"

"You said there were three things that might happen with this kind of killer. What was the third?"

Julian sighed.

"The third is that sometimes, and I mean rarely, the murderer has had enough, has managed to kill or suppress whatever demons drove him or her, and simply stops killing. They go to their graves at a ripe old age with their secrets intact. They literally get away with murder."

Alex shook her head. "All I can say is that in my black-and-white world, there's a special place in hell for those psychotic assholes. They may not get what they deserve in this world, but they sure as shit are going to get it in the next one."

CHAPTER 45

Brenda sat in the first pew St. Stephen's Catholic Church, enjoying the relative quiet prior to the commencement of Sarah's funeral service. The casket was simple—a light cherry stain with small brass accents, as Sarah had directed. A basket of freshly cut daisies lay below it, awaiting the arrival of the mourners, who were to place one flower each on Sarah's casket as they came to pay their respects. Brenda examined her daisy. Such a basic flower, but it was exquisite in its simplicity. Like Sarah herself.

Brenda smiled, remembering words Sarah had imparted to them in their youth. "Remember, children, you don't need to be fancy, rich, or famous to have a positive impact on the world. Success starts with getting up in the morning and making a promise to yourself to be the very best person you can be that day. Kindness, character, and integrity. Giving more than you take. That will make you successful in everything you do."

She glanced at the flower again and whispered, "I'm going to continue to make you proud, Sarah, as God is my witness. And I'll talk to Linda today. She's going to make you proud, too."

Brenda's thoughts were interrupted by a small group of eightysomethings slowly making their way toward her. Brenda got up to meet them, arms outstretched.

"Thanks for coming," she managed before breaking down once more. In the end, it was they who comforted her as they sat together, waiting for the service to begin.

"Ladies and gentlemen, in preparation for landing, we ask that you stow your tray tables and place your seats in the upright position. This plane is turning right around and heading back to Providence from Boston upon your deplaning, so please help us flight attendants out and clean the area around you, including the pocket on the back of the seat in front of you. Thank you."

The plane landed, and Linda was the eighth person to disembark. As she exited the Jetway into the airport, one of the female gate attendants commented, "Ma'am, you look stunning in that color."

"Well, thank you very much," Linda said, inclining her head in response. When she looked up, she saw that she was walking toward the passengers waiting to board the plane, and one man in particular caught her eye. Tall, dark, and handsome—Italian, she presumed. He looked tired, and his shirt was unironed. Two days of stubble clung to his chiseled face, and she couldn't help but wonder if he might be Jonathan's replacement, the next Mr. Sterling. A little frumpy, but we could definitely spruce him up. It wouldn't take much, she found herself thinking.

As if sensing her scrutiny, the man locked eyes with Linda, sending a shiver down her spine. She was unsure sure what it was—sexual tension...or the fact that he had the look of a hunter seeking prey—but he held the same expression she wore when searching for her perfect date. Either way, she couldn't hold his gaze and felt compelled to avert her eyes.

Continuing away from the gate toward the taxi stand, she glanced back to find him watching her intently, an inscrutable expression on his face.

ᛉ

Alex was in the stall when she heard the bathroom door bang open.

"Alex, are you in here?"

"Dolores? Is that you?"

"Oh, good, you *are* in here."

"What the hell?" Alex asked. "Seriously, you couldn't wait until I was back at my desk?"

"Well, they told me you were in here, and I needed to talk to you right away."

"Clearly," Alex said sarcastically as she flushed the toilet and came out to wash her hands. "What's so important that it couldn't wait two minutes?"

Dolores was practically jumping up and down.

"I have a cut on my leg that I got while gardening last week. It's healing nicely."

Alex burst out laughing and looked at Dolores with a wrinkled brow.

"I'm really glad to hear that, but what does that have to do with anything?"

"Skin cells regenerate all the time. It's the largest organ we have in, or on, our bodies, did you know that?"

"Again, fascinating, but why is that important to me?"

"Skin cells regenerate for several days after our hearts and brains stop functioning."

"You mean after we die, skin cells keep growing for a while?"

"Yes. That's exactly what I mean."

Alex dried her hands. "That's amazing. Thanks so much for coming into the bathroom to tell me that." Alex opened the bathroom door and walked out, Dolores trailing closely behind her.

"I don't think you're getting what I'm saying, Alex. The heart attack killer uses an in—"

Alex stopped and turned around so suddenly that Dolores bumped into her.

"You were about to say that the heart attack killer uses an injection to murder but that we couldn't find any needle marks."

"Yes…" Dolores answered, her eyes wide and tone suggestive, willing Alex to continue her thought process in order to arrive at the same conclusion Dolores had.

"Because after death, the skin kept generating cells, thereby potentially covering up any needle marks."

"Yes. On skin that's exposed every day—arms, legs, feet—the skin cells keep regenerating after death for a couple of days but usually not enough to hide a needle mark. However, if an *extremely* thin needle were used and the injection were made under the hairline, where skin-cell generation is protected, the coroner might miss the injection site upon autopsy, especially if the procedure were done several days after death."

Alex was nodding her head. "And how long after death were the autopsies done in each of the other cities' heart attack deaths?"

Dolores opened a file she'd been carrying. "Baltimore—three days; New York—five days; and Philadelphia—four days."

"Is that enough time for the skin to have created enough new cells to hide a small injection sight under the hairline?"

Dolores smiled broadly. "You bet."

"What about our own Mr. Donaldson? You said the family wouldn't allow you to shave his head?"

"I contacted them and told them that by allowing me to shave Mr. Donaldson's head, they might be helping the police stop a serial killer. When I put it that way, they were kind enough to agree."

Alex grabbed both of Dolores's shoulders. "And?"

"I found this." Dolores opened the file folder once more to show Alex a close-up of a shaved scalp. A tiny hole was clearly visible above his left ear.

"Oh my God," Alex breathed.

"Mr. Donaldson had been dead only two days, so the injection site was not yet covered by new skin. Another day or two, and I never would've found this."

Alex hugged Dolores hard and said, "You're the best!" before running down the hall to call Julian and Vinny.

"Alex, wait! There's something else you need to know," Dolores yelled.

Alex turned and retraced her steps, flushed and out of breath. "What?"

"This injection was made directly into the left temporal artery. It's like a highway that leads directly to the brain and the heart."

"Okay, so what?"

"It's not an obvious choice for an injection. It takes great skill and precision to inject there without causing unwanted problems for the person being injected. It's a small artery, and the recipient would have to be very, very still to ensure success."

"What are you saying, Dolores?"

"I'm saying that the victims would have had to have been heavily sedated, maybe even paralyzed, when the injection occurred. And the drugs that are being used in these crimes aren't easily obtainable by anyone outside the medical community. If you combine that information with the fact that the perp must have exact knowledge of the human body in order to complete these appalling acts, I'm thinking that she might be at the very least a nurse but more likely a physician."

⅄

Vinny boarded the plane and ran his hand over his chin as he buckled up for the short flight from Boston to Providence. I need to shave soon. I must look like a homeless guy, he thought.

His phone chirped.

"Vinny Marcozzi."

"Hey, Vin, it's Steffy. You were right. The hangers in the closet were all exactly four inches apart, and the bathroom looked as if it had never been used. Shampoo and everything lined up perfectly. Also, he had sex before he died."

"That matches with the other poor saps who died. I don't suppose there were any prints?"

"We're running them through IAFIS now."

"You probably won't get a hit. We haven't so far."

"All right. Well, I'll let you know if we do. Oh…also, I got the security footage. The camera was facing away from the vic's door, but there are several people walking in the hallway before and after the murder, so you can check it out and see what you think. Maybe something'll pop. I'm sending it as an e-mail attachment right now."

"Thanks, Steff. Talk to you soon."

As the plane taxied toward the runway, Vinny immediately went to his e-mail account and downloaded the footage. Tilting his phone sideways to enlarge the picture for review, he touched the large arrow to play the video.

Steffy was right. There were at least seven people in the hallway around the time of death, but only one captured his attention.

A tall, curvy brunette was walking—no, strutting—down the hallway, hips swaying rhythmically as if to a song only she could hear. A travel suitcase trailed behind her, and as she approached the elevator, she slowly turned and looked directly at the camera. A secretive smile sat on her lips as she raised one eyebrow and winked at Vinny.

"Oh my God," Vinny whispered, reaching to press the flight attendant call button. He had to turn the plane around and try to catch the woman who'd locked eyes with him prior to getting on the plane. Midreach, he remembered that he held no official status as an FBI agent and therefore possessed no authority to order the plane grounded.

Instead, he forwarded the footage to Alex and phoned her as well, but the call went straight to voicemail. "Alex, our perp's in Boston, and I think we have her on the security footage I forwarded to you. We're about to take off, so I'm going to have to turn off my phone, but I'll call you when I get to the hotel. In the meantime, review the footage, and you'll see who I mean. She got off the flight from Providence—Delta 875—as I was getting on. Check the flight manifest."

Vinny rang off and put his phone in airplane mode while an annoyed flight attendant looked on. He wasn't much of a praying man, but he did take the time to send a mental note to the man upstairs, asking for a break in finding this cocky, insane bitch.

CHAPTER 46

As the priest droned on about resurrection and life everlasting, Brenda found her thoughts wandering. Forty-eight people. That's what it comes down to? That's it? As Brenda counted the heads in the church, her eye fell on the stunning brunette seated in the last pew, head bowed reverently. Brenda excused herself from the octogenarian throng who'd comforted her and made her way back to sit next to Linda.

"It's about damn time, Lin. Where you been?"

"I got here as soon as I could," Linda whispered back.

A stereotypical church lady, right down to her sagging stockings and pinned-on hat, stood up on bowed legs and started crooning "Ave Maria." Brenda winced and leaned toward Linda.

"Lin, I got to talk to you about a diary I found in Sarah's house."

"Okay."

"Listen, I know you're going through a rough time with that asshole Jonathan—excuse me, Lord, for swearin'," Brenda said, looking up as she added the last part, "but do you remember seeing a lady named Dr. Amelia Clarke when you was a kid?"

Brenda felt Linda stiffen before she answered. "Yes, why?"

Brenda squirmed. She was about to say something she could never take back, something that might forever change her relationship with the only family she had left in the world. But she had to say it.

"'Cause in Sarah's diary, she said that Dr. Clarke thought that you—"

"That I what?" Linda had turned to Brenda and was staring directly into her eyes, causing Brenda to momentarily lose her nerve. Then she thought of Sarah and the promise she'd made to take care of her foster sister. If Linda required help, then Brenda needed to assist her in getting it. And help could start only if Brenda knew the truth.

"That you might have had something to do with your family's deaths," Brenda said breathlessly, looking down at the floor.

Her comment was met with silence, although Brenda could feel Linda's eyes boring into her.

"What do *you* think?" Linda finally asked, returning her steady gaze to the front of the church.

Brenda didn't know what to say…because she didn't know what to think.

"You think I killed them." It was a statement versus a question, and Linda's voice didn't waver as she spoke.

Brenda turned to her friend and took her hand. "Why didn't you tell me you had a sister who died in the fire that night?"

"I don't know. I guess sometimes it's easier to forget than to relive a memory."

It was an honest answer, and Brenda had no response. They both focused on the church lady as she reached the song's pinnacle.

"Aaaaaa-ve Mariiiiii-ia."

"Jonathan left me, you know," Linda said flatly. Her tone left Brenda confused.

"Didn't you cheat on him? Do you care that he left?"

Linda gave Brenda a sidelong glance that admitted nothing. "He took Catherine with him."

"God, the bastard!" And then, facing upward, she said, "Sorry, Lord. Lin, what're you gonna do?"

"I'm going to find him, get my daughter back, divorce him, and maybe kill him."

Brenda chuckled. "That's the spirit, Lin. That's the tough girl I know." But Linda wasn't laughing. Not even smiling.

"Lin, look at me." Linda turned, and Brenda took note of the vacancy in her eyes, a darkness that was new...or had it always been there? "Linda, I'm worried about you. Are you okay? I mean...really okay?"

Linda continued to stare through Brenda and finally answered, "No, Brenda. I think I'm definitely not okay, but the problem is that I don't know how to fix me. I told Sarah that I'd done some things and that I was trying to stop. It's true. I try, but I can't seem to. It's just that he won't leave me in peace, no matter what I do for him."

"For who, Lin?"

Linda looked all around her. "My father. He's here now. I can feel him all around me, like a black haze that won't lift. Can you see it? Sometimes I can see his face too, but not right now." She turned to Brenda and grabbed her hands, clutching them like a drowning person would. "He's not a good man, Brenda."

Brenda was becoming scared. "He's dead, Linda. You know that, right?"

Linda shook her head. "Of course I know he's dead, Brenda. I killed him. But he haunts me like the sick, crazy fuck he was when he was alive."

Memories came flooding back to Brenda from their childhood together. The Christmas she and Linda got matching sweaters from Santa and wore them for a week straight before Sarah insisted on washing them. The broken arm Brenda received in reward for climbing onto the roof when Linda had become too scared to come down on her own. The time they had tried to make dinner for Sarah and had accidentally set the house on fire, resulting in a grounding that had been unprecedented in Sarah's household.

Brenda put her arm around Linda's shoulders and drew her close. "Did you know that Sarah was a teacher before she started accepting foster kids?"

Linda smiled. "No, I didn't, but I guess it doesn't surprise me. She was so good with kids, especially the troubled ones."

"And did you know that she'd lost a baby, too?"

Linda turned to Brenda as her face crumpled. "No, I didn't know. Poor Sarah." Tears ran down her face, and she let them. "She deserved better."

"Well, you rest easy, Lin, cause she's in heaven now, living it up," Brenda said, rocking Linda back and forth the way Sarah used to.

The church lady had finished, and one of Sarah's lifelong friends, Trudy Donegan, was approaching the pulpit to give a eulogy.

"Lin?"

"Yeah?"

"Did you really kill your father?" Brenda asked, looking straight ahead and continuing to cradle Linda's shoulders while rocking her.

Linda pulled away and turned toward Brenda. Taking both of Brenda's hands in her own while her eyes filled with tears, Brenda saw once more the child with whom her own life had become so intertwined.

"Would you hate me if I did?"

Brenda's breath caught in her throat as the world tumbled out of control. Her idol, her perfect friend—sometimes aloof, sometimes playful, but always loyal and kind to Brenda—had committed the ultimate crime.

When Brenda found her voice once more, it was weak and tentative. "And your mother and sister?"

Linda looked at her for a moment and then looked away, focusing on Sarah's casket.

"Oh my God," Brenda whispered as she withdrew her hands from Linda's.

Trudy finished her eulogy with a prayer. "Sarah, I know you're up there looking down on us heathens. We'll be with you soon, but until then, may we all follow in your footsteps, as goodness knows, you led a life to be proud of."

"Why?"

Linda turned to Brenda. "It had to be done."

"But why?"

"Which one?"

Brenda felt like she was going to vomit. Feeling dizzy and not knowing how to proceed, she latched onto Trudy's prayer and thought, what would Sarah do?

"You said your dad wasn't a good man. What did you mean by that?"

"Have you ever read the book, *Where the Wild Things Are?*"

"Sure, all the time when I was a kid, before you came to Sarah's. Why?"

"I've never read it, but it sat on my nightstand in the same place for about six years or so. I would stare at it while my father was raping me. That and those fucking tortoiseshell-rimmed reading glasses."

Brenda blanched and suddenly felt very cold. "That's why you killed him."

Linda turned to her. "He killed me first, didn't he?" Then she faced the front of the church again.

"My mother knew and did nothing about it. For six years." She turned to face Brenda once more. "Six *years*, Brenda."

Linda's mouth twisted, and then she said, "My sister was five years old when she died. The same age I was when my father started coming into my room almost every night. I couldn't let her go through what I had. I needed to protect her. Do you understand?"

Brenda did understand. Just as Linda had protected her sister by killing her, Brenda suddenly knew that she would protect Linda by keeping her secret. After all, it was a long time ago, and although the act of murder was wrong in God's eyes, Linda had endured a hellish torture for a long time. Besides, what would happen to little Catherine if her mother went to jail? It's not like Linda's going around killing people now, Brenda thought.

"I understand," Brenda nodded.

"Do you hate me, Bren?"

"Never, Lin. I don't like what'cha did, but I understand why you did it. Besides, I could never hate you."

Chapter 47

Vinny's knee had a mind of its own as it bounced up and down incessantly during the flight to Providence. He had debated calling his asswipe of a boss, Joanna, to tell her what was going on in an effort to become "official" on the case, thereby allowing him to use the full force and resources of the FBI. However, if he were wrong, if the woman he saw in the security footage was not the same woman he'd seen at the airport, he'd be dooming himself to a life chained to a desk doing scut paperwork. He needed to get off the plane and hear back from Alex regarding the woman's name. Then they could look into her background and see if it matched the killer they were hunting. He reflected on the look the woman on the hotel security tape had given the camera. Pure confidence. Almost a challenge. Catch me if you can, she'd been saying to Vinny.

Alex returned to her desk after conversing with Dolores and immediately began investigating drugs that might be used to sedate and/or paralyze someone. She was shocked to learn that entire websites were dedicated to the subject of how to commit the perfect murder.

"Who writes this shit?" she wondered aloud, her eyebrows knit in concentration as she read about a legal drug called succinylcholine that can paralyze and kill within minutes by suffocation if it's not applied appropriately. Horrified to learn that succinylcholine, or sux for short, was the main ingredient used by many doctors for putting people under anesthesia for surgery, she also discovered it was one of three additives used in lethal injections given to death-row inmates.

"This must be what she used. No wonder Dolores thinks she's a doctor… no one else could know half of this crap," Alex said to no one in particular.

She leaned back in her chair, shaking her head, "God, this woman is truly and completely insane."

Her phone pulsed, indicating she had a voicemail. She'd turned her phone to vibrate while she was in the bathroom and had forgotten to activate the ringer after her discussion with Dolores.

Alex pressed play and immediately heard Vinny's frantic voice.

"Alex, our perp's in Boston, and I think we have her on the security footage I forwarded to you. We're about to take off, so I'm going to have to turn off my phone, but I'll call you when I get to the hotel. In the meantime, review the footage, and you'll see who I mean. She got off the flight from Providence—Delta 875—as I was getting on. Check the flight manifest."

Alex searched for the footage Vinny had indicated he'd sent but couldn't find it. She checked her e-mail and texts but saw nothing, so she called Vinny back and left him a message.

"Vin, you said you forwarded me the footage, but there's nothing in my inbox or in my texts. I think in your excitement you simply forgot to actually send it. So, when you get this message, send the footage to me. In the meantime, I'll work on getting the names from the flight manifest. Get back here as soon as possible, okay?"

Alex replayed Vinny's message to ensure she had the right flight number and then called Delta headquarters in Atlanta, Georgia.

After being on hold for an interminable length of time, Alex was politely but firmly told that she'd need to obtain a subpoena in order to secure names from the flight manifest. She had then calmly explained that this was a police matter and time was of the essence, to which the southern-accented woman named Charlotte had responded, "Oh, bless your heart, why didn't you tell me? In that case, you'll need to obtain a subpoena in order to secure names from the flight manifest."

"I'm never flying Delta again," Alex said firmly and slammed down the phone.

Turning her attention toward doing what Charlotte had suggested, obtaining a subpoena, she marched to Kevin's office and flopped into a chair, updating her chief on Dolores's findings as well as Vinny's recent discoveries. He listened attentively and then said, "Sounds like enough to get a subpoena. I'll call Judge Hadid. He's a reasonable guy and tends to go with our hunches as long as we don't cross the line. We're not crossing any lines, are we, Alex?" Kevin looked at her, eyebrows raised.

She gawked at him innocently. "Me? Cross a line? Kevin, please."

As she sauntered out of his office, she said, "Let me know when you have it."

He yelled after her, "You're welcome!"

◢

Julian entered the church just as a vocalist was finishing a mediocre version of "Ave Maria." Not wanting to interrupt the service already in process, he tapped his way to the back left pew and took a seat. After the song, he listened to a woman named Trudy talk about her childhood shared with Sarah, cementing in Julian's mind what an incredible person Sarah had been.

Inclining his head slightly to the right, he heard whispering and mumbling. Using a skill he'd acquired over the years since becoming blind, he tuned out all extraneous noise and focused only on the speech, discerning the words "mother did nothing about…six years" and then "do you hate me?"

"As you approach to pay your respects, will everyone please take a daisy from the basket in front of Sarah's casket and place it on her coffin in remembrance of her? Thank you. Please note that burial will follow this service at the Pine Grove Cemetery here in Lynn. Directions can be found in your programs. Please join us."

Julian rose and tapped his way down the aisle toward the front of the church, where he assumed Sarah's coffin was. His cane accidentally tapped the person in front of him in line.

"Watch it, buddy!"

"Oh, excuse me. I'm sorry. Couldn't see where I was going," Julian said, smiling.

"Oh, it's me who should be sorry, mister. I didn't know you was blind," Brenda said, touching Julian's arm.

"Julian, what a lovely surprise! I got your voicemail and was going to visit while I was here in Boston…but what are you doing here?" Linda gushed, sidling up against Julian.

"Well, Sarah was clearly a very special lady, and I felt a weird kind of connection with her, having been there when she passed. I thought it was only right that I come today. Plus, quite frankly, I thought I might run into you."

Brenda watched her friend warily as she listened to Julian speak. She'd never seen Linda so focused on someone's face, so engaged in what was being spoken. She wondered if this was the man with whom Linda had cheated on Jonathan.

"Hey, Lin, who's this?"

"Oh, I'm so sorry. Where are my manners? Brenda, this is my good friend Dr. Julian Stryker. He's been…helping me through some difficult times."

Brenda looked Julian up and down. "Yeah, he sure does look like he could do that. Good to meet'cha. I guess if you're a friend of Lin's, then you're a friend of mine."

"And, Julian, this is my very best friend, Brenda Forsythe. She and I grew up together in Sarah's house. She knows all my secrets." Linda gave Brenda a look and winked.

Julian gave Brenda a slight bow and said, "My pleasure," before turning his attention once again to Linda.

"Linda, I was hoping you and I might spend some time together while you're here to further our discussions."

"Is that what they're calling it these days? 'Furthering your discussions?' That's a hoot!" Brenda snorted, covering her mouth when she remembered where they were.

Julian started to respond, "No, Brenda, I think you're misunder—"

But Linda interrupted him by taking his arm and saying, "I'd like that very much. How about I come to your office following this service? In fact, I could drive us there."

"What about Sarah's actual burial, Lin? You're coming to that, aren'tcha?" Brenda asked in disbelief.

Linda turned to Brenda and took her hands. "Brenda, Sarah was sick for a while, and I said goodbye to her in my own way some time ago. I'm not sure I actually want to see her body go into the ground. It might bring up some bad memories for me, you know?"

Brenda couldn't read Linda right now. She wasn't sure if Linda was being truthful or whether she just wanted to spend time with Julian. Brenda shook her head and said, "Whatever ya want, Lin."

They each placed their flowers on Sarah's casket, Brenda and Sarah kneeling and Julian standing behind them.

As they made their way to their respective cars, Brenda pulled Linda aside and said, "I hope you know what you're doing, Lin. He's a looker, but it's not worth jeopardizing custody of Catherine."

"What do you mean?"

"I'm no rocket scientist, but I do know that if you start sleeping around before your divorce is done, then a court might think Jonathan is the better parent for Catherine to live with full-time."

"It's not like that with Julian and me, Bren." Linda gazed at Julian, whose face was turned toward the late morning sun. "He's different. He understands me and appreciates me for what I am on the inside."

Brenda shook her head. "Does he feel the same way?"

Linda smiled, her eyes bright. "He came down here to see me, didn't he?"

After Vinny's flight landed in Providence, he jumped into a cab and directed the driver to get him to the Hilton immediately. The driver took him at his word and left tire marks on the asphalt as they screeched away from the curb. Vinny checked his phone and listened to Alex's voicemail indicating he'd not actually sent the hotel security footage.

"Dammit! Idiot!" he said to himself as he found the footage and sent it to Alex in an e-mail. He also texted her, telling her to check her e-mail now.

He arrived at the hotel to find the crime scene cordoned off per police protocol. The body had been processed, photographed, and removed for autopsy. Flashing his FBI badge, he talked to the detective in charge and then walked the scene himself. Satisfied that all aspects matched those of the heart attack killer, he approached a uniformed officer to take his leave and laughed.

"What's so funny, sir?" the cop asked.

"I never thought to ask what the poor schmuck's name was who died."

"Jason Quinn."

"Hmm. That sounds familiar. Was he in the news recently?"

"A couple of years ago now, sir. He changed his name to Brian Bosch. He was a reporter for the *National Informer.* Not much of a loss if you ask me, but it certainly wasn't a good way to go."

Vinny had heard nothing after the name Brian Bosch.

⚓

In a cab on his way back to the airport, Vinny called Alex.

"Are you sitting down?"

Alex sat down in her desk chair. "I am now. What's up?"

"The latest vic was none other than Brian Bosch, a.k.a. Jason Quinn. Guess I won't be finishing my interview with him."

"That's cold, Vinny, even for you. Have a heart, will you?"

"Hey, there's no love lost between you and the press, Alex. And don't pretend the world isn't a slightly better place without him in it."

"Yeah, yeah. Do you think the perp targeted him because of who he was or his profession?"

"No. My gut says this was an opportunity kill. Otherwise I think she would've let us know in some way. She's too egotistical to do otherwise."

"Makes sense. Anything interesting at the scene?"

"It all fits the killer's MO. Everything in its place, tortoiseshell glasses on the nightstand, et cetera, et cetera."

"Great. Get back here, then. If she's really in Boston, I'll need your help running down all the names on the flight list."

"Have you looked at the footage I sent?"

"Yeah. The footage is grainy, but I feel like I've seen her before somewhere. And how about that wink at the end of the tape? Wow, she wants to be caught."

"You think so? I think she's telling us that she's just getting started. Either way, I'm on my way back to the airport to catch the next flight back to Boston."

Alex's phone vibrated. She drew it away from her ear and saw a text from Kevin indicating the flight manifest was attached in an e-mail.

"Hold on, Vinny."

Alex opened the attachment and went right to the bottom—154 people on board Delta flight 875 from Providence to Boston. She sighed heavily and returned the phone to her ear.

"A hundred and fifty-four people on the flight, Vin! Get back here fast. I'll start on the list."

⋏

Julian's phone was in his briefcase, which sat on the floor next to his desk. He had, as was his custom, placed it there upon arriving back at the office. While he visited the bathroom, he had left Linda chatting with Jesse in the outer office. The phone vibrated several times as Alex's call traveled the miles between their two locations. Unanswered, the call went through to Julian's voicemail, whereupon Alex left a message, updating Julian on the latest murder, its location, and Dolores's opinion that the killer was not only a woman but a physician.

CHAPTER 48

D r. Linda Sterling sat on the edge of Jesse's desk, laughing and chatting with him about the latest disaster on *America's Got Talent*. Julian emerged from the bathroom in time to hear Linda say, "Well, I don't watch the show, Jesse, but it sounds like so much fun! I'll put it on my list to binge watch the next chance I get."

Julian tilted his head. Her voice sounded different, more even, under control. Then again, the last time he'd seen her in his office, she'd been under extreme stress. Perhaps this was the Linda that had it all together. Maybe Lizzie had overreacted in her assessment of Linda's behavior prior to coming to Boston. Either way, Julian just wanted to chat for a few minutes to satisfy himself that Linda was in a good mental place, both as a person and as a physician.

"Well, you two seem to be getting along," Julian said, smiling.

Linda laughed. "Jesse and I were just gossiping about the latest TV dramas, right, Jess?"

"Uh-huh. You know, Julian, I was wrong about Linda. She's a dream."

Linda furrowed her brow. "What do you mean?"

Jesse raised his eyebrows. "You have to admit, Linda, you were not very nice the first time you were here."

"Oh, that," she scoffed, waving her hand in the air. "It was a bad day. What can I say? We all have them. The important thing now is that we're all friends. We are friends, right, Julian?"

"Sure, Linda. Why don't we go into my office for a bit?"

"Anything you say. You're the doctor."

Jesse watched as Linda's hips swayed themselves into Julian's office and sank slowly into the worn leather of his couch. She kicked off her shoes and winked at Jesse. "Why don't you close the door, Jess? We'll be out in a while."

Jesse looked to Julian for direction, who barely nodded his head. Linda seemed casual, nonchalant, as if she didn't have a care in the world. She struck Julian as being completely in control, something he knew was paramount to her.

"You seem happy today, almost carefree, Linda."

"Yes. It's a good day. I got something off my chest today with Brenda, and I have to admit that I feel somewhat liberated. And I had a great night's sleep last evening."

"Do you mind telling me what you shared with Brenda?"

Linda opened her mouth to respond, and an icy black wind blew through her, chilling her to the bone. Her body shook uncontrollably as her father's face loomed large in front of her, and without speaking, she knew he was there to warn her.

He's going to help us, Daddy. I told you before that Julian understands. I trusted Brenda, and you were okay with that. Please let me trust Julian.

Her father didn't respond, but his eyes bore into hers with an intimidating stare. Suddenly, and for the first time, tortoiseshell glasses appeared around his eyes, causing her to recoil in fear.

"Linda? Everything okay?"

"Um…yes. It's fine. I can't share with you what I told Brenda, but it made me feel better."

"Linda, I'm going to get right to the point. I'm worried about you. You clearly feel a great need for control and recently have felt out of control. That can leave someone feeling pretty vulnerable. Is that how you feel?"

That was *exactly* how she felt—vulnerable. But how could she tell this wonderful man without giving away her secrets?

"My husband and I are getting divorced."

Julian had expected her to try to regain command of the conversation by changing the subject, and he was ready for it. "How do you feel about that?"

Linda shrugged. "He was only good for one thing. Well…two, actually," she said, smiling. "He's a good father to my darling Catherine, but he can be replaced."

"Replaced. That's an interesting choice of words to apply to a man who you supposedly loved, married, and had a child with."

"Is it? Well, it's not my fault he's a sniveling coward of a man who can't even stand up to his own wife."

"Did you want him to stand up to you? Or did you always want to be in control?"

"You mean like I am right now?"

"Are you in control right now?" Julian asked, lifting his head as he spoke.

"You tell me, Dr. Stryker. Am I?" She raised herself slowly from the leather couch and walked directly toward Julian, who sat perfectly still in his chair. Her perfume wafted his way, and he could feel the heat of her body as she leaned in toward him.

Linda abruptly stood as a quick knock sounded and the door to Julian's office briskly opened.

"Hey, Julian, sorry to interrupt, but—" Jesse caught himself as he took in the scene. Linda had been leaning over Julian, who was seated rather comfortably in the regular chair he used with patients. Jesse squinted at Linda, who simply bit her lip and smiled slyly in response. She slowly brought her finger to her lips in a *shh* gesture.

"Yes, Jesse, what is it?" Julian asked.

Jesse paused and then said, "Danny and Mrs. Sheehan are here. I normally wouldn't have interrupted, but she only has a few minutes before her shift starts at the nursing home. She and Danny wondered if they could drop off the paperwork for Rosey Tech and say a quick thanks."

Julian did some quick strategizing in his head. He hadn't planned the Sheehan's visit, but the timing couldn't have been more perfect. Linda was clearly riding a recent high that was sure to crash soon based on the little time he had spent with her. If he wanted her to realize that she needed professional help beyond a couple of visits with him, then he would have to create a situation that might break through her façade of nonchalance.

"Sure, send them in. You don't mind, do you, Linda? After all, you know the Sheehan family."

Before she could respond, Sharon and Danny walked through Julian's door.

"So sorry to interrupt, Dr. Stryker, but Danny and I wanted to thank you for getting him into the program at Rosey Tech. We just came from a tour there, and it's just incredible! Danny is—" Sharon stopped speaking as she recognized Linda.

"Oh my God! Dr. Sterling! How great to see you! What're you doing here?"

Linda slipped her shoes back on and stood up straight.

"Dr. Stryker and I are friends. I'm here on a social call while I'm in Boston."

Julian couldn't help but notice Linda's change of tone when addressing Mrs. Sheehan. The raspy, seductive voice she had employed while approaching his chair had been replaced by crisp and authoritative speech.

"Well, it's great to see the two doctors who helped my boys! Thanks to both of you, our family's moving forward in a positive way. I left the paperwork with Jesse, Dr. Stryker. Okay, I gotta go. Say thanks, Danny."

Danny Sheehan waved and said, "Thanks for everything, Doc. I hope I'll see you soon." And they were gone.

Jesse, who'd been standing in the doorway, waited until the Sheehans had left before he addressed Julian. "Do you need anything, Dr. Stryker? Anything at all? If you do, just yell. I'm right outside your door." While he was speaking, he glanced at Linda, who had turned away from him.

Julian understood Jesse's underlying message and figured Jesse had seen Linda's body language upon opening the door. "I think we're good right now. Thanks, Jess."

"Okay, but I'm right outside."

"Got it," Julian said with a smile, thinking that sometimes Jesse could be a bit overprotective.

As the door closed, Linda turned to Julian. "Did you plan that?"

"The Sheehan visit? No. But how did you feel when you saw them?"

"Like shit. Like the crappy doctor I am."

"Because you couldn't save Jimmy?"

"Because I can't seem to save any of them. Another one will die within the next two weeks."

"Linda, I'm going to ask you a difficult question. Do you feel that you're capable of continuing to care for your patients?"

"Of course."

"Without causing yourself harm?"

"What's that supposed to mean?"

"Linda, have you been hurting yourself on purpose as a punishment?"

"As a punishment for what?"

"You tell me."

"You mean for not being able to save my patients? You think I'm cutting myself as a punishment for killing my patients?"

"I didn't say anything about cutting...or killing."

CHAPTER 49

A lex sat at her desk with four first-year detectives surrounding her.

"Does everybody understand? Put everything else on hold until we've run down these hundred and fifty-four names. I want to know everything about these people: names, birth dates, marriages, divorces, occupations, kids, arrests, warrants, what they had for breakfast, lunch...everything. Got it? And I want it in the next twenty minutes."

"Alex, there's no way we can—"

"Twenty minutes!" Alex repeated, staring down the newbie who'd dared talk back.

Scattering to their respective desks, they began typing furiously on their computers. Acting on Dolores's advice, Alex had already identified four physicians on Delta flight 875 and had their names scrawled on the notepad in front of her. Three of the four doctors were women, so she started with them. Googling them alphabetically, she quickly discovered that none of them had a prior police record except Betsy Brennan, who had an unpaid speeding ticket in Pennsylvania. She then went to www.whitepages.com, entered all three names, and printed out their personal and professional phone numbers and addresses.

Working methodically, she called Betsy Brennan's home number and got an answering machine. Leaving no message, she hung up and dialed Dr. Brennan's office number.

"Good afternoon, Dr. Brennan's office. Nora speaking. How may I help you?"

"Hello, Nora. My name is Alex Hayes, and I'm a detective with the Boston Police Department. I'm currently working on a case, and I need your help. Can you please tell me if your boss has been in Baltimore, New York, and Philadelphia in the past year?"

"What? I don't understand. Why are you asking me—"

"Listen, Nora. I know this is coming out of the blue, but I really need your help. Please just tell me if Dr. Brennan has been in those cities in the last year?"

"Um…well, I guess it's okay that I talk to you. I'd need to check her schedule, because of course I can't remember off the top of my head whether or not she's been in…where did you say?"

"Boston, New York, Baltimore, Philadelphia, and Hartford. Oh…and Providence."

"Rhode Island?"

"Yes, Providence, Rhode Island."

"Well, I can tell you with certainty that she hasn't been in Providence. I'd definitely remember that."

"What about the other cities?"

"I'm checking. Um…no, she's been to Cincinnati, Topeka, and Springfield, though. Does that help?"

"Immensely. Thanks so much for your time."

Alex hung up and dialed the next doctor's home number.

"Kramer residence, Bradley speaking."

"Hello, Bradley. Is Dr. Kramer home?"

The little boy giggled. "Which one?"

"What do you mean?"

"Both my parents are doctors. Which one do you want?"

"Oh. Um…Dr. Cynthia Kramer."

"Nope. She's at work."

"Thanks. I'll call her there."

As Alex dialed Dr. Kramer's office number, she wondered what it was like to have both parents as doctors. She wondered how often the child got to see them.

"Dr. Kramer's office."

Alex repeated her introduction and was disheartened to learn that Dr. Kramer had traveled exactly one time in the past year and that had been to go to her college reunion in California.

She stared at the last name on the list—Linda Sterling. Nice name for a doctor, Alex thought distractedly as she dialed Dr. Sterling's office number.

"Hello, Dr. Linda Sterling's office. Lizzie speaking. How may I help you?"

Chapter 50

Linda knew she'd been caught. Her father's entire body floated before her, as if he wanted to say something but his mouth wouldn't open. Darkness descended, and her hands wandered to her hair. She started pulling out strands, one by one, and placing them delicately on the coffee table. She had removed thirty before Julian spoke once more.

"Linda?"

"Yes?"

"Why did you say that you're killing your patients?"

"Because that's what I do best. Killing."

"Who says?"

"Daddy."

Her voice had shifted once again. It was smaller and reminded Julian of the version of Linda he had met in the restaurant.

"Your father told you that? That killing is what you do best?"

"Yes."

"Why would he say that?"

Linda paused in her hair pulling to straighten out the strands and then layer them in a crisscross pattern, making a mosaic of hair on the wooden table. She thought it was pretty. Her father loomed over her, critically examining her work.

"Linda, does your father still hurt you?"

"Yes, sometimes. But only when I don't listen."

"Did he hurt you as a child, Linda?"

"No, never. Daddy loved me. I was his little Pippin."

"And how often did he love you, Linda?"

"Almost every night."

"Linda, how long did your father molest you?"

Linda looked up from her artwork. Her father bent toward her, breathing heavily on her cheek as his hands encircled her lean neck.

"What do you mean?"

"I believe that your father molested you, Linda. Perhaps for a while. I think you need to talk to someone about it, because I'm afraid it's affecting your work and your personal life."

Linda couldn't breathe. Her father's hands squeezed, choking her larynx, threatening to crush it.

"Linda, are you okay? Linda?" Julian asked more anxiously, leaning forward in his chair. "Jesse!"

Jesse burst through the door. "Oh my God! Linda, stop!"

Jesse rushed over to Linda, who had taken a scarf, wrapped it around her neck several times, and was pulling it tighter and tighter, strangling herself.

"What the hell's going on in here?" Jesse demanded once he had freed Linda. "That's it! You're done here, Julian."

Julian held up his hand to Jesse. "Linda, are you okay? Do you want to continue?"

A raspy-voiced Linda responded, "Yes."

"Not a good idea, Julian. How about you let me call—"

"Jesse, I appreciate your caring, but please leave, and let us continue. I'll be fine."

Jesse glared at Linda and then turned to Julian, who once again nodded almost imperceptibly. As Jesse reluctantly left the room, Julian held out his hand to Linda and said, "The fact that you just self-harmed in front of me suggests that you want me to help you. Do you understand?"

"I do want your help, Julian. I do. I'm just so tired," she finished, taking his hand.

Chapter 51

Alex slammed down the phone and yelled, "Bingo!" before picking it up once again to dial Julian. He hadn't responded to her last voicemail, and to Alex's frustration, the call went to voicemail again.

"Julian, call me right away. The name of our killer is Sterling—Dr. Linda Sterling—and it turns out that she's here in Boston for a funeral. I just got off the phone with her assistant, who verified that she's been in every city there was a murder and—get this—on the exact same dates! Vinny's on his way back from Providence, and I'm sure you want to be in on the takedown. Call me, dammit! Where are you, anyway?"

Alex googled the dead woman's name that Lizzie had given her over the phone and came up with a list of Sarah Turnbulls. But only one had passed away recently, so she clicked on that Sarah, and an obituary popped up. Scanning the article, she found the name of the church and cemetery where services were being held. She noted the address, grabbed her jacket, and yelled, "Stop the search, plebes! I found her!" as she rushed out the door to her vintage car.

The engine roared to life as Alex glanced at her watch—12:02 p.m. The church service had been at eleven and had probably lasted about forty minutes. Then a twenty-minute ride to the cemetery, Alex reasoned, would have the procession arriving a little before she did. She gunned her engine and wound through lunch-hour traffic to get onto Route 1, crossed the Tobin Bridge, and pulled slowly into the cemetery at 12:18 p.m.

Only one burial service was in progress, so Alex parked the car, tucked her gun into a hip holster, and, not wanting to arouse undue notice, casually sauntered over.

"O God, the life of the living, the hope of the dying, the salvation of all that trust in thee, mercifully grant that the soul of thy servant and handmaid, Sarah Turnbull, delivered from the darkness of her mortality, may rejoice with thy saints in perpetual light. Through our Lord. Amen."

Alex looked on while the small yet sincere group of mourners performed the sign of the cross. No one stood out to her in any way. Most were over eighty years old, and the few that were younger seemed of a lower socioeconomic class. Nope, no doctors here, she thought.

As the crowd dispersed, one woman remained at the gravesite, sullen and alone. Alex advanced slowly, not wanting to startle or alarm her.

"I'm sorry for your loss," Alex offered.

Brenda looked up. "Aw, thanks. That's nice of ya. Did you know Sarah, or are you with the cemetery?"

"No, no. I didn't know Sarah, but I know someone who did."

"Oh yeah? Who?"

"Linda Sterling. Is she here?" Alex asked, glancing around.

"Lin? No, she left with her new boyfriend. Some doctor." When she said the word *boyfriend*, she put air quotes around it. "Who did you say you were again?"

"Just a friend of Linda's. Thanks for your time. Hey, do you know where she and her boyfriend went?"

"Uh, I dunno. A hotel, maybe?"

"And what was this guy's name?"

"Uh…let's see. It was. J—" Brenda's eyes narrowed. "Wait a minute. Who are you exactly, and how do you know Linda?"

Alex pulled out her badge and held it up. "Alex Hayes, Boston PD. I'm looking for Linda Sterling because she's a person of interest in some recent homicides we're investigating."

"Homicide…as in murder?"

"As in murder."

"Recent?"

"What?"

"Were the murders recent?"

"Within the last year. Why do you ask?"

Brenda looked down. "No reason."

Alex stepped forward and tilted her head until Brenda finally looked her in the eye.

"Is Linda a good friend of yours?"

"Yeah. She's my very best friend."

"I see. Is there something you want to tell me?"

"No."

"What's your name?"

"Brenda Forsythe." Brenda looked down again, noticing how scuffed her faux patent-leather slingbacks had become.

"Well, Brenda, I want you to understand something. I'm looking for Dr. Sterling because I think she can help me figure out who's been killing men up and down the northeast corridor."

Brenda's eyebrows came together as she struggled to understand. "Why would she be able to help you?"

"Well, we believe that our killer is a doctor, and since Dr. Sterling is one too, well, we thought she might be able to answer some questions for us."

"Like what?"

"Well, I want to talk to her about the drugs that are used in the murders, drugs that only a doctor would know about. And because Linda is also a psychiatrist by training, I'm hoping she can explain to me why the murderer leaves the hotel rooms where she kills so neat, or why the killer leaves tortoiseshell-rimmed glasses on the nightstand, or why—"

Brenda looked up sharply as she backed away from Alex. "What did you just say?"

"Which part?"

"The glasses," Brenda said breathlessly as the area around her started to spin out of control.

"I said that the murderer leaves tortoiseshell-rimmed glasses on the nightstand."

Brenda flashed back to her conversation with Linda during Sarah's church service in which Linda had described her father's molesting her.

"*Where the Wild Things Are sat on my nightstand in the same place for about six years or so. I would stare at it while my father was raping me. That and those fucking tortoiseshell-rimmed reading glasses.*"

With tears in her eyes, Brenda sat down hard on the grass next to Sarah's grave. Sensing that something had shifted, Alex joined her, and after a few minutes had passed, she reached out and placed her hand over Brenda's.

"Brenda, something tells me that you're a good person and an extremely loyal friend. The best thing you can do for Linda right now is to tell me everything you know that might help us find her before she hurts someone else. Or herself."

The look in Brenda's eyes was so heartbreaking that Alex didn't know if she could push this potential witness any further. But she knew she had to.

"Brenda, do the right thing for the men who've died because of Linda. I promise that I just want to talk to her right now. That's all."

"How many?"

"How many what?"

"How many people has she killed?"

"Six so far."

"That's not true." Brenda was crying.

Alex sighed. "I know you don't want it to be true, Brenda, but it is."

"No, that's not what I mean. She hasn't killed six people. She's killed at least nine...if you count her family."

Chapter 52

"I know you're tired, Linda. I can hear it in your voice. Why don't you go into the bathroom, rinse your face, and then we can regroup and start planning which therapist you're going to see and how you're going to move forward in a positive way. Okay?"

Linda smiled and stroked Julian's hand, lingering a bit with her touch. "Okay, Julian. I'll be right back."

When he heard the door close, Julian leaned back in his chair and breathed out heavily. Linda's condition was much worse than he'd thought. The fact that she'd self-harmed in his presence was such a pathetic cry for help that he felt perhaps she should be committed immediately. He pressed the sound button on his watch.

"The time is twelve forty-two p.m."

My lunch with Alex is going to have to be moved, he thought grudgingly. He removed his phone from his briefcase to call Alex and was alerted to two new voicemails. Placing the phone on the desktop, he commanded it to play the first voicemail.

"Julian, there was another heart attack murder in Providence last night, and Dolores is pretty sure the killer is a physician based on how she's killing. Call me."

Julian winced. Another death. The killer's unraveling. We've got to get this woman, or she's going to kill again soon, he thought.

He then commanded the phone to play the second voicemail.

"Julian, call me right away. The name of our killer is Sterling—Dr. Linda Sterling—and it turns out that she's here in Boston for a funeral. I just got off the phone with her assistant, who verified that she's been in every city there was a murder and—get this—on the exact same dates! Vinny's on his way back from Providence, and I'm sure you want to be in on the takedown. Call me, dammit! Where are you, anyway?"

☈

Linda splashed cold water on her face and spoke to herself in the mirror.

"I knew Julian would understand. Everything's going to be okay," she said aloud.

"You are so much more stupid that I ever gave you credit for." Her father's countenance appeared before her in the mirror, completely obliterating her own.

"I've always said that you were surrounded by idiots, but now I find that you, my dear, are indeed the queen of all idiots."

Linda's eyes narrowed as she spat out, "You will *not* speak to me like that!"

"I'll speak to you however, whenever, and wherever I please, and you'd do well to remember that!" His head came forward and smashed into hers, sending her reeling backward into the wall. Regaining her balance, she stifled a sob.

"Leave me alone! Please, just leave me alone." Touching her hand to her forehead, she felt blood. Glancing at the mirror, she was confused to find that it was cracked.

Quicker than a bolt of lightning, he was suddenly everywhere, smothering her with his omnipresence as he used to do with his body. She gasped for air.

"Daddy, stop. I can't...I can't...breathe!"

"You know what you need to do, Pippin," he whispered in her head as he caressed her hair.

"It's so easy. Just finish it. Your final release."

"I don't want to. I can't. He's helping me," she rasped before falling to the tiled floor. "Daddy, I need air!"

"And you'll have air, Pippin, once you complete your task. Just...one...more!" With that, he grabbed her hair and smashed her head against the floor, leaving her flirting with passing out before he disappeared.

⚐

The hair on Julian's neck stood on end, and his breath caught in his throat. The killer's unraveling, his own thoughts echoed in his head. She's going to kill again soon.

Julian quickly reached for his cell phone to call 911, but his unsteady hands dropped it. Feeling around for it with his foot, he inadvertently kicked it further out of reach. He rose slowly to avoid making his chair creak and quietly felt his way toward the door to the reception area.

"Where are you going?" Linda asked as she exited the bathroom. Her voice was altered—confident, calm, gravelly. Gone were the tears and fatigue he'd heard only minutes before.

"I was going to get us some coffee," Julian bluffed.

"Really? How thoughtful...but I don't want any coffee."

She strolled over to where Julian was standing, hand outstretched toward the doorknob. She gingerly took his hand and interlaced her fingers with his. "Let's sit for a while and chat, shall we?"

"Well, Linda, I actually have a full afternoon of patients. In fact, my next one should be here shortly. Let me just check with Jesse and—"

Linda's laughter cut him off. "Oh, Julian. Aren't you just so precious? Let's check your schedule right here on your phone." She led him over to where his phone had fallen to the floor, its screen still showing the recent voicemails.

"What's this?" she asked. "Two new voicemails? Let's play them."

"No, Linda...don't!"

"Who's Alex?"

"What?"

"That's who the voicemails are from. Who's Alex?" Linda repeated, a little more urgently.

"She's my girlfriend."

The floor under Linda felt as if it shifted. "Your girlfriend?"

"Yes. Linda. I—"

"Stop," she whispered. Withdrawing her hand from his, she raised her eyebrows and leaned in so that her body was pressed against him. Her lips brushed against his as she whispered, "Well, isn't that a game changer? Why don't you have a seat at your desk, Dr. Stryker."

Linda's sudden shift caught Julian off guard, and he wasn't sure how to proceed as he felt his way to the chair.

"Linda, you and I were working on getting you better, right? How about we return to our earlier discussion of how best to do that?"

Linda approached him from behind and bent to his left ear. After a playful nibble, she whispered, "You seem nervous, Dr. Stryker."

"No, not at all, Linda. I just think that your needs would be best served by—"

She laughed—a short, harsh bark. "Oh, we're way past that, Dr. Stryker. My needs were never a concern in this entire ridiculous fiasco."

"What do you mean, Linda?"

"And stop saying my name so much, Dr. Stryker. I know why you're doing that."

"Doing what?"

"You're saying my name because you're trying to engage me, draw me in, to pretend that we're friends. Like you have my best interests at heart. C'mon, *Julian*. Psych 101. You'll need to do better than that. It's almost insulting."

Julian dipped his head, desperately wishing that Jesse would perform one of his best tricks—an untimely and unexpected entrance.

"That's better," she breathed. "A little contrition was all I needed."

She pushed his chair away from the desk, hiked up her skirt, and straddled his lap. Running her hands through his hair, she grabbed two fistfuls and pulled him to her for an unreciprocated kiss. Pulling away, she tilted her head, examining his face.

"Do you think I'm pretty?"

"Physically?"

"Yes."

"I have no idea."

"Do you think your girlfriend is pretty?"

"Yes."

"How do you know?"

"Because I've felt her face a hundred times, and each time, I feel beauty."

"Will you feel my face?" She grabbed his hands and tried to force him to touch her face. He resisted and then pulled his hands away completely.

"No, Linda."

"Call me Pippin."

"Absolutely not. Enough!" He tried to rise from the chair but was stymied by her full weight holding him down.

"Linda, get off me."

She threw back her head and laughed. "That's funny. That's what I used to say to my father in my head. Of course, I never said it out loud. I wonder what would have happened if I had." Her tongue darted into his ear and then traced its outer edge.

Julian set his mouth. "Linda, you just made good progress by acknowledging that your father sexually abused you when you were a child. Go sit on the couch, and we can further our conversation."

"Let's make love, Julian—right here, right now." Linda seized Julian's hand, and before he could stop her, she had placed it under her shirt.

Julian violently withdrew his hand and took a deep breath. Just as he was about to yell for Jesse, Linda's left hand clamped down hard across his mouth, and she whispered harshly, "It doesn't feel very good to be powerless, does it, Julian? That's what I felt like for so many years before I finally did something about my problem. I took control and put my world back in order, just like I'm doing now. Now, here's what's going to happen. You're going to do exactly as I say, because I have a syringe in my other hand that I can very easily inject into you. Do you understand?"

Julian paused, determining whether or not she was lying. After a beat, he nodded.

"Do you know what's in the syringe, Julian?"

He nodded again. Linda withdrew her hand. "What's in it, Julian?"

"Succinylcholine...to paralyze me."

Linda sighed. "No, I'm afraid we won't have time for that. We're going to have to go straight for the big finish."

Julian physically recoiled. "Potassium chloride?" he asked breathlessly.

"Ding, ding, ding! He's our big winner, Don. Please tell him what he's won!" Linda said, imitating a game-show announcer. "Well, Linda, for getting the right answer, Julian has won an all-expenses-paid trip to hell!"

Linda kissed Julian full on the mouth and bit his lip as she was pulling away, drawing blood. "You're going to like hell, Julian. It's always warm there, and you can do whatever you want."

Chapter 53

"Listen, Brenda, I want you to come with me."

Brenda's body stiffened as she wiped her eyes. "Am I in trouble?"

"No, no. I need your help, though. You've done such a good job helping me that I want you to come down to police headquarters so we can talk to you more about Linda and where she might be."

"I told you she went with her new boyfriend."

Alex smiled. "You did tell me that, but we don't know who he is or where they might be. Does this boyfriend know about her past?"

Brenda thought for a moment. "I'm not completely sure, but I don't think so. Lin said that he likes her for what she is on the inside."

"A monster?" It slipped out before Alex could stop it. Brenda glanced at her sharply and then shrugged. "I guess I can see why you'd think that. But I want you to know that Lin wasn't always like that. And—" Brenda broke off.

"And what?"

"Well, she had a pretty good reason for killing her father."

"And what was that?"

"He raped her almost every night for six years."

Alex blew out air. "Do you have a picture of Linda with you, by chance?"

"Yeah, sure." Brenda dug through her purse and removed her phone. Scrolling through pictures, she came to the one the bartender had taken when Linda had first returned to Boston and they had met at the bar.

Brenda smiled weakly as she handed the phone to Alex. "She's beautiful, ain't she?"

Alex glanced at the photo, first at Brenda, whose smile was warm and real, and then at Linda, who seemed to be holding something back from the camera. "Yes, she's very pretty. Wait a minute."

Alex took out her iPhone and opened the attachment in Vinny's e-mail that showed the security footage from the Providence murder. She fast-forwarded it until the point at which Linda looked directly at the camera and winked. Pausing the tape, she turned her phone to Brenda and said, "Is this Linda Sterling?"

Not understanding that she was seeing footage related to the most recent murder, Brenda smiled and said, "Yep, that's her. Always looks like a million bucks. Ya know, she always smiles like she knows somethin' we don't. Where'd ya get that recording, anyway?"

Alex's brows were furrowed as she stared at Brenda and ignored her question. She shifted her gaze down as she repeated what Brenda had said.

"'Smiles like she knows something we don't.' I've heard that before."

Alex looked again at the still frame of Linda winking at the camera.

Her face looks familiar to me. I've seen Linda before, Alex thought. But where?

"Linda's always been something of a puzzle, I guess," Brenda went on, ignorant of the fact that Alex's thoughts were elsewhere.

Shopping? At a mall?

"Ya think ya know somebody and then find out they done stuff like murder. I still can't believe it, really."

At the precinct, perhaps?

"Hey, do ya think we could stop somewhere for lunch? I didn't eat this morning on account of the fact that I was in charge of Sarah's funeral, and now I'm starving."

Alex instantly raised her head and slapped the ground next to her.

"That's it! The restaurant! That's where I've seen her! I was at a restaurant with Kevin, and he said the same thing—that she smiled like she knows something we don't. She was with Juli—" Alex's voice trailed off as the full impact of realization dawned. "Oh my God!"

"What? Who's Kevin? What restaurant?" Brenda asked.

Alex frantically exited her e-mail and pressed the photo icon to access her own pictures. She found one of Julian dressed in his best suit, looking debonair and mugging for the camera.

"Does this man look familiar to you, Brenda?"

"Hey, that's him! That's Linda's new boyfriend. Really handsome, and blind—did I mention that? Why do you have his picture? Is he in trouble, too? Did he help Linda kill people? He seemed so nice."

Alex shook her head. "We gotta go. You're coming with me. Let's go—now!"

Alex rushed to her car with Brenda in tow. Jumping into the front seat, Brenda barely had time to buckle her seat belt before Alex peeled out of the cemetery parking lot.

She drove to Julian's office in record time, lights flashing but sirens silent. The last thing she wanted to do was scare this psychotic bitch into hurting Julian.

On the way, she dialed Julian's phone, which went to voicemail again. She considered calling Jesse to warn him but was afraid he'd either make the situation worse or end up getting hurt himself.

"Omigod...omigod...omigod!" Alex mumbled under her breath.

"Why are we going so fast?" Brenda asked, gripping the armrest with her right hand while her left hand clutched her purse.

"Your...friend is with my boyfriend."

"He's your boyfriend?" Brenda asked, clearly confused. "Linda led me to believe that he was her boyfriend."

"Yeah, well, she's a little nuts, so..."

"You don't need to worry," Brenda said. "She won't hurt him or anything."

Alex looked directly at Brenda. "You are kidding, right?"

Brenda blanched as she reconsidered what she'd just said. Alex returned her focus to the car, which had reached 110 miles per hour.

CHAPTER 54

Julian's cell phone vibrated on the desk. The screen read ALEX.

"Oh, there's your girlfriend again. She's kind of needy, isn't she? Calling you three times in a row."

Julian knew that Alex would be at his office any minute to pick him up for lunch. She was probably calling to tell him she was on her way.

"Should we listen to the message?" Linda teased, reaching for the phone.

"No. Let's just talk, like you suggested, Linda," Julian said calmly, stalling for time. "Tell me more about hell, Linda. I know you've been there already."

"You got that right. Hmm, let's see. Hell is being betrayed by the very people that are supposed to love you. My asshole father and my sniveling bitch of a mother."

"Why do you call your mother that?"

"Because she knew, Julian. She knew! She used to come down the hallway while my father was grinding away and stand outside my door. Can you imagine? She knew!" Linda stood up from Julian's lap and started to pace around the office. "What kind of a mother does that?"

"A very broken one."

"Yeah. Whatever. She didn't stand up for me when it counted. I blame her almost more than him. He had a sickness, an abnormal brain. She doesn't have an excuse except that she was a fucking coward!"

"Yes, she was, Linda. But perhaps your father was abusing her as well. Has that occurred to you?"

Linda abruptly stopped pacing and faced Julian. "What do you mean?"

Julian shrugged. "He might have been abusing her physically, mentally, or emotionally, somehow using her knowledge of his abuse with you as leverage in the marriage. Of course, you couldn't see that as a child, but as an adult, as a physician, as a psychiatrist, surely you can entertain that possibility now."

Linda stared at the floor. "I never thought of that, actually."

"You were too wrapped up in your own pain to see it before now, Linda, and that's understandable. That's why you're here, isn't it? To work through your pain so that you can move forward in your life?"

Linda nodded her head enthusiastically. "Yes, yes, that's why I'm here. You do understand."

"Of course I do, Linda. Please put down the syringe and let's finish what we started. There's still a good way out of this for you. Just put down the needle. Please."

Linda looked at the syringe in her hand as if she didn't quite know how it had come to be there. Julian listened intently as she deliberately walked up behind where he sat perfectly still, his hands folded neatly on the desktop. Her breath was heavy on his neck as his blood pulsed wildly in the vein against which she held the syringe.

"Are you scared, Julian?"

"Are you, Linda?"

"All the time."

Without warning, the door burst inward, and Alex yelled, "On the ground! Now!"

Julian tried to move but Linda's strong, steady hand had twisted the fabric of his collar and held it fast.

Adrenaline fueled Alex's voice. "Julian, you okay?"

"Yes, we're fine, Alex."

"Good. Just so you know, Julian, I have my forty-five pointed at Linda's chest, and Jesse's here, too. Linda, put down the syringe, and let's talk."

Julian felt the slight pressure of the needle poised at his carotid artery. He knew he must remain calm and motionless or the potassium chloride could be injected, even by accident. Holding his hands up slowly, he placed them palms down on the desktop.

"Linda, Alex is right. Let's talk. But first, please put the needle down."

"Shut up, Julian! Of course you're going to side with her. She's your *girlfriend.*" Keeping eye contact with Alex, she leaned down quickly and whispered in his ear. "I could've been your girlfriend, Julian. It could have been me." She bit his ear hard. Julian grimaced at the pain but didn't move.

"Enough, Linda! Enough people have died. What is it? Nine now?"

Linda's eyes widened. "Yes," Alex continued. "I know that you killed your family. I understand killing your parents, but why your sister? Was that just for fun?"

Linda sneered. "No, you sick fuck. I killed her because my father was about to take her on as his next special project. Believe me, I did her a favor."

Jesse was in disbelief. "You killed your own sister?"

"Oh, is that so hard to believe? Does that change your opinion of me? Oh no!" she spat sarcastically.

"Linda, do you remember reciting the Hippocratic oath when you became a physician?" Julian asked, his hands closing into fists on the desk.

The sudden change of subject caught everyone unaware.

"What?"

"This is my favorite part of the oath: 'Most especially must I tread with care in matters of life and death. Above all, I must not play at God.' You've been playing at God recently, Linda. You're playing at it now. I know you care very, very much about your patients and about your skill as a physician. You don't want to jeopardize all of that. Your patients need you. Please, put the needle down."

"Linda?" came a weak voice from behind Jesse.

"I told you to stay in the car!" Alex hissed at Brenda without taking her eyes from Linda.

Brenda ignored Alex. "What in God's name are you doin', Lin? What *is* all this?" She gestured with her hands while taking in the entire situation with her eyes. "Oh my God! What happened to your forehead? Is that...oh my God…is that glass?" Brenda's face twisted as her voice broke, and she started sobbing.

Linda openly regarded her friend of so many years, and a chasm opened within her. Tears welled up as her control started to crumble. "Oh, Brenda. I'm sorry. I'm so sorry."

In response, Brenda simply stared, her melancholy brown eyes desperately searching for answers that Linda could never provide. Slowly shaking her head, she asked with sincerity, "How did it ever come to this? You and Sarah were everything to me."

Tears rolled freely down Linda's face now although her rock-steady hand never wavered from Julian's neck.

Brenda looked despairingly at Linda and whispered, "What would Sarah say?" as she took a step toward Linda, whose face contorted in anguish.

"Stop, Bren. Stop! Don't come any closer. I just have to do this one last thing. Just this last one, and then order will be restored. Don't you understand? I'll be free."

"Who says, Lin? Your dad? He's dead, Lin. You killed him along with the rest of your family and all of those innocent men. Enough, Lin."

"They weren't innocent! None of them! They killed me first!" Linda screamed, her voice echoing wildly out of control. "They killed me first! Why doesn't anyone understand that?"

Her frantic eyes searched her onlookers ferociously, desperate to make someone—anyone—understand.

"My father created me! He created me, then he defiled me, and then he recreated me into this!" Her left hand gesticulated violently as her right hand maintained constant vigil at Julian's carotid artery.

"Okay, okay, Linda. Let's take a break," Julian soothed.

Linda's breathing slowly calmed as a full minute ticked by. The tableau was frozen—Julian seated at the desk, head bent; Linda behind him, ever watchful. Alex was a statue of focus, aiming her gun at Linda's heart as Jesse stood closely behind her. And finally there was Brenda off to Alex's left, staring vacantly at her foster sister and former hero.

As Linda absorbed the scene, a beautiful tranquility blossomed inside her, filling the black void. Calm serenity emanated from her core, and for the first time she could remember, she felt completely at peace. Looking at each person in turn, she finished by gazing lovingly at Julian. With tears in her eyes, she raised the syringe, smiled, and said, "This is for you, Daddy."

The thin needle penetrated the vein as Alex squeezed off four rounds from her Smith & Wesson .45 caliber pistol.

Brenda collapsed in fear as Jesse ran for cover.

Julian and Linda crumpled to the floor in a heap, facing each other, bodies entwined like lovers.

Chapter 55

Vinny slept slumped in a chair next to the hospital bed. Alex sat next to him, anxiously awaiting the awakening. After an interminable length of time, Julian slowly roused and groaned.

"Julian, it's me, Alex. I'm here, and so is Vinny."

Julian's head wobbled like a bobblehead doll. He tried to speak, but the words wouldn't come out right.

"Shh. Don't try to talk yet. The doctor said it would take another hour or so for the anesthesia to wear off after the surgery."

Julian groaned again and made a face.

Alex laughed. "Are you confused?"

Julian attempted speech one more time and ended up drooling.

"Please stop," Alex said, cleaning his chin. "Let me explain what happened and why you're here. I don't know how much you remember, but let me start by apologizing. I didn't mean to shoot you."

"Wha? Wha?" Julian's head was swimming.

"Yeah, your own girlfriend shot you. Don't you love the irony?" Vinny asked, rubbing his eyes and yawning.

"And I feel terrible about it. I'm so sorry."

Julian's groggy hands probed his bandaged left shoulder, which sent shooting pain down his arm.

"The good news is that the surgeon got the bullet out. It's currently at a picture shop, where it will be mounted and framed for posterity."

"Shut up, Vinny. You're not helping," Alex said, elbowing him in the ribs.

"Au contraire, my friend. I think I'm helping a lot. Listen, bud. I gotta go. My boss called me about an hour ago and told me—get this—that she owes me an apology. An apology! That I was right about the heart attack killer and she was wrong. Can you believe it? I got to get my ass back to DC to hear that in person. On a more serious note, though, I'm sorry I wasn't here when that bitch bit it. I would've enjoyed watching that. Glad you're gonna be okay. Okay, I need to go. Until the next time, my friend."

Vinny leaned in for an awkward hug and then vanished.

Julian's head was starting to clear somewhat. Although memories were still fuzzy, he remembered being seated at his desk as shots rang out and—

"Leh-leh—"

"Linda? Are you asking about Linda?"

"Yeh."

Alex took his hand. "She killed herself, Julian. I'm sorry. I know you were trying to help her."

"H-h-ow?"

"Well, I was aiming for her when I accidentally shot you. But before the bullets could do any damage to her, she'd injected herself with potassium chloride. We tried to save her, but you know how quickly that stuff works. She injected it into a vein in her arm, so it traveled very quickly to her heart. I don't know if she ever planned on killing you at all or whether it had always been meant for her. I guess we'll never know."

Julian turned his head away. Such a waste, he thought. "Ben-a?"

"Brenda? She's okay. Rattled, but okay. She lost her entire family in the last week. She's a tough lady, though. She'll get through it. In fact, she told me that she's going to look up all of her former foster brothers and sisters and try to get them together for a reunion of sorts."

Julian vowed to follow up with her as soon as he was able and offer his services free of charge if she needed them.

The door was suddenly thrown open, and Julian recognized the heavy footsteps of his good friend Jesse. Additional footsteps accompanied Jesse's, however, and Julian's eyebrows came together in confusion.

"Yes, it's me, Julian. How are you feeling?"

"He can't talk yet," Alex responded.

"Oh real-ly," Jesse said with a smile, rubbing his hands together. "Well, it isn't often I get the chance to speak to the great Dr. Stryker without his being able to respond, so let me start with this." Jesse paused, took a deep breath, and then threw his arms around Julian, causing him to wince in pain. "Oh my God, I thought you were going to die! I'm so glad you're okay!" Jesse withdrew, wiping tears from his eyes.

Julian managed a small smile, which drew immediate consternation from Jesse. "How dare you make light of my feelings!" Jesse playfully hit Julian's leg. "Don't worry...I'll get you back. Oh, where are my manners? Julian, this is Oliver. Oliver, this is my sometimes boss, usual friend, and always a pain in my ass—Julian."

Julian managed a nod as Jesse stage-whispered, "This is the Thai guy."

"I think he got it, Jesse. Skedaddle," Alex said, inclining her head toward the door.

"Okay, see you back at the office soon. Oh, and I've been taking care of that mongrel you call a dog. He misses you terribly, so get out of here soon."

As Jesse and Oliver closed the door, Alex took Julian's hand.

"Not many girlfriends get to apologize for shooting their boyfriends. We both need to find a less dangerous line of work."

Julian shook his head.

"No? Why not?"

In response, Julian stuck out his lips for a kiss.

"Ah, I get it. Because then we wouldn't have this time alone." Alex leaned in, kissed Julian for a long moment, and whispered, "I'm glad you're okay."

As she pulled away, she said, "You know, some couples go away for the weekend. Some couples don't have to get shot to spend some alone time together. Just a thought."

Julian smiled and said, "Ah luh you."

Alex wiped a tear from her eye and sighed. "I love you too, Julian...so much."

Julian felt sleep tugging at his eyelids. The last thing he remembered before falling asleep was Alex saying, "You know, getting shot is one way of avoiding lunch with my mother, but she's not going to wait forever. So, we've rescheduled for next week."

About the Author

Elizabeth B. Splaine received her bachelor's degree in psychology from Duke University and her master's degree in healthcare administration from the University of North Carolina at Chapel Hill. She spent ten years working in health care before switching careers. She is now an opera singer, voice teacher and writer. *Blind Order* is the second book in her series of Julian Stryker thrillers.

Made in the USA
Middletown, DE
09 November 2022

14372272R10186